Andy McNab joined the infantry as a boy soldier. In 1984 he was 'badged' as a member of 22 SAS Regiment and was involved in both covert and special operations worldwide.

During the Gulf War he commanded *Bravo Two Zero*, a patrol that, in the words of his commanding officer, 'will remain in regimental history for ever'. Awarded both the Distinguished Conduct Medal (DCM) and Military Medal (MM) during his military career, McNab was the British Army's most highly decorated serving soldier when he finally left the SAS in February 1993. He wrote about his experiences in two phenomenal bestsellers, *Bravo Two Zero*, which was filmed in 1998 starring Sean Bean, and *Immediate Action*.

His novels, *Remote Control*, *Crisis Four*, *Firewall* and *Last Light*, were all bestsellers. Besides his writing work, he lectures to security and intelligence agencies in both the USA and the UK.

Also by Andy McNab

Non-fiction
BRAVO TWO ZERO
IMMEDIATE ACTION

Fiction
REMOTE CONTROL
CRISIS FOUR
FIREWALL
LAST LIGHT

LIBERATION DAY

ANDY McNAB

BANTAM PRESS

LONDON · NEW YORK · TORONTO · SYDNEY · AUCKLAND

TRANSWORLD PUBLISHERS
61–63 Uxbridge Road, London W5 5SA
a division of The Random House Group Ltd

RANDOM HOUSE AUSTRALIA PTY LTD
20 Alfred Street, Milsons Point,
New South Wales 2061, Australia

RANDOM HOUSE NEW ZEALAND
18 Poland Road, Glenfield, Auckland 10, New Zealand

RANDOM HOUSE SOUTH AFRICA (PTY) LTD
Endulini, 5a Jubilee Road, Parktown 2193, South Africa

Published 2002 by Bantam Press
a division of Transworld Publishers

A catalogue record for this book is available from the British Library

ISBNs 0593 046188 (cased)
0593 048237 (tpb)

Typeset in 11/13½pt Palatino by
Falcon Oast Graphic Art Ltd

Printed in Great Britain
by Mackays plc, Chatham, Kent

1 3 5 7 9 10 8 6 4 2

Dedicated to all victims of terrorism

LIBERATION DAY

1

TUESDAY, 6 NOVEMBER 2001, 23:16 hrs

The submarine had broken surface ten minutes earlier, and its deck was still slippery beneath my feet. Dull red torchlight glistened on the black steel a few metres ahead of me as five of the boat's crew feverishly prepared the Zodiac inflatable. As soon as they'd finished it would be carrying me and my two team members across five kilometres of Mediterranean and on to the North African coast.

One of the crew broke away and said something to Lotfi, who'd been standing next to me by the hatch. I didn't understand that much Arabic, but Lotfi translated. 'They are finished, Nick – we are ready to float off.'

The three of us moved forward, swapped places with the submariners, and stepped over the sides of the Zodiac on to the anti-slip decking. Lotfi was the cox and took position to the right of the Yamaha 75 outboard. We bunched up near him, each side of the engine. We wore black bobble hats and gloves, and a 'dry bag' – a GoreTex suit – over our clothes with rubber wrists and neck to protect us from the cold water. Our kit had been stowed in large zip-lock waterproof bags and lashed to the deck along with the fuel bladders.

I looked behind me. The crew had already disappeared and the hatch was closed. We'd been warned by the captain that he wasn't going to hang around, not when we were inside the territorial waters of one of the most ruthless regimes on earth. And he was willing to take even fewer risks on the pick-up, especially if things had gone to rat shit while we were ashore. No way did he want the Algerians capturing his boat and crew. The Egyptian navy couldn't afford to lose so much as a rowing-boat from their desperately dilapidated fleet, and he didn't want his crew to lose their eyes or bollocks, or any of the other bits the Algerians liked to remove from people who had pissed them off.

'Brace for float-off.' Lotfi had done this before.

I could already feel the submarine moving beneath us. We were soon surrounded by bubbles as it blew its tanks. Lotfi slotted the Yamaha into place and fired it up to get us under way. But the sea was heaving tonight with a big swell, and no sooner had our hull made contact with the water than a wave lifted the bow and exposed it to the wind. The Zodiac started to rear up. The two of us threw our weight forward and the bow slapped down again, but with such momentum that I lost my balance and fell on to my arse on the side of the boat, which bounced me backwards. Before I knew what was happening, I'd been thrown over the side.

The only part of me uncovered was my face, but the cold took my breath away as I downed a good throatful of salt water. This might be the Mediterranean, but it felt like the North Atlantic.

As I came to the surface and bobbed in the swell, I discovered that my dry bag had a leak in the neck seal. Sea-water seeped into my cheap pullover and cotton trousers.

'You OK, Nick?' The shout came from Lotfi.

'Couldn't be better,' I grunted, breathing hard as the other two hauled me back aboard. 'Got a leak in the bag.'

There was a mumble of Arabic between the two of them, and a schoolboy snigger or two. Fair one: I would have found it funny too.

I shivered as I wrung out my bobble hat and gloves, but even wet wool keeps its heat-retaining qualities and I knew I was going to need all the help I could get on this part of the trip.

Lotfi fought to keep the boat upright as his mate and I leant on the front – or bow, as Lotfi was constantly reminding me – to keep it down. He finally got the craft under control and we were soon ploughing through the crests, my eyes stinging as the salt spray hit my face with the force of pebble dash. As waves lifted us and the outboard screamed in protest as the propeller left the water, I could see lights on the coast and could just make out the glow of Oran, Algeria's second largest city. But we were steering clear of its busy port, where the Spanish ferries to'd and fro'd; we were heading about ten Ks east, to make landfall at a point between the city and a place called Cap Ferrat. One look at the map during the briefing in Alexandria had made it clear the French had left their mark here big time. The coastline was peppered with Cap this, Plage that, Port the other.

Cap Ferrat itself was easy to recognize. Its lighthouse flashed every few seconds in the darkness to the left of the glow from Oran. We were heading for a small spit of land that housed some of the intermittent clusters of light we were starting to make out quite well now as we got closer to the coastline.

As the bow crashed through the water I moved to the rear of the boat to minimize the effects of the spray and wind, pissed off that I was wet and cold before I'd even started this job. Lotfi was the other side of the outboard. I looked across as he checked his GPS and adjusted the throttle to keep us on the right bearing.

The brine burned my eyes, but this was a whole lot better than the sub we'd just left. It had been built in the 1960s and the air con was losing its grip. After being cooped up in diesel fumes for three days, waiting for the right moment to make this hit, I'd been gagging to be out in the fresh air, even air this fresh. I comforted myself with the thought that the next time I inhaled diesel I'd be chugging along ninety metres below the Mediterranean, back to Alexandria, drinking steaming cups of sweet black tea and celebrating the end of my very last job.

The lights got closer and the coastline took on a bit more shape. Lotfi didn't need the GPS any more and it went into the rubber bow bag. We were maybe four hundred metres off the shore and I could start to make out the target area. The higher, rocky ground was flooded with light, and in the blackness below it, I could just about make out the cliff, and the beach Lotfi had assured us was good enough to land on.

We moved forward more slowly now, the engine just ticking over to keep the noise down. When we were about a hundred metres from the beach, Lotfi cut the fuel and tilted the outboard until it locked horizontal once more. The boat lost momentum and began to wallow in the swell. He'd already started to connect one of the full fuel bladders in preparation for our exfiltration. We couldn't afford to mince about if the shit hit the fan and we had to do a runner.

His teeth flashed white as he gave us a huge grin. 'Now we paddle.'

It was obvious from the way they constantly took the piss out of each other that Lotfi and the one whose name I still couldn't pronounce – Hubba-Hubba, something like that – had worked together before.

Hubba-Hubba was still at the bow and dug his wooden paddle into the swell. We closed in on the beach. The sky was perfectly clear and star-filled, and suddenly there wasn't a breath of wind. All I could hear was the gentle slap of the paddles pushing through the water, joined now and again by the scrape of boots on the wooden flooring as one or other of us shifted position. At least the paddling had got me warm.

Lotfi never stopped checking ahead, to make sure we were going to hit the beach exactly where he wanted, and the Arabic for 'right' I did know: 'Il al yameen, yameen.'

The two of them were Egyptian, and that was about as much as I wanted to know – not that it had turned out that way. Like me, they were deniable operators; in fact, everyone and

12

everything about this job was deniable. If we were compromised, the US would deny the Egyptians were false flagging this job for them, and I guessed that was just the price Egypt had to pay for being the second biggest recipient of US aid apart from Israel, to the tune of about two billion dollars a year. There's no such thing as a free falafel.

Egypt, in its turn, would deny these two, and as for me, they probably didn't even know I was there. I didn't care; I had no cover documents, so if I was captured I was going to get stitched up regardless. The only bits of paper I'd been issued with were four thousand US dollar bills in tens and fifties, with which to try to buy my way out of the country if I got in the shit, and keep if they weren't needed. It was much better than working for the Brits.

We kept paddling towards the clusters of light. The wetness down my back and under my arms was now warm, but still uncomfortable. I looked up at the other two and we nodded mutual encouragement. They were both good lads and both had the same haircut – shiny, jet black short-back-and-sides with a left-hand parting – and very neat moustaches. I was hoping they were winners who just looked like losers. No one would give them a second look in the street. They were both in their mid-thirties, not tall, not small, both clear-skinned and married, with enough kids between them to start up a football team.

'Four-four-two,' Lotfi had smiled. 'I will supply the back four and goalkeeper, Hubba-Hubba the midfield and two strikers.' I'd discovered he was a Man United fan, and knew more than I did about the Premier League, which wasn't difficult. The only thing I knew about football was that, like Lotfi, more than seventy-five per cent of Man United's fans didn't even live in the UK, and most of the rest lived in Surrey.

They hadn't been supposed to talk about anything except the job during the planning and preparation phase, in a deserted mining camp just a few hours outside Alexandria, but they couldn't help themselves. We'd sit around the fire after

13

carrying out yet another rehearsal of the attack, and they'd gob off about their time in Europe or when they'd gone on holiday to the States.

Lotfi had shown himself to be a highly skilled and professional operator as well as a devout Muslim, so I was pleased that this job had got the OK before Ramadan – and also that it was happening in advance of one of the worst storms ever predicted in this part of the world, which the meteorologists had forecast was going to hit Algeria within the next twelve hours. Lotfi had always been confident we'd be able to get in-country ahead of the weather and before he stopped work for Ramadan, for the simple reason that God was with us. He prayed enough, giving God sit reps several times a day.

We weren't going to leave it all to Him, though. Hubba-Hubba wore a necklace that he said was warding off the evil eye, whatever that was when it was at home. It was a small, blue-beaded hand with a blue eye in the centre of the palm, which hung around his neck on a length of cord. I guessed it used to be a badge, because it still had a small safety-pin stuck on the back. As far as the boys were concerned, I had a four-man team with me tonight. I just wished the other two were more help with the paddling.

The job itself was quite simple. We were here to kill a forty-eight-year-old Algerian citizen, Adel Kader Zeralda, father of eight and owner of a chain of Spar-type supermarkets and a domestic fuel company, all based in and around Oran. We were heading for his holiday home, where, so the int said, he did all his business entertaining. It seemed he stayed here quite a lot while his wife looked after the family in Oran; he obviously took his corporate hospitality very seriously indeed.

The satellite photographs we'd been looking at showed a rather unattractive place, mainly because the house was right beside his fuel depot and the parking lot for his delivery trucks. The building was irregularly shaped, like the house that Jack built, with bits and pieces sticking out all over the place and surrounded by a high wall to keep prying eyes from seeing the amount of East European whores he got shipped in for a bit of Arabian delight.

Why he needed to die, and anyone else in the house had to be kept alive, I really didn't have a clue. George hadn't told me before I left Boston, and I doubted I would ever find out. Besides, I'd fucked up enough in my time to know when just to get the game-plan in place, do the job, and not ask too many questions. It was a reasonable bet that with over 350 Algerian al-Qaeda extremists operating around the globe Zeralda was up to his neck in it, but I wasn't going to lie awake worrying about that. Algeria had been caught up in a virtual civil war with Islamic fundamentalist groups for more than a decade now, and over a hundred thousand lives had been lost – which seemed strange to me, considering Algeria was an Islamic country.

Maybe Zeralda posed some other threat to the West's interests. Who cared? All I cared about was keeping focused totally on the job, so with luck I'd get out alive and back to the States to pick up my citizenship. George had rigged it for me; all I had to do in exchange was this one job. Kill Zeralda, and I was finished with this line of work for good. I'd be back on the submarine by first light, a freshly minted US citizen, heading home to Boston and a glittering future.

It felt quite strange going into a friendly country undercover, but at this very moment, the president of Algeria was in Washington DC, and Mr Bush didn't want to spoil his trip. Given the seven-hour time difference, Bouteflika and his wife were probably getting ready for a night out on the Tex Mex with Mr and Mrs B. He was in the States because he wanted the Americans to see Algeria as their North African ally in this new war against terrorism. But I was sure that political support wasn't the only item on the agenda. Algeria also wanted to be seen as an important source of hydrocarbons to the West. Not just oil, but gas: they had vast reserves of it.

Only fifty or so metres to go now, and the depot was plainly visible above us, bathed in yellow light from the fenceline, where arc lights on poles blazed into the compound. We knew from Lotfi's recce that the two huge tanks to the left of the compound were full of kerosene 28, a domestic heating fuel.

On the other side of the compound, still within the fenceline and about thirty metres from the tanks, was a line of maybe a dozen tankers, all likely to be fully laden, ready for delivery in the morning. Along the spit, to the right of the compound as I looked at it, were the outer walls of Zeralda's holiday house, silhouetted by the light of the depot.

2

The view of the target area slowly disappeared as we neared the beach and moved into shadow. Sand rasped against rubber as we hit bottom. The three of us jumped out, each grabbing a rope handle and dragging the Zodiac up the beach. Water sloshed about inside my dry bag and trainers.

When Lotfi signalled that we were far enough from the waterline, we pulled and pushed the boat so that it faced in the right direction for a quick getaway, then started to unlash our kit using the ambient light from the high ground.

A car zoomed along the road above us, about two hundred metres away on the far side of the peninsula. I checked the traser on my left wrist; instead of luminous paint, it used a gas that was constantly giving off enough light to see the watch face. It was twenty-four minutes past midnight; the driver could afford to put his foot down on a deserted stretch of coast.

I unzipped my bergen from the protective rubber bag in which it had been cocooned and pulled it out on to the sand. The backpacks were cheap and nasty counterfeit Berghaus jobs, made in Indonesia and flogged to Lotfi in a Cairo bazaar, but they gave us vital extra protection: if their contents got wet we'd be out of business.

The other two did the same to theirs, and we knelt in the

shadows, each checking our own kit. In my case this meant making sure that the fuse wire and homemade OBIs hadn't been damaged, or worse still waterlogged. The oil-burning incendiaries were basically four one-foot square Tupperware boxes with a soft steel liner, into the bottom of which I'd drilled a number of holes. Each device contained a mix of sodium chlorate, iron powder and asbestos, which would have been hard to find in Europe, these days, but was available in Egypt by the shedload. The ingredients were mixed together in two-pound lots and pressed into the Tupperware.

All four OBIs were going to be linked together in a long daisy chain by one-metre lengths of fuse wire. Light enough to float on top of oil, they would burn fiercely until, cumulatively, they generated enough heat to ignite the fuel. How long that would take depended on the fuel. With petrol it would be almost instantaneous – the fuse wire would do the trick. But the combustion point of heavier fuels can be very high. Even diesel's boiling point is higher than that of water, so it takes a lot of heat to get it sparked up.

But first we had to get to the fuel. All fuel tanks are designed with outer perimeter 'bungs', walls or dykes whose height and thickness depend on the amount of fuel that will have to be contained in the event of a rupture. The ones that we were going to breach were surrounded by a double-thick wall of concrete building blocks, just over a metre in height and about four away from the tanks.

Lotfi and Hubba-Hubba had been rehearsing their tasks so often they would have been able to do them blindfolded – which, in fact, we had done some of the time during rehearsals. Training blindfolded gives you confidence if you have to carry out a job in the dark, such as dealing with a weapon stoppage, but it also makes you quicker and more effective even when you can see.

The attack theory was simple. Lotfi was going to start by cutting out a section of the wall, three blocks wide and two down, facing towards the target house. Hubba-Hubba had turned out to be quite an expert with explosives. He would place his two frame charges, one on each tank, on the side facing the sea and opposite where I was going to lay out and prepare my four OBIs.

As the frame charges cut a two-foot square hole in each tank, the fuel would spew out and be contained in the bung. The ignited OBIs would float on top of the spillage, burning in sequence along the daisy chain, so that we had constant heat and constant flame, which would eventually ignite the lake of fuel beneath them. We knew that the kerosene 28 fuel oil rising in the bung would spark up when the second of the four OBIs ignited, which should happen as the fuel level reached just less than half-way up the bung wall. But we wanted to do more than just ignite the fuel within the bung: we wanted fire everywhere.

The burning fuel would disgorge through the cut-out section in the wall and out on to the ground like lava from a volcano. The ground sloped, towards the target house. As soon as Lotfi had shown me the sketch maps from his recce, I'd seen that we could cut the house off from the road with a barrier of flame. I hoped I was right; two hundred policemen lived in barracks just three kilometres along the road to Oran, and if they were called to the scene we didn't want to become their new best mates.

Just as importantly, we could make what happened tonight look like a local job – an attack from one of the many fundamentalist groups that had waged war on each other here for years. That was why we'd had to make sure the equipment was homemade, why all our weapons were of Russian manufacture, and our clothing of local origin. The traser might not be regular Islamic fundamentalist issue, but if anyone got close enough to me to notice my watch, then I really was in the shit, so what did it matter? In less than two hours from now, Zeralda would be dead, and the finger of blame would be pointing at Algeria's very own Islamic extremists, who were still making this the world's most dangerous holiday venue.

They didn't like anyone unless he was one of their own. We hoped that our attack would be blamed on the GIA, the Armed Islamic Group. They were probably the cruellest and most screwed-up bunch I'd ever come across. These guys had been trained and battle-hardened in places like Afghanistan, where they'd fought with the mujahadeen against the Russians. After that, they'd fought in Chechnya, and then in Bosnia and anywhere else they felt Muslims were getting fucked over. Now they were back in Algeria – and this time it was personal. They wanted an Islamic state with the Qur'ān as its constitution, and they wanted it today. In the eyes of these people, even OBL (Osama Bin Laden) was a wimp. In 1994, in a grim precursor of attacks to come, GIA hijacked an Air France plane in Algiers, intending to crash it in the middle of Paris. It would have worked if it hadn't been for French anti-terrorist forces attacking the plane as it refuelled, killing them all.

Unlike me, all the equipment in my bergen was dry. I peeled off my dry bag, and immediately felt colder as the air started to attack my wet clothes. Too bad, there was nothing I could do about it. I checked chamber on my Russian Makharov pistol, pulling back the topslide just a few millimetres and making sure, for maybe the fourth and last time on this job, that the round was just exposed as it sat in the chamber ready to be fired. I glanced to the side to see the other two doing the same. I let the topslide return until it was home tight before applying safe with my thumb, then thrust the pistol into the internal holster that I'd tucked into the front of my trousers.

Lotfi was in a good mood. 'Your gun wet too?'

I nodded slowly at his joke and whispered back, as I shouldered my bergen, 'Pistol, it's a pistol or weapon. Never, ever a gun.'

He smiled back and didn't reply. He didn't have to: he'd known it would get me ticking.

I made my final check: my two mags were still correctly placed in the double mag holder on my left hip. They were facing up in the thick bands of black elastic that held them on to my belt, with the rounds facing forwards. That way I would pull down on a mag to release it and they would be facing the right way to slam into the pistol.

Everyone was now poised to go, but Lotfi still checked – 'Ready?' – like a teacher at the airport on a school trip, making everyone show their passports for the tenth time. We all nodded, and he led the way up to the high ground. I fell in just behind him.

Lotfi was the one taking us on target because he was the only one who had been ashore and carried out a CTR [close target recce]. Besides, he was the one in charge: I was here as the guest European, soon to be American, terrorist.

There was a gentle rise of about forty metres from the tip of the peninsula where we'd landed to the target area. We zigzagged over sand and rock. It was good to get moving so I could warm up a little.

We stopped just before the flat ground and sat and waited for a vehicle to make its way along the road. Lotfi checked it out. No one said it, but we were all worried about the police being stationed so close, and whether, because of the terrorist situation here, they constantly patrolled their immediate area for security. I was still happy to stop and catch my breath. My nose was starting to run a little.

Lotfi dropped down below the ledge and whispered in Arabic to Hubba-Hubba before coming to me: 'Just a car, no police yet.'

The wet T-shirt under my pullover was a bit warmer now, but it was just as uncomfortable. So what? It wouldn't be long before it was black tea and diesel fumes again, and, for about the first time in my life, I'd be proactively planning a future.

I pulled back my pullover sleeve and glanced down at my traser. 00:58. I thought of Mr and Mrs B. Just like the Bouteflikas, they too were probably having a wash and brush-up while they talked about what on earth they were going to talk about over the Tex Mex. Probably something like, 'Oh, I hear you have lots of gasoline in your country? We wouldn't mind some of that, instead of you giving it to the Italians to fill up their Fiats. And, oh, by the way, there'll be one Algerian fewer for you to govern when you get back. But don't worry, he was a bad 'un.'

As the sound of the vehicle faded in the direction of Oran, we all raised our heads slowly above the lip to scan the rock and sandy ground. The constant noise of crickets, or whatever they called them here, rattled into the night.

The fuel compound was an oasis of yellow light and bright enough to make me squint until my eyes adjusted. It was just under two hundred metres to my half-left. From my perspective the tanks were sitting side by side, surrounded by the bung. To the right of them was the not-so-neat row of fuel trucks.

The perimeter of the compound was guarded by a three-metre high chain link fence, sagging in places where the trucks had backed into it over the years.

In the far corner of the compound, by the gate that faced the road, was the security hut. It was no more than a large garden shed. The security was for fire watch just as much as for stopping the trucks and fuel disappearing during the night; the depot had no automatic fire system in the event of a leak or explosion. Lotfi told us there was a solitary guy sitting inside, and if the whole thing sparked up it would presumably be his job to get on the phone.

That was good for us, because it meant we didn't have to spend time neutralizing any fire-fighting apparatus or alarms. What was bad was the police barracks. A complete fuck-up on our side was only a phone call and three Ks away. If we got caught it would be serious shit. Algeria wasn't exactly known for upholding human rights, no one would be coming to help us, no matter what we said, and terrorists were routinely whipped to death in this neck of the woods.

22

3

The target house was to the right of us, and closer than the compound. The wall that surrounded it was a large, square, high-sided construction of rendered brick, painted a colour that had once been cream. It was built very much in the Muslim tradition of architecture for privacy. The main door faced the fuel tanks, and we knew from the satellite that it was rarely used. I couldn't even see it from where I was, because the lights in the compound weren't strong enough. From the shots Lotfi had taken during the CTR, I knew it consisted of a set of large, dark, wooden double doors rising to an apex, studded and decorated with wrought iron. The pictures had also shown a modern shutter-type garage door at the side, facing away from us towards the road. A dirt track connected it with the main drag.

Inside the high protection was a long, low building. It wasn't exactly palatial, but showed that the fuel and teabag business paid Zeralda well enough for him to have his own little playpen.

Double doors from quite a lot of the rooms opened on to a series of tiled courtyards decorated with plants and fountains, but what the satellite photographs hadn't been able to show us was which room was which. That didn't really matter, though.

The house wasn't that big and it was all on one floor, so it shouldn't take us long to find where Zeralda was doing his entertaining.

The metalled road flanked the far side of these two areas and formed the base of the triangular peninsula.

Lotfi moved back down into the dead ground and started to scramble along in the darkness to his left, just below the lip. As we followed, two cars raced along the road, blowing their horns at each other in rhythmic blasts before eventually disappearing into the darkness. I'd read that eighty per cent of men under the age of thirty were jobless in this country and inflation was in high double figures. How anybody could afford fast cars was beyond me. I could only just about afford my motorbike.

We got level with the tanks and moved up to the lip of the high ground. Hubba-Hubba took off his bergen and fished out the wire cutters and a two-foot square of red velvet curtain material, while we put on and adjusted the black and white check *shemags* that would hide our faces when we hit the hut. I wouldn't be taking part directly because of my skin colour and blue eyes. I would only come into the equation when the other two had located Zeralda. It wouldn't matter that he saw me.

When Hubba-Hubba got his bergen back on and his *shemag* around his head we checked each other again as Lotfi drew his pistol and did his school-trip routine, with a nod to each of us as we copied.

Breaking the operation down into stages, so that people knew exactly what to do and when to do it, made things easier for me. These were good men but I couldn't trust my life with people I didn't know very well and whose skills, beyond the specifics of this operation, I wasn't sure about.

Following Lotfi, with me now at the rear, we moved towards the fenceline. It was pointless running or trying to avoid being in the open for the thirty or so metres: it was just flat ground and the light in the compound hadn't hit us directly yet as the arc lights were facing into the compound, not out. We would get into that light spill before long, and soon after that we'd be attacking the hut, so fuck it, it didn't really matter. There was no other way of crossing the open ground anyway.

There came a point where, bent over as we tried instinctively to make ourselves smaller, we caught the full glare of the four arc lights set on high steel posts at each corner of the compound. A mass of small flying things had been drawn to the pools of light and buzzed around them.

I could hear the rustle of my trousers as my wet legs rubbed together. I kept my mouth open to cut down on the sound of my breathing. It wasn't going to compromise us, but doing everything possible to keep noise to a minimum and make this job work made me feel better. The only other sounds were of their trainers moving over the rocky ground, and the rhythmic scrape of the nylon bergens over the chirp of the invisible crickets. My face soon became wet and cold as I breathed against the *shemag*.

We got to the fenceline behind the shed. There were no windows facing us, just sunbaked wooden cladding no more than a metre away.

I could hear someone inside, shouting grumpily in French. '*Oui, oui, d'accord.*' At the same time there was a blast of mono-tone Arabic from a TV set.

Lotfi held the red velvet over the bottom of the fence and Hubba-Hubba got to work with his cutters. He cut the wire through the velvet, moving upwards in a vertical line. Lotfi re-positioned the velvet each time, the two men working like clockwork toys, not looking remotely concerned about the world around them. That was my job, to watch and listen to the sounds coming from the shed in case its occupant was alerted by the smothered 'ping' each time a strand of chain-link gave way.

The telephone line snaked into the compound from one of the concrete posts that followed the road, which looked like a slab of liquorice running left and right. There was a sign, in both Arabic and English, to be careful of the bend. I knew that if I went to the right I would hit Oran about ten kilometres away, and if I went left I would pass Cap Ferrat and eventually hit Algiers, the capital, about four hundred Ks to the east.

Hubba-Hubba and Lotfi finished cutting the vertical line as the one-sided conversation continued inside the shed, then carefully pulled the two sides apart to create a triangle. I eased my way slowly through, so my bergen wouldn't snag. I got my fingers through Lotfi's side of the fence to keep it in position and he followed suit, taking hold of Hubba-Hubba's side while he packed the cutting kit. When he was through as well, we eased the fence back into place.

We put our bergens on the ground behind the shed, to the accompaniment of the monotonous Arabic TV voice, and the old guy still gobbing off in French.

It flashed through my mind that I had no idea what had been happening in Afghanistan this past week. Were the US still bombing? Had troops gone in and dug the Taliban out of their caves? Having been so totally focused on the job in the mining camp and then stuck in the submarine, I didn't have a clue if OBL was dead or alive.

We used the light to make final adjustments to each other's *shemags*.

Everyone carefully checked chamber for the last time. They were becoming like me, paranoid that they were going to pull a trigger one day and just get a dead man's click because the topslide hadn't picked the round up due to the mag not being fully home.

Lotfi was hunched down and bouncing on the balls of his feet. He just wanted to get on with it and hated the wait. Hubba-Hubba looked as if he was at the starting blocks and unconsciously went to bite his thumbnail, only to be prevented by the *shemag*. There was nothing we could do but wait until the old guy had finished his call; we weren't going to burst in half-way through a conversation. I listened to the French waffle, the TV, the buzz of the mozzie things around the lights,

26

and our breathing through the cotton of the *shemags*. There wasn't even the hint of a breeze to jumble the noises together.

Less than a minute later, the guard stopped talking and the phone went down with an old style ring of a bell. Lotfi bounced up to full height and checked Hubba-Hubba was backing him. He looked down at me and we nodded in time before they disappeared around the corner without a word. I followed, but stayed out of the way as Lotfi pulled open the door and the TV commentator was momentarily interrupted by a single shouted instruction and the sort of strangulated pleas you make to two weapon-pointing Arabs in *shemags*. I saw a sixty-something bloke, in baggy, well-worn trousers and a tattered brown check jacket, drop a cigarette from between his thumb and forefinger before falling to his knees and starting to beg for his life. His eyes were as big as saucers, his hands upturned to the sky in the hope that Allah would sort this whole thing out.

Hubba-Hubba stuck the muzzle of his Makharov into the skin at the top of the old boy's balding head and walked around him using the weapon as a pivot stick. He reached for the phone and ripped it from its socket. It fell to the floor with one final ring, the noise blending with the scrape of plastic-soled shoes on the raised wooden floor as they dragged him over to a folding wooden chair.

I could see that he had been watching Al Jazeera, the news network. The TV was black and white, and the coat-hanger antenna wasn't exactly state-of-the-art, but I could still make out the hazy nightscope pictures of Kandahar getting the good news from the US Air Force as tracer streamed uselessly into the air.

The old boy was getting hysterical now, and there were lots of shouts and pistols aimed his way. I guessed they were telling him, 'Don't move, camel-breath,' or whatever, but in any event it wasn't long before he was wrapped up so well in gaffer tape he could have been a Christmas present.

The two of them walked out and closed the door behind

them, and we retrieved the bergens. Things were looking good. 'Train hard, fight easy' had always been shoved down my neck, even as an infantry recruit in the 1970s, and it was certainly true tonight. The other half of the mantra, 'Train easy, fight hard – and die', I pushed to the back of my head.

We crossed the hard crust of sand that had been splashed with fuel over the years, and compressed by boots and tyres, heading for the tanks no more than fifty metres away. The trucks were to my left, dirty minging old things with rust streaks down the sides of their tanks from years of spillage. If the sand and dust now stuck to them was washed off, they would probably fall apart.

I clambered over the bung, feeling safe enough to pull off the *shemag* as the other two got on with their tasks. After I'd extracted the four OBIs I checked at the bottom of my bergen for the nine-inch butcher's knife and pair of thick black rubber gloves that came up to my elbows. They were the sort that vets use when they stick their arm up the rear end of large animals. I knew they were there, but always liked to check such things. Next out was the thirty-metre spool of safety fuse, looking a bit like a reel of green washing line. All the kit we were using was in metric measures, but I had been taught imperial. It had been a nightmare explaining things to the boys during rehearsals.

Lotfi and his mate, God, started to play stonemasons on the bung, taking a hammer and chisel to the elevation that faced the target house, which was hidden in darkness, no more than two hundred metres away. This was a problem because of the noise Lotfi was making. But, fuck it, there was no other way. He just had to take his time. But at least once the first block was out, it would be a lot easier to attack the mortar. It would have been quicker and safer, noise-wise, to blow a hole in the wall at the same time as the tanks were cut, but I couldn't have been sure that the right amount of wall had been destroyed, allowing the fuel to gush out before it was ignited.

I laid the four OBIs in a straight line on the floor as Hubba-Hubba and his mate, the evil eye protector, assembled and checked the frame charges from his bergen. These were very basic gizmos, eight two-foot-long strips of plastic explosive, two inches wide, an inch thick, taped on to eight lengths of wood. He was making sure the PE had connected by rolling more in his hands before pushing it into the joints as he taped the wood together to make the two square frame charges. He had pushed two dodgy-looking Russian flash detonators into the PE on the opposing sides of each charge, then covered them with yet more PE. Both charges had then been wrapped in even more tape until they looked like something from kids' TV. It was bad practice using the dets like that, but this was a low tech job and these sorts of details counted. If the charges didn't detonate we'd have to leave them, and if they looked sophisticated and exotic it would arouse suspicion that maybe the job hadn't been down to GIA.

Just to make sure they'd jump to the wrong conclusion, I'd made up a PIRA [Provisional IRA] timer unit to detonate them. They were dead simple, using a Parkway timer, a device about the size of a 50p piece that worked very much like a kitchen egg-timer. They were manufactured as keyrings to remind you of when your meter was about to expire. The energy source was a spring, and the timers were reliable even in freezing or wet weather conditions.

I watched as Hubba-Hubba disappeared to the side of the tanks facing the sea with his squares of wood and left me to sort out the OBIs. I heard the clunk as the first frame charge went on to the tank, held in place by magnets. He was placing them just above the first weld marks. Steel storage tanks are maybe half an inch thick at the bottom, due to the amount of pressure they have to withstand from the weight of fuel. There is less pressure above the first weld, so the steel can be thinner, maybe about a quarter of an inch on these old tanks. The frame charges might not be technically perfect, but they'd have no problem cutting through at that level, as long as they had good contact with the steel.

I heard the magnets clank into position on the second. He

was doing everything at a walk, just as we had rehearsed. This wasn't so that we didn't make a noise and get compromised, but because I didn't want him to run and maybe fall and destroy the charges. We'd only made two, and I had no great wish to end this job hanging upside down in an Algerian cell while my head was on the rece iving end of a malicious lump of four-by-two.

I laid the green safety fuse alongside the OBIs that I'd placed in the sand a metre apart. The safety fuse between each OBI would burn for about a minute and a half, just like when Clint Eastwood lit sticks of dynamite with his cigar. A minute and a half was just a guide, as it could be plus or minus nine seconds – or even quicker if the core was broken and the flame jumped the gaps instead of burning its way along the fuse. That was the reason why I hadn't connected the fuse in advance, but kept it rolled up: if there was a break in the powder it could be too big a gap for the flame to jump, and we'd have no detonation.

Once an OBI was ignited by the fuse it would burn for about two and a half minutes. That meant that as soon as the first one sparked up there would be about another minute and thirty before the next one did. Which meant two of them burning together for a minute, and by the time the first had burnt out, the third would be ignited, and so on to the fourth. I needed the sort of heat generated by two of these things burning at once to make sure the fuel ignited.

I opened the Tupperware lids of the OBIs and fed the safety fuse over the exposed mixture in each of the boxes. They were now ready to party.

Hubba-Hubba was looking over his shoulder as he moved slowly backwards towards me, unreeling another spool of fuse wire as he went. This was now connected to one of the frame charges via two detonators. It wasn't the same kind of fuse I'd been using. This was 'fuse instantaneous', which goes off with the sound of a gunshot because the burn is so fast. There's a little ridge that runs along the plastic coating so at night you can always distinguish it from the straightforward Clint

Eastwood stuff. He cut the fuse from his spool without a word, and went back to do the same with the second charge.

The PIRA timer unit would initiate the fuse instantaneous, which would burn at warp speed to a four-way connector, a three inch by three inch green plastic box with a hole in each side. I didn't know what the small worn-out aluminium plate stuck to its base called it in Russian, but that was the name I knew it by. All this box did was allow three other lengths of fuse to be ignited from the one – Hubba-Hubba's two lengths of fuse instantaneous to the two charges, and my safety fuse for the OBIs.

Hubba-Hubba was now unreeling the fuse instantaneous from the second charge back towards me as I took the safety fuse and cut it from the reel six inches back from the first OBI, making sure the cut was straight so the maximum amount of powder was exposed to ignite it in the four-way connector. I then pushed the end of it into one of the rubber recesses, giving it a half-turn so that the teeth inside gripped the plastic coating. Hubba-Hubba placed the two fuses instantaneous next to me and went to help Lotfi.

I cut his two lengths of fuse in the same way before feeding the lines into the connector as the sound of Lotfi's rubber mallet hitting his chisel filled the air and the navigation lights of an airliner miles up floated silently over us.

I checked the three lines that were, so far, in the connector to ensure the three lines into it were secure before cutting a metre length of the ridged fuse instantaneous and placing it in the last free hole. This was the length that went to the timer unit, a three-inch-thick, postcard-sized wooden box.

Then, as I lay on my stomach and started to prepare, a vehicle drove along the road from the direction of Oran.

The noise got louder as it came round to the base of the peninsula. I could tell by the engine note and the sound of the tyres that it wasn't on the road any more, it was going cross-country.

Shit, police.

I heard a torrent of Arabic whispers from the other two a few metres away. I got their attention. 'Lotfi, Lotfi! Take a look.'

He got on to his knees, then slowly raised his head. Instinctively I checked that my Makharov was still in place.

I got up and looked over their heads. The vehicle was a civilian 4x4, heading for the house. The headlights were on full beam and bounced up and down on the garage doors set in the compound wall. As it got closer to the building the driver sounded the horn.

Shit, what was happening? My information was that no one would be moving in or out of the house tonight. George had said that when we hit this place Zeralda would definitely be in there. He'd assured me the intelligence was good quality.

The wagon stopped and I could just about hear some rhythmic guitar music forcing its way out of the open windows. Was the int wrong? Had the target just arrived, instead of coming in yesterday? Was this another group of mates come to join in the fun? Or was it just a fresh batch of Czechs or Romanians with bottle-blonde hair being ferried in for the next session? Whatever, I wanted to be in the house for no more than half an hour, not caught up directing a cast of thousands.

I watched as the garage shutter rattled open. I couldn't tell if it had been operated electronically or manually. Then the vehicle disappeared inside and the shutter closed.

We got back to business. With the timer unit in my hand and the bergen on my back, I climbed over the bung, feeling more than a little relieved.

The other two were still attacking the wall and Hubba-Hubba seemed to lose patience, kicking it with the flat of his foot to free a stubborn block.

I opened the top of the timer unit and gave it one more check. Basically it consisted of a fifteen-metre length of double-stranded electric flex coming out of a hole drilled in its side. Attached to the other end was a flash det, a small aluminium cylinder about the size of a third of a cigarette, that fitted over the fuse instantaneous. To keep it in one piece in transit, I had rolled up the flex and put an elastic band around it. Inside the box there was a twelve-volt battery beside the Parkway timer, the small rectangular type with the positive and negative terminals on top and next to each other. Both items were glued to the bottom of the box.

Soldered flat on to the timer unit was a small panel pin, protruding like a minute hand beyond the dial of the Parkway. It was no more than half an inch long, and had been roughened with emery cloth to make a good electrical contact. Also soldered on to it was one of the two strands of flex that came into the box. Another panel pin, which had also been emery clothed, was sticking out from the bottom of the box, between the Parkway timer and the battery at the 0 on the Parkway dial. That, too, had a small length of wire soldered on to it, leading to the negative terminal of the battery. The other strand of flex was soldered directly to the positive.

The Parkway wasn't set, so I'd pushed a wedge of rubber eraser down over the vertical pin to stop the two making contact. If they did, it would complete the circuit and initiate the flash det.

I lay there for another ten minutes or so until the other two had finished. It would have been a bit quicker if I'd gone and helped, but you never, ever lose control of the initiation device until you're ready to leave the area. I wanted to know that every second we were by the tanks, the eraser was still covering that panel pin. The faint sound of Al Jazeera floated through the air. I could feel the wetness of my clothes cold against my skin now that I'd stopped moving.

It was time to connect the flash det and the timer to the device. I held up my hand and showed the boys the wooden box. They knew what was about to happen, and got up and left for the cut in the fenceline. I knelt down by the fuse instantaneous to fit the flash det, checking the eraser was still in place before feeding the fuse into the small aluminium tube. I made sure the fuse end couldn't get any further inside, so it would initiate, then taped the whole lot in place. There was a crimping tool that would have done the job much better, but it had to look low-tech.

I then unwound the wire from the elastic as I climbed back over the bung. This was very bad drills. I had connected the initiation device to the charges and was climbing about: if I dropped it, I'd turn the whole job into a gang fuck as the charges took out the tanks as well as me. But fuck it, this was the only way to do it tonight as far as I was concerned.

I lay as flat as I could in the sand, even forcing my heels down, with the extended wires running over the bung, before removing the top of the box.

To arm the device, I turned the Parkway dial to 30. Then I gave it another one or two minutes for luck, all very high-tech stuff.

I let go of the dial and could hear the ticking as the spring began to unwind. I had tested this unit over and over again and, give or take five seconds, it was always on time over the half-hour. The panel pin that was attached flat to the dial had maybe an inch and a half to travel before connecting with its vertical twin.

All that remained was for me to take off the rubber wedge and replace the wooden lid on the timer unit so no dirt could find its way between the two pins. I joined the others. All being well, fragments of the timer unit would confirm that tonight's devastation was the work of an old and bold ex-muj who'd been up to no good. It would just underline what the security guy told them.

As we went past the hut the door was open and an Al Jazeera newscaster was taking us through more fuzzy black and white pictures of the night's events in Afghanistan. We made our way to the cut in the fenceline and Lotfi pointed to his *shemag* as a signal for me to cover up. I tucked the cotton around my mouth and saw the security guy, still bound up with tape, now lying in the sand below the lip. He had shit his baggy trousers big-time, but he'd live through the night.

34

Hubba-Hubba knelt down and gave him a few highlights in rapid Arabic from the GIA party political broadcast, then at Lotfi's nod we all left him praying noisily to himself through the gaffer tape and ran directly towards the house.

Lotfi pulled out the alloy caving ladder from his bergen and unrolled it in the sand. Hubba-Hubba moved round to the other side of the wall facing the road to check the garage door. Why climb the wall if there was an easier way through?

I gave the heavy wrought-iron door handle a twist. It turned, but the door wouldn't budge. Hubba-Hubba came back shaking his head. We were going to need the caving ladder after all. Made from two lengths of steel cable with alloy tube rungs in between, the whole thing was about nine inches wide and fifteen feet long, designed for cavers to get up and down potholes, or whatever they do down there.

Lotfi brought out the two poles we'd picked up at the hardware store, the telescopic jobs you can stick a squeegee on if you want to clean high windows. Like all the other kit except for the timing unit, this should be coming back with us; but if anything got left behind, it couldn't have a B&Q label on it.

He taped them together to make one long pole, just slightly shorter than the wall itself. Lotfi used it to lift the large steel hook that was attached to one end of the wire ladder, and eased it over the top of the wall.

I checked chamber on my Makharov yet again, and the others copied. Then, after a *shemag* check, we were ready to go. I stepped closer. 'Remember, if we have a drama – no head shots.' I'd been boring these two senseless for days about this, but it was imperative we didn't fuck up Zeralda's head. I didn't know why, but I was starting to make an educated – well, sort of – guess.

I checked traser: with luck, just over twenty-two minutes left before the tanks became infernos. I tapped Hubba-Hubba on the shoulder. 'OK, mate?'

He started to climb, with me steadying the waving ladder under him. Caving ladders aren't climbed conventionally; you

35

twist them through ninety degrees so that they run between your legs and you use your heels on the rungs, not your toes. Back at the mining camp, watching these two trying to get up and down had been like a scene in a slapstick comedy. Now, with so much practice, they glided up and down like chimpanzees.

Hubba-Hubba disappeared over the top of the wall and I heard a faint grunt as he landed the other side. Then came the slow metallic creak of bolts being gently prised open, while Lotfi retrieved and rolled up the ladder before stashing it back in his bergen along with the poles.

The door opened and I moved through into a small court-yard, hearing at once the gentle trickle of one of the ornamental fountains. I couldn't see it, but knew from the sat photos that it was in front of me somewhere.

Lotfi followed close behind me. It was very dark in here, with no lights on at all this side of the house. The building's irregular shape meant that light from another part of the build-ing could easily be hidden. If we hadn't seen the car turn up, we wouldn't have known there was anyone at home.

I felt leaves against my *shemag* as I stood by the compound wall, looking and listening as my face became wet with condensation once more. Hubba-Hubba closed the door behind us, bolting it shut so that if we screwed the job up and Zeralda was able to do a runner, it would take a while for him to escape.

Once they had got their bergens back on, I was going to lead. I wanted to be in control of my own destiny inside this cage. Pulling out my Makharov, I followed the building around to the right. I still couldn't see anything, but I knew from the sat pictures that the floor of the courtyard was paved with large tiles in bold blue North African patterns.

We left the soothing sound of the fountain behind and rounded a corner, past a set of french windows behind closed wooden shutters. Maybe four metres in front of me, light spilled from a second set of doors on to a wrought-iron garden set, with a mosaic pattern on the circular table. I stopped to try to control my breathing, and heard faint, intermittent laughter ahead.

I eased off my bergen and left it on the ground, then got down on my knees and put out my hand to make sure the others were going to hold it right there.

I crawled to within a couple of feet of the french windows, and could suddenly hear guitars and cymbals. I smiled when I recognized Pink Floyd.

I lay down and craned my neck until I could see what was happening beyond the glass. As soon as I'd done it, I wished I hadn't. The whole room was a haze of cigarette smoke. Zeralda was naked and covered in either oil or sweat, I couldn't make out which, and his fat, grey-haired body and almost woman-sized breasts were wobbling about as he wrestled on a big circular bed. In the blue corner was a very frightened boy who couldn't have been any more than about fourteen, with a crew-cut and ripped T-shirt.

In all there were three boys in the room, all in different states of undress, and another adult, younger than Zeralda, in his thirties maybe, with greased-back hair, still clothed in jeans and white shirt but with bare feet. He seemed to be a spectator for now, sitting in a chair, smiling and smoking as he watched the one-sided bout. The other boys looked as scared as their friend, starting to realize what they'd let themselves in for.

I moved my head away to have a think about what I'd just seen. It had never crossed our minds that Zeralda's fun and games involved boys; we'd been told it was women.

When I was far enough from the window I stood and walked back to the others. Our heads closed in and I quickly checked traser: eleven-ish minutes to go before the device went off. Before that happened we needed to be in on target and for Zeralda to be dead. That way, we'd have contained the situation before there was any sort of follow-up by the fire brigade or, even worse, the two hundred policemen.

The nylon of their bergens rustled gently as they moved in

37

for me to whisper. 'He's in there with another man and three young boys.'

Hubba-Hubba raised his shovel-like hands in disbelief. 'Boys? No women? Just boys? Young boys?'

'Yep.'

There was a collective Arabic mutter of disapproval. Hubba-Hubba could only just about control his breathing. 'I will do it, let me kill him.'

4

Lotfi wasn't going to let that happen. 'No, we have our tasks.'

Hubba-Hubba was still in a state of disgust. 'How many?'

'For definite, two men, three boys. That's all I've seen.'

Lotfi had a change of heart. 'Then I will kill the other one.'

Hubba-Hubba agreed. I was starting to worry. 'No, only the target. Just the target, OK, we're just here for him. No one else, remember?' Doing things outside your limits of exploitation can lead to horrendous fuck-ups elsewhere. We didn't know the whole story, just this little bit. I felt pretty much the way he did, but . . . 'Just the target, no one else.'

Lotfi said he would lead, as the colour of my eyes and skin could still be a problem for a little while longer. I caught his shoulder. 'Remember. If there's a drama—'

He finished my sentence. 'No head shots.'

I tapped my traser. We had less than six minutes.

I could hear Hubba-Hubba still murmuring quietly to himself about what Zeralda was getting up to as there was a burst of laughter from inside the room, and I remembered that his own sons were nearly as old as these boys.

We stopped just short of the door. I could hear a little Arabic waffle, then more laughter from inside the room. Then I heard a young voice, clearly pleading: whatever was going on in there, he didn't like it. I felt a surge of anger.

Traser told me there were four minutes left on the Parkway timer. I undid the top flap of my bergen, dug out the rubber gloves and started to put them on. Those two, and their invisible mates, had better get their finger out once we were inside: we didn't have much time.

Hubba-Hubba picked up a wrought-iron chair and hurled it against the windows. The noise of smashing glass was followed by startled screams from inside, and then by even louder screams of aggression as he and Lotfi kicked out the remaining glass and pushed their way through. Even Pink Floyd were no match for this lot.

The next distinguishable sound I heard was begging, this time from the men. I didn't want to know what was going on in there now, or how Lotfi and his mate were choosing to control the situation. I heard more breaking glass, the racket of furniture being pulled about.

A split second later the loud crump of the devices made me duck instinctively as what looked like sheet lightning filled the sky. There was a renewed frenzy inside; more furniture being hurled about, and the screams became wails.

All at once the boys' cries ceased, as if a switch had been thrown.

I checked my *shemag*, took the bergen in my left hand and the Makharov in my right, and poked an eye round the corner to see what was happening. The room reeked of cannabis smoke. Pink Floyd were still going for it next door.

Both men were on the floor, being kicked and stamped on by Lotfi, who was alone in the room with them. Zeralda was about to collect a boot in the teeth.

'Not the face,' I yelled. 'Not the face!'

Lotfi turned, his huge black eyes wide and quivering. I jumped through the french windows, my trainers crunching on shards of broken glass. I dropped the bergen and put my gloved left hand on his shoulder, keeping a good grip on the

Makharov with my right, and my thumb on the safety in case he totally lost control and I had to stop him.

I gave his shoulder a squeeze and eased him away from the whimpering and bloodstained heap on the floor. I had to speak up to be heard over the music. 'Come on, mate, remember why we're here . . .'

I understood what was disturbing him and liked him for it, but not so much that I'd let him jeopardize the job. He moved back against the wall as I looked down to check out Zeralda's head. I caught the other one looking into my eyes. I guessed that he knew I wasn't an Arab, that this wasn't a GIA attack. Bad decision on my part, not waiting until Lotfi had finished and called me in. It was just one of those fuck-ups that happen once on the ground. And a totally bad decision on his part, having ears and eyes: no matter what the reason for no one else being killed in the house, he would have to die.

He seemed in control, even if his overfed face didn't look that good; most of the blood that should have been inside his head was now on the front of his shirt.

I kicked Zeralda over on to his back. His face wasn't too bad. He had a few teeth missing and blood leaking out of his mouth and nose, but not much else. His eyes were closed and his body wobbled as he, I presumed, tried to explain why I should keep him alive.

I stepped back, raised the Makharov, and double-tapped him in the chest. After a couple of jerks, he wobbled no more.

Zeralda's mate's eyes were shaking in their sockets now, just like Lotfi's, but there was no gasp of horror or any begging from him as the music took over again, punctuated by the distant cries of the boys from somewhere else in the house.

Hubba-Hubba came back into the room.

'Where are the boys?'

'Bathroom.' Hubba-Hubba pointed back the way he'd come.

'Get them out of here before the fuel cuts us off. Give them the car. Go, mate, just get them out of here. This fucker stays, I want him to watch.'

41

Lotfi had pulled the greaseball on to the bed and was yelling abuse at him. He let fly with his fist, punching him hard in the mouth for good measure.

As Greaseball tried to separate his hair from the blood on his face I made sure he saw me take out the butcher's knife. He began to get the message. His brown eyes bulged and shook some more.

I pulled Zeralda by the arm and rolled him back over on to his stomach, then sat astride him and grabbed a fistful of his hair in my left hand. I yanked it back and positioned the knife below his Adam's apple.

I looked up to double-check that Greaseball was watching, and then started to cut. I had prepared myself for days by telling myself that this was going to be shocking, but this wasn't the time to be shocked. I had a job to do.

The knife was razor sharp, and I felt little resistance once it got through the first layer of skin and I pulled back on his head to make the cutting easier. I was beginning to feel a little light-headed. Maybe it was because of the cloud of wacky baccy that still hung in the air, but I doubted it. Pink Floyd were still at full pitch, singing about the happiest days of our lives.

Greaseball closed his eyes but Lotfi thrust his pistol against his ear, uttering in Arabic. His eyes opened again, just in time to see blood stream from his dead friend on to the tiles, and flow between his own feet dangling from the bed. It was too much for him; he vomited on to the bedding as he tried desperately to keep his feet off the ground, as if it was on fire.

He started to gob off in vomit-soaked Arabic to Lotfi, but halted abruptly as a blinding light burst through the haze of sweet-smelling smoke that still filled the air.

It came from the area around the tanks. The OBIs had done their stuff. The fuel was burning good-style: I could see the leaves on the trees outside, which were higher than the perimeter wall, reflecting the bright orange flames.

I concentrated on the job in hand, working at the top of his spinal column like I was cutting a section of ox-tail.

Lotfi had got fed up with his supporting role and was pistol-whipping the other paedophile. If he hadn't before, Greaseball now got the message: he was in deep shit. He started begging, his legs and red-stained soles up by his chest, his hands down between them trying to protect himself as he lay on the bed. 'Please, please, I'm a friend. I'm a friend . . .' something like that, anyway. His English sounded pretty good; I just couldn't hear too clearly with the music this loud.

I yelled at Lotfi: 'Turn that fucking noise off, it's doing my head in.'

He kicked his way past the furniture that had been thrown around the room, and seconds later the music stopped, just as Greaseball tried wiping the vomit from his mouth before realizing his hands were bloodstained.

Hubba-Hubba appeared in the doorway and for a moment looked appalled by what I had nearly finished.

'What?'

'Glasses,' he said.

'What?'

'One of the boys needs his glasses.'

I couldn't believe what I was hearing. 'Fuck him, just get rid of them. We're running out of time.'

'He can't. He needs them, they're difficult to get. Really expensive to buy here.'

He rooted around on the floor next to the bed, then pulled back the blood-soaked covers as I finished what I'd come to do.

I grabbed the top sheet, pulled it from under Greaseball, and wrapped Zeralda's head in it.

Hubba-Hubba stood over the headless body. 'Can you turn him over?'

'What?'

'Turn him over. They could be under him. You have the gloves.'

I did as I was told. The precious glasses were under his legs, one lens cracked and bloodstained.

Hubba-Hubba picked them up between his thumb and

forefinger as if he was holding a scorpion. 'They can go now, I'll put them in the car.'

Lotfi hadn't returned, but I knew what he was up to.

I wiped the knife blade on the bed and put it back into the bergen, then pulled out a black bin liner and threw in the shrouded head.

And that was it. I'd never cut off a man's head before, and I hadn't been looking forward to it one bit. But after seeing Zeralda with the boys, I'd had all the incentive I needed. In fact, I felt pretty good as I turned to Greaseball.

The roar of burning fuel now filled the night. Flames licked higher and higher, brushing against the sky. The police could only be minutes away.

Greaseball raised himself up from the bed. 'You can't kill me, I am too important. No one but Zeralda is to be killed – you know that, don't you? You can't kill me, that is not your decision to make, you are just the tools.'

I looked him straight in the eye, but said nothing, feeling angry and deflated as he spat out some vomit. Then he almost smiled. 'How do you think your people knew that he would be here tonight? You cannot kill me, I'm too important. You need me. Now, stop being stupid and crawl back into your kennel until required.'

Windows were being smashed about the house now, to feed the fire we were going to start in here. Lotfi and Hubba-Hubba would be stacking furniture for good measure. This was the bit they'd really loved during the training.

Lotfi pulled the last of the squeezy bottles from his bergen. They'd been half filled with boiled washing up liquid, then topped up with petrol and given a good shake. He gave the bed a squirt, then saved the rest for Zeralda. One match and this place would be an inferno.

Greaseball made a run for it into the house and Hubba-Hubba started after him.

'Leave him. Not enough time.'

The phone rang and we all jumped.

It could have been anyone – maybe the police, maybe one of Zeralda's family, or one of his paedophile mates. Whatever, Hubba-Hubba turned and gave the phone a good old squirt as well.

'Come on,' I shouted, 'time to move. Let's light up, let's go, let's go!'

I shouldered my bergen, and heard the rush of fuel being ignited in the room next door. Lotfi ran past me and out into the courtyard. I followed as Hubba-Hubba transformed the bedroom into a furnace.

There was no great plan for the next bit – just run down to the boat and get out to sea for a pick-up and some hot sticky black tea and a noseful of diesel fumes.

As I ran through the perimeter door I saw the flaming fuel from the bung flowing out of the breach and down the incline, exactly like it said in the script. The sky was bright orange. After all that practising, all that rehearsal, it looked just beautiful. I stood there for what seemed like ages, looking at the flames as the heat gently seared my skin. I was almost sorry that we wouldn't be around to see the best bit. As the flames flowed under the fuel trucks, they, too, would soon be joining in the fun, with luck just as the police arrived.

Lotfi gave me a shove, and our shadows followed us until we got over the lip. Once we hit the sand it was simply a case of turning right and following the shoreline to the Zodiac.

As I scrambled down the hill I felt nothing but exhilaration. At long last I'd earned my US passport – and the right to a whole new life.

5

FRIDAY, 16 NOVEMBER, 11:56 hrs

I sat on the T, the smart aluminium commuter train that had brought me from Logan airport into Boston and, after a quick change, north towards Wonderland.

Wonderland always sounded to me like some kind of glitzy shopping mall; in fact, it was only the drop-off point for people from the northern suburbs heading into Boston. Today, though, no destination could have been better named. Carrie had been lecturing at MIT this morning, so was picking me up here instead of at the airport, then taking me to her mother's place in Marblehead, a small town about twenty miles north along the coast. Her mother had lent us the granny annexe, while she carried on with her B-and-B business in the main house. Carrie and I lived there alone now that Luz had started high school in Cambridge. To me it was home, and it was a long time since I'd felt that way about anywhere.

The other passengers looked at me as if I'd just escaped from the local nuthouse. After two days of travelling back from Egypt, my skin was greasy, my eyes stung, and my socks, armpits and breath stank. As some kind of damage limitation before I saw Carrie I was brushing my teeth and swallowing the foaming paste as I looked out of the window. It wasn't going to transform me into Brad Pitt on Oscars night but it was the best I could do.

I picked up the nylon holdall near my feet and put it on the empty seat beside me. I needed to check just one more time that the bag was sterile of anything that could link me to the job before she picked me up. My hand passed over the smooth, rounded shape of the Pyramids snowstorm shaker I'd bought her at Cairo airport, and the hard edge of the small photo album she'd lent me for my weeks away. 'If you don't look at it and think nice things about me every day, Nick Stone,' she'd said, 'don't even think about coming back.'

I opened it and felt a grin spreading across my face, as it did every time I saw her. She was standing outside Abbot Hall in Washington Square, Marblehead, on the start of what she'd called my US Heritage Induction Tour. Abbot Hall was the home of 'The Spirit of '76', the famous portrait of a fife and drum at the head of an infantry column during the revolutionary war. She wanted me to see it because she said it embodied the spirit of America – and if I was going to become a US citizen one day, it was my solemn duty to damned well admire and be moved by it. I said I thought it looked more like a cartoon than a masterpiece, and she pushed me outside.

Her short brown hair was being buffeted by the wind blasting off the Atlantic as I pressed the shutter. She looked like GI Jane in green fatigue cargoes and a baggy grey sweater. She certainly didn't look in her late thirties, even though a certain sadness in her smile, and a few small creases at the corners of her mouth and eyes, told anybody who was paying attention that the last couple of years had not been easy on her. 'Nothing PhotoShop can't handle,' she said, 'once I've scanned them into the PC.'

It was rare to see her expression so relaxed, even when she was sleeping. Normally it was much more animated, most often frowning, questioning, or registering disgust at Corporate America's latest outrage. She had good reason to look weighed down. It had been hard for her and Luz since the two of them had come back from Panama, one without a husband, the other

47

without the man who'd become her father. Since Aaron's death there hadn't been a day when he didn't come into her conversation. I still tended to cut away from stuff like this, but the way she saw it, he'd been her husband for fifteen years and dead for only a little over one.

In the whole of my life as a Special Forces soldier, and later, as a 'K' working on deniable operations for the Intelligence Service, I'd always tried to turn my back on the guilt, remorse and self-doubt that always followed a job; what was done was done. But watching her trying to deal with it moved me more than I'd thought possible.

I'd been sent to Panama in September 2000 to coerce a local drugs racketeer into helping the West. Carrie and Aaron had been my local contacts; they'd been environmental scientists running a research station near the Colombian border, and on the CIA payroll as low-level intelligence gatherers. I was staying at their house when the racketeer's boys came looking for me, and Aaron had paid the price.

There hadn't been many days since when I didn't wonder if there'd been something more I could have done to save him.

There was another photograph of Carrie in her mother's kitchen at Marblehead. She was cooking clam chowder. Just to one side of her was a framed black and white portrait of her with her father, George, a handsome, square-jawed all-American in a uniform, probably taken in the early sixties.

I gazed at the one of her standing outside her college. Carrie had been encouraging me to give the place a try; I'd always loved medieval history, and had been reading quite a lot about the Crusades lately. I'd told her I wasn't sure the whole mature-student thing was me, working in Starbucks, being bollocked by an eighteen-year-old team leader. I hadn't quite got round to telling her that my formal education had ended when I was fifteen, so the college was unlikely to take me on as a janitor, let alone enrol me on one of its courses.

I guessed there was quite a lot of stuff, one way or the other, that I hadn't told Carrie. There was my trip to Algeria, for a start. It wasn't the job itself; I wouldn't have said a word about that anyway. It was the fact that I'd promised her I'd never get involved in dirty work again. The carrot George had dangled in front of me was irresistible; with American citizenship papers in my pocket, I'd be free to work at whatever I wanted. But I wasn't sure Carrie would appreciate the method behind the madness.

The story I'd told her was that I'd been offered three weeks' work escorting thrill-seekers into Egypt. After the 9/11 attacks, tourism to the Middle East had all but dried up, and the few travellers still brave enough to go wanted minders. Carrie agreed it was a good idea for me to make some money before I started the long process of applying for citizenship. Until that happened, all I could do were menial jobs, so money would be tight. I hadn't a clue how I was going to explain to her why my citizenship had come through so fast, but I'd cross that bridge when I came to it. I sat and looked out at the dull grey day as ice-covered trees zoomed past along the side of the track and vehicles in the distance with cold engines tailed exhaust fumes behind them. It wasn't a good start to us being together, but it was done now. I should just look to the future.

After two days of mincing around, ninety metres below the Mediterranean, following the North African coastline, we'd finally made it back into Alexandria. The weather had closed in as predicted about ten hours after we got on board, not that we knew, so far below water. A Chrysler MPV was waiting at the dockside; somebody took my bergen, and that was the last I saw of it. For the next week I just had to wait in a hotel room in Cairo while the head I'd brought back was confirmed as Zeralda's. If not, we might have been sent back to get the correct one.

I still didn't know why I'd been asked to bring back Zeralda's head and I still didn't care. All that mattered was that George was coming to Boston in a few days' time, and I'd be getting Nick Stone's shiny new US passport, social security number and Massachusetts driver's licence. I was about to become a real person.

I looked around the train. Most of my fellow travellers had now got bored looking at the dickhead cleaning his teeth and wiping the foam that ran down his chin, and were buried in their papers. The front pages were plastered with the war in Afghanistan, reporting that everything was going well and there were no casualties. Northern Alliance fighters were silhouetted against the sunset as they stood watching US Special Forces soldiers carrying enough kit on their backs to collapse a donkey.

I looked out and chewed on my brush. To my right, and running parallel with the track, was the coast road, also cutting through the icy marshland. We were overtaking a taxi, his side windows festooned with patriotic imagery; there was even a little Stars and Stripes fluttering from his aerial. I couldn't see the driver, but knew he just had to be an Indian or a Pakistani. Those guys didn't want to leave anything to chance in these troubled times.

The marshland petered out, and whitewashed, weather-boarded houses sprang up either side of the train, then the blur of supermarkets and used car lots also draped in the Stars and Stripes. I felt my pulse quicken with anticipation. I didn't have to work for the Firm any more, didn't have to do any more jobs for George. I really felt I'd been given a new start, that life was coming together. I was free.

6

I shoved the toothbrush into my brown nylon holdall as the train came to a halt and people stood and got their hats and coats on. The automatic doors drew back to reveal the signs for Wonderland Station, and I stepped out of the carriage, hooking the holdall over my shoulder. I got an immediate and fierce reminder that I wasn't in North Africa any more. The temperature was several degrees below zero. I zipped up my fleece jacket, which did nothing to keep out the bitter wind as I joined the throng heading for the barrier.

She was standing by a ticket desk, dressed in a green nylon Puffa jacket and a Russian style black sheepskin hat, her breath billowing about her face as we both waved and smiled.

I got through the barrier and threaded my way through the crowd. Taking her in my arms, I planted a big, exaggerated kiss on her forehead, hoping that the toothpaste routine hadn't been in vain. I ran my fingers gently down her cheek as I drew back and we exchanged huge smiles.

Her large green eyes stared into mine for several seconds, then she hugged me hard. 'I missed you big-time, Stone.'

'Me too.' I kissed her again, properly this time.

She linked her left arm in mine and rubbed her free hand up and down my stubble. 'Come on,' she said. 'Places to go, things to do. Mom's at a church meeting until this evening so you don't have to say hello until later. Gives us a little time.' She rested her head on my shoulder as we walked outside. 'But we're not going home just yet. There's something I want you to see on the way.'

We weren't quite in step: the leg she'd broken in Panama had left her with a slight limp. I grinned like an idiot. 'I'm all yours.'

The dog-track parking lot was used by commuters during the day. The November air had already worked its magic on line upon line of windscreens and frozen them white.

I looked down at her face poking out from the sheepskin. 'How's Luz?'

'Oh, she's fine. She says hi. She might be coming back next week – with a new friend.'

'It'll be good to see her. Who's the lucky boy?'

'David somebody, I think.' She turned to me. 'But you're not to—'

'I know.' I held up my hand to swear the oath. 'No jokes, don't worry, I won't embarrass her . . .' If I did, though, it wouldn't be the first time.

We reached the main drag and waited for the lights, along with ten or so other pedestrians heading for the lot. 'So, how was your trip? I notice I didn't get a card of the Pyramids like I was promised.'

'I know, I know. It's just that I thought by the time I got back into Cairo and posted it I'd be here. Especially this time of year . . .'

'Not to worry. You're back, that's all that matters.'

The traffic stopped and the bleeper on the crossing ushered us across.

'Did you get hit by the storms?'

'We were much further south.'

'I was worried.' Those little lines appeared at the corners of her eyes. 'Six hundred people died in the floods in Algeria . . .'

I looked straight ahead. 'Six hundred? I didn't know.'

We'd just got in among the cars when she stopped and faced me, her arms pushed in under mine and linked around my waist. 'You stink like a camel, but it really is good to have you back all the same.' She kissed me lightly on the lips, her skin cold but soft. 'You know what? I don't want you to go away ever again. I like you right here, where I can see you.'

We stayed wrapped in each other and I fought the urge to tell her the truth. Sanity prevailed. I would find a time and a place to do that, but not now, not yet. She was too happy, I was too happy. I wanted to keep the real world outside.

She let me go. 'Magical-mystery-tour time.'

We got to her mother's Plymouth sedan. Carrie hadn't got round to buying a car since she'd got back: she'd been too busy. She'd arranged the transportation of Aaron's body from Panama to Boston, then the cremation, before returning to Panama to scatter his ashes in the jungle. After that, she'd had to get Luz settled into high school, and herself into her new job. She'd also had to set up house – then change her life around again when a not-too-reliable Brit turned up begging for a spare room.

We split as she went to the driver's side of the Plymouth, reaching into her bag for the keys and hitting the fob. The car unlocked with a bleep and a flash of the indicators. I pulled open the door, threw my holdall into the back and climbed in, as Carrie closed her door and put on her belt. That frown of hers had reappeared, the one that went along with the raised eyebrow and slight tilt of the head.

The engine turned over and we rolled out of the parking space. She cleared her throat. 'I've been thinking about a whole bunch of stuff while you were away. There's something very important I want to say to you.'

I reached across and pulled off her hat before running my fingers slowly through her hair, as she negotiated the Plymouth over the potholed tarmac. We hit the main drag and turned left up the north shore for the ten miles to Marblehead.

'Good important or bad important?'

53

She shook her head. 'Not yet. It'll be easier for me to explain when we get there.'

I nodded slowly. 'OK. Tell me some other stuff, then.'

Luz liked her new school, she said, and had started to make some really nice friends; she was staying over with one of them for the rest of the week to give us time together. She also told me how her mother's B-and-B had picked up a little since September. Oh, and that she thought there might be a part-time job for me at the yacht club as a barman. I wanted to tell her that I didn't need a job pulling pints of Samuel Adams for weekend water warriors. Come Wednesday, I was going to be a *bona fide*, flag-waving citizen; the US was my oyster, and all that sort of thing.

Marblehead old town was like a film set: brightly painted wooden houses with neat little gardens sitting on winding streets. Cornish fishermen had settled there in the 1600s, maybe because the rocky coastline reminded them of home. The only fishermen there now dangled lines off the backs of their million-dollar boats in the Boston yacht club.

Marblehead today was where old Boston money met new Boston money. Carrie's mother had been born there, and was blessed with plenty of the old stuff. She'd come back ten or so years ago, after her divorce from George, and took in B-and-B guests because she enjoyed the company.

Carrie made a couple of turns that took us off the main street and we came to a stop on a small road that ran along the water's edge. Tucker's Wharf jutted just a little into the water, with old weatherboarded buildings either side, now restaurants and ye olde shoppes. 'This is it,' she announced. 'We're here.'

We got out, zipped up against the cold, and Carrie took my arm as she walked me towards a wooden bench. We sat and looked out over the bay at the large houses the other side.

'Mom used to bring me here when I was a kid,' Carrie said. 'She called it Marblehead's gangway to the world. That sounded pretty magical to a ten-year-old, I can tell you. It made me think my home town was the centre of the universe.'

It sounded pretty magical to me, even now. The place I'd grown up in was the centre of a shit-heap.

'She used to tell me all kinds of stories of fishing boats setting off from here to the Grand Banks, and crews gathering to join in the revolutionary war and the war of 1812.' She smiled. 'You're not the only history buff around here. I hope you're impressed.' The smile faded slowly as her thoughts turned elsewhere. She looked into my eyes, then away, across the water. 'Nick, I don't really know where to start with this.'

I gave her hair a stroke. I didn't know where this was going, but I guessed it had to do with Aaron. I had a sudden flash of him sitting under guard in that store room in Panama, smoking. His nose was bloodied and his eyes were swollen, but he was smiling, maybe feeling happy with himself that he'd helped the rest of us escape into the jungle as he enjoyed his last cigarette.

I hadn't had a clue how I was going to get him out of there. I was unarmed; my options were about nil. Then he had made the decision for me. The door burst open and Aaron launched himself into the night.

As he slithered into the darkness there was a long burst of automatic fire from inside the house. Then the guard got to the door and took aim with a short, sharp burst.

I had heard an anguished gasp, then a chilling, drawn-out scream. Then the sort of silence that told me he was dead.

'I brought him here, you know, soon after we'd met. We came up from Panama one vacation. I knew it would scandalize my parents. Turned out they had a whole lot of other stuff on their minds. George was too busy fighting whoever were the designated bad guys that year to notice I was there. I shouldn't have been surprised. He couldn't even remember Mom's birthday. So back we went to Panama to study while the folks got divorced.' She smiled wistfully. 'Jeez, I'd gone to all that trouble to round off my rebellious years by getting laid by my teacher, and my straitlaced parents were too busy messing up their own relationship to pay any attention . . . Shit,' she said, rolling her eyes. 'Maybe I shouldn't be encouraging you into college.'

I gave her a squeeze. 'I spent my rebellious teenage years nicking cars, and the ones I couldn't get into I'd just smash up. I think they're over now.'

Suddenly she pressed herself against me. 'I hated you being away, Nick. It scared me. I guess it made me realize how much I've got used to having you around. After Aaron died I told myself I'd be very careful about laying myself open to that sort of pain again.'

I lifted a hand to her face and brushed a tear from her cheek.

'I was worried about being with you, Nick. Dependability isn't exactly high on your résumé.'

I gave my résumé, as she called it, a quick glance. This time last year I'd been living in sheltered housing in Camden, had no money, had to line up to get free food from a Hare Krishna soup-wagon. All my friends were dead apart from one, and he despised me. Apart from the clothes I stood up in when I arrived in Panama, my only other possessions were in a bag stuck in Left Luggage at a London railway station. She had a point.

'And no sooner have we settled down here than you take off again. Not much for a girl to brag to her mother about, is it?' She paused. 'Then there's Kelly. What if we don't get on? What if she and Luz don't get on?'

I was Kelly's guardian: she was the other woman in my life I was busy disappointing. She was thirteen and not nearly as grown-up as she liked to think she was. I'd be seeing her at Christmas down in Maryland. Not on Christmas Day itself, because she was doing the family thing with Josh and his children, her new family, but I'd be seeing her on Christmas Eve. 'Carrie, I—'

She placed a finger to my lips. 'Sssh . . .' She turned and looked me straight in the eye. 'I *was* worried, but I'm not worried any more. I don't care about the past. You're a tour guide now, a barman, whatever – I don't care, as long as you're good at it. The last few weeks have been good for me. They gave me time to think, and I realized something. I can finally think about what's ahead. It's like I was just treading water the last year, my life was on hold.

'That's what I want to tell you, Nick. I want us to be together – really together.' She looked down, then up again and into my eyes. 'New Carrie, new Nick, new life. That's why I wanted to bring you here. Tucker's Wharf, gangway to the world. Gangway to the future.

'You've been so patient about Aaron. I know I'll never get over him, but I am ready to move on, and that's the important thing. I want the future to be about us.'

'I don't know what to say.'

'Then don't. You don't need to say anything.'

We stood up and walked arm in arm for about twenty minutes until we reached a small protected cove.

'Little Harbor.' She swept her hand across the bay. 'Mom always called this the place where it all began. The founders, some of them her family, put down their roots here in 1629. The settlers cut back the forest to build tiny thatch-roofed cottages and fishing boats. I can still hear Mom saying, "From here, strong-hearted men set out to fish uncharted waters." I loved her stories of the founding families. They were gutsy, venturesome, in search of personal liberty, a plot of land, a place by the sea . . .'

'They had a point.' I was surprised to hear myself saying it out loud. 'Marblehead is pretty much my fantasy, too, you know.' I hadn't known places like this existed when I was bunking off school in Peckham.

'Tucker's Wharf was about departures, Nick. This is about arrivals. It's our new start. I feel we're at the start of something, and I wanted to bring you here to tell you that. I've never shared this place with anyone, not even Aaron.' She smiled again. 'Ready for some more history? Our ships traded with the known world, dried fish for clothing, tools, gold and silver.

Everybody prospered and there were two big news stories – war with the French, and pirates. They harassed the coast for decades.'

She hesitated for a moment, embarrassed. 'I got you this.' From under her coat she produced a carefully wrapped gift, tied with shiny blue ribbon. She beamed. 'Go on, then, open it. It won't bite.'

I removed the ribbon as delicately as I could.

A General History of the Robberies and Murders of the most Notorious Pirates by Captain Charles Johnson.

She could barely conceal her delight as I flicked through the pages, pausing at each illustration.

'It was first published in 1724. I had to get this edition from a little place in New York. I know it's not the Middle Ages, but there's a whole lot about ships from New England being boarded en route to London. I knew you'd like it. And, besides, it's to remind you of everything I've been boring you about just now.'

I closed the book. 'You haven't been boring me. I loved every word of it.'

We got back into the car and drove to Gregory Street. The house had been in the family for years. Built in 1824, it was originally a fisherman's cottage overlooking the sea. Various extensions and rebuilds over the years, probably during the Golden Age she was talking about, had turned it into a spacious family home. A wooden pineapple was nailed above the front door as a sign of welcome. They were all over the place in this part of the world. A couple of hundred years ago, sailors returning from long voyages would place a pineapple by their door to show they were back and people were welcome to come and visit. I would normally have made some quip about that, but thought better of it today.

She swung the car into the gravelled driveway and headed towards a white Taurus parked in front of the annexe, next to my covered-over Yamaha 600 motorcycle.

Carrie didn't seem too concerned. 'I thought Mom wasn't

expecting anyone until Saturday. Oh, well, I'll go see if she remembered to put out the cookies and coffee. Got to look after the guests!'

As we got closer I could see Massachusetts plates. The vehicle was so clean and sterile it had to be a hire car.

She parked beside it and we both got out. She threw her keys at me over the roof. 'Tell you what, why not take a shower and I'll be right back? And make sure you shave. We have some catching up to do.' There was a smile before she nodded at the annexe. 'Go.'

Excited, she ran back down the drive towards the front of the house as I went into the annexe. It was huge, much bigger than the last house I'd lived in, and tastefully furnished in dark wooden furniture that had been in the family for generations. I always felt as if a photographer from *Homes and Gardens* would appear at any minute to take pictures of me reclining by the log fire. I didn't spread myself around too much, though. I didn't have much to spread.

She had made a big effort for my homecoming. There were flowers, and a bottle of champagne on the mantelpiece. Leaning against it was a plain white card that said in her distinctive, large and neat handwriting, 'Welcome home.'

I put my holdall on the floor in the bedroom, went into the en suite and got the shower sparked up while I undressed. The hot water ran down my smelly body and I did something I hadn't done for a while. I started to think seriously about the future.

I got to work with the soap and razor before stepping out to dry myself with soft white towels.

I heard the front door shut. 'I'm in here . . .'

The bedroom door opened and she stood in the frame, tears running down her red face.

I had a bad feeling about this, and it had to do with the Massachusetts-plated Taurus parked in the driveway. 'Carrie?'

Her green eyes, just as red as her face, stared at me as I moved forward to comfort her.

'George is here. Tell me what he's saying isn't true, Nick.' Her eyes searched mine, and I had to look away.

'What's he saying?'

'That you've been working for him.'

'Carrie, come and sit down—'

'I don't want to sit down.'

'I have something to tell you.'

'Then tell me, before I go crazy,' she said, and I could hear her starting to lose control. 'What are you going to tell me? Why won't you simply say that my father is lying?'

'Because it's not that simple,' I said.

'It *is* simple! It's fucking simple!' She could no longer keep the panic out of her voice. 'He says you work for him. But that's not true, is it, Nick? Is it? You've been in Egypt, haven't you, as a tour guide? Christ, Nick, are we living a lie here?'

I shrugged. I didn't know what to say.

Carrie looked at me as if I'd knifed her. 'You bastard!' she gasped. 'You fucking bastard!'

'You don't need to know this shit,' I said. 'My work for him is finished. I've done one job for him. I only did it to get my citizenship. George has got me a US passport. We can—'

'We nothing,' she snapped. 'We don't exist any more.'

'But—'

'You don't understand what you've done to me, do you?'

The next few seconds seemed to pass in slow motion. Carrie moved towards the door, anger and sadness etched across her face. She stopped and looked at me for a long time, as if she had something to say but couldn't find the words. Then she was gone.

I didn't move. I told myself I needed to give her some space. In truth, I just didn't have the bollocks to go after her.

Then the decision was made for me. The engine of the Plymouth fired up and the car shot down the drive.

7

A gang of seagulls screeched overhead and dived into the water just forty metres away as I ran towards the front of the house.

The sea was choppy; there was a wind getting up that made the yachts in the bay bob agitatedly at their moorings, and their rigging sound like the rattle of a hundred cages.

I opened the insect screen and as soon as I was through the heavy wooden front door I was hit by the overbearing heat. Her mother kept the temperature at a solid ninety degrees, day and night.

George called out from the rear, 'In the kitchen.'

My Timberlands clunked on the dark hardwood floor of the hallway and I passed the loudly ticking grandfather clock.

George was sitting, straight backed, at the old pine rectangular table. A dozen or so photographs of boats were stuck to a corkboard behind him, and he was looking down at a picture frame in his hands. Little doilies and smelly candles sat on every scrap of surface.

'You know what they say about New Englanders and the cold, Nick?'

I shook my head.

'When the temperature hits zero all the people in Miami die.

But New Englanders, they just close the windows. Trust my ex-wife to be different.'

If he was extending a hand of friendship, I wasn't shaking.

Just like in the old picture of years ago, square-jawed and muscular, George was still looking like something off a recruitment poster. The only difference now was that his short back and sides was greying. His face was cold and unyielding. This setting of New England family domesticity didn't suit him at all.

'What the fuck are you doing here, George? We were supposed to meet downtown Wednesday, remember?'

'Our plans have changed, Nick. We're not talking about a holiday booking.'

He pursed his lips and picked up a framed photograph from the Welsh dresser. I could see it was of the three of them. Carrie must have been about ten years old in her blue checked school-girl summer dress. He was in his medal- and badge-festooned military uniform, holding a certificate, with his wife standing proudly beside him. I'd told Carrie when I first saw it that they looked the perfect family. She'd laughed. 'Then hellooo . . . meet the camera that lied.'

'You could have sent somebody. You didn't have to come in person. You know I wanted to keep her out of this.'

He didn't answer as I looked down at him. He was a man who had never let power and success go to his clothes. He was dressed in his civilian uniform, a brown corduroy sports jacket with brown suede elbow pads, white button-down collar shirt, and a brown tie. There had been one addition since 11 September: he now had a Stars and Stripes button badge pinned to his right lapel. But, these days, who didn't?

At last he looked up. 'She didn't even give you time to dry your hair.' There was just a hint of a smile as he thought of his daughter fucking me off, as he placed the frame carefully on the tabletop. 'I've done you a favour, son. She needed to find out some time. And I happen to think she deserved to know.' He bent down and picked up a leather folder from beside his feet. 'Maybe this will help. Compliments of the US Government.'

He went and poured himself some coffee from the percolator while I sat opposite his chair at the table and unzipped the folder. 'It's not as if it's a bad thing you've done, you've nothing to be ashamed of.' He turned round and gestured towards the mug in his hand. I accepted with a grudging nod. Carrie's mother would go ape if the wood got marked so I took two pineapple-motif coasters from the pile in the centre of the table as George continued, now with his back to me. 'This isn't a war of choice like Vietnam or Kosovo. This is a war of necessity. It's in our yard now, Nick. Carrie should be proud of you.'

I glanced into the folder and saw my passport, driver's licence and other documents. 'This could have waited, George.'

'What you did for us out there, it had to be done, Nick. This is not the time to be showing the world we're nice guys. This outreach thing that's going on, every schoolkid gets a Muslim pen pal, that kind of thing, it makes no sense. This isn't a time to hug, this is a time to be feared.'

I flipped through the passport and there was something wrong, big-time wrong. These weren't Nick Stone's documents; they belonged to someone called Nick Scott, who had the same face as me. I looked up sharply. George was still pouring creamer. 'I didn't want a new name, I wanted my own back.'

He came and sat down with the two mugs of coffee, passing one across the table then waving my last words aside. He kept the other in his huge left hand, his veteran's onyx signet ring glinting on his wedding finger. He took a tentative sip; too hot – the mug went on the coaster. 'Do you know over six hundred people died in floods over in Algeria two days ago? You were lucky to get in-country before the storms.'

I cupped my hands around the mug and felt the heat. 'I heard something.'

'You know why? Because the drains had been blocked to

63

stop terrorists planting bombs under the streets and killing people. Kind of ironic, isn't it?'

I didn't know where this was headed, but I wasn't feeling good about it. I just wanted to get out of here and go and find Carrie.

'Know what my job is nowadays, Nick? To make sure we don't have to block our drains. You've helped me do that, and the first thing I want to say today is thank you.'

This was really starting to worry me. I picked up the dull-looking brew with not enough creamer, and took a sip.

'For years, we've been fighting this war with our hands tied. Now people are looking for scapegoats because America doesn't feel safe any more. America says, "The government should have known, the CIA should have known, the military should have known. Thirty billion of our tax dollars spent on intelligence, why didn't anyone know?" ' He paused to lift his mug. 'Well, here's the news. On nine-eleven America had the exact level of protection that it was willing to pay for. We've been telling government for years that we need more money to fight this thing. We told them this would eventually happen but Congress wouldn't give us cash. Doesn't anyone watch C-Span any more to see what their own government is doing? Maybe they're just too busy watching Jerry Springer. What do you think?'

I shrugged, not really understanding what he was on about, not that it mattered. I just got the feeling the place we were going to wasn't one where I wanted to be.

'Did any of the complainers see the intelligence chiefs talking about the new terrorism? We kept telling Congress, live on TV, there wasn't enough money to build intelligence networks in the areas where these scum are operating – and that they needed to untie our hands so we could deal with this situation. We've told them for years that this is a clear and present danger within America's borders that needs to be taken on and defeated but, hey, guess what? Congress just said no, looking at ways of saving a nickel.'

64

He took a long, slow breath of frustration before continuing. 'So why didn't America demand more protection from their Congressmen? Because they were watching one of their two hundred other channels and didn't catch the news. Didn't catch Congress telling us we didn't need more capability. Telling us we were just looking for something to replace Cold War. Know why Congress did that? Because they think that's what the people think, and they don't want to upset them, because they don't want to lose their vote. Now everything is different. Now we have all the nails we need to shut the stable door, but the horse has already bolted.

'Goddamn it, Nick, why didn't things change after the terrorist attack on the USS *Cole*? Seventeen American sailors came home in body-bags – why didn't that open their eyes? And what about the bombing of the air force base in Saudi Arabia? Or the embassy staff in Africa? Or our soldiers mutilated and dragged through the streets of Somalia? Why wasn't anybody letting us do anything then?

'Because those guys up on the Hill were just too damned busy worrying about the civil rights of paedophiles and rapists, worrying about interest rates on credit cards that the voters use to buy widescreen digital TVs to make them feel life is good. But those home-movie centres don't seem to get C-Span. Nobody knows what's going on, and that's just how Congress wanted to keep it. Then they have the gall to ask us: "Why did they attack the innocent people? Why didn't they go after the military?" Well, the answer is, that's a done deal, but no one took any notice.'

He picked up his mug and looked genuinely sad, the first time I had ever seen him like that. He seemed to be lost in his own world for a while until I cut in. 'So now what?'

'Now?' The mug went down. 'We've got the money. A billion-dollar down-payment. The problem is finding a way to fight these people. They don't have anything to defend. It's not like the Cold War, or any war, that we've seen before. There's no real estate to fight over, and the notion of deterrence doesn't

65

apply to these guys. There's no treaty to be negotiated, no arms control agreement that's going to guarantee our security. The only way we can deal with them is to hit them hard and fast and take them down. You know it's crazy – only a few months ago, they were saying a hundred million for the Navy was too much . . .'

He paused and reflected. I wasn't too sure if this was all part of the performance: George might be sad, but he still had a job to do. 'But, hey, you can't unring a bell, Nick. I'm here because I want you to work for me. For us. Nick Scott would be your cover name.'

I shook my head. 'The deal was one job. You agreed on that.'

'Events have taken a serious turn these last couple days, Nick.' His voice was steely, his gaze level. 'Al-Qaeda have upped the ante, these guys are just programmed for trouble. I can't tell you how unless you commit. But I can tell you, this is the front page of the threat matrix the president gets to read every day. These are scary days, Nick. Yesterday's ran to thirty pages.' He looked down at the table and traced a figure of eight with his mug. 'You know what? At the moment I feel like a blind watchmaker, just throwing the components into the case and waiting to see what works.'

I didn't look up, because I knew he was waiting, his eyes ready to ambush mine.

'I need your help, Nick.' It was a challenge, not an entreaty.

'Things are good here with Carrie.'

'Are they?' He gave an exaggerated frown. 'I don't think she took it too well. She's like her mom.'

The arsehole. Divide and rule. He'd done it on purpose. I forced myself to stay calm. 'You didn't tell her everything, did you?'

'Son, I don't even tell God everything. I'll leave that until I meet him face to face. But, right now, I see it as my duty to make sure there's a big fucking bunch of al-Qaeda ahead of me in the line.'

He stood up and turned his back to me again as he placed

the framed picture back on the dresser. Maybe he didn't want me to see how proud he was of the way he'd delivered his lines. 'The secret of combating terrorism is simple – don't get terrorized. Keep a clear head and fight back on their terms. That's the only way we're going to win this war – or, at least, contain it, keep a lid on it. But we can only do that if we take the battle to them, with every means at our disposal. And that's where you come in, Nick. I need to stop the drains getting blocked – and fast. Do you want to know more, Nick, or am I wasting my time here?'

I looked at him and took another mouthful of coffee. 'I'd like to know what happened to Zeralda's head.'

There was a bit of a smile. 'It came back here and was presented to his cousin in Los Angeles on a silver salver. By all accounts it kind of freaked him out.'

'What about the greaseball who was there with him? Was he the source? Is that why no one else was to be killed?'

'Greaseball?' He managed to complete the smile. 'I like it. Yes, he was and still is a source, and a good one – too good to lose just yet.' The smile faded. 'Nick, have you ever heard of *hawalla*?'

I'd spent enough time in the Middle East to know it, and when I was a kid in London, all the Indian and Pakistani families used it to send cash back home. 'Like Western Union, but without the ADSL lines, right?'

He nodded. 'OK, so what we've got is a centuries-old system of moving money, originally to avoid taxes and bandits along the ancient Silk Road, and nowadays to avoid the money laundering laws. A guy in San Francisco wants to send some cash to, say, his mother in Delhi. So, he walks into one of these *hawalla* bankers, maybe a shopkeeper, maybe even working in the money markets in San Fran. The *hawallada* takes his cash and gives the guy a codeword. The *hawallada* then faxes, calls or emails his counterpart in Delhi, maybe a restaurant owner, and gives him the codeword and the amount of the transfer. The guy's mother goes into the Delhi restaurant, says the

67

codeword, and collects. And that's it – takes less than thirty minutes to move huge sums of money anywhere in the world, and we have no track of it.

'These *hawalla* guys settle their debts and commissions among themselves. In Pakistan, business is huge. There's maybe five, six billion dollars US sent back there every year by migrant workers just from the Gulf states. But only one billion goes through normal banking channels. Everything else goes via *hawalladas*. These guys work on total trust, a handshake or a piece of paper between them. It's been going on for centuries, must be about the second oldest profession. It even gets a mention in the New Testament.' He gave me a wry smile. 'Carrie's mother is a very religious woman. You know the tale of Ananis and Safia?'

As if. I shook my head.

'Go read some day. These *hawalla* guys were hiding money that they were due to give to Peter, so they were deemed sinners. And when they were confronted with their shame they just fell down and died.' There was a pause. 'That's what you did for us, Nick: you made Zeralda fall down and die. This *hawalla* network has been used to funnel money to the terrorist groups in the Kashmir valley. It's been used by the heroin trade coming out of Afghanistan, and now it's here, in the US.

'This is not good, Nick. Zeralda was a *hawallada*, and we reckon he'd moved between four and five million dollars into this country for terrorism in the last four years. You can be sure the legit banks are doing their bit now and cracking down on laundering all around the world, but with *hawalla* we can't check accounts or monitor electronic transfers.

'Well, we've got to close it down. Al-Qaeda is retreating and regrouping their assets in both manpower and cash. We've got to turn off the faucet, Nick, and we've got to do that before al-Qaeda moves all its funds to safe harbours. Money is the oxygen for their campaign in this country – your new country. I say again, am I wasting my time here, Nick?'

I really needed room to think. 'What happened to the cousin in Los Angeles?'

'Let's put it this way, we didn't stand in his way when he jumped on the first plane he could get out of the States. All he left behind was a few clothes, a pair of leather motorcycle gloves, a Qur'ān, and maybe sixty pages of Arabic text off the Internet. All his accounts are frozen, but we're not after his money. We want him to go spread the news of what happened to the other half of the transaction route. He's back in Algeria, a very scared man, and much more use to us there than he would be sitting in a penitentiary.'

The coffee was almost cold. I took another sip to buy myself some more thinking time.

'See, Nick, you were the key. The key that switched on the power of terror. Bringing back that head showed these guys that for us anything is possible as well. They've got to know we're coming for them, that they shouldn't start reading any long books, know what I mean?'

He liked that one and took another swig himself. 'As Rumsfeld just told the world, Nick, there will be covert operations and they'll be secret even in success.'

'Did you know beforehand that Zeralda was into boys? We were briefed it was just hookers.'

'As I said, even God doesn't know everything I know. I wanted to make sure you guys finished the job. Not being mentally geared up for it, then seeing something as sick as that would make it ... shall I say less confusing? I just figured you'd be thinking it could be your own kid. Am I right?'

I nodded. The expression in those boys' eyes had reminded me of the way Kelly looked when her parents were killed.

'Nick, I understand what you want from life now, but things have changed for all of us since September, and everything's ratcheted up again in the last twenty-four hours. My grandfather was only here a year before fighting for this country in the First World War. My father did the same in the Second, because he wanted this country to remain free. I've done the

69

same all my life, and even found myself crying on nine-eleven – and that's not a place I often go to.

'Do this new job for me, and I guarantee you'll get a Nick Stone passport. All you'll need to do is swear your oath of allegiance and that's it, you're one of the seven hundred thousand new Americans this year.' He switched on the kind of expression you normally only see in stained-glass windows. 'You're one of us now, Nick. All the people you love live here. Think about Kelly. What world do you want her to grow up in? The kind of place where you freak out every time she flies here to see you? Who knows? It'll take a while, but Carrie will understand. Think about it, Nick, just think.'

I'd done my thinking. I'd heard all I needed to hear.

I stood up, handing him the empty mug. 'No. I've done my bit. We had a deal and my only job now is to make things right with Carrie.'

8

I ran out on to the street. I didn't need to be Oprah Winfrey or Dr Phil to work out where she had gone – I mean, where do you go when the man you've poured your heart out to turns round and headbutts you?

I found the Plymouth and walked down into Little Harbor. She was sitting on the beach, staring out at the houses on the other side of the bay. My footsteps crunched on ice as I approached.

'Carrie, I'm so sorry . . .'

She turned very slowly to face me. 'How could you?' Her voice was weary, defeated, empty even of the bitterness I expected and, I guessed, deserved. 'How do you think this makes me feel? I trusted you.'

'I'm not turning into your dad. It was just that once. One job. It's over now.'

'Of all people . . . He caused Aaron's death, remember? The same man who was going to blow up an American cruise ship just so the White House would have the excuse to march back into Panama. Doesn't that mean anything to you?'

I hated it when she looked at me like that. It was as though she could see right through me, and it wasn't a view I'd ever much enjoyed.

'I'm so sad, Nick. I'm feeling bereaved all over again. I feel so goddamn stupid; I thought we had something good happening here.'

I sat down beside her. 'Look, I'm sorry I couldn't tell you, but what could I have said to make it sound all right?'

'The truth, that's all I needed and always need from you. The truth I can handle, the truth I can work with, but this . . .' She turned away, tears running down her face.

I thought about Zeralda's head, and gave mine a shake. 'Carrie, you remember how it was in Panama. You know how these jobs work. There are some truths you really don't want to know . . .'

'This has been the story of my life, Nick. I just can't risk it all happening again. I know it's selfish of me, but I don't think I can take it any more. That man is responsible for so much pain in my life. He sacrificed me and my mom by dedicating himself to his double-dealing world. But even so, I allowed myself to be sucked in, and because of it my husband was killed. I kid myself I blame George for Aaron's death, but do you know what? Really, I blame myself. I let my own father exploit me, the way he exploits everyone.

'In Panama, he knew I was desperate to get a passport for Luz so we could get back to the States. But I've never gotten anything from him for free. Even as a little girl, I always had to earn it first.'

I watched her as her eyes concentrated on the water but her mind was elsewhere. 'Aaron was right all along. He told me that once it started and George knew we were desperate for the passport, it would never stop because George wouldn't let it. And you know what? He was right, because here we are again. How can I let myself be with you until I know you've no longer got even a toe in that world?

'I've made the mistake of depending on you. Depending on you being there when I wake up in the morning. And, worse still, Luz has started to get used to you being around, too. I'm not going to run the risk of having to tell her that another person she loved, that she relied upon, is lying in some ditch with a bullet in the back of his head . . .'

I reached out to touch her but she stiffened and moved away.

'You could have applied for citizenship. You could have gone back to school, had a home, you could have had me. Doesn't any of that mean anything?'

I didn't answer her immediately. 'I can't think of anything I'd like more. It's the full fairytale, for me.' I didn't know how she did it, but I always found myself saying things to her that I thought I'd kept well buried. 'Perhaps the real truth is that I can't quite believe there's a place for me in your perfect world. Remember what I said to you in the jungle? My world may look like a pile of shit –'

'– but at least you sometimes get to sit on the top of it . . .'

I looked at her, hoping for even a hint of a smile, but I hadn't come close.

'That's not the issue here.' Her voice was still sad and tired. 'You lied to me, Nick, that's the long and the short of it. Nothing's changed. You betrayed what I thought we had. Oh, God, when I think what I said to you today, I feel so ridiculous.'

My heart was pounding as I stood behind her, trying to think what I could say. 'We just need time, Carrie. We just need time . . .'

She shook her head. The tears were running off her face now and on to her Puffa jacket, staining the nylon a darker green. 'You'd better go. Both of us have got to do some thinking. I don't think I can just now. When you're ready to come back to me on my terms, Nick, give me a call.

'Until then, if it has to be you who does my father's dirty work for him, Nick, it has to be you. I'll never forget what you did for us in Panama. I'll always admire the man you are, and I'll always love the man you might have allowed yourself to be. But don't expect Luz and me to come and put flowers on your grave . . .'

9

Navigation lights flashing in the gloom, an American Airways jet thundered down the runway and took off, quickly disappearing into dense low cloud. I turned back from the window and looked at George. His finger was jabbing a copy of the *Boston Globe* so I could see the front page pictures of dead Taliban scattered across Afghanistan.

'A wounded animal is the most dangerous of all, Nick. There will be another strike; it's just a matter of where and when.' He gave me a look of such intensity that I began to realize I was going to be going sooner than later. 'We've received A grade int in the last few days that they're putting something together for Christmas. But we have no idea of the target – and that's where you come in.'

We'd come straight to the Hilton at Logan airport, and it had already been getting dark when we arrived. He had booked the room well in advance. The arsehole had known precisely how Carrie would react when she heard the truth, and had still been in the kitchen, waiting for me, when I got back to the house. He didn't exactly have to twist my arm to get me working for him again. I'd already made up my mind on the walk back to Gregory Street – or, rather, it had been made up for me. The fact was, I had nowhere else to go. What was I going to do?

Check into a motel down the road and try to patch things up with her over the next few months, between pulling pints at the yacht club? Go back to the UK? There was nothing for me there except trouble; George would make sure of that. No, if I wanted to stay in the US to see Kelly and perhaps really get a life, I had to play by his rules. My immediate objective had to be to earn a real passport, and when the job was over, just see which way the wind was blowing. Well, that was where my half an hour of thinking had taken me, and it had seemed to make some kind of sense at the time.

'You have to ask yourself, Nick, which is scarier, the noise or the silence? Even before nine-eleven, we knew that there were al-Qaeda active service units out there, and they haven't gone away.' He was sitting at the desk to the left of the TV and mini-bar; the chair had been turned to face the bed where I was lying against the headboard.

'You got anything on them?'

'If only . . .' He jabbed at the newspaper again. 'The word is they'll all have mad eyes and beards – not so. This side of the Atlantic they're just ordinary, respectable people. Computer technicians, accountants, realtors; sometimes even born and raised here.' He looked around the room. 'Even hotel re-ceptionists, some of them married with two point four children, an MPV and a mortgage.

'They don't have to hide themselves in ethnic ghettos, Nick. They live in our neighbourhoods, shop in our malls, wear Gap, hey, even drink Coke.' He took a can from the minibar and lifted the ringpull. 'These folks are well-spoken, intelligent pillars of the community. They come here as kids, lie low, blend in, bide their time – classic sleepers. But they don't even have to be foreigners. Guys are converting to Islam by the hundred in our own prisons and, believe me, they're not turning into Allah's answer to Billy Graham . . .'

He sat back, the can resting on his knee. 'We don't know who, or how many, are in the ASUs. All we know is these sons of bitches are ready and waiting to press the button on December twenty-fourth.'

He pulled some papers from his alloy briefcase, and a fistful of airline tickets for Nick Scott.

'These are copies of stuff found by Special Forces in Afghanistan, transcripts from tactical interrogations of prisoners, and more in-depth material from al-Qaeda, rendered in Pakistan.' He sat back in the chair while I scanned the first few pages. 'It confirms three things. One, al-Qaeda have the knowhow to build radiological bombs. Two, they've gotten their hands on substantial quantities of radioactive material in the US. And three, they plan to use it December twenty-fourth. Dirty bombs – you know what I'm saying, don't you?'

I knew what he was saying. These things had radioactive material packed around conventional explosives. When detonated, the immediate explosion would cause just as much damage as a conventional weapon, but it would also blast radiation into the surrounding atmosphere. An area the size of Manhattan – or bigger, if the wind blew – would have to be cordoned off while they sandblasted buildings, replaced tarmac, bulldozed contaminated earth – and for years after, the queues of cancer victims would grow outside every hospital. Dirty bombs are a perfect terrorist weapon; they don't just blow you up, they rip out the nation's heart.

George was reading my thoughts. 'We're talking Chernobyl, Nick. Chernobyl, in our own backyard . . .' He paused, holding up his hands, fighting back the words. 'And if that happens, they've won. No matter what happens after. Just imagine what will happen if a truck with maybe four thousand pounds of homemade explosive and radioactive waste drives at ninety into the White House railings, right on to the lawn, maybe into the house itself. Now, imagine another heading into Rockefeller Plaza, when you can't move for Christmas shoppers, and another, say, on Wall Street. Or maybe not trucks, maybe twenty people on foot, in malls across Boston, carrying two, three, four pounds of contaminated HE in a carrier bag or strapped under their winter coats. Imagine them detonating all at the same time. Imagine that, Nick. I do, and haven't slept for weeks.'

He squeezed the empty can of Coke like he was throttling the life out of it, and this time it wasn't part of the act. 'According to these documents, their guys have been stealing and storing isotopes for two years, the stuff used in hospitals and industry. We're talking a big enough stockpile to make either a lot of small devices or maybe five or six Oklahomas – we could be talking of both truck and pedestrian attacks.'

He leant forward, elbows on knees. 'We have one straw to grasp at. These guys are on a suicide mission. But,' he raised his right index finger, '*but* – they're not going to do a damned thing until they know family business is taken care of.'

'You mean, the ASUs won't commit until they get confirmation that Dad has a new Landcruiser with all the trimmings?'

'Exactly. They may be crazy, but they're not stupid. So, here's my thinking. The set-up funds for these attacks have been coming into the US for nearly three years, and they'd have had everything in place before hitting the WTC because they'd know the shutters would come down straight afterwards.

'We know from the Zeralda connection that al-Qaeda channelled the cash to their ASUs in the US via three *hawalladas* based in the South of France. These guys would also get the compensation money to the ASUs' families, via their counterparts in Algeria.' He smiled for the first time since we'd entered the room. 'But that isn't going to happen now, since you did your John the Baptist trick with Zeralda. All *hawallada* activity has come to a halt in Algeria, and other al-Q money-movers have followed suit.

'So, the way it looks is that these French *hawalladas* have a mass of cash – around three million US – which they still have to get to the families. If not, no attack.

'We know from our source in France that an al-Qaeda team is on its way there – they're going to physically package up the money and take it back to Algeria.' He paused, to make sure I got the message. 'Your job, Nick, is to make sure that doesn't happen.'

In George's language, we had to 'render' them. In mine, once we had identified the three *hawalladas* with the help of information from the source, whom I'd be contacting once I got into France, we were to lift them, drug them, and leave them at a DOP [drop off point]. From there, they'd be picked up and taken aboard an American warship that would be anchored near Nice on a goodwill visit. Once on board, a team of inter-rogators would get to work on them straight away, to find out who their US counterparts were. There'd be no time to bring them back to the States, it had to be done in theatre. They'd not enjoy coming round in the belly of that warship; the inquisition would be doing their stuff to protect their own flesh and blood back home, not some far-off bit of desert or jungle. It makes quite a difference. Once the *hawalladas* had been sucked dry, maybe they'd have their heads chopped off, too. I didn't want to know, and I didn't much care.

'The FBI and CIA are doing everything they can to locate these ASUs,' George said. 'But as far as I'm concerned, these *hawalladas* are the quickest route to fingering the guys sitting at home in New Jersey or wherever with a truckload of caesium wrapped around some homemade explosive.'

'What if the source doesn't come up with the goods?'

George waved this aside. 'Everything's in a state of flux. Just get down there, meet up with the two guys who'll be on your team, and wait for my word on the source meet.'

He looked me directly in the eye. 'So much depends on you, Nick. If you succeed, none of these guys gets to see December fourteenth, let alone twenty-four. But whatever happens, that money must not make it to Algeria.'

He sat back in his chair once more and spread his hands. 'And it goes without saying, this has to be done without the French knowing. It takes time to go through all that human rights and due process bureaucratic crap – that's time we don't have.'

'And we have to make sure the rendered *hawalladas* still have their heads on, so they can chat to you people, right?'

George helped himself to another Coke. I didn't notice him offering me one. 'I don't have to tell you this, Nick. If someone hits you and then threatens to hit you some more, you've got to stop them. Period.'

The can went into the bin and he started collecting together the stuff on the bed and put it back into his briefcase. The briefing was over. 'You leave in the morning. Enjoy the flight – I hear Air France have some great wines.'

He stood up, tightened his tie, and buttoned up his jacket. 'We have a lot of catching up to do if we're to win this war, Nick, and you're now part of that catch-up.'

He turned back half-way to the door. 'Until they kill you, of course, or I find someone better.'

He gave me a big smile, but I wasn't sure he meant it as a joke.

10

WEDNESDAY, 21 NOVEMBER, 10:37 hrs

I sat in the *laverie* on boulevard Carnot, watching my sheets tumble about in the soapy water, deafened by the constant roar of traffic that drowned even the drone of the washing machines. I was waiting to RV with the source. The RV was to take place across the busy boulevard at Le Natale brasserie at eleven, either inside or at a pavement table, depending on where the source decided to sit. She was calling that particular shot, and I didn't like it.

The mid-morning temperature had climbed into the low sixties. The thinnest clothes I'd brought with me from Boston were what I was wearing now, jeans and a blue Timberland sweatshirt, but judging by one or two of the passers-by, I wouldn't have been out of place in winter furs.

Le Natale was a *café-tabac* where you could buy a lotto ticket and win a fortune, put all the winnings on a horse, watch the race while eating lunch or just throwing coffee down your neck, then buy your road tax and a book of stamps on the way out.

I had picked the launderette for cover. The sheets had been bought yesterday after I'd recced this area. You always have to have a reason for being somewhere.

George had told me three days ago that the source would be

supplying me with details of a pleasure boat that was parking some time soon, somewhere along the coast. On board would be the al-Qaeda team, an as yet unknown number of people, who would be collecting the money from three different *hawalladas* before taking it back to Algeria. We were to follow the collectors, see who they picked up the money from, then do our job the same day. There was no time to waste. George wanted them in that warship ASAP.

I was the only one in the *laverie*, apart from the old woman who did the service washes. Every few minutes she hitched up her shabby brown overcoat and dragged her slippered feet across the worn lino tiles to test the dampness of the clothes in the tumble dryers. She kept dabbing the clothes against her cheeks and seemed to be complaining to herself about the lack of drying power every time. She'd then close the door and mumble some more to me while I smiled back at her and nodded, my eyes already returning to the target the other side of the plate glass window, or as much of it as I could see through the posters for *Playboy* and how '*super economique*' the machines were.

I'd been in the South of France four days now, having left Boston on the first flight to Amsterdam, then on to Paris before finally arriving here on the eighteenth. I got myself a bed in a hotel in the old quarter of Cannes, behind the synagogue and the fruit and cheap clothes market.

Today was the day the covert three-man team I commanded was about to take the war to al-Qaeda.

My washing machine was spinning like mad as a stream of people moved in and out of the brasserie doors, buying their Camel Lights or Winstons along with their paper as the world screamed past in both directions.

The money we were after from the *hawalladas* had been made here in Europe. Al-Qaeda and the Taliban between them controlled nearly seventy per cent of the world's heroin trade. The *hawalla* system had been used very successfully to move that cash to the US to finance the ASUs.

The old woman pulled her weary body up once more, mumbling to herself as I pretended to look interested in a man on a moped who was weaving in and out of the traffic with only one hand on his handlebars. The other was holding a plastic coffee cup. His helmet straps flew out each side of his helmet as he tried to take a gulp at the same time as cutting up a Citroën.

This was a good place to watch the RV before making contact, and it hid me from the CCTV camera mounted outside on a high steel pole. It seemed to be monitoring the traffic on the incredibly busy four-lane boulevard that connected the autoroute with the beach, but for all I knew it might be movable. I wasn't taking any chances. There was not only al-Qaeda and the *hawalladas* to worry about, but French police and intelligence surveillance as well.

Since this was a totally deniable operation, every precaution had to be made to ensure the security of our team. The French had vast experience fighting Islamic fundamentalism. They had an excellent human intelligence network in North Africa and could discover that we were operating on the Riviera at any time. It didn't matter how or why; they might have monitored the al-Qaeda money movement, and we'd get caught in the middle. Then we would be really in the shit, as no one would be coming to help us. In fact, George would probably help the French to convict us as terrorists to cover his arse. I still wondered late at night why the fuck I did these jobs. Why did I not only take them on but get fucked over by the very people I should have had most reason to trust? The money was good – well, it was now, working for George. But I still couldn't come up with the answer, so last night I used the same mantra I'd always muttered to stop me thinking too much about anything. 'Fuck it.'

This meet with the source was the first of many high-risk activities my team was going to undertake in the next few days. I had no idea who this woman was; for all I knew, the French, or even al-Qaeda, might already be on to her, and I'd be caught up in a total gang fuck on day one.

The café had large, clear windows, unobstructed by posters or blinds, which was something else I didn't like. It was too easy for people to see in, especially people with telephoto lenses. A red canvas awning protected some of the outside tables for those who wanted to keep out of the sun. Two customers sat at different tables reading newspapers under it, and a couple of women seemed to be comparing the hairstyles of their little puffed-up poodles. The Riviera's morning routine was just generally mooching along.

A few of the women had to be Italian. They didn't so much walk as glide in their minks, but maybe they were simply steering clear of the poodle shit. Everyone in Cannes seemed to own one of the heavily coiffed little shitters, and trotted them along on their fancy leads, or looked on lovingly as they did a dump in the middle of the pavement. I'd already had to scrape three loads off my Timberlands since arriving, and had now become a bit of an expert at the Cannes Shuffle, dodging and weaving as I walked.

To my right, the boulevard headed gently uphill, getting steeper as it passed two or three kilometres of car dealerships and unattractive apartment blocks before hitting Autoroute 8, which took you either to Nice and Italy, about an hour away, or down to Marseille and the Spanish border.

To my left, and about five minutes' walk downhill, lay the railway station, the beach and the main Cannes tourist traps. But the only part of town I was interested in today was where I was right now. In about fifteen minutes the source should be turning up wearing a red pashmina and a pair of jeans; she was going to sit at a table and read a month-old copy of *Paris-Match*, one with a picture of Julia Roberts on the cover.

I didn't like the physical set-up for this meet. I'd taken a coffee and croissant inside the café yesterday for a recce and could see no escape route. It wasn't looking good: large, un-obstructed windows letting the world see what was happening inside, and an exposed pavement outside. I couldn't leap off a fire escape at the back, or go to the toilets and climb out of the window if anyone came barging through the main door. I would have to go for the virgin ground of the kitchen. I had no choice: I had to make contact with the source.

The tumbler door opened behind me on to a batch of very flowery patterned sheets. I shifted my weight on to my left buttock and adjusted my bum-bag, which hung over the fly of my jeans and contained my passport and wallet. The bag never left me, and to help make sure it stayed that way I'd threaded a wire through the belt. Pickpockets in the crowds down here used Stanley knives to slit belts and straps, but they'd have had a tough job with this one.

The old woman was still mumbling away to herself, then raised her voice to me, looking for my agreement on the crap state of the machines. I turned and did my bit, '*Oui, oui,*' smiled and turned my eyes back towards the target.

Tucked down the front of my jeans was a worn-out 1980s Browning 9mm with a thirteen-round mag. It was a French black-market job, which, like all the team's weapons, had been supplied by a contact I had yet to see, whom I'd nicknamed Thackery. I hadn't laid eyes on him; I just had this picture in my head of a clean-shaven thirty-something with short black hair. The serial number had been ground out, and if the Browning had to be used, ballistics would link it to local Italian gangs. There were enough of them around here, with the border so close. And, of course, I had bought myself a Leatherman. I'd never leave home without one.

As I checked up and down the road and across once more at the café, the world was buzzing around me and my new girl-friend in the launderette. Schoolkids raced around on motor scooters, some with helmets, some without, just like the police on their BMWs. Small cars were driven like ballistic missiles in both directions. Christmas decorations were rigged up across the boulevard; the most popular number this year was white lights in the shape of stars and lighted candles.

I thought about how much things had moved on since Logan.

'All the people that you care about live here.' George had known exactly what he was doing even before he got me to take Zeralda's head. Blind watchmaker, my arse.

I scanned up and down the boulevard for the hundredth time, looking for anybody wearing red on blue, checking to make sure no one else was lurking around waiting to jump me once I'd made contact.

I had a contingency plan if there was a problem before the meet. My escape route was out of the *laverie* service door, which was open. It was lined with bags of left washing and lost socks and underwear, and led through a small yard into an alleyway. At the end was a low wall, which led into the back-yard of the perfumery on the boulevard to my left. From there I'd slip into an adjacent apartment block and hide in the base-ment garage until the coast was clear.

I checked traser. Four minutes to eleven. To my left I caught a flash of red among the pedestrians on the kerb, waiting to cross in the direction of the café. I hadn't seen it before; she must have come from one of the shops or the other *tabac* further down the hill. She'd probably been sitting having a coffee, doing pretty much what I'd been doing. If so, it was a good sign; at least she was switched on. I kept the patch of red in my peripheral vision, not searching for the face in case there was eye contact.

There was a gap in the traffic and the pashmina made a move. It was a man; he had a mag rolled up in his right hand and a small brown *porte-monnaie* – or fag-bag, as a few of my new fellow countrymen called them – in his left. If I was wrong, I'd soon be finding out.

Once over the road he went up to an empty pavement table and took a seat. As in all French cafés, the chairs were facing the road so the clientele could people-watch. He got settled and laid the mag out flat on the table. I continued to watch through the traffic. A waistcoated waitress went over and took his order as he brought a packet of cigarettes out from the fag-bag.

I couldn't see much of his face, owing to the distance and the volume of traffic between us, but he was wearing sunglasses and was either dark-skinned or had a permatan. I'd find out later. I didn't look at him any more now. My gaze shifted elsewhere; there were more important things to check. Was it safe to approach him? Was anyone else about, waiting to fuck up my day?

I ran through my plan once more in my head: to go and sit near him, order coffee and, when it felt safe, come out with my check statement. I was going to point to Julia and say, 'Beautiful, isn't she?' His reply would be, 'Yes, she is, but not as much as Katharine Hepburn, don't you think?' Then I was going to get up and go over and sit by him and start talking Katharine. That would be the cover story: we just met and started talking about film stars because of the cover of the magazine. I didn't know his name, he didn't know mine, we didn't know each other, we were just chatting away in a café. There must always be a reason for being where you are.

I still felt uneasy, though. Meeting inside the café would have been bad enough, with nowhere to run, but outside was even worse. He could be setting me up for a snapshot that could be used against me, or maybe a drive-by shooting. I didn't know this character, I didn't know what he was into. All I knew was that it had to be done, no matter what was out there; if everything went to plan, I would come away with the information we needed.

I stood up, adjusted my sweatshirt and bum-bag, and nodded to the old woman. She folded some jeans and mumbled something as I set off left, downhill towards the town centre. There was no need to watch Pashmina Man. His window for the RV was thirty minutes, he was going to be there until eleven thirty.

Everything seemed normal as I passed the perfumery. Women were doing their sniff tests on overpriced bottles, and young men sporting the Tintin look, with plucked eyebrows and waxed-up hair, were wrapping their purchases in very expensive looking boxes. The *tabac* further along wasn't that packed. A few old boys were drinking small beers and buying lotto tickets. I couldn't see anything out of the ordinary.

I reached the pedestrian crossing about fifty metres further downhill and, once on the RV side of the road, I headed back up towards the red pashmina past the news stand and *pâtisserie*. Only in France could a man wear one of these things and not even get a second glance.

As I approached I got a glimpse of him in profile, sipping espresso, smoking and watching the world pass by a little too intently. He looked familiar, with his slicked-back hair, slightly thinning on top, and round, dark face. I got a few paces closer before I recognized him, and almost stopped in my tracks. It was the greaseball from Algeria.

11

I ducked into the first doorway to my left, trying my hardest to look interested in the glass display cabinets along the wall while I collected my thoughts. The elderly shopkeeper gave me a smile and a genial 'Bonjour'.

'Bonjour, parlez-vous anglais?'

'Yes.'

'Just looking, thank you.'

He left me alone as I looked at the array of wooden and plastic pipes and all the paraphernalia you need to smoke one. I turned my wrist and checked traser: 11:04. Greaseball still had twenty-six minutes to wait until the RV was closed, and I was in no rush. I took my time. I needed to think.

I didn't want to meet up with him, source or not, especially outside, especially if he was a known face. That was bad professionally: I needed to be the grey man.

I turned to the door and gave the old man a mechanical 'Au revoir', straight from the phrasebook, wishing that what little time I'd spent at school had been at French lessons.

Without looking in the direction of the RV I went back out into the street, turned right towards the pedestrian crossing, over the road, and pushed my shoulder against the door of the tabac. It was a dreary place, the walls covered in dark brown carpet to complement the dark wooden floors. The old men in here had half a dozen Gauloises on the go, the haze of smoke adding to the gloom. I sat back from the window so I could keep an eye on Greaseball, and ordered myself a coffee.

He'd lit up another cigarette. The pack was on the table with the lighter on top, next to his *porte-monnaie*. He ordered something more, and as the waitress turned to go back into the café I took my paper napkin and wrapped it round the espresso cup before taking a tester sip. Greaseball started to get a little agitated now, checking his watch for the fifth time in as many minutes. There were three more minutes to go until eleven thirty, and once again he checked through the café window to see if there was anyone seated inside on his own, before twisting round again and making sure the mag was flat and easy to spot.

I poured my change on to the table from my small brown coin purse and left eleven francs, which were collected with a grunt by the old guy running the show.

Greaseball checked his watch once more, then leant across to ask the waitress cleaning the next table for the time. Her reply seemed to confirm what he feared, because he got to his feet and checked up and down the road again as if he knew what he was looking for. It was eleven thirty-four before he packed away his cigarettes and finally headed up the hill.

I picked up the cup for the last time, gave the lip a quick wipe before leaving with the napkin, and followed him from my side of the road as trucks and vans blocked him from view for split seconds. I needed to make a little distance and be right on top of him in case he got into a car. If he did, I could stop him before he moved off. I would have to approach him at some time, but not yet. First of all I needed to make sure no one else was following him – or me.

I couldn't see anything suspicious: no one talking to themselves with their eyes glued to the back of Greaseball's head; nobody leaping into or out of cars in a desperate measure to get behind him, or concentrating so much on not losing him in a crowd that they took a slide in dog shit or bumped into people and lamp posts.

Dicing with death, I crossed the road then focused on his brown suede loafers, which perfectly matched the fag-bag. He had bare, hairy ankles. No socks: very South of France. He walked with Julia in his right hand and the bag in his left.

I didn't want him to have any opportunity to turn and make eye contact, since he'd be unlikely not to recognize me. And, given the circumstances of our last meeting, I guessed he might be a tad nervous when he did.

I checked constantly to my left at the shops and apartment-block entrances for somewhere I could go if he stopped. It's not an easy bit of tradecraft, because by the time the target has turned and looked back you have to be static if in view or, better still, hidden. And you can't afford to draw attention to yourself in the process.

He turned left, off the main, and became unsighted. I quickened my pace to get to the corner, did the Cannes Shuffle, and crossed the road. No way was I turning into dead ground without first checking what was waiting for me.

Looking left and right for traffic as I crossed, I had the target once more. He was still on the left-hand side of the road and wasn't checking behind him. He was walking purposefully: he wasn't running from something, he was going to something.

Once on the other pavement I turned left and went with him. He was a bit further away now, but that was fine because the road was a lot narrower, just a normal street lined with houses and apartment blocks. There weren't many real people here, so a little distance was a help.

Looking ahead and keeping the red in my peripheral vision, I could see the large blue neon sign ahead for an Eddie's on my side of the road. The supermarket took up the ground floor of an apartment block. It was one of a chain called E. Leclerc. I didn't actually know what the E stood for, but it had been a boring four days so I'd made up the name, along with Thackery's.

There was a *rotisserie* van at the kerb with its sides open, selling freshly cooked chicken and rabbit. A flock of small cars were trying to force themselves into impossible spaces and double-park around the shop. They bumped up on to the kerb, and into each other. People didn't seem to care much about their paintwork down here.

Greaseball crossed towards the store and disappeared up the road immediately before it. I quickened my step. As I got to the junction I saw him easily beyond the chaos of shoppers, moving up the road. It was very narrow here, just single track, and quite steep now that we'd got further up the hill. There were no pavements, just iron fences and stone walls either side, flanking houses and apartment blocks. Some of the buildings were quite new and some needed a lick of paint, but they all had one thing in common, and that was the amount of ironwork that covered every point of entry.

He kept to the left. I followed, allowing him to become temporarily unsighted now and again as the road twisted uphill, in case he stopped. We were the only two on this stretch of road and I didn't want to make my presence too obvious. If he'd disappeared by the time I got round the corner, the drills for finding him would be long, laborious and boring, but I had no choice. I'd have to find a place to hide and wait for him to reappear. If I had no luck I'd have to contact George and tell him the bad news. I'd lie, of course, and say I'd seen something suspicious around the RV. He would have to get his finger out in quick time and do whatever he did to get another RV organized.

I wasn't worried any longer that he was going to a car, because he wouldn't have parked this far from the RV. The thought did cross my mind that he'd pinged me and was moving around the town a bit to confirm I was following him. What that would mean to me, I didn't know – maybe a reception as I turned a corner. But I had no option, really. I had to follow and contact him once we were somewhere safer and less exposed.

The old terracotta roofs that overlapped the walls here and there each side of me would have been there for donkey's years before the dull cream apartment blocks that had sprung up on every available patch of land since the sixties. They were no more than five or six storeys high; quite a few of the balconies had towels, duvets or washing hanging off them; one or two had barbecues. I could hear the drone of the traffic from the main drag off to my right.

Greaseball took off the pashmina to reveal a blue checked shirt. He wasn't the only one getting hot; I was starting to leak around my face and down my spine as I made my way uphill. We passed some more apartment blocks, which seemed a little the worse for wear, and Greaseball stopped for a car to squeeze past. He rummaged in his fag-bag. There was a not-too-good-looking block opposite, with a line of cars nosy-parked in front.

I carried on towards him, head down, not making eye contact. He might be pinging me this very moment, waiting for me to betray myself. The car accelerated past me and I had to stop to let him through as Greaseball disappeared into the covered, mosaic-tiled porchway.

There was no time to be subtle. I only had one chance. I ran towards him and got there just as he turned the key in the glass-and-brass-effect main door. He had his back to me but he could see me in the reflection of the glass.

'Beautiful, isn't she?'

He spun round, leaving the key in place. His eyes were bulging and his arms fell to his sides as he moved back against the glass. My left hand grabbed the hem of my sweatshirt, ready to pull it up and draw down the Browning. His eyes darted after it. He had a good idea of what that was all about. For several moments he just stared at me in horror, then he stammered, 'You? *You?*'

I wasn't surprised he'd remembered me. Some things stay with you for ever.

Even from a couple of feet away I could smell his heavy aftershave, mixed with the odour of heavily lacquered hair. I said again, 'Beautiful, isn't she?' and nodded at the magazine in his hand. There was still no reply.

'Answer me. *Beautiful, isn't she?*'

At last I got something. 'Yes, but Katharine Hepburn . . .' His face wobbled. He realized he'd fucked up. 'No, no, no, please. Wait, wait. She is, yes, she is, but not as much as Katharine Hepburn, don't you think?'

It was good enough. 'Where are you going?'

He half turned and pointed. He'd shaved this morning, but already had shadow.

'Is there anybody in there with you?'

'*Non.*'

'Let's go in, then. Come on.'

'But . . .'

I shoved him through the door, and into the dark foyer. The rubber soles of my Timberlands squeaked on the grey phoney-marble floor. A baby was crying in one of the ground-floor flats and I could smell frying as we headed for the lift. He was still flapping big-time. There was some heavy erratic breathing going on in front of me as he cradled his pashmina in his arms. I was going to reassure him about my intentions, but then thought, fuck it, why bother? I wanted to keep him on the back foot.

The small, box-like lift arrived and we got in. The smell changed. Now it was like the *tabac*. He pressed for the fourth floor and the thing started to shudder. I was standing behind him, and could see the sweat trickle down from his neck hair on to his shirt collar as I tapped him on the shoulder. 'Show me what's in the bag.' He was only too eager to comply, and held it up for inspection over his shoulder. There was nothing in there that I hadn't seen already: a pack of Camel Lights, a gold lighter and a small leather money pouch. The keys were still in his hand.

The lift climbed so slowly it was hard to tell if it was moving at all. Looking at him from the rear, I could see that his jeans were a bit too tight around his gut. His love handles flopped out each side, straining against his shirt, and folding over his waistband. A gold Rolex and a couple of thin gold bracelets dangled from his left wrist on to his perfectly manicured hand. He also had a matching pair of bracelets on his right wrist, and a signet ring on his little finger. All in all, he looked like an over-the-hill gigolo who thought he was still twenty-one.

He zipped up the bag and wiped the sweat from his neck. 'There's no one here,' he assured me. 'I promise you.'

The lift doors opened and I gave him a shove into a semi-dark landing. 'Good. What number?'

'This way. Forty-nine.'

I squeezed behind him, my right hand ready to draw down on my 9mm again as he placed the key into the cylinder lock in a dark brown varnished door. It opened into a small room, maybe ten by ten. The sun was trying hard to penetrate the net curtains covering the glass sliding doors of the balcony, and not quite succeeding. He walked in while I waited where I was, hand on my pistol grip. He turned back towards me, arms sweeping around the room, 'Look, you see, everything is OK.'

That was his opinion. He might be Mr Gucci out on the boulevards, but this place was a tip. To my left was a door into the kitchen. It was fitted with 1970s faded blue and white veneered units that had been worn down in places to the chipboard. An ashtray overflowed on to a half-eaten baguette. The sink was piled high with dirty pans and dishes.

I closed the door with my heel as I walked in and motioned to him with my head. 'Bolt it.'

I moved aside as he obeyed, breathing heavily.

There was another door to the left. 'Where does that go?'

'The bedroom and bathroom. '

He started to walk towards it, eager to please. 'Let me go and—'

'Stop, we go together. I want to see every move you make. Got it?'

I followed a few steps behind him as his loafers squeaked

94

over the light grey mock marble. Both of the other rooms were in a similar state. The bedroom just fitted the bed, and the rest of the floor was covered with newspapers, dirty underwear, and a couple of Slazenger tennis bags still in their Decathlon sports-shop carrier. He didn't look the tennis type, but the two used syringes that lay on top of the bags were very much his style, which was why he tried to kick it all under the bed without me seeing. He was obviously contributing energetically to al-Qaeda's heroin profits.

A pair of wardrobes were packed with brightly coloured clothes and shoes, all looking new. The bedroom stank of aftershave and cigarettes, but not as badly as the tiny bathroom did. It had a faded yellow sink, toilet and a typical French half-bath with a hand-held shower. Every surface was covered with bottles of shampoo, cologne and hair colour. The bath had enough pubic hairs around the plug-hole to stuff a mattress.

'You see everything is correct. It is safe.'

I didn't even bother to check if he was embarrassed as we walked back into the living room. I squeezed around the furniture and went over to the patio-style window that led on to the balcony overlooking the road we had just walked up. A couple of tennis rackets leant against the railings, and a pair of scrunched-up beach towels hung over the balustrade.

By now he was sitting nervously on a green settee, which had probably been installed at the same time as the kitchen. It was against the left-hand wall, facing a dirty Formica wall unit that was dominated by a huge TV and video. Everything was covered in so much dust I could even see his fingermarks around the controls. VHS tapes and all manner of shit was scattered around the shelves. A small boombox-type CD player stood on a shelf above the TV, surrounded by a sea of discs lying out of their boxes. The videotapes had no titles, but I could guess the sort of thing he was into watching.

The rectangular waxed-pine coffee table at the centre of the room was covered with more old newspapers, a half-empty bottle of red wine, and a food plate that had doubled as an ashtray. I was beginning to feel greasy as well as grubby in this guy's company.

I got to the point, so I didn't have to spend too much more time around him. 'When will the boat be here?'

He crossed his legs and placed both hands around his knees, feeling a little more comfortable now it seemed I wasn't going to take his head off. 'Tomorrow night, at Beaulieu-sur-Mer, it's towards Monaco.'

'Write it down.' I knew where it was, but wanted to make sure I had the right place. He leant forward, found a pen among the mess on the table, and wrote on the edge of a newspaper, in a scrawl that any doctor would have been proud of.

'There is a port, a marina, I think you call it. It's not far. Her name is the *Ninth of May*. It's a white boat, quite large. It's coming in tomorrow night.' He ripped off the edge of the paper – 'Here' – and pushed it towards me.

I looked out of the window and down into the garden of one of the original houses opposite. An old man was tending a vegetable patch, attaching bits of silver paper to bamboo sticks. I kept watching him. 'How many are going to be on board?'

'There are three. One will always remain with the boat, while the other two collect the money. They're going to start on Friday, the first of three collections. They'll make one a day, and leave for Algiers with the money on Sunday. They are trying to close their accounts here in France – before you do it for them, no?'

I turned back to Greaseball. He rummaged around in his bag and dragged out a Camel. With an elegant flick of a lighter, he sat back and let smoke curl out of his nostrils. He crossed his legs once more and laid his left arm along the back of the settee as if he was running the show. He was starting to get a bit too confident. 'Where are they going to collect the cash, then, Greaseball?'

He choked on his cigarette and smoke blew uncontrollably from his nose and mouth. 'Greaseball?' Composing himself, he took another drag and this time exhaled slowly, smiling at his new name. 'Where? That I do not know, and I won't until tomorrow night, maybe. I'm not sure yet. But I do know they're only going to use public transport, buses, that sort of thing. It's safer than Hertz. Conductors don't keep records.'

It made sense to me. 'Do you know how much money?'

'Anything between two point five and three million American.'

He took another drag and I went back to watching the old guy dig around his vegetable patch, thinking about the number of suicide bombers' families with Landcruisers with all the trimmings that could be funded with that sort of cash.

'Are they collecting from *hawalladas*?'

'Yes, of course. These guys on the coast, the ones who will be handing them the money, are *hawalla* people.'

I moved back one of the net curtains so I could get a clearer view.

'What time will the boat arrive?'

'Did you know this is where the money was collected to finance the attack on the American embassy in Paris?' He took another drag and sounded almost proud. 'Can you imagine what would have happened if that had been successful too?'

'The boat, what time?'

There was some shuffling as he adjusted himself in his seat. 'In the evening some time, I'm not too sure.' There was a pause and I could hear him stubbing out his cigarette and pulling another from the pack. I turned as he gave the lighter a flick and looked at the CDs on the wall unit. It was obvious he was a big Pink Floyd fan.

'Zeralda liked me to bring a new tape for him each trip. I'd collect the boys too, of course.' He cocked his head to one side, measuring my reaction. 'Did you see me drive back to the house that night? I was hoping you would have finished the job by then. But he kept calling on my cell. He didn't like to be kept waiting . . .'

The fucker was smiling, taunting me.

I pulled the sliding glass panel with my sweatshirt cuff to let in some air, and was greeted by the sound of traffic from the main drag, and the old boy outside clearing his passages. I resisted the temptation to go over and give Greaseball a good smack in the teeth and looked outside again instead. 'So you two liked the same music as well as the same boys?'

He blew out another lungful of smoke before he replied. 'You find it distasteful – but are you telling me it's worse than cutting off a man's head? You don't mind using people like me when you need to, do you?'

I shrugged my shoulders, still looking out at the old man. 'I'm here because it's my job, believe me. And distasteful isn't a strong enough word for what I think about you.'

I heard what sounded like a snort of derision and turned back to face him.

'Get real, my friend. You may hate me, but you're here, aren't you? And that's because you want something from me.'

He was right, but that didn't mean to say I was going to share his toothbrush. 'Have you got anything else for me?'

'That's all I know so far. But how do I inform you about the collections?'

'I'll come here at eleven tonight. Make sure you're here, and no one else is. You have a bell that rings downstairs, yeah?' He nodded and sucked the last mouthful out of his Camel. 'Good. Open the door.'

He moved towards the exit. I went over to the coffee table and took the marina address, as well as the newspaper. Beaulieu-sur-Mer – I did know it, and so would anyone else if they picked up the paper. The imprint was clear to see on the pages beneath. As I bent down I could see the lower shelves of the wall unit and did a double-take at some Polaroids. I knew he liked rock music, but this was something else. Greaseball was in a bar, drinking with one of the guitarists from Queen. At least, that's who it looked like. Whoever it was, he had the same mad curly hair.

Greaseball was trying to work out what had caught my eye as I waited for him to pull back the bolt. 'Those people, the ones on the boat . . . Are you going to do the same to them as you did to Zeralda?'

I checked my 9mm to make sure it was concealed as he opened the door and glanced outside. I didn't bother to look back at him. 'Eleven. If you don't know by then, I'll be back in the morning.' I went past him, my left hand ready to pull up the sweatshirt.

As I walked towards the lift I saw the stairwell and decided to go that way instead, just to get off the floor more quickly. I elbowed the light switch as I passed it. A couple of floors down, I was smothered in darkness. I waited for a moment, then pressed the next one.

I reached the ground floor and headed for the main door as a young woman in red tracksuit bottoms and pullover was packing a crying baby into a pram on the landing.

Out in the sun again, I had to squint as I checked the bell-push for number forty-nine. There was no name by it but, then, who would want to own up to living in a place like this? As I walked away, I wondered how I was going to break the news to Lotfi and Hubba-Hubba that Greaseball was the source.

12

As I headed back along boulevard Carnot, I knew I'd have to move from my hotel. It was far too close to Greaseball's flat, and I didn't even want him to see me, let alone find out where I was staying.

I stopped at the launderette and picked up my sheets. They were now on top of the washing machine, still wet. As I shoved them into the black bin liner the old woman gobbed off at me for leaving them in when there were about four other people waiting. I'd obviously breached the *laverie* protocol big-time, so I just smiled my apologies to everyone as I finished my packing and left.

I set off down the hill towards the beach. I had to contact George and give him a sit rep, and that meant going to the Mondego, a cyber café, and getting online. He needed to know where the collectors were going to park up their boat and, later on, where they were going to collect the cash. My surroundings got very smart very quickly. Luxury hotels that looked like giant wedding cakes lined the coast road, La Croisette, and Gucci shops sold everything from furs to baseball caps for dogs. I tipped the sheets into a street bin, hanging on to the plastic bag. As I carried on walking, I screwed up the newspaper I'd taken from Greaseball's apartment inside it.

This might have been the upscale end of town, but anything that stuck out of the pavement, like a parking bollard or a tree, was decorated with fresh dog piss and a couple of brown lumps.

New cars, motorbikes and scooters were crammed into every possible, and impossible, space, and their owners, the customers in the cafés, looked extremely cool and elegant in their sunglasses, smoking, drinking, just generally posing around the place.

There were quite a few homeless around here as well. Fair one: if I was homeless I'd want to sleep in a warm place with lots of good-looking people about, particularly if they were the sort to throw you a few bob. A group of four or five dossers were sitting on benches alongside a scruffy old mongrel with a red polka-dot scarf around its neck. One guy had a can of beer in his coat pocket, and as he bent over to pat the dog the contents were spilling on to the ground. His wino friends looked horrorstruck.

I'd never used this café to get online: normally, I drove to Cap 3000, a huge *centre commercial* on the outskirts of Nice. It was only about forty-five minutes away, driving within speed limits, which I was meticulous about, and always crowded. But this time I needed to tell George what I had found out immediately. I was leaving Cannes now anyway, so wouldn't need to come here again.

The place looked quite full, which was good. A group of twenty-somethings wearing designer leather jackets and shades posed near their motorbikes and scooters, or sat on shiny aluminium chairs and sipped small glasses of beer. Most had a pack of Marlboro or Winston on the table with a disposable lighter on top, alongside a mobile that got picked up every few seconds in case they had missed a text message.

I wove my way through the temple of cool, past walls lined with boring grey PCs, towards the rows of gleaming drinks optics and the steaming cappuccino machine that stood at the black, marble-topped bar.

I pointed at the nearest PC and tried to make myself heard above the beat of the music. 'I want to get online. . . . Er, *parlez-vous anglais?*'

The guy behind the counter didn't even look up from unloading the dishwasher. 'Sure, log on, pay later. You want a drink?' He was dressed in black and sounded Scandinavian.

'*Café crème.*'

'Go, sit down.'

I headed to a vacant PC station, perched myself on one of the very high stools, and logged on. The screen information was all in French, but I'd got the hang of it by now and went straight into Hotmail. George had set up an account for me that was registered in Poland. The user name was BB8642; George was BB97531, a sequence of numbers that even I couldn't forget. He was as paranoid as I was, and he'd gone to quite a lot of trouble to make our correspondence untraceable. I wouldn't have been surprised if he'd fixed it for Bill Gates to erase our messages personally, as soon as they'd been read.

Signing in, I made sure the font size was the smallest possible so nobody could read over my shoulder, and checked my mailbox. He wasn't getting information on this job from anywhere else. He just wanted it from me. I was his only line of information: anything else would have been dangerous. There was no other way of making contact: I'd never had a phone number for him, even when I was with Carrie, never even knew where he lived. I wasn't sure if she did, these days.

George's email asked me if I'd got his present, and said I mustn't open it until Christmas. He was referring to the kit left for me at the DOP, and the drugs we were going to use to help the *hawalladas* on their way to the warship.

I tapped away with my index fingers.

Hello, thanks for the present, but I'm not too sure if I can wait till Christmas. Guess what? I just saw Jenny and she said that Susanna is coming to town on business, arriving tomorrow night. She'll be in town until Sunday and has three meetings while she is here, one a day starting Friday. Jenny is finding out the details so she can arrange for all of us to get together and try that place you are always talking about, the one that serves great White Russians. I have so much to tell you. You were right, Susanna's business is worth anything between 2.5 and 3 mill. Not bad! You'd better get in there quick before some stud moves in. I know she likes you! I'm around tomorrow, do you want to meet up for a drink, say 1 p.m.?

My coffee arrived and I took a sip of froth without picking it up. This was the second email I'd sent George since arriving in-country. Each time any contact was made, a colour was used for authentication. The first was red, this one was white, the third, the brush contact tomorrow at one, would be blue. Then I'd start the colour sequence again. All very Stars and Stripes, all very George, but these things needed to be simple or they were forgotten. Well, by me, anyway.

George now knew that I had met the source, the boat was coming in on Thursday night, and I wanted a brush contact tomorrow to pass over the collection details. Things like that are far too sensitive to send in clear, even if Bill Gates was in the good lads club.

I finished the email 'Have a nice day'. After all, I was nearly an American now.

Signing out of Hotmail, I reopened with the addresses I used to contact Lotfi and Hubba-Hubba.

Anyone checking the subscriber would discover he lived in Canada.

There was nothing in my mailbox from these two, which was good news. Like me, they were just waiting for the time to meet up and get on with the job.

I invited each of them for coffee at four o'clock today. They'd be checking their boxes at one-ish, so they'd get the message in plenty of time.

I wrapped a napkin around the coffee cup and took a sip while I worked out what to do next. I had to check out of the

103

hotel, then go to Beaulieu-sur-Mer and do a recce before the boat arrived. I'd need to look at the vital ground before meeting up with Lotfi and Hubba-Hubba at the safe house at four.

I took another slow sip. This was going to be my last quiet time before I started running around like a crazed dog.

I wondered what Carrie was doing now, and spent a minute or two just staring at the keyboard, trying to shake that last image of her at the harbour out of my head. In the end I just logged off, and wiped the keys and cup rim clean with the napkin.

My hotel was right next door to a synagogue, and above a kosher takeaway pizza joint called Pizza Jacob. It had been perfect, not only because it was cheap but because the ageing manager took cash. My fellow guests were a bunch of dodgy-looking comb and pencil salesmen, trying to save money by sleeping in a room with no TV or phone, and very thin blankets.

I checked out and threw my holdall into the boot of the dark blue Renault Mégane. The bin liner, still containing the bits of Greaseball's newspaper I hadn't already chewed up and swallowed, joined a couple of paper cups, three empty Coke cans and napkins in the passenger footwell. I made what must have been about a sixty-point turn and eventually managed to squeeze out of the small and crowded car park at the rear. I put on my sunglasses and dark blue baseball cap before I emerged on to the street. The sun was bright, but it wasn't what I was shielding myself from. CCTV cameras were everywhere along this coastline.

I'd sort myself out a new hotel when I needed it, and if I had time.

13

I hit the coast road, turned east, and headed towards Nice, flanked by the railway tracks and the sea. About a K outside Cannes I pulled up, bumping the car half up on to the kerb behind a row of others belonging to a bunch of rod fishermen down on the beach. Bad parking was so common here it didn't draw a second glance, and it meant I could check to see if I'd picked up any tracking devices in the last twenty-four hours.

I wasn't expecting anything just yet, but I'd still taken precautions. I'd bought a little pot of silver enamel modelling paint and a brush, and had coated all the retaining screws on the bumpers and the numberplates. If anybody had been tampering they would have had to cut the paint.

I looked round the wheel arches and underneath the chassis. Then I had the bonnet up and checked the engine compartment.

If I found a device, I'd simply walk away, and that would be the end of the job as far as I was concerned. The other two would have to carry on.

But everything was fine. I got back behind the wheel and carried on along the coast road, passing through all sorts of places I'd heard about in songs.

The sea was almost totally still today, and shimmered in the sunlight. It all looked just like the South of France should look, except that the sand was heaped up in gigantic mounds. They imported it by the truckload from North Africa, and now was obviously the time of year when they gave the beach a makeover before the new season.

Nobody was sunbathing but quite a lot of people were out blading, walking their dogs and just generally enjoying the space. Stony beach took over again as I neared Nice proper. I skirted the airport and Cap 3000, my email centre and the place where the brush contact would happen tomorrow.

The airport was right at the edge of the city, virtually on the beach. A new terminal was under construction, and large pictorial banners told me how wonderful it would be for the future of the area.

I drove into the city along a wide dual carriageway, punctuated by palm trees. The automatic sprinkler system threw up a series of pint-sized rainbows along the central reservation. The traffic was funnelled between glass and steel hotels and more construction sites. It got busier and busier, until it turned into the Wacky Races, with the contestants stopping and starting like maniacs, slaloming from lane to lane and leaning on their horns.

I switched on the English-speaking Riviera Radio and listened to an Alan Partridge soundalike make his link from the closing bars of a Barbra Streisand weepy into a string of commercials for financial and yachting services. Before long I even knew the price of a barrel of Brent crude, and what was happening on the Nasdaq. It was obvious what type of Brit expat they were broadcasting to: the very rich kind. But I always listened to it because they had a review of the US papers in the afternoon, and carried the BBC World Service hourly.

I hit the Promenade des Anglais, the main drag along the coast. It was a glamorous stretch, lined with palm trees and glitzy old-world hotels. Even the buses were immaculate: they looked as though someone had just given them a good polish before they were allowed into town. I carried on round the harbour, which was heaving with pleasure cruisers and ferries en route to and from Corsica, and started to see signs for Beaulieu-sur-Mer.

The road wound uphill until only the cliff edge and a hundred-foot drop separated it from the sea. As I got higher I could see mountain ranges inland that seemed to go on for ever. I guessed Riviera Radio was right when it said you could be on the beach in the morning, and skiing in the afternoon.

Nice disappeared behind me as the road snaked along the cliff. I felt like I'd been caught up in a Sunday afternoon black-and-white movie; I expected to turn a corner at any moment, and meet David Niven in an Austin Healey coming the other way.

I took a steep left-hander, and Villefranche and its huge deep-water bay lay spread out below me. Home of the US Sixth Fleet until France decided to pull its military out of Nato, it was one of the biggest natural harbours in the world. American and British warships still dropped anchor there when on a courtesy visit – or when spiriting away heavily anaesthetized *hawalladas*.

The dull grey shape of the warship dominated the bay with its large registration number stencilled in white paint on the back. It had more domes and antennae than the *Starship Enterprise*, and a helipad on the back big enough to take a jumbo jet.

The crew wouldn't have a clue what was happening. The most they'd know was that an area was out of bounds, and some important guests were on board. Only the captain and a few officers would have been told what the goodwill visit was really all about. The guests were probably getting a sit rep from George this very minute, using the information I'd just sent. They'd be sparked up now making their final preparations in some small, steel-walled room, out of screaming distance from the crew. I really hoped we were going to make it all worth their while.

Beyond the warship was Cap Ferrat. It looked very green, and very opulent, with large houses surrounded by trees and high fences. I made my way round the bay, through Villefranche and past a small left-hander that hairpinned up to the mountains. Up that road and just over sixteen Ks away, on the other side of a couple of small villages and the odd isolated house, was the DOP. It was an illegal tipping area, full of rusting freezers and household waste. It looked like it could host the biggest jumble sale on the planet, and was just the place I needed.

A few minutes later I was in Beaulieu-sur-Mer. The harbour was the other side of the town, so I followed signs to the *gare*. It was a small cream-coloured building with a taxi rank and flower beds that were so manicured they looked like they had a personal stylist. After a couple of circuits, I found a spot and parked. I got out and retrieved my digital camera from my holdall.

The Mégane was a perfect vehicle for this sort of job: it was a dark colour, a popular make, and about as nondescript as they come, once I'd peeled off the sticker from the dealership the hire company had bought it from. It was also small enough to park quickly, but big enough to hide a body in the boot. Which was why, as well as my personal kit, I had two rolls of silver gaffer tape in the boot. Lotfi and Hubba-Hubba also had some; we wanted to make sure that once we got a body inside a vehicle it was there to stay.

All three vehicles had been played about with so that the reverse and brake lights could be cut out. It was simple enough: we just sliced through the leads and added an on/off switch to the circuit. When we drove a *hawallada* into the DOP with the lights out, the last thing we wanted was for the brake or reversing lights to kick in and show everyone around what we were up to. For the same reason, all the interior lightbulbs had been removed. We'd have to return the cars to Alamo, or wherever the other two had got theirs from, in the same condition we'd hired them, but it wouldn't take more than an hour or so to change everything back.

I wandered around between the post office and the station,

making like a tourist, taking the odd snap while the taxi drivers stood around their Mercedes, preferring to talk and smoke rather than take a fare.

The *gare* was immaculate, as French railway stations always are. I glanced at the timetables – regular services in both directions along the coast, either back to Nice, Cannes and Marseille or on to Monaco and Italy.

I bought myself nine francs' worth of percolated while-you-wait coffee from the machine and tried not to over-excite three small white hairy dogs that were tied by lengths of string to the news-stand on my left. They looked at me as if it was lunchtime. I stepped around them and went to look at the postcards carousel. Cards are a really good source of information for people like me, because they usually have shots of locations you can't get to easily. It's a Standard Operating Procedure for most intelligence operators to collect them as they travel round the world, because the agencies want these things to hand. If there's an incident, say, at an airport in the middle of Nowhereland, they just have to open their files and they've got a collection of visuals to refer to until more information is gathered.

I picked up several pictures of Beaulieu-sur-Mer, which showed the marina from different angles and heights, all shot in fantastic sunlight, with beautiful women and sharply chiselled men strolling among the boats. Next to the carousel was a display of town maps, so I picked out three different ones. The vendor had a big round face and an annoyingly happy smile. I gave him my 'Merci, *au revoir*' and walked away with the change, which the French never seem to put into your hand, but always on the counter, in case you've got some disease.

I went back to the car.

The marina was larger than I'd expected from the postcards. Two or three hundred shiny masts rocked and glinted in the sunlight.

Just before turning through the entrance, I saw bus stops on either side of the road and a glass phone box. Whoever was on the boat had chosen their location well: there were buses to both Monaco and Nice, and the rail station was just a ten-minute walk away. The phone box was certainly going to be a bonus for us.

The large blue sign welcomed me, thanked me for my visit, looked forward to me coming back again, and gave me a list of available shops and services. I took a right on to the access road, a short avenue with neatly trimmed hedges on either side. There was a mini-roundabout ahead of me, and beyond that, the world's largest supply of pleasure craft. I turned left towards the car park.

14

A one-storey, flat-roofed building housed a parade of shops and cafés that ran for maybe a hundred metres each side of the mini-roundabout. I bumped slowly over a succession of sleeping policemen, past fancy restaurants with glinting glasses and dazzlingly white linen tablecloths, all laid out for lunch. It was just after midday, so they'd be full pretty soon, once the punters had emerged from the clothes shops, carrier bags bulging with Lacoste polo shirts and jumpers.

Coffee drinkers sat at café tables just a few metres from the water's edge, probably wishing they were sitting aboard the sleek and beautiful boats just out of reach to my right instead. The craft all seemed to have English names like *Suntreader* or *Kathy's Dreams*, and it was obviously the time of day for their owners to be out on deck, to take an aperitif and enjoy being envied.

I reached the point where the parade merged with a series of administration buildings that bordered the car park. I pulled up next to the deserted beach, by a sign saying 'Petite Afrique', probably because that was where the sand came from. I was alongside a little play area, which was half-way through being given a facelift.

Thanks to the postcards and what I'd seen so far, I now had

a pretty good sense of how the boats were arranged. From the mini-roundabout, a central pier ran straight out into the middle of an open square, with four smaller piers branching off each side at right angles. Another three piers jutted out from the quay by the shops, and three more from the opposite side. The place was jammed with row after row of boats, their masts, with whatever bits and pieces they had hanging off them, towering up to the sky. I had no idea where the *Ninth of May* was going to find room to park up; it didn't look like there was a space to be had.

My first priority was to find a single OP that would cover the whole area, so no matter where this boat parked, I'd be able to get eyes on and trigger the collectors as they left to pick up the cash. If that couldn't be done, I'd have to find a number of different ones.

I could already see two routes out of this place, apart from the sea. There was the access road I'd come in on, and a foot-path to the right of the shops, which led up to a terraced garden.

I left the Mégane, hitting the key fob before walking back past the shops towards the roundabout and the central pier. Ambling around with my camera in hand, I particularly admired the terraced garden. It was nearly as long as the parade, and was packed with small palm trees and exotic, semi-tropical plants set in light, dry soil – well worth a couple of photos. A shiny green hedge ran along the back of it, hiding the road, but I could now see there was a way through, because a man walking his dog along the path had just headed up some steps and disappeared.

The majority of the boats seemed to have red ensigns hanging off the back. A lot were registered in the Cayman Islands. I heard a group of Brits sitting on the back bit of a huge motor boat, enjoying a beer and listening to Riviera Radio. There was quite a lot of activity aboard, and not just the clinking of glasses. Decking was being pulled up, cleaned and varnished, and chrome was being polished until you could see your Gucci sunglasses in it.

There was an incessant *ching ching ching* of steel rigging and the one thing I did know that hung off boats, radar reflective balls, as I wandered along, snapping away, playing the tourist. When I got to the mini-roundabout I could see the rest of the shops. There was a tyre replacement centre, several chandlers and a high-tech yard with yachts up on blocks and shrink-wrapped in white plastic as if they'd just come off the supermarket shelf. There was also another set of stone steps that led directly to the road.

I turned left at the mini-roundabout on to the main pier, which was built of grey concrete slabs. As I got to the first set of branches, I looked down the line of boats. Every two or three parking spaces there was a shared utilities station, with pipes and cables feeding the rear of each vessel with power, water and a TV aerial. I saw the occasional satellite dish too, weighted down by sandbags and breeze blocks so the boat-owners could get Bloomberg to check if the markets were performing strongly enough for them to buy the next size up.

The yachts nearest the parade were large enough to keep most America's Cup teams happy, but the further I walked along the pier, the closer I got to the really big boys, until I was among the kind of vessels that had radar domes the size of nuclear warheads on the back and only needed a splash of grey paint to be confused with battleships. One even had its own two-seater helicopter. No doubt about it, I was in the wrong job and had been fostered by the wrong family. I'd always said to myself I should find out who my real parents were, and I realized that now was the time I should start trying.

From the end of the main pier I looked back once more to the garden, working on the theory that if I could see a possible hiding place from where I was now, I could probably see down here from up there. I took more pictures. The only place that looked possible as a one-size-fits-all OP was to the far right of the marina, above the flat roof of the administration building, and among the bushes that were about level with the car park. I wandered back, feigning interest in the boats but really looking under the piers to check how they were constructed. Huge concrete pillars rose out of the water, topped with T flanges, on which sat the concrete sections.

A thin film of oil coated the water at the rear of the boats, a hundred different shades of blue and orange swirling in the sunlight. I could see shoals of tiny fish fussing around the pillars quite easily through the clear water. I didn't know how yet, but I had to get on board the *Ninth of May* and plant the device that was going to stop it reaching Algeria with the cash. Getting wet might be the only way to do it.

As I walked back towards the car park I could hear British, French and American voices settling down for lunch. Waiters and waitresses hovered with expensive-looking bottles of water and wine, and baskets of freshly cut baguette. I was beginning to feel quite hungry.

I stopped at a *tabac* and inspected another carousel of post-cards as I tucked into a jumbo-size Snickers bar. I listened to a group of twenty-something Americans drinking beer at one of the tables outside. It had been a lot of beer, judging by the number of empty glasses and the content of their conversation. And, judging by their severe haircuts, tattoos and tight polo shirts, they had to be on shore leave from the warship at Villefranche.

'No way, man, we should fucking nuke 'em, man, this very p.m.!'

Another guy started chanting, 'USA, USA, USA,' getting very worked up. The others chorused their agreement and swigged some more Kronenbourg. It must have been hell being stuck in the Mediterranean instead of bobbing up and down on the Indian Ocean, waiting to hose down the Afghan mountains with cruise missiles.

I rotated the spinner. These cards weren't as good as the ones at the station, but then I caught sight of something in a display case that I knew would make Lotfi's day – a baseball hat with

114

an arm sticking out of the top of it, holding a hammer. When you pulled a piece of string the hammer swung down on to the peak. I couldn't resist it: it would send him ballistic. I went inside and handed over a hundred francs. It was pretty outrageous, but as she was selling Hermès scarves for those windy days on the waves for a couple of thousand, I guessed I got off pretty lightly. No wonder all the shops had alarm boxes with yellow strobe lights above their front doors.

The sailors were still honking as I came out. 'We shouldn't be kicking back here, man, we should be kicking some Bin Laden ass right now.'

I looked beyond them to the central pier, and stepped back rapidly into the doorway. Two white vans with blue light bars and riot grilles over the windows had pulled up, and were spilling out heavily armed men in navy blue jumpsuits on to the quay.

I suddenly got very interested in the latest issue of *Paris-Match* as an estate car, also with a blue light bar, stopped next to the vans. The word 'Gendarmerie' was emblazoned along the door panels.

Not flapping just yet, and still engrossed in the contents of the magazine rack, I checked chamber. If they were here for me, they didn't yet know where I was: otherwise why get together for a briefing at the rear of the vehicles?

I watched as the Americans continued to develop the Kronenbourg plan of attack on Bin Laden, unaware of what was happening just past the roundabout.

It couldn't have anything to do with me. But, just in case, I moved out on to the pavement and turned left, away from them, heading for the staircase that would take me up to the terraced gardens.

The American table-thumping slowly faded out of earshot. They'd probably never know how much Bin Laden ass they were about to kick, if George's plan hit the target.

I found the concrete steps at the end of the block that led up to the higher ground. They were well worn and there was no notice to say they were private. If I did get challenged I'd just play the dickhead tourist.

The steps took me up on to the roof, which was covered in red asphalt and formed a balcony. There was even a set of railings to stop you falling into someone's soup on a windy day. The roundabout was in dead ground from here, which was good; I couldn't see them, they couldn't see me. A stone wall, about a metre high, ran the length of the path, against which concrete benches had been installed at ten-metre intervals, facing in the direction of the marina for a nice relaxing view. Nearer the road, an old man with a wheelbarrow was giving some weeds the good news with a spade.

The dirty white top of a truck zoomed past above me and beyond the hedge, heading for Nice. This looked good so far: not only should I be able to see the entire marina, once I'd got into the bushes a few metres above me, but I could be over the hedge and on to the main drag in no time.

A bench stood directly in front of the bushes where I would probably try to establish the OP. Someone had sprayed 'I fuck girls!' in English across the back of it in blue paint. After my morning with Greaseball, it was a breath of fresh air.

I glanced up towards the gardener, and down in the direction of the *gendarmerie*, but both were out of sight. I slipped over the bench and on to stony ground above it.

Moving into a possible OP site from the front was something that I would never normally do: it leaves sign in the very place you are trying not to draw people's attention to. But it didn't matter here; there was enough human and dog sign about already.

I scrabbled up the bank and into the bushes, settling behind a large palm bush that branched into a perfect V at about head height. The field of view wasn't bad; I could see the whole of the marina, and the binos would get me right on to the *Ninth of May*, wherever it parked. I could also see all three exit points.

The vehicles by the roundabout were now deserted and the jumpsuits had split into two groups, each with a hyperactive

116

spaniel on a lead. I watched as the dogs scurried about the piers as if they were demented, darting, stopping, pointing their noses towards the backs of the boats. It had to be drugs; they were carrying out spot checks or looking for some kit that had been smuggled in. I sat and thought about the three million dollars US that was headed towards the *Ninth of May*, a vast amount of US bills that would be contaminated with drug residue, as most US cash is. Tens of thousands of them bundled together would send even a half-bored sniffer dog crazy.

Was that what they were aiming for now? Were they checking for the cash? No, they couldn't be. They would be more proactive, there would be a lot more support. This looked like a routine operation.

I let them get on with it, and stood up to take a look over the four-foot-high hedge. There was a tarmac pavement, and beyond that a narrow strip of garden on the level ground before the road, and, maybe fifteen metres downhill, about ten nose-in parking spaces. Just over a hundred metres further was the marina's main entrance.

I took off my sun-gigs and sat back in the OP, taking a few pictures of the target area before checking traser. There was plenty of time before the safe house meet to stay static and tune in to the place. Could I be seen, for example, from the pavement above or the path in front if somebody walked past?

I listened to the traffic, which was constant but not heavy, and started to visualize what I wanted the other two to do when I triggered the collectors off the boat.

I looked down at the jumpsuits and dogs as they worked their way round the marina, and wondered if French intelligence were on to the collectors as well. Their External Security Service hadn't messed about in the mid-eighties when Greenpeace's *Rainbow Warrior* had parked up for the night in Auckland, New Zealand, as it campaigned against French nuclear testing in the Pacific. DGSE's Operations Division, using divers from their Swimmer Combat Command, just blew up the boat, no fucking about. I was glad these people weren't allowed to operate on French soil – but then again, we weren't either, and these were strange times.

15

I continued to play about with ways we could take the collectors from the boat to wherever they were going to pick up the money. I needed a half-decent plan I could present to the other two at the safe house. We needed a structure, orders that would be the template for the operation. It would change as more information was gathered or the collectors did something we didn't expect, but at least we would have something to guide us.

A few old women gossiping at warp speed in high-pitched French were walking behind me with their dogs. I could hear claws scratching the tarmac as they moved past.

I sat for nearly an hour as the police dogs wagged their tails and sniffed like mad things down in the marina. The old guy was still digging his way downhill, unperturbed by the activity going on below us. I wasn't worried; he shouldn't see me, and if he did, so what? I'd just pretend to have a piss and hope he wouldn't be back to tend this part of the garden for another three days.

When I checked traser again it was one forty-seven. The safe house was no more than an hour away, so I'd stay a little longer. Time spent on reconnaissance is seldom wasted.

A bit of a wind had got up, and the boats were swaying from

side to side now. The cry of a seagull took me straight back to the Boston yacht club, and the thought that I could be working there now, pulling pints of Samuel Adams in a place where the dogs weren't allowed to shit, and I wouldn't have to spend all day in a bush.

Just after two o'clock, a while since the jumpsuits had gone, I decided to make a move, thinking it was a shame that the gardener hadn't made it this far along. It would have been a good test of the position.

Not wanting to destroy the very bit of vegetation behind me that was hiding me from the road, I moved right, along the hedgerow about four or five metres, and, after checking the other side, climbed over. I pulled the peak of my cap down some more and replaced my gigs as I followed the pavement back to the marina entrance. Once at the roundabout, I turned left, past the shops and café on the way to the car. I played the tourist as ever, taking a lot of interest in the boats and how wonderful they were, looking around and enjoying myself as some more Kronenbourgs were being summoned from the *tabac*. The boys were going to have to wait a while before they kicked some al-Qaeda butt.

I drove back towards Nice. Hubba-Hubba and Lotfi would both have checked their emails at one-ish, and be on their way to the safe house. Each of us had no idea where the other was staying, and, just like on the Algerian job, we didn't know what names we were using as cover.

We'd come into France at different times, but had been operating as a team for the last four days. I alone knew how to contact George. Anything they didn't need to know I wouldn't be telling them, just in case they ended up hanging upside down as a nice man read them their horoscopes with a length of two by four on the soles of their feet.

Even though I hardly knew these guys, I couldn't help liking them. It was obvious that they knew each other well, and they made me feel as if I'd been sort of adopted by them. But operational security was something we all understood and, fuck it, I'd never see them again after Sunday, so we weren't exactly aiming to be friends for life.

In preparation for this job I'd cut the TAOR [tactical area of responsibility] into three areas, allocating one for each of us to familiarize himself with in depth, or at least as much as we could in such a short time. Then we had a day in each other's areas. Hubba-Hubba had to recce the area from Monaco to the west side of Nice, ending at the airport. I took over from there to the west side of Cannes, and Lotfi took from Cannes down to St-Raphaël, about twenty Ks along the coast. We'd now read enough guidebooks and travel information on our TAOR to start our own holiday company. But it had to be done; from the moment the boat arrived, we needed to be able to operate as if we'd lived in this part of the world for years. We could have done with a few more weeks to bed in properly, but as usual we were victims of life's two fuckers: not enough information, and not enough time.

We now had to learn how the buses and trains worked here, even down to the fare structure. If Greaseball was right, it was highly likely that we'd find ourselves following these people on public transport. At the very least, we'd need to have the correct change or tokens ready so as not to draw attention to ourselves.

To operate successfully, a team like ours had to achieve three goals. The first was to establish efficient communication and information flow within the unit, and then separately between the unit leader and the command structure.

The second was to limit the chances of discovery by outsiders, by minimizing the number of communication links between the members. That meant no phone calls, no meetings other than at the safe house, and even then only when operationally necessary. There had to be no other communication other than my contacting them by their individual email, and no marked road maps, in fact nothing on paper. Everything had to be committed to memory. The less of a trail we left, the better our chance of survival.

121

The third goal was to limit the damage that might be done if one member of the team was discovered and removed from the network, which meant minimizing the number of direct links with each other, and only sharing information on a need-to-know basis. That was why we had split up and done our own thing so far: if one of us got lifted, he didn't know where the other two were, he didn't know their full names, he didn't know anything apart from my Canadian email address.

Working within these constraints had meant that we had to sacrifice efficiency in communications, intelligence gathering and planning, but it kept us alive. Now, as the job started kicking off, we had no choice but to operate more visibly as a team, which made us more effective, but more vulnerable to discovery.

My route took me back into Nice along the Promenade des Anglais. I reached the centre of town and turned right, away from the beach, heading north. I flicked on Riviera Radio and got the same boring voice I'd heard at the marina. He was waffling his way through a badly worded commercial for easily fitted security shutters for the home and office. Then there was a review of the American newspaper headlines. It was all doom and gloom and people dying of anthrax. For about the hundredth time since I'd left, all I could do was hope that no one I knew was affected.

It wasn't long before the five-star shopping areas and hotels and palm trees gave way to freight depots, grime-covered warehouses and dirty cream, rectangular sixties or seventies apartment blocks built far too close to each other.

I followed the road round a sharp left-hand bend and over the railway lines, then hit the maze of high-speed feeder roads to the motorway. I drove beside the river. At this time of the year it was just a hundred-metre-wide stretch of sandstone-coloured rock and rubble, in the centre of which a trickle of water wound its way down towards the sea.

Beautiful nineteenth-century houses that had once lined the banks were now towered over by DIY superstores and warehouses. There were no palm trees round here, that was for sure. There were no shiny buses, either.

Autoroute 8 appeared ahead of me now as I crossed the river. It ran along a viaduct, a couple of hundred feet high, that straddled this part of the city before disappearing into a tunnel in the direction of Monaco.

It would have been a lot quicker and easier if we'd allowed ourselves to use the autoroute, but that wasn't going to happen unless the shit really hit the fan. The toll booths had cameras and, besides, the police always hung around these places checking car tax and insurance. For all we knew the booths might also have face-recognition technology on the cameras.

All three of us had to avoid leaving sign. We were careful to pick cafés and shops with automatic doors, or ones we could push open with a shoulder. Even drinking coffee was a major challenge, as it had to be done without leaving prints, and every attempt had to be made to prevent leaving DNA. It wasn't so much what they could do with any of the information we might leave in our wake right now, it was what it could tell them later: this stuff stays on computer for ever.

I remembered a job I'd been on with the Regiment in Northern Ireland, when we were trying to get some finger-prints to connect a suspect with a bombing campaign. This guy was so good, he wore gloves most of the time, and when he didn't, he took care to remove all print traces.

In the end, we risked everything to follow him, just waiting for him to slip up. He went into cafés several times and had a cup of coffee, but wiped the cup and the spoon every time before he left. If it was a paper cup, he took it home with him. And he didn't just throw stuff like that out with his household rubbish, he burnt it in his garden.

It took weeks, but we got him in the end. One day he used a teaspoon, stirred his coffee, put it down and forgot to wipe it. The moment he left, the team was straight in.

There was no way I was going to make the same mistake. Everything I touched I wiped, or if the prints weren't wipable, I'd keep it with me and destroy it later. Even taking cash from an ATM was a pain. All three of us had had to do it a lot, since we paid cash for everything. When we took money out, we did so from the same area – I used Cannes – so that no pattern of movement could be established. I never used the same ATM twice; I wasn't giving anyone a known location to stake out and lift me. The only routine I followed was that I always got money out at night, varying the time and slipping on a hat and sunglasses and standing an arm's length to the side so the ATM camera didn't get me. Even then, I had to make sure I didn't leave a print. It was the same when it came to buying stuff from a shop or café – it was vital not to go to the same place twice. It was all a major pain in the arse, but if things went noisy, I wanted to leave the French police as few pieces of our jigsaw puzzle as possible. I knew that prison visiting wasn't high on George's list of priorities.

I drove under the viaduct, past the huge concrete funnel that belched smoke from the city's incinerator. I was now in L'Ariane, very near the safe house.

Areas like these, Hubba-Hubba had told me, were called *banlieues*, the suburbs. That word had always conjured up the image of nice three-bed semis with privet hedges near the commuter station. But here it meant ghetto; high-density tower blocks where *les immigrés*, mostly North African, had taken refuge. L'Ariane had the reputation of being one of the most deprived and violent *banlieues* in France, after those that ringed Paris. Hubba-Hubba had told me plenty of his auntie's horror stories; it was a no-go area for the authorities, out of bounds even to ambulance crews and firemen, who didn't dare set foot in the place without police protection – and just one glimpse of a *gendarme* was all it took to spark a riot. I couldn't think of a better place for a safe house.

I passed a burnt-out car that hadn't been there three days ago. Apart from that, everything else looked the same – a grim, rat-infested, litter-strewn warren of graffiti-sprayed concrete and satellite dishes.

I took the first turning left into the estate and parked outside the kebab-cum-cleaner's-cum-pâtisserie-cum-laundry. I got out of my car immediately so it looked as if I had a reason to be here – which, in fact, I did, though it wasn't one I wanted anyone to know about. I worried about the Mégane; the roads were packed with vehicles, but mine was four or five years newer, and still had its plastic hubcaps.

I'd only been here twice before: when we'd got together on the twentieth to sort out the recces and divide the areas, and again earlier today, to deliver the kit I'd picked up from the DOP.

16

I'd tucked my pistol into the front of my jeans. I worried about having just one mag with me, but then again, if I needed more than thirteen rounds to protect myself, I was beyond help and should probably be pulling pints at the yacht club.

As I closed the door, a young Muslim woman appeared, eyes lost in the shadows of her headscarf, shoulders drooping under the weight of two plastic carrier bags full of cans and breakfast cereals. She was blending in here a lot more easily than I was.

I went to the boot and got out my bag, locked up and headed straight for the entrance to the nearest block of flats on my side of the road. The mosaic tiles decorating the front of the building had crumbled away long ago. The concrete underneath was now decorated with a blend of French and Arabic graffiti that I didn't understand.

The security locks and intercom system had been trashed years ago. The entrance hall stank of piss, the floor was littered with cigarette butts. Shouts came from the floor above me, and a barrage of loud French rap. At least I was out of sight of the road. Anyone watching would assume I was visiting someone in the block, and since I was a white stranger, that probably meant I was there for drugs. Because I was alone and without armed back-up, I couldn't be a policeman.

I headed straight out of the back door and into a square flanked by four identical blocks. It had probably looked wonderful when it was full of shiny little Dinky-toy vehicles in the architect's model. I could still make out the markings of a car park, but now the place looked more like a storage area for the incinerator next door than the forecourt of a Citroën dealership. It was littered with burnt-out cars and rotting food that seemed to have been flung out of the upper-storey windows. Windblown rubbish was heaped in drifts against the walls of every block and, for some reason I couldn't work out, dead pigeons seemed to be lying everywhere. Maybe someone was shooting them from a window with an air rifle, or perhaps they'd eaten some of the food. A couple of seriously macho rats darted from body to body.

I strode purposefully across the square, putting in an anti-surveillance route to make sure I wasn't being followed.

I entered the next block to the blare of music and kids screaming upstairs. There was a strong smell of cooking. Two guys who looked as though they'd just got off the bus from Kosovo were in the entrance hall ahead of me, surrounded by kids with bobble hats and baggy jeans. The kids were in the process of paying for whatever it was these guys were selling them. The men froze, the foil wraps in their hands, and stared me out, waiting to see my next move. The kids couldn't have cared less, they just wanted the wraps.

It was pointless turning back. I just acted as if I belonged, didn't give a shit what was going on, and walked past. The moment they realized I wasn't concerned they carried on with the deal. I pushed open a door and hit the road.

I worked my way through a maze of small alleyways. Hollow-eyed men in shell-suit tops and jeans hung out on every corner, smoking and occasionally kicking a stray ball back to their kids, who looked like smaller versions of their dads. These people had no work, no prospects, no future. It didn't matter what colour they were, in this part of town everyone was burnt-out, just like the cars.

127

I turned towards the last block. On my first visit I'd thought it had been condemned; the place had scorch marks licking up from every window. Breeze blocks filled the window frames on the first few floors. This was my last checkpoint before heading for the RV; I was clear, nothing behind me, and everything looked normal, or as normal as anything could look around here. A Muslim woman came out on to a landing above me and gave the family duvet a good shake.

I crossed the debris-covered road and headed for the RV, one of the three farmworkers' cottages that crouched in the shadows of the estate. I imagined the owners sitting here fifty years ago, minding their own business, watching their chickens and sheep go down to the river for a drink. Next thing they knew, they were living in the middle of a dustbin of a housing project, as the city swallowed them up and introduced them to the brave new world of high-rise living. The far one now belonged to Hubba-Hubba's aunt. He'd paid for her and her husband to go back to North Africa for two months and see their family before they died, so the house was ours for the duration.

I checked the position of the Browning; I really wanted to check chamber as well, but couldn't. In a place like this there would be eyes everywhere.

I made my way along a stretch of dried mud that might once have been grass. The cottages had been painted dark beige many years ago. The faded green shutters on the furthest one were closed, the windows covered with metal grilles. Litter blown from the road had piled up against the bottom of the rusty, sagging chain-link fence that surrounded them. Beyond it was a concrete path and a dilapidated chicken coop that had last seen an egg in the fifties.

I could hear an exchange of rapid and aggressive French from the flats behind me. The duvet shaker was giving someone inside her state-of-the-nation address. I checked that the first tell-tale was in position. It was: a new black bin liner, half filled with newspaper, had been placed by the gate inside the

128

fence. That meant Hubba-Hubba was in the house, hopefully sponsoring the RV. A glance at traser told me it was four minutes to four. All being well, Lotfi would also be in position.

When Hubba-Hubba had arrived he'd have put out the bin bag for Lotfi and me to see as we made our approach. Hubba-Hubba would have got here about three; Lotfi thirty minutes or so later.

If the bin liner hadn't been there, I'd have just kept walking and gone to the emergency RV in twenty-four hours' time – Cannes at McDonald's, or McDo as it was called down here. The place was always packed with schoolkids and office workers, much to the disgust of the French food police. If any one of us failed to show we'd be in the shit, but the job would still go on. We had no choice: there was too much at stake for it not to.

I went through the gate with my bag over my left shoulder, leaving my right ready to react with the Browning, and walked up the pathway.

As I reached the door of the furthest cottage, I checked again that I wasn't about to be jumped on as I took off my sun-gigs. I looked for the two match heads that should be protruding from the bottom of the door. They had to be where I could see them without adjusting the angle of my head as I approached; I didn't want to make it obvious that I was looking for something.

They were exactly where they should be, one sticking out an inch from the right-hand corner of the door, and the other on the left, by the frame. That told me that both Hubba-Hubba and Lotfi were inside; the door hadn't been opened and closed without the tell-tales being replaced.

I knocked on the door and watched. After a few seconds, the spyhole darkened. I lowered my eyes, but kept my face in line with it, to indicate that everything was OK, that nobody was against the wall and out of view with a weapon aimed at my head. Eyes are a good tell-tale; they can't be seen from a distance, so nobody can see what's going on.

The matches disappeared from view, four bolts were pulled back, and the handle turned. The door opened and three rubber-coated fingers appeared around its edge as it was pulled inwards. I walked in without any greeting, and it was closed behind me. The bolts were slid back into place.

I took two steps over the wooden floorboards of the cramped hallway and on to a worn, Persian-style rug. I followed the smell of freshly brewed coffee into the dimly lit living room, past furniture draped in doilies and faded black-and-whites of kids with gummy smiles gathered together on a sideboard in cheap chrome frames. Lotfi was standing by a wooden-armed settee, part of an ancient, flower-patterned three-piece suite. It was covered in clear plastic sheeting, which reflected the few beams of light that managed to defeat the shutters behind him. The coffee stood on a low table in front.

He wore jeans and a cheap striped cotton shirt, the sort where the pattern fades after just a few washes, but that wasn't what made me want to grin. He was also wearing Marigolds, and a dolphin-patterned shower cap over his heavily gelled hair. Hubba-Hubba knew that the boy was taking his personal security very seriously, but had taken the piss out of him mercilessly the last time we'd all met.

I put my bag on the rug and got out my own gloves, the clear plastic ones I'd picked up from a filling station.

Lotfi watched me as I put them on and muttered, 'Bonjour,' in a low voice. I knew he was waiting for my face to break into a smile.

I unzipped my bag, removed my Nike cap and replaced it with the hammerhead baseball cap I'd bought at the marina. Then I stood smartly to attention, trying to keep a straight face as I pulled down on the string.

Lotfi watched impassively as the hammer moved up and down on the peak and I heard Hubba-Hubba try not to snigger by the door. 'This is serious, Nick.' He pointed behind me. 'Please, do not be a fool like him.'

I turned. Hubba-Hubba was sporting a plastic Groucho Marx big-nose-moustache-and-glasses set. The two of us snorted with laughter, like a couple of kids. We couldn't help it. It really had been a boring four days, and I was feeling sort of all right to see them again.

Hubba-Hubba held up his hands, to give me the full benefit of his ridiculous flower-patterned gloves, and that only made things worse.

Behind their disguises, both of them still had very neat hair and moustaches. Hubba-Hubba had broken out slightly and not shaved for a few days. His teeth gleamed in the murky light as we enjoyed our moment of stupidity, and Lotfi tried not to understand why it was so funny.

After a moment or two, I decided that kindergarten was over. We had things to do. 'Is the escape clear?'

Hubba-Hubba nodded, and the Groucho Marx kit slid down the bridge of his nose. That started me off again, and this time even Lotfi joined in.

The escape route was into the cellar via the kitchen, then through into the next-door cottage. A mat had been glued over the trap-door, so that when it was closed it would be concealed. Apparently it was a leftover from the Resistance in the Second World War.

We sat down around the coffee table to the sound of crumpling plastic that Hubba-Hubba had bought from a DIY store. We couldn't afford to leave behind anything like hair or clothes fibres that might be used against us. The sheeting and our other precautions wouldn't do a one hundred per cent job, but you can only do your best.

'I'm afraid we may have a problem, Nick.' Lotfi nodded towards Hubba-Hubba, his expression serious. 'I'm getting worried about him. He's turning into a weird beard.'

'A what?'

'Weird beards – you know, Talib. He's turning into Taliban.'

Hubba-Hubba took off his big nose and glasses, shaking his head as he poured the coffee into three blue flower-patterned cups. 'We have to make allowances, Nick. He doesn't get out much these days.' He gave me a theatrical wink.

I sipped my coffee. This was nothing instant from a jar, it was hot, sweet Arabic stuff. It always tasted to me like perfume, but it was good all the same. I could hear kids running around on the road, and mopeds buzzing past, sounding like turbo-charged sewing machines.

'We're operational from tomorrow,' I said, in a low voice. 'The boat's going to park up at Beaulieu-sur-Mer some time tomorrow night. I don't know yet where the collections are going to happen, or precisely when, but I'm told there are going to be three of them; one a day, starting Friday. I've got another source meet tonight, and hopefully I'll get the collection addresses then.'

Lotfi was silent for a moment, digesting this information. Finally, he spoke. 'Berth, Nick.' He smiled. 'You berth a boat.'

I smiled.

'Berth, OK. I'll try to remember that one.'

'And the French don't have marinas,' Hubba-Hubba added. 'They have *ports*.'

17

I watched the two of them drop enough sugar cubes in their cups to make their spoons stand up. I decided to treat myself to one. Then I pulled out the camera from my bag, together with the postcards and maps I'd got from the news-stands, and a couple of sets of leads. I nodded at Hubba-Hubba. 'OK, smartarse, let's see if you can spark up Auntie's telly . . .'

He stood up and pressed the on button. After a minute or so there was an electronic squelch and a picture appeared: some high-octane Italian quiz show with everyone's arms flying everywhere. They looked as though they'd be getting their kit off any minute. I went round the back and rigged up the connecting wires so we could have a good look at the pictures I'd taken, instead of having to crowd around the digital display on the back of my camera like schoolboys with a copy of *Mayfair*.

I took another sip of coffee as I marshalled my thoughts. 'OK. These are orders for the stakeout of Beaulieu-sur-Mer, and the take of the collectors from the target boat, the *Ninth of May*, to the *hawalladas*, then the *hawalladas*' lift and drop-off. We'll just call the marina BSM from now on, OK?'

They both nodded, probably pleased to be spared my bad pronunciation. Their French, of course, was perfect.

I held out my now empty cup to Hubba-Hubba, who was

already doing refills. 'OK, then, the ground . . .' I fiddled with the buttons on the back of the camera to bring up one of the pictures of the marina. 'BSM – I know you've been there, but I'm going to give these orders as if you haven't so we all know where we stand.' I explained the layout of the town, the main coast road, railway line, station, bus stops and phone box.

Lotfi got out his prayer beads and started to feed them, one by one, between his right thumb and forefinger. It sounded like the ticking of a clock.

'Before I carry on,' I took a breath, 'the source is the man we left behind in Algeria, the runner from the house. The Greaseball.'

They exchanged glances and their faces fell.

'That's obviously why no one else in the house was to be touched.' I paused, knowing very well what was going through their minds. 'I thought you should know, that's all.'

It felt good wiping some of his slime off me, spreading the shit about a bit.

The two of them looked at each other again and I could sense they, too, felt contaminated.

'As I said, I don't know the locations or timings of these collections, but I have another Greaseball meet tonight, so hopefully we'll know then.

'OK, let's have a look at the target area in detail – the marina, the port, whatever you want to call it.' I threw a glance at Lotfi. He managed a smile as I flashed up the entrance sign, and showed them the pictures I'd taken of the way that the piers, the shops, and the OP were positioned. 'It will make more sense when you go down there to see it again for yourselves. Any questions?'

They had none. Or maybe, as they studied the postcards and maps, sitting on plastic sheeting and trying to pick up the small coffee cups with rubber-gloved fingers, they had other things on their mind, apart from Lotfi's shower cap.

'OK, situation so far: the *Ninth of May* is coming in tomorrow

134

night, Thursday. All I know about it is it's a white pleasure boat, quite large.

'There will probably be three of them on board; one will always stay on the boat, while the other two collect. They're planning one collection a day for three days, starting Friday, and aiming to leave for Algeria with the money on Sunday some time after the last collection. So, we should be getting out of here by Monday, and by then Friday's *hawallada* should already have had everything he knows dragged out of him. By the time we're flying into the sunset Monday night, the first of the ASUs could already be having their doors kicked in by the FBI as they sit down to watch Jerry Springer.'

Lotfi lifted his head towards heaven. '*In-sha'allah.*'

I knew what it meant, and smiled. 'If God wills it.'

Lotfi came down from the sky and looked at me as if I should be replying, so I dusted off some ropy Arabic. '*As-salaam alaykum.*'

I wasn't too sure I'd used the right reply, but it got me a smile and a '*Wa alaykum as-salaam*' in return as he looked over to Hubba-Hubba. I turned to him and caught him smiling back.

'Hey, I think my Arabic's getting pretty good, these days. What do you reckon?'

Hubba-Hubba gave a slow nod. 'It's better than your English.'

They laughed and took sips of coffee as I joined them, thinking they were probably right. I got back to the orders before they took the piss out of me even more. 'The collectors will use public transport – trains and buses. Possibly taxis, but unlikely. Any questions?' I looked at each of them in turn, but they stayed silent. 'OK then, enemy forces – as normal, everyone and everything. During my recce today, the police came into the marina with dogs for what looked like a drugs search. It wasn't targeted at specific boats, but it's something we should be aware of.

'Friendly forces – basically, that's us. There's probably just a handful of people on board the warship who know what's happening, but you know they won't help us. If we're in the shit, don't expect any help.'

They gave each other a knowing nod.

'The mission.' I paused. 'The mission is in two parts. One, identify the *hawalladas* and deliver them to the DOP. Two, ensure the money never makes it to Algeria.' The mission is always repeated so there is no doubt, even though I kept having the feeling that these two were way ahead of me. 'The mission. One, identify the *hawalladas* and deliver them to the drop-off point. Two, ensure the money never makes it to Algeria.'

I knew by the look on Lotfi's face that I'd fucked up.

'What's wrong?'

'*Hawallada*. Not *hawalladas*. It is uncountable, both singular and plural – there is no S.'

Hubba-Hubba nodded his agreement.

'*Hawallada* it is. But I get to keep "parked" and "marina", right?'

They thought that was a reasonable trade.

'OK, then, let's have a look at how we're going to do it.' I looked them both in the eye: fun time had ended, and they understood. 'I see this happening in five phases. Phase one, the OP on the *Ninth of May*. Two, placing the device. Three, taking the collectors to the *hawallada*. Four, the hit and drop-off at the DOP. Finally, phase five, preparing for the next day. Any questions?'

I paused for a few seconds to let that sink in. They drank a little more brew.

'Phase one – the OP.' Hubba-Hubba refilled as Lotfi got back to work on his beads. I showed them the pictures of where my car would be parked on the road behind the hedgerow. They would find somewhere within comms distance when they did their own recces tomorrow. 'I want you, Lotfi, to get in position on the town side of the marina. Check out the closing times of those shops.'

He nodded.

'Hubba-Hubba, I want you to check out the other side's timings and find a lie-up position towards Monaco. I'll need the shop closing times when we meet tomorrow for the confirmation orders.'

It had been more important for me to find an OP position than spend time in the target area looking at shop signs.

I went through how I saw the OP being checked out tomorrow night and, of course, what we were going to do if anything went wrong. 'Questions?'

I took a couple of sips of coffee as Lotfi's beads clicked away in his hand and Hubba-Hubba's cup made gentle contact with the table. They both shook their heads.

'Phase two – placing the device on the boat. I'm probably going to have to approach it from under the pier, or just walk straight on, but I won't decide until I know exactly what the boat looks like, and where it's going to be parked. If I can't get it in place tomorrow night, I'll keep trying until I do.'

I nodded at Hubba-Hubba. 'You need to run me through the device after this.'

Lotfi grimaced. 'You are a very brave man, Nick. Do you really think it was a good idea for him to play with explosives? He can only just tie his shoelaces. Even that I had to teach him.' He slapped Hubba-Hubba across the back of the head. '*Boooom.*'

'OK, then, phase three – taking the collectors, who we will call Romeo One and Two, to the *hawallada*. Nothing should happen until about six a.m. Friday at the earliest. There aren't that many buses or trains until around that time anyway. If the Romeos are moving around they'll want to use pedestrian traffic as cover and before six it's going to be a bit thin on the ground.'

I told them how we were going to take the Romeos, by bus, train and taxi, even a hire car in case Greaseball was wrong. Hubba-Hubba checked the coffee pot as I continued. 'As I said before, it's unlikely they'll use taxis, so we need to make sure we know the drill for getting a bus or a train. Make sure you've got the right change. Find out how you get a ticket, and how it all works down here.'

They looked disappointed, but then I realized it was because the brew had run out.

'No matter how we take the Romeos, at least one of us has to be there when they meet up with the *hawallada*. Otherwise there's going to be no lift, and we fail. Any questions?

'OK, then, let's have a look at how we're going to carry out the lift. We don't know what languages they speak, if they're young or old, or where we're going to be able to do it. It will be think-on-our-feet time. If there is only one of us in a position to hit the *hawallada*, it's going to be tough. And remember, even after injection they could be kicking about for another couple of minutes.'

We all gave this some thought.

A car horn honked and was joined by several others. The noise got louder as the vehicles came up the road towards us.

We jumped to our feet, unpeeling ourselves from the plastic. I immediately started to erase the pictures from the camera. 'What the fuck's that?'

Lotfi gathered up our brew kit and moved with it down into the escape. Hubba-Hubba was at the shutters as I went to the back of the TV and pulled out the wires. He raised his Marigolded hand. 'It's OK, it's OK . . . Calm.'

Lotfi came back into the room and I went with him to the window. A parade of six- or seven-year-old Mercedes and Renaults was moving slowly along the road, decorated with ribbons and bouquets. Lotfi laughed. 'A wedding.'

I couldn't see a bride or groom, but felt glad that somebody in this shit-hole was having a good time.

We got back to business on the settee. 'Once the *hawallada* is in the DOP, the ready-for-pick-up marker is put in place – are we OK with that?' There was more nodding. Hubba-Hubba sat back into the plastic, spreading it over the back of the settee. Lotfi just played with his beads.

'Good. Phase five. Once the first *hawallada* is left at the DOP, we split up, refuel, feed our faces, and get back in position to wait for the next collection. The timings will depend on when we get the *hawallada* to the DOP. We should try to do it as soon as it's dark, so we have more time to prepare for the next day. But who knows? We could spend all night trying to lift him, and if we don't succeed, I'll decide whether we stay with him on day two, or go and get the trigger on the boat and take the Romeos to the second *hawallada*. That way, at least we have two IDs instead of just one. Questions?'

They shook their heads.

'OK, then, support. Radios?' I pointed at Hubba-Hubba.

'Yes, I have laid everything out for you to check, and I now have more batteries. More batteries than I'm shaking a stick at.'

Lotfi laughed. 'More batteries than you can shake a stick at . . .' He turned to me, his eyebrow raised. 'You see, Nick? This boy needs help.'

I gestured at Hubba-Hubba. 'Thanks, mate. I'll go down and do a final check of the kit after this. In the meantime, do you both remember the phone number? I'll start – zero four.'

Hubba-Hubba went, 'Ninety-three, forty-five.' Lotfi picked it up for the four numbers after that.

'Great. Phone cards?' I reached into my bum-bag and pulled out my wallet and phone card, and they produced theirs. The phone booths here worked on cards that you could buy anywhere, and ours were all worth a hundred francs.

'OK, last thing, insulin pens?'

Hubba-Hubba nodded. 'Downstairs.'

'Good. After we've finished here, I want you two to go and do your recces of BSM. Hubba-Hubba, make sure you finish by ten tomorrow morning. Lotfi, you go between eleven thirty and one thirty, because I want us all clear of the area before the boat comes in. We will meet back here tomorrow at nineteen hundred unless you hear from me online before sixteen, telling you otherwise. Can you make email at that time of day?'

They nodded. Lotfi sparked up. 'I will pray before leaving. It could be the last time for a few days, or for ever. Who knows these things but God?'

I watched him shove the coffee table to the side of the settee while Hubba-Hubba went into the kitchen to start on the washing-up.

I leant against the wall while he prepared himself, watching as he took off his trainers. 'Ramadan started on the sixteenth of November, right? So how come you're working, eating and drinking – I thought someone like you would have stopped by now.'

He placed his trainers neatly beside him. 'To a Muslim, saving life is mandatory. If he or she does not have strength to do so without food, then it is mandatory to break the fast. Saving life, that is what we are doing, no? Do you think Muslim doctors stop work?'

It made sense to me. 'If they did, most of the hospitals across Europe would close down.'

He started to adjust his shower hat.

'By the way, I read that article in the *Tribune* you told me about. I didn't realize the Virgin Mary gets more mentions in the Qur'ān than she does in the Bible.'

He tucked in two rogue strands of hair. 'Jesus is also revered in the Qur'ān.'

'I've never really had much time for him. I could never be arsed to get out of bed on Sundays.'

He rewarded my glibness with a quiet smile. 'So what gives you conviction, morals, fulfils your life?'

I hated being asked questions by people who were so squared away. 'I guess I just get by day to day, you know how it is.'

'No, I don't know. That's a sad thing, Nick. I feel sorry for you. There is so much you have missed.' He gave me a stare so penetrating that I found myself looking away, checking on Hubba-Hubba behind me. 'It must be painful being so empty inside . . .'

140

'I like to keep things simple, just seems better that way.' I was starting to wish I hadn't opened my mouth.

'Simplicity is good, Nick. Emptiness is not.' His expression softened again. 'But there is always time to learn, time to fill yourself. You know, both the Bible and the Qur'ān trace a common lineage back to Abraham and Adam. There really is a lot we all can learn from them. Maybe you should read them one day, they have made many people whole.'

I smiled. He smiled back, knowing there was more chance of me being struck by lightning.

He turned his back to me so that he was facing east, in the direction of the TV. As he went down on his knees, I couldn't resist asking, 'Is that why the world's so full of justice, mercy and compassion?'

'I see you took your time reading that article, didn't you?'

He didn't look back, but I could see the fuzzy reflection of his face in the TV screen. 'Justice, mercy and compassion, that would be perfect, don't you think? But when I think of people like the ASUs in America, who use my religion as a vehicle for their own selfish anger, I see no justice, and find it difficult to feel mercy and compassion. But God has helped me overcome these things. You see, these people, these ASUs, they call themselves Muslims. But they are not truly so. In associating their acts with the will of God, they are guilty of *shirk*. This is the most unforgivable sin. So it is my duty as a true Muslim, someone who really has submitted himself to God, to send those who are sinning in his name before his angels, for their book of destiny to be weighed.'

I thought he and George should get together one day over a coffee. They'd have plenty to talk about.

'At this time, God will decide what becomes of them. He decides everything, all our destinies.'

'That's Kismet, right?'

He turned back towards me as a car with a dodgy exhaust rattled past the window. 'What do you know of Kismet, Nick?'

'Not much.' I grinned. 'I saw the film when I was a kid.

Loads of your mates flying around on magic carpets, that sort of stuff.'

'You make jokes to cover up so many things, don't you?'

I shrugged, fighting back another stupid remark.

'Kismet, justice, mercy and compassion. You have been studying a little bit more than that article since we last spoke, haven't you? Here is something else for you to think about.' He turned back to the TV, sat on his heels and rocked slightly from side to side to adjust himself. He looked completely ridiculous in his shower cap, but spoke with such dignity I found myself hanging on his every word. 'In Sura 28:88, the Qur'ān says: "And cry not unto any other god along with Allah. There is no god save Him."

'Now where have we heard these words before? We sound the same, and we are the same, in so many ways, except that the Bible has stories about our God written by many people, sometimes hundreds of years after the event, while the Qur'ān holds God's very words, spoken directly to the Prophet.

'That's why one in five people on the planet is a Muslim, Nick. We feel closer to God.'

I shifted myself away from the wall. 'Well ask him to keep an eye on us over the weekend, will you? We might need a hand.'

'Of course. But you know true believers are always triumphant over non-believers, in the end. Maybe you will be able to put a good word in yourself, one day.'

18

I went into the kitchen. Hubba-Hubba was rubber glove deep in washing-up suds as he cleaned the brew kit.

'See you down there.'

He nodded as he tackled a stubborn coffee stain. His auntie would have been proud of him. The sounds of Lotfi at prayer floated in from the living room as I lifted the trap-door and went down the wooden ladder into the musty coolness of the cellar. It wasn't that big, maybe three metres by three, but high enough to stand up in. In the far corner was a coarse green blanket laid out with all our equipment in very straight lines.

Hubba-Hubba really did like order. Squared up with the edge of the blanket were our radios, binoculars, and the drug packs we'd need to subdue the *hawallada*.

I knelt in the dust of the stone floor and checked the radios first. They were small yellow Sony walkie-talkies, the sort of things designed for parents to keep track of their kids on ski trips or in the mall. We had two each, one on our bodies, one as a back-up in the boot of each car. If there was a drama with anyone's radio, they could either get their own spare or go to another vehicle, take the key hidden behind the rear licence plate, and help themselves to a replacement.

The Sonys only had a communications distance of about a K

and a half, virtually line of sight. It would have been better to have a longer distance set in case we got split up during the follow, but at least it meant we couldn't be listened to out of that range. Taped to the bottom of each were eight AA batteries: two lots of stand-by power. Attached to a socket was a mobile phone hands free with a plastic earclip. The jack was taped firmly in place so it didn't fall out when someone was sending, because sod's law dictated that that was exactly when it would get pulled out, and we'd be in loud time, treating the world to a running commentary on what we were up to.

The row of three rectangular grey plastic cases, each about seven inches long and three wide, contained enough anaesthetic to send an elephant to sleep. They were disguised as diabetics' insulin kits. I opened one to check the thin green autopen, sunk into its hard plastic recess. It was already loaded with a needle and cartridge. Also bedded into the plastic were another three needles that simply clicked on to the bottom of the pen, and another three cartridges. Once you had it against the target's skin, you pressed the trigger, and the spring inside would shoot the needle forward and inject the drug, which in this case wasn't insulin but ketamine. Alongside them was a card holding six nappy pins, with big pink plastic caps. The *hawallada* wouldn't be too worried about the colour: the pins were to prevent their tongues falling down their throats and choking them. Depressed ventilation was a side effect of this stuff, so their airway had to be kept clear at all times.

I started to check the other two kits, making sure that each also contained a scratched and worn steel MedicAlert bracelet as cover, warning anyone who was interested enough to check that we were, strangely, all diabetic.

Ketamine hydrochloride – street name 'Special K' or 'K' – is still used as a general anaesthetic for children, persons of poor health, and small furry animals. It is also a 'dissociative anaesthetic', separating perception from sensation. Higher doses, the sort we were going to give, produce a hallucinogenic effect. It can cause the user to feel very far away from their body. They enter what some people call a 'K-hole'; it has been compared to a near death experience, with the sensation of rising above one's body and finding it difficult to move. I had that feeling most mornings, but the amount these *hawallada* would be getting, they'd be waving through the space shuttle window.

In powder form, ketamine looks a little like cocaine; street users snort it, bung it in drinks, or smoke it with marijuana. Our *hawallada* were going to be getting it in liquid form, jabbed into the muscle mass of their arse where there was little risk of us hitting a blood vessel and causing permanent damage.

The three sets of green binos were small x8, the sort that fits into a coat pocket. We needed them in case we couldn't close in on the boat for the trigger and had to get eyes on the target from a distance.

All these items were important, but none more so than the dark blue plastic cylinder that lay at the centre of the blanket. About eighteen inches long and three in diameter, it came apart if you twisted it in the middle. A length of fishing line had been fed through a small hole that we'd burnt with a hot skewer just by the join, and was held in position by a strip of insulation tape on the outside of the casing, which had been folded back on itself to make a tab for easy removal.

The cylinder looked like it had come from a stationery shop, and was normally used for storing rolled-up drawings. Now it was full of some very exotic high explosive taken from a consignment made in Iran and sent to GIA in Algeria, but intercepted by the Egyptians on the way. I'd collected it at the same time as the insulin kits from the DOP, when I first got in-country.

Like everything else on this job, the components from which the pipe bomb was constructed were normal everyday items that could be bought cheaply and without raising eyebrows. Hubba-Hubba had bought all the kit he needed from DIY stores: wooden clothes pegs, emery paper, drawing pins, a small soldering set, wire, superglue, insulation tape. The

145

last item on the shopping list had come from a phone shop.

I felt a little guilty about giving Hubba-Hubba this task instead of doing it myself. I got on well with these people, yet here I was, jeopardizing his security by making him buy all the kit and build the device. But that was just how it was; as team commander I wasn't going to compromise myself if I didn't have to, and he knew the score.

I heard footsteps behind me as the praying continued above, and saw Hubba-Hubba's trainers coming down the ladder. He still had his gloves on, and the cuffs of his rolled-up sleeves were wet. He came and knelt down beside me.

'No offence, mate,' I tapped one of the radios with my right index finger, 'but you understand that I have to check everything.'

He nodded. He was a professional; he understood the mantra – check and test, check and test. 'You had better take a look at this, then. One of my best, I think.'

He carefully untwisted the cylinder and pulled it apart at the centre. The inside was packed with eight pounds of the mustard-coloured high explosive, with just enough space in the centre for the pager and initiation circuit, which were glued on to a rectangle torn from a cornflakes packet. The pager was glued face down, so that with the back cover removed, the two AA batteries and the rest of the workings were exposed. He laid the opened device back on the blanket.

The sweet, almost sickly pick 'n' mix smell of the HE hit my nostrils. 'Where did you make it?'

Hubba-Hubba moved his head back to try to avoid the smell. 'In a Formula One motel, just off the autoroute. People only stay for the night and move on, so it was a good choice. It only took me two hours to make, but the rest of the night to get the smell out of the room!'

His smile didn't last long. 'Nick . . . the source, Greaseball. I don't like it, why are we using such a man? Afterwards maybe we should—'

'Time to stop thinking about that, mate. I feel the same

way, but the sad fact is, he's worth more alive than dead. Just think of the int he's given us so far. He's the one who's getting us to the *hawallada*. And that's what we're here for, aren't we?'

He looked down at the kit, his eyes scanning each item on the blanket as he nodded in grudging agreement.

'Listen – arseholes like that? It's not worth getting worked up about. I'm sure when he's no longer any use he'll be history. There'll be quite a queue.'

Hubba-Hubba's brow creased. 'Do you have children, Nick?'

I dodged the question. 'I understand, believe me. His day will come.' I pointed at the pager with a plastic-covered finger. 'Come on, take me through this thing.'

He explained that the power to initiate the device would be generated when the bleeper notified the owner they had a message, hopefully from us. 'This pager either bleeps or vibrates, depending on the user's choice. I have diverted the notification power by rewiring it, so that when it receives our call the power is sent to the detonator instead of making the thing beep or vibrate.'

It didn't have to be a pager; anything that generated enough power to initiate the detonator could have been used. Psions or Palm Pilots do the job, especially if you know the exact date and time you want the device to initiate – someone making a speech next month, say, or even next year. All you have to do is set the alarm on the schedule programme for the time and day, place the device, leave it, and when the notification sparks up, *boooom*, as Lotfi would say.

I could see the two thin wires coming out of the end of the pager, one disappearing into the PE where the det was buried. The other was glued along the top jaw of the wooden clothes peg, which was, in turn, glued down next to the pager. I knew what it was doing there but waited for Hubba-Hubba to explain. It was his fireworks party.

'Four kilos is a lot of high explosive, Nick, but it is not going

147

to turn the boat into a Hollywood fireball – unless you can locate it to ignite the fuel, of course.'

He was right. It would all depend on where I could place the thing.

'The clothes peg, Nick, that's the circuit breaker, your safety catch. To stop you going bang.'

I couldn't help but smile at his understatement as I checked the two AA batteries. Between the nipple of the top battery and its connection in the pager was a sliver of clear plastic cut from the pager's packaging, in case someone called a wrong number while I had this thing shoved up my jumper. It would stay there until just before I went to place the device. I wouldn't want to waste time opening the cylinder and messing about with bits of plastic when I got on the boat: I'd want to just get on board and get this thing hidden and armed as quickly as possible.

Hubba-Hubba picked up a splinter of wood and used it to trace the circuit, following the det wire glued along the top of the peg then tucked under the top jaw.

'I wrapped the wires around the drawing pins and soldered them. It is an excellent connection.'

The wire leading from the drawing pin in the lower jaw disappeared into the PE.

For the time being, these two pins were separated by another piece of plastic, to which Hubba-Hubba had fastened the other end of the fishing line. He let me admire the circuit for a few more seconds. 'It is good, yes?'

I nodded. 'Did you emery the pinheads?'

He raised his hands in a gesture of disbelief. 'But of course! As I said, it is an excellent connection. Before moving to the boat, you take out the battery breaker and close the device, OK? After checking this safety catch is in place, of course.'

'Of course.'

'Then, once you have placed the device, gently pull on the fishing line. Once the pinheads make contact, the circuit will be complete and it is time for you to leave the boat with quick feet!'

148

Any one of us three could shove our phonecard into a call box, ring the pager number, then tap in ten digits. Once contact had been made, we'd get *'Message bien reçue'*, which I supposed was the French for 'Bang'. And that would be that; the boat, the people, the money, gone. I only hoped I'd be the one in the phone box outside the marina by the bus stop, watching the boat leave. I'd detonate as soon as the *Ninth of May* was safely in open water and, with any luck, some of the millions would be washed ashore at my feet.

There was one question we didn't yet know the answer to: how far out to sea would the pager initiate?

Hubba-Hubba gave his handiwork one more check. 'It is all yours now.'

I twisted the cylinder back together as carefully as he'd undone it, and left it on the blanket. Upstairs, Lotfi was still praying at warp speed. Hubba-Hubba leant down to put the device back in line and I checked the rest of the kit.

'Still warding off that evil eye thing?' I nodded at the pendant, which was swinging by his chin: the small, beaded hand with an unblinking blue eye in its palm.

'Of course. I've had it since I was a baby. In Egypt, many children have charms pinned to their coats as protection. You see, Westerners think nothing of saying about a child, "Hasn't he grown?" or "Isn't he looking so healthy?" But these things are taboo where we come from. That is because the evil eye could make the child sick. That is why we only give compliments related to character, things you cannot easily measure, and even then only in a way that shows there is no malice or envy intended.'

'So the evil eye can't hear, right?'

'Something like that. For instance, someone might see me driving later tonight and feel envious, and if they had the evil eye they could cause me to crash, maybe even die. But this,' he tapped his chest, 'this has stopped such things happening to me for over thirty years. You should get one. In this world, they are more practical, perhaps, than that...' He

149

looked upwards as the sound of Lotfi's prayers drilled their way through the floor.

I stood up. 'On this job,' I said, dusting myself down, 'I reckon we can use all the help we can get.'

Lotfi was just dotting the Is and crossing the Ts with God as I got my bag and Hubba-Hubba went to the door to check the spyhole. I heard a bolt being drawn back as I pulled off my gloves and stuffed them into my bag. 'Right, I'll see you later.'

Hubba-Hubba nodded *'Au revoir'* before checking the spyhole once more. He gave me a thumbs-up, and I walked out into the darkness. I heard a dog barking off a balcony somewhere.

I retraced my earlier route, with the bag back over my left shoulder and my right free for the Browning. There were no street lamps, and the only light came from the windows above me. Behind them, adults and kids hollered at each other, music blared, more dogs barked.

I got to the door of the last block of flats, but made no attempt to stop and look out. I didn't want to draw attention to myself. I walked straight out, keeping my head down and my eyes up as I hit the key fob and the Mégane's indicators flickered. I locked myself in and drove off immediately, as you would in this part of town.

Two consecutive right turns got me back on to the main road. I wasn't worried about anti-surveillance yet as they wouldn't be following me around here. They'd wait at the exits from the estate.

Once on the main, I kept my speed normal and drove into the city centre, heading for the coast and the Promenade des Anglais. There was still plenty to do. I needed to get something to eat, get back to Greaseball and, with luck, get the addresses, then go and see exactly where they were.

I saw the bright yellow lights of a Shell garage as I approached the city centre, and drove on to the forecourt. Whenever there is an opportunity to fill up, no matter how little fuel is needed, it must be taken. Watching the vehicles drive past, I went through the routine of filling up with a plastic glove on, to stop the horrible petrol smell on my delicate skin. I messed about with the petrol cap, making mental notes of passing cars, their plates, make and colour, and number of passengers, hoping that I'd never see them again. French numberplates comprised a group of numbers, then two or three letters, then another group of numbers. The easiest way to try to register them was just to take note of the letters and the last set of numbers.

As the unleaded flowed, I continued moving my eyes about to see if there were any cars parked up with people in, looking, waiting for me to move out of the forecourt. But it was just the normal evening commuter crowd, trying their hardest to get home to whatever French people did in the evening – which, as far as I knew, was just eat.

Filling up with exactly fifty francs' worth, and with my hat and head down for the security cameras, I paid cash and didn't have to wait for change. Then, driving over to the air and water section with a new batch of gloves, I checked for any devices that might have been placed while I was at the safe house.

I hit the coast road towards Cannes, and was nearly blinded by oncoming headlights and flashing neon as I drove along the Promenade des Anglais. Near the airport, the first of the happy-hour hookers had started her shift, complete with leopardskin bomber jacket, sparkly silver spray-on pants, and the world's highest white platform boots. At least, I thought they were the world's highest until I saw one of her colleagues, leaning against the wall in a long black coat and huge black vinyl platforms. She was chatting away on her mobile, maybe taking a booking from someone in one of the business hotels that satellited the airport. A couple of days earlier, Riviera Radio had reported that the French girls had complained to the police about East Europeans taking all their trade, when they had no visas and no right to be here. The police had responded by rounding everyone up, and the commissioner said he was embarrassed as a Frenchman to have to report that the East

European girls were considerably better looking than their French counterparts, and that was probably the reason there'd been complaints.

Leaving the airport behind me, I hit more neon at Cap 3000 and carried on along the coast towards Juan-les-Pins, deciding to pick up a pizza on the way to Cannes. The place was a seasonal beach town, living off its past glory from the sixties and seventies, when Brigitte Bardot and the jet set used to come down for a cappuccino and a pose of a weekend. It still had its moments, but right now three-quarters of the shops were closed until Easter or whenever the season started again. Restaurants were being refurbished and bars were getting repainted.

19

I cruised around the sleepy town. Strings of Christmas lights twinkled across the streets, but there was nobody at home to enjoy them. A few bars and cafés were still serving a small number of customers, but the majority of the hotels looked dead. Several shops had whitewashed windows, like bandages across next season's facelift.

I drove down a tree-lined main, looking for a takeaway pizza place that was open, and did a double-take at the two men walking towards me. For a moment I even wondered if I was hallucinating, but there was no doubting who it was in the long leather coat, smoking and chatting as he went.

I jerked my head down instinctively so that the peak of my cap hid my face. I didn't know if Greaseball had seen me, and I didn't want to check. There was no reason why he should have: my headlights should have blinded him temporarily anyway.

I took the next right and threw the Mégane up on to the kerb, then made my way quickly back to the main. I looked up to my left and they were still in sight, walking away from me. They were the only other people around; cigarette smoke drifted behind them in a cloud. Greaseball's mate was taller than him, maybe six foot, and had a bush of dark curly hair, cut just above the shoulder. He was wearing a dark, three-quarter-length coat over what looked like jeans. I couldn't see that much of him from behind, but would have bet good money on him being the man I'd spotted in the Polaroids back at Greaseball's flat. They talked quietly and earnestly to each other as they moved up the road.

They stopped and Greaseball turned towards the kerb; I could see the glow of his cigarette. He took one last drag as he nodded to his companion, then threw the stub into the gutter. The other man was definitely Curly from the Polaroid. He took something from his coat pocket, checking around him as he did so. It must have been small, because I couldn't see a thing. They shook hands and quickly hugged before parting; whatever it was, it was being posted. Maybe this was who gave Greaseball his fixes. Curly turned immediately left, down a side road, while Greaseball carried on another few metres up the street, before disappearing into what looked like a restaurant or bar. A sign hung on the wall outside, but it wasn't illuminated.

I crossed the street, to get a better view of the place, and checked the road Curly had gone down. As I closed in, I could see that the sign showed a belly-dancer with a veil and low-cut bikini top. There was no sign of Curly, and it looked as though Greaseball was now being entertained by the 'Fiancée of the Desert'.

The outside of the building looked as if someone had gone berserk with a truckload of plaster, flinging handfuls at the wall to make it look ethnic. Ornate grilles covered two small windows each side of the door, through which I could just make out shadows bobbing about in the glow.

I went back across the street, head down, checking left and right. There was no traffic, just a mass of tightly parked cars. I tried to see what was going on inside, but couldn't make out much through the small, square window. I couldn't see Greaseball anywhere.

Carrying on past the solid wood door, I peeped inside the

next window as casually as I could. I still couldn't see anything but low light and tablecloths.

It looked as if a pizza would have to be binned for a few hours. I went to the top of the street, and stopped in a doorway on the opposite side. Three scooters screamed past with their engines at bursting point. The riders looked about fourteen.

The street lights and decorations cast a haphazard pattern of shadows, so it was easy to find a corner to lurk in, in the doorway of a lingerie shop. It was probably the best place not to arouse any suspicion in this country; if Greaseball could get away with wearing a pashmina, I could probably wear this kit without anyone batting an eyelid.

Diners finished their meals. Groups and couples kissed, laughed and went their separate ways, but still no sign of Greaseball.

After two hours I was quite an expert on basques and suspenders. The only people on the street now were old men and women taking their dogs out for a last dump before bedtime. Only the odd vehicle came in either direction.

A Lexus glided up the road from my left and stopped outside the restaurant. The alloy wheels and bodywork were so highly polished you could see the Christmas decorations in them. The driver stayed put with the engine running as his passenger finished off a telephone call. When he finally got out, I could see he looked like a dark-skinned version of George Michael, with a goatee beard and flat, short hair. As he slid into the restaurant, the car moved further along the road and parked up. The driver, also dark, had a shaved head that gleamed as impressively as the Lexus. I could tell that he was already bored with waiting.

Fifteen minutes later, the door opened and Greaseball emerged into the glow of the Christmas lights. He turned towards me and I moved back into the shadows. If he got level with me, I'd have to sit down, hide my face and pretend to be pissed. But it would be difficult for him to see me over the parked cars from the other side of the road.

I waited for him to pass, then came out on to the pavement and followed. The Lexus was still there, waiting for George Michael to stop filling his face. The driver had the interior light on, trying to read a paper; this probably wasn't his idea of the perfect night out. Greaseball turned left, heading for the taxi rank at the railway station.

I watched as he got into the back of one and moved out on to the main, towards Cannes. I checked traser: nine thirty-seven, not long to go before the meet. He must be going home. It was pointless rushing back to my car since I was pretty much certain where he'd be at eleven. Besides, I didn't want to scream around after him and get stopped by the police for jumping a red.

I headed back in the direction of the Fiancée of the Desert.

At ten forty-five, having finally grabbed something to eat, I turned the Mégane up boulevard Carnot and made my way past Greaseball's apartment block.

I took a few turns, methodically checking out the area for people sitting in cars or lurking in shadows before parking outside Eddie Leclerc's.

I moved into an alleyway behind the shop and waited to see if anyone was following me up the hill. I just stood as if I was having a piss between two large skips full of cardboard boxes, and let ten minutes go by.

I could still hear vehicles on the main drag as I walked up the hill, but at this time of night it was no longer a constant drone. Otherwise, there was just the occasional burst of music from a TV, or a dog barking.

There were lights on in a couple of the apartments on Greaseball's floor. I checked traser. I was a couple of minutes early, but it didn't really matter. I hit the bell with the cuff of my sweatshirt over my thumb. I heard crackling, and a rather breathless 'Hello, hello?'

I moved my face nearer the small grille and said, 'It's me, it's eleven.'

There was a buzz at the door. I pushed it open with my foot, then pressed the intercom again. The door buzzed once more and the intercom crackled again. 'Push the door,' he said.

I gave the handle a rattle, but didn't move. 'Nothing's happening. Come down, I'll wait here.'

There was a moment's hesitation, then, 'Oh, OK.'

I slipped into the hallway and closed the door gently behind me, then moved to the side of the lift, by the door to the stairs, and drew down the Browning, making myself feel better by checking chamber before packing it back into my jeans.

The lift rattled its way up the shaft. I eased open the door to the stairs and hit the light plunger with my elbow, just in case he had friends waiting to move in behind me once I'd got up to the apartment.

The stairwell was empty. I closed the door as the light went out and waited where I was for the lift to come back down. It stopped and Greaseball walked out, expecting me to be at the front door. There were no keys in his hand. How did he plan to get back into his flat?

I drew down in preparation, and whispered, 'I'm here.'

Greaseball spun round. He could see the weapon down at my side and his eyes flickered in alarm.

I said, 'Where are your keys?'

He looked confused for a second, then smiled. 'My door is open. I rushed down to meet you.' He looked and sounded genuine enough.

'Is anyone with you?'

'No, *non*.' He gestured. 'You can see.'

'No. Is there anyone with you upstairs?'

'I am alone.'

'OK, let's go.' I ushered him into the lift and, just as before, stood behind him in a cloud of aftershave and alcohol. He was dressed as he had been earlier in the day, except for the pashmina, and still had his leather jacket on. He wiped his mouth nervously. 'I have the – I have the—'

'Stop. Wait until we get inside.'

157

The lift stopped and I moved him out. 'Off you go. You know what to do.' He headed for Flat 49, with me three paces behind, the weapon held alongside my thigh.

20

He hadn't lied: the door was still open. I touched him gently
with the pistol on the side of his arm. 'In you go, and leave this
as it is.' He did as he was told, and even opened the door that
led into the bathroom and the bedroom, to prove the place was
deserted.

I stepped inside and it was immediately obvious that the
magic cleaning fairy hadn't paid any surprise visits since this
morning. I turned the light off above me with the Browning's
muzzle, then pushed down the button that released the dead-
bolt so I could close the door with my heel. I raised the
Browning, ready to go into the room.

The moment the door was shut, I reactivated the deadlock. I
didn't want anyone making entry with a key while I was clearing the apartment.

He was standing by the table. 'I have the addresses . . .' He
had to force his hand into his jeans, which were straining to
hold in his gut.

'Turn the light out.'

He looked confused for a second, then understood. He
reached for his Camels before moving to the switch; then we
were plunged into darkness. A street light across the road
glowed against the old man's garden wall. Greaseball was

nervous; the lighter wouldn't keep still as he tried to direct the flame towards the tip of his cigarette. The shadows that flickered across his face made him look even more like something out of the Hammer House of Horror than he normally did.

I didn't want the darkness for dramatic effect. I just didn't want anyone to see a silhouette waving a pistol about through the net curtains.

'Now close the shutters on these balcony windows.'

I followed the red glow in his mouth as he pulled down on the canvas strap that controlled the wooden roller shutters, and began to lower them. 'I really do have—'

'Wait, wait.'

Once the shutters were down I watched the glow of ash move back towards the settee, and listened to him wheezing as he tried to breathe through his nose with a mouth full of cigarette. He knocked into the table and I waited for the sound of him sitting down.

'You can turn the light back on now.'

He got up and walked past me to hit the switch.

I started to clear the flat, with him in front of me as before. I glanced at the wall unit for another look at Curly. The Polaroids weren't there. A dog barked its head off on the balcony above us as we entered the bedroom. It looked as if he had decided against tennis, after all. The bags, along with the syringes, had gone from under the bed. The flat was clear: there was no one here but us.

As I moved towards the living room, I pushed the Browning back into my jeans and stood by the door. He collapsed back on to the settee, flicking his ash at an already full plate.

'You have the addresses?'

He nodded, pushing himself to the edge of his seat and reaching over the coffee table for his pen. 'The boat, it will be at Pier Nine, berth forty-seven. I'll write it all down for you. I was right. There are three collections, starting Friday in Monaco—'

I lifted my hand. 'Stop. You've got the addresses in your pocket?'

160

'Yes, but – but . . . the ink's bad. I'll write them again for you.'

'No. Just show me what you've got in your pocket.' His excuse sounded too apologetic to be true.

He managed to squeeze his hand back into his jeans, and produced an A5 sheet of lined paper that had been torn from a notebook and folded three or four times. 'Here.' He leant towards me with the sheet in his hand, but I pointed at the table. 'Just open it up so I can read it.'

He laid it down on top of yesterday's *Nice Matin*, and turned it round towards me. It wasn't his writing, unless he'd been to neat lessons since this morning. This was very even and upright, the sort that schoolgirls in my comprehensive used to practise for hours in their exercise books. And it belonged to a Brit or an American. The first address contained the number 617; the one didn't look like a seven, and the seven didn't have a stroke through it.

Monaco was marked 'Fri'. Nice marked 'Sat'. Here in Cannes was labelled 'Sun'. 'Who gave you these?'

He shrugged, visibly annoyed with himself, and probably shaken because he knew he'd fucked up when he flapped at the beginning and got too eager to give me the addresses so I would go away. 'No one, it's my—'

'This isn't your handwriting. Who gave it to you?'

'I cannot . . . I would be—'

'All right, all right, I don't want to know. Who cares?' I did, really, but there were more important things to worry about right now and, besides, I thought I already knew. 'Do you know the names of the collectors – or the *hawallada*?'

He shook his head and sounded breathless, probably because of the amount of nicotine he was inhaling. He couldn't have been more than forty years old, but he'd be dead of lung cancer long before sixty.

'What about the collection times?'

'This is all I was able to find out.'

'How do I know these are correct?'

'I can guarantee it. This is very good information.'

I went over to crazy-threat mode. 'It had better be, or you know what I will do to you, don't you?'

He leant back in the settee and studied my face. He wasn't flapping now, which surprised me. He smiled. 'But that's not really going to happen, is it? I know things. How do you think I've survived so long?'

He was absolutely right. There wasn't a thing I could do about it. These people can screw you about as much as they want. If they provide high-quality intelligence, nothing can happen to them unless people like George want it to. But what sources often fail to understand is that they're only useful while they can provide information. After that, nobody cares. Apart from Hubba-Hubba and Lotfi; I was sure they would continue to care a great deal.

He studied me for a long time and took another drag of his cigarette. The smoke leaked from his nostrils and mouth as he spoke. 'Do you know what slim is?'

I nodded. I'd heard the word in Africa.

'That's me – slim. HIV positive. Not full-blown Aids yet. I pump myself with antiretrovirals, trying to keep the inevitable from happening, but it will come, unless. . . . Well, what do I care what you do to me? But I used to wonder about Zeralda. I used to wonder if he had slim . . .' He was trying to hide a smile but couldn't stop the corners of his mouth from turning up. 'Who knows? Maybe he did, maybe he didn't. Maybe he did, but didn't know it. Slim has a way of doing that. It just creeps up on you.' He flicked some ash angrily on to the plate. 'Maybe you should have a check-up yourself. There was a lot of blood, wasn't there?'

Taking more nicotine into his lungs, he sat back and crossed his legs. He was enjoying this.

I didn't let him know that I wasn't that fussed by Zeralda's splashed blood. I knew that I had about the same risk of contracting the disease from it as being struck by lightning on the same day I won the lottery.

I stared back at him. 'If you don't care about dying, why

were you so scared in Algeria? And why were you scared earlier?'

He started to smoke like Oscar Wilde on a bad day. 'When I go, my friend, I plan to go – how do you people say? – with a bang. Let me tell you something, my friend.' He leant forward and stubbed out his second butt end. 'I know there is no hope for me. But I do plan to end my life the way I wish to, and that certainly isn't going to be at a time of your choosing. I still want to have a lot more living before slim really gets me – then bang!' He clapped his hands together. 'One pill and I'm gone. I don't want to lose my figure – as you can see I'm still the prettiest boy on the beach.'

I picked up the newspaper and folded it around the note-book page, making sure it was nice and secure, then rolled it up, as if I was on my way to the building site. 'If you're lying about these addresses, I'll get the green light to hurt you bad, believe me.'

He shook his head, and extracted another cigarette. 'Never. I'm too valuable to your bosses. But you, you worry me, you have been out of your kennel too long.' He jabbed a nicotine-stained finger at me. 'You would do it of your own accord. I felt that in Algeria.' There was the single click of his lighter and I heard the tobacco fizz. 'I know you don't like me, and I suppose I can understand that. But some of us have different desires and different pleasures, and we cannot deny ourselves our pleasures, can we?'

I ignored the question. I opened the door and he got to his feet. I left with the newspaper in my hand, wanting to get out of there quickly so I could resist the overwhelming urge to splatter him against the wall.

21

I dumped the newspaper, still with the piece of paper inside, in the footwell of the passenger seat, and took one of the pairs of service station clear plastic gloves from the glove compartment and put them on. Then, bending down into the footwell, I fished out the piece of paper and read the addresses, holding it by just one edge.

The first was Office 617 in the Palais de la Scala, at place du Beaumarchais, Monaco. I remembered the building from my recce. It was just to the side of the casino and the banking area, not that that meant much: the whole of Monaco was a banking area. The de la Scala was Monaco's answer to the shopping mall, with real marble pillars and bottles of vintage champagne that cost the same as a small hatchback. It was also next to the Hôtel Hermitage, the haunt of rock stars and fat-cat industrialists.

The Nice address was on Boulevard Jean XIII, which a quick check of the road atlas told me was in an area called La Roque, near the freight depot that I had passed to get to the safe house and with a railway station, Gare Riquier, no more than seven hundred metres away. The last one, I knew very well. It was along the Croisette in Cannes, just by the PMU betting shop-cum-café-cum-wine bar, facing the sea and cheek by jowl with

Chanel and Gucci. Women in minks sat there with old Italian men whose hands wandered under the fur like ferrets as they bet on horses, drank champagne, and generally had fun until it was time to be escorted back to their hotels. The only difference between the women in minks and the ones who worked the road near the airport was the price tag.

I was tempted, but it was far too late to go into Monaco to do a recce of the Palais de la Scala. For a start, the mall would be closed, but that wasn't the main reason. Monaco has the highest *per capita* income in the world, with security to match. There's a policeman for every sixty citizens, and street crime and burglary simply don't exist. If I went into Monaco at this time of night for a drive-past of the target area, I'd be picked up and recorded by CCTV, and could very well be physically picked up at a road block. Drive in and out of Monaco three times in a day and there's a high possibility you'll be stopped by the police and asked why. It was all designed to make the inhabitants feel cocooned and protected, and that didn't just mean the racing drivers and tennis stars who lived there to avoid tax. The population also included others who had made their money from the big three: deception, corruption, and assassination.

I decided to leave the recce for the morning, and take a look at the Nice address on the way to BSM where I planned to spend the rest of the night. That meant parking up overnight somewhere, and joining the morning traffic queues into the principality, but it carried far less risk. I folded the piece of paper and placed it inside another glove, then hid it under the seat, pushing it right up into the upholstery.

I hit the coast road. It was much less busy now; just the odd Harley or two thundering along as their riders took advantage of the deserted tarmac.

As I approached Nice, the whole coastline seemed to be bathed in neon. It reminded me of the United States, a never-ending stream of shocking pink and electric blue.

There was heavier traffic in both directions along the

Promenade des Anglais, and the whores were doing good business with kerb crawlers near the airport. Quite a few bars were still open for diehards.

I turned inland on the same road as I'd used to go to the safe house, and headed for La Roque, on the east edge of town. It turned out to be just a big sprawl of apartment blocks, much like those around the safe house, only cleaner and safer. There were no scorch marks above the windows, no bricked-up buildings, no burnt-out cars. There were even supermarkets, and a street market, by the look of the boxes of damaged fruit and vegetables that were piled up in the main street. A rubbish truck lumbered along, bedecked with yellow flashing lights, and collectors in fluorescent jackets moved among the dossers rooting through the debris.

I pulled over to check the map. Boulevard Jean XIII was the second option right, so I overtook the rubbish truck and turned right. Cheap shoe shops, thrift shops and grocery stores were both sides of me. Maybe this was where Lotfi and Hubba-Hubba had bought their outfits. A few takeaway pizza joints were still open, flanked by lines of mopeds with boxes on the back, ready to zip off to an apartment block with a large *quatre fromages* and some special deal chicken dippers.

The building turned out to be not a house but a shop front covered completely by a large pull-down shutter plastered in graffiti. Huge padlocks anchored it to the pavement.

I hung the next right at the junction, just two shop fronts along, then right again, taking a quick look at the back of the shop. I found rough, broken tarmac and crushed Coke cans, and hundreds of signs that I presumed said, 'Fuck off, don't park here, shop owners only.' Big skips lined the long wall that ran along the rear of the parade of shops.

I drove along the back of the parade. There was no need to park, and it wouldn't be wise to spend too long hanging around commercial premises at this time of night. It might attract attention, or even a couple of police cars. At least I knew where it was; I'd do the recce the night before the lift.

166

Turning right again after about a hundred metres, I was back on the boulevard; I turned left, back the way I had come, towards the sea and BSM. Nice harbour was a forest of lights and masts. As I drove round it, I noticed an Indian restaurant, the first I'd seen in France. I wondered if it was full of expats throwing down pints of Stella and prawn cocktail starters while the cook added a little squirt of Algipan to the vindaloo, to give it that extra zing.

I reached the marina at BSM at just after one thirty, and drove into the car park between the harbour and the beach. The world of boats was fast asleep, apart from a couple of lights that shone out of cabins rocking gently from side to side in the light breeze. Dull lighting came from tall, street-style poles following the edge of the marina. These ones were a bit fancier, branching out at the top into two lights per pole, though a few of the bulbs were on their last legs and flickering. Luckily for me, they'd been designed not to give out too much light, or no one would have been able to get to sleep.

My only company in the car park was two cars and a motor-cycle chained to the two-foot-high steel tubing set into the ground to stop vehicles parking in the flower bed.

With the engine off, I opened my window and listened. Silence, save for the soft chink of the rigging. I felt under the seat for the piece of paper and put it into my bum-bag. I got out, making the Browning comfortable as I headed towards the admin end of the parade. Quickly climbing the concrete steps, I got to 'I fuck girls', jumped up on to the OP, and settled myself in for the remainder of the night, having first buried the addresses in the earth at the base of the palm tree. I needed to be detached from it, in case I'd been seen by some well-meaning member of the public and got lifted by the local police for dossing in a public place.

It was going to be a pain in the arse staying up here for the next seven hours, but it had to be done. The car was a natural draw point if people had surveillance on me, so I didn't want

167

to sleep in it. Also, from here I could see anyone trying to tamper with it.

I brushed some of the stones from under me as I leant forward against the palm, and alternately watched the car and studied the layout of the marina.

The addresses were in my head by now; I didn't need the information any more. That bit of paper was for George. The handwriting, the fingerprints on it, even the paper itself could be useful to him, either now or later. After all, this was going to be a long war.

It started to get quite nippy at about four o'clock. I dozed off for a few minutes now and again, having pulled the baseball cap down as far as it would go, and curled my arms around myself, trying to retain some warmth.

22

THURSDAY, 22 NOVEMBER, 07:27 hrs

My eyes stung more and more and my face got colder, which kept me checking my watch. It was still dark. I retrieved the addresses from their hiding place and moved along the hedge before jumping over, then walked along the road to the entrance, down to the roundabout, and past the shops and cafés. Everything was still closed; the odd light could be seen behind the blinds of a couple of the smaller boats as they got the kettle on for the first brew of the day.

I got my washing kit from the car; there was a freshwater shower by the beach on the other side of the car park. I washed my hair and gave myself a quick once over with the tooth-brush. I'd spent a third of my adult life out in the field, sleeping rough, but today I couldn't afford to look like a dosser. I wouldn't last five minutes in Monaco if I did. Also, I couldn't walk around in swimwear, or go bare-chested anywhere but the beach. No camper vans, either.

A comb through my hair and a brush-down of my jeans and I was ready. I went back to the Mégane and hit the road, with the heater going full blast to dry my hair. Monaco was twenty-ish minutes away if the traffic was good.

I hit Riviera Radio just in time for the eight o'clock news. The Taliban were fleeing the bombing campaign, Brent crude was down two dollars a barrel, and the day was going to be sunny and warm. And now for a golden oldie from the Doobie Brothers . . .

I disappeared into a couple of mountain tunnels, the bare rock just a few feet away from me, and as I emerged into the gathering daylight I put my hat back on and made sure the peak was down low for the trip into the principality. The first people I saw were policemen in white peaked caps and long blue coats down to their knees, looking like they'd come straight from the set of *Chitty-Chitty Bang-Bang*.

The road was quite congested, with a hotchpotch of numberplates. There was a lot of French and Italian traffic, but just as much from the principality, with red and white diamond chequered shields on their plates.

As I reached the small roundabout just a few hundred metres beyond the end of the tunnel, I had to run a gauntlet of motorcycle police parked up on either side of the road. Three of them, in knee-length leather boots and dark blue riding trousers, were checking cars both in and out of the principality, scrutinizing tax and insurance details on the windscreens as their radios gobbed off on the BMWs beside them.

The road wound downhill towards the harbour, past three or four CCTV cameras. They were everywhere, the rectangular alloy boxes swivelling like robotic curtain twitchers.

Sunlight was starting to bounce off the clear water in the harbour, making the boats shimmer as I got down to sea level. Some yachts were the size of P&O cruisers, with helicopters and Range Rovers parked on the deck so that the owners didn't have to worry about phoning Hertz when they parked up.

High on the other side of the harbour was Monte Carlo, where all the casinos, grand hotels and fat cats' condos were clustered. That was where I was heading. I followed the road as it skirted the port, and couldn't help imagining myself as one of those Formula One drivers who raced along this stretch of tarmac each year, made millions, then came and lived here to make sure none of it leaked back into the tax system. Good work if you can get it.

Monaco hadn't struck me as a particularly attractive place. It was full of boring, nondescript apartment blocks smothering the grand buildings that had gone up in the days before people wanted to cram into the principality and save some cash. The banks held twenty-five billion dollars on deposit, which wasn't bad for a population of thirty thousand people. The whole place could fit into New York's Central Park and still have some grass to spare. Money even washed over into the streets, where public escalators took you up and down the steep cliffs that started less than a hundred metres from the water's edge. There was no shortage of rich people wanting to live there, and the only way to accommodate them had been upwards. On the recce a few days ago, I'd walked past a primary school housed on the first floor of an apartment complex. Its terrace had been extended, and covered over with green felt flooring to create a playing-field.

There were just as many little whippety dogs in waistcoats, and poodles with baseball caps here, but there was no need for the Cannes Shuffle. Even the pavements were part of the fairy tale.

The harbour fell away as I drove up the hill towards the casino. Opposite me, on the far side of it, was the palace where the Prince and all his gang lived. Flags fluttered from every tower and turret. The architect must have been Walt Disney.

I hit the perfectly manicured lawns of the casino. Even the giant rubber plants around it were protected, cocooned in some kind of wax covering in case of a freak frost. A fairy-tale policeman directed me out of the path of a Ferrari that was being reversed out of the valet park, so some high-roller could drive the quarter-mile or so back to his yacht after gambling the night away.

I turned left, past the Christian Dior and Van Cleef jewellery shops and more protected rubber plants. Across a junction in front of me was Place du Beaumarchais, a large grassed square

171

with walkways and trees. To my right was the Palais de la Scala, an impressive six-storey pile built in the old French style, with pristine cream paintwork and shuttered windows.

I followed the edge of the square, and turned right into an underground car park just before the de la Scala entrance, squeezing in next to a sleek, shiny Acura sports car with New Jersey plates. How it had got there, I didn't have a clue; maybe it had been driven off one of the yachts.

Back up at street level I walked across to the shopping mall. The sun was just reaching over the tops of the buildings, and I put on my sunglasses to complement the hat for the short walk under the security cameras.

I pushed my way through the door of the mall with my shoulder, and my nostrils were immediately assaulted by the smell of money and polish. I took off my glasses. Small concession shops lined both sides of the marble corridor, selling champagne and caviar. First stop on the left was the glass entrance to the main post office, its interior as grand as a private bank. The corridor went on for about forty metres, then turned left and disappeared. Just before the corner there was a cluster of tables and chairs outside a café. Large decaffs and the *Wall Street Journal* seemed to be the order of the day. Power-dressed people moved among them with a click of their heels.

Half-way down on the right was a Roman-style marble pillar and door. A sign announced it was the reception area for the offices that made up the five floors above.

I walked towards the café, glancing at a large Perspex display that gave details of who owned or rented the office space upstairs. One glance told me they all started with Monaco – the Monaco Financial Services Company, Monaco this, Monaco that. They were all spaced out, showing who was on what floor, but I was walking too fast and my mind was working too slowly to spot who occupied 617.

I carried on past the blur of brass plates. Double glass doors opened into the reception area. An immaculately dressed dark-haired woman operated the desk. A wall-

172

mounted camera swivelled behind her as she spoke on the telephone.

I took a seat at a vacant table at the café, looking back towards the reception area. A waiter immediately materialized and I ordered a *crème*. He wasn't too impressed with my attempt at French. 'Large or small?'

'Large one, and two croissants, please.'

He looked at me as if I'd ordered enough to explode, and disappeared back into the café.

I looked over to my right to see what was round the corner. A very smart-looking cobbler's shop sold shiny belts and other leather goods, and a dry-cleaner's had a row of ballgowns on display. Opposite the cleaner's was a china plate shop. This part of the corridor was only about fifteen metres long, and ended with another glass door. I could see sunlight reflecting off a car windscreen outside.

My order arrived as well-dressed people at other tables finished off their coffee and sticky buns before work. The loudest voice I could hear, however, was English home counties. A woman in her early forties with big hair was talking to an older companion. They wore enough makeup between them to fill a bomb crater. 'Oh, darling, it's just too awful ... I can't get salopettes long enough for my legs in London. The only place seems to be Sweden, these days. I mean, how ridiculous is that?'

Others talked quietly, almost covertly, into their mobile phones, in French, Italian, English, American. All the English speakers used the same words during their conversations: 'deal', 'close' and 'contract'. And no matter which nationality was talking, they all ended with '*Ciao, ciao*'.

23

I finished my milky coffee as two suits stopped at the plastic-covered board and checked it out before pressing a buzzer. One bent his head towards the intercom, then they both disappeared through the doors immediately to the left inside the reception area.

I'd seen nearly everything in here I needed to. I picked up the napkin, cleaned my hands and wiped the cup, even though I'd only touched the handle. Leaving an outrageous sixty-six francs and a tip, I went out the way I'd come in.

This time, my eyes hit the sixth-floor sign and ran along the row of small plates: 617 was apparently the home of the Monaco Training Consultancy, whoever they were. I walked on and exited the building.

The sun shone bright above the square now, so I put on my gigs and pulled my peak down. Cars, motorbikes and scooters were crammed like sardines into any available space around the square. Gardeners pruned the bushes and a couple of guys in Kevlar gear were just about to take a chainsaw to some branches of the large leafless trees. Sprinklers lightly sprayed the grass as women dressed in furs floated past, their dogs wearing matching fashion accessories. I took a right at Prada and went round the back of the building as the chainsaw sparked up behind me. I wanted to see where the exit by the dry-cleaner's emerged.

The narrow road this side of the building was about sixty metres long, with a few small shops developing pictures or selling little paintings. I turned right again, along the back of de la Scala, and found myself in the building's admin area. Some shutters were up, some were down; behind them were private parking spaces and storage areas for the shops. Most of the space was taken up by the loading bay for the post office. It was very clean and orderly, and the postal workers wore smart, well-pressed blue uniforms and white socks. I felt as though I'd wandered into Legoland.

The dry-cleaner's entrance was just past the loading bay. I glanced through the glass doors and could see all the way to the café, and the point where the corridor turned right towards the reception.

Beyond the dry-cleaner's, on the other corner of the Palais de la Scala and about twenty feet above the ground, was a camera. At the moment it wasn't angled in this direction because it was too busy monitoring the junction below it. I hoped that wasn't going to change. I walked back to the Mégane the way I'd come.

I squeezed away from the Acura and went and had a look at the railway station before heading for Nice and Cap 3000. It was time to prepare for the brush contact with my new mate Thackery that I'd arranged yesterday in my email to George.

I drove into the retail park at just after ten thirty. I put on my disposable gloves, retrieved the addresses from under my seat, then pulled the paper from its own protective wrapping. I ran through the addresses in my mind before unfolding it, testing myself; this was the last time I was going to see them. Then I folded it once more, and rolled it tightly enough to be able to squeeze it back into the thumb of the glove, ripped off the excess polythene and shoved it into the pocket of my jeans.

I got out and locked my door as an airliner touched down on

the runway a couple of hundred metres away. For a moment it had looked as though it was going to land on the beach.

Most of the complex was dominated by the Lafayette retail company, with its huge department store and gourmet supermarket, and the spaces around it were filled with shops selling everything from smelly candles to mobile phones.

As I walked through the automatic glass doors, a loudspeaker above me knocked out some bland Muzak. There weren't many Santas about, but plenty of twinkling lights and Christmas novelty stalls. One sold a whole range of multicoloured velvet headwear, from top hats to jesters' caps with bells. Escalators carried hordes of shoppers with gigantic plastic bags bulging at the seams between the two levels. This was the only place that I'd used more than once. It was large, busy, and I considered it a reasonable risk. I had to get online, and a café was too intimate. So long as I never used a card or an ATM, this place should be OK.

Four shiny new Jaguars from the local dealership were parked up in the atrium, windscreens groaning with promotional material. To the left of them was the entrance to Galeries Lafayette, the two-storey department store.

The rather bored-looking Jaguar salesman sat behind the cars, at a white plastic garden furniture set, complete with parasol. He was surrounded by piles of shiny catalogues, but had his nose stuck firmly in *Nice Matin*. Perhaps he realized that November isn't the time to buy cars; it's the time to buy socks and slippers and Christmas stuff for your mum.

First things first. I went to the sandwich shop and got myself a Brie baguette and a very large hot coffee, and took both with me to Le Cyberpoint. This wasn't a shop, but a collection of telephone-cum-Internet stations, each with a conventional telephone, linked to a small touchscreen and metal keyboard, with a big steel ball for the mouse. There were eight of them, mostly being used by kids whose parents had dropped them off with a phonecard to shut them up for an hour or so while they did the shopping.

I put my coffee on top of the machine, to relieve my burning fingers and allow me to shove some crusty baguette down my neck before pushing the phonecard into the slot and logging on. Muzak played in the background, too low to hear and too loud to ignore, as Hotmail hit me with enough adverts in French and English to fill a whole night's TV viewing. There was nothing from George. He'd be waiting for the addresses that I'd give to Thackery at one o'clock, and had nothing new to tell me.

I closed down, and pulled out my phonecard, which still had sixty-two francs left on it. As I picked up my coffee, I spilt some down the machine and jerked back to avoid any dripping on me. Visibly annoyed with myself, I gave the screen, keys and mouse a good wipe down with the napkin that they'd wrapped round the baguette, until I'd left no fingerprints. With a fistful of soggy paper and a suitably apologetic look on my face, I left Le Cyberpoint and headed back to the car, stopping on the way to buy a roll of 35mm film and a red and yellow jester's hat with bells on.

There was only an hour before the brush contact, so I turned the Mégane's ignition key and hit Riviera Radio, then slipped on the polythene gloves. I tipped the film out of its plastic canister, and replaced it with the rolled-up addresses.

Marvin Gaye was interrupted by an American voice. 'We now go to the BBC World Service for the top-of-the-hour news.' I checked traser on the last of the bleeps, and it was dead on. A suitably sombre female brought me up to speed on the bombing of Kabul, and the progress of the Northern Alliance. I turned it off, hoping that Thackery had been well trained and was doing exactly the same.

At thirty-two minutes past the hour I checked the canister in my jeans, the Browning, my baseball cap and bum-bag, and headed once more into Cap 3000. It was a lot busier now. The gourmet food hall was doing a roaring trade, and it looked as though the Jaguar rep had led the charge. He was still at the garden table, but sitting back with a glass of red wine and a

177

filled baguette the size of a small torpedo. I headed left and through the ground-floor perfume department of Galeries Lafayette. Menswear was directly above me, up an escalator, but going this way gave me time to check my arse and make sure no one else was wanting to join us.

I went into the book department to the right of the smelly counters, and started to check out the English-language guides to the area, not picking them up but tilting my head to scan the spines.

When I'd satisfied myself that no one was taking more interest in me than was healthy, I walked deeper into the store, took the escalator up to the first floor, and worked my way back to the men's section. I hit the bargain rails of cargo trousers and took a pair, plus some jeans. Then I minced along the coat rail and chose one in dark blue padded cotton. It would stop me freezing to death at the OP, and not make the noise that nylon would every time I shifted position.

I moved from table to table, comparing prices, before picking up two sweatshirts. As far as I knew, you couldn't leave fingerprints on fabric. The only thing I was doing differently from any other browser was snatching a look at traser whenever I could. I had to be on my start line at precisely twelve minutes past. The contact wasn't exactly at one o'clock, but twelve minutes after. Surveillance teams are aware that humans tend to do things at the half, quarter, or on the hour.

At the same time, I was also keeping a running total of my expenditure. I wanted to make sure I had enough cash on me to cover the cost of this kit. I didn't want any scenes at the checkout that people might remember later.

At eight minutes past one I headed over to the maze of shelving in the underwear department. Calvin was doing a nice line in flannelette pyjamas and long johns this season, but they weren't really my style. I moved on, glancing at the four or five other people in my immediate vicinity. None of them was wearing blue. I picked up four pairs of socks after sifting

178

through the choices and checked traser. Three minutes to go.

Still no glimpse of blue. I draped my purchases over my left arm as I agonized over a shelf full of T-shirts and fished the canister out of my jeans. A man brushed past me from behind, and gave me a big *'Pardon'*. That was OK: it gave me extra cover to check traser. Two minutes to go. Michael Jackson's 'Thriller' was interrupted by somebody gobbing off over the Tannoy about the bargain of the day.

I was walking back towards my start line when I spotted a blue chunky turtleneck jumper ahead of me, no more than ten metres away. It was two sizes bigger than it needed to be, and making its way towards the other end of the socks and under-wear aisle, the other start line. This wasn't the sort of Thackery I'd imagined: this one looked straight out of a garage band. He was in his late twenties, with peroxide blond hair, gelled up and messy. He, too, had a bag in his left hand. He was hitting the start line; it had to be him. One minute to go. I toyed with a selection of boxers on the edge of the underwear department, but my mind was focused on what was about to happen.

Twenty seconds to go. Adjusting the clothes on my arm, I transferred the canister into my right hand as I started to walk down the aisle. Thackery was now about six metres away. Between us, an old man was stooped over a pile of thermals.

There was another announcement over the Tannoy, but I hardly heard it. I was concentrating completely on what needed to happen during the next few seconds.

Thackery's eyes were green, and they were looking into mine. The contact was on. He was happy with the situation; so was I.

I headed straight along the aisle, aiming for the suits, but my eyes were on his hand. Two metres to go. I stepped around the old man, and relaxed my grip on the canister.

I felt Thackery's hand brush against mine, and the canister was gone. He carried on walking. He'd done this before.

I decided against the suits, but had a quick look at the

overcoats before heading to the cash desk on the far side of the floor. I didn't know what Thackery was doing, and didn't care. My only job now was to pay up and get out, and that was exactly what I did.

24

A wrecked car was burning nicely in the square, dangerously close to one of the apartment blocks. Flames were licking at the first-floor balconies, but nobody seemed to care. An old mattress had been chucked on to the roof, its burning foam adding to the column of thick black smoke. I tossed the bin liner containing all my crap on to the fire; it was too good an opportunity to miss and I stood against a wall and watched it turn to ash. Kids ran round the car like Indians around a wagon train. They threw on wooden pallets and anything combustible they could find, while their parents shouted at them from the windows above.

As I approached the house, Hubba-Hubba's bin liner was exactly where it should have been, and the matches were under the door. Lotfi looked up from the settee by the coffee table as I entered the living room. Wearing a matching green shower cap and gloves, he muttered, '*Bonjour*, Nick,' with a very straight face, daring me to comment on his new hat. I just nodded extremely seriously as Hubba-Hubba threw the bolts behind me.

As I bent down to get my own gloves out of my bag, I saw Hubba-Hubba's trainers stop a few feet behind me. He gave me a cheery '*Bonjour*', but I didn't look up until I'd slipped on my new multicoloured velvet jester's hat, then given a shake of the head for the full benefit of the bells. I tried to control my laughter, but failed as Hubba-Hubba moved into view. He was wearing a pair of joke glasses with eyeballs bouncing up and down on springs. Lotfi looked at us with a pained expression, like a father with two naughty children.

We all took our places around the coffee table. Lotfi got out his beads, ready to start threading them through his fingers as he thought about his next conversation with God. Hubba-Hubba took off his glasses and wiped the tears from his eyes before playing mother with the coffee. I kept my hat on, but what I had to say was serious.

'I've got the location of the boat in BSM from Greaseball. I've also got the three addresses from him, but he doesn't know the names of the *hawallada* or the times of the collections.' I looked at the two of them. 'You ready?'

They both nodded as I tried the hot sweet brew. Then they closed their eyes and listened intently as I gave them the Palais de la Scala address.

They were immediately concerned. 'I know what you're thinking. I couldn't agree more. It's going to be a nightmare. But what can I say?'

Well, I did know what to say: the address, three more times. I watched their lips moving slightly as they repeated it to themselves.

I gave them the second address three times, then the third. They opened their eyes again once I'd finished, and I told them about the recces.

On the build-up for the Algeria job, when we were in Egypt, sitting around a pot of coffee just like we were now but without the clowns' get-up, I'd told them about the seven Ps: 'Prior planning and preparation prevents piss-poor performance.' They liked that one – and it was funny afterwards, listening to Hubba-Hubba trying to get his tongue around them in quick time.

'OK, then, the *Ninth of May* is going to be parked up at berth

182

forty-seven, pier nine. Forty-seven, pier nine. That's the second one up on the left-hand side of the marina as you look at it from the main road. Got that?'

Lotfi turned to Hubba-Hubba and gave him a quick burst of Arabic, and for once, I understood the reply: '*Ma fi mushkila, ma fi mushkila.*' No problem, no problem. Hubba-Hubba waved his gloved hands around the room as he traced the outline of the marina and pinpointed the pier.

I gave them the confirmatory orders for the stake-out, from placing the device to lifting and dropping off the *hawallada*.

Lotfi looked at the ceiling and offered his hands and beads to his maker. '*In'sha'allah.*'

Hubba-Hubba gave a sombre nod, which looked ridiculous, given the way we were dressed. Lotfi's beads clicked away as kids on scooters screamed up and down the street.

'OK, then. Phase one, finding the *Ninth of May*. Lotfi, what are the closing times for the places you looked at?'

'Everything is shut by midnight.'

'Great – and yours, mate?'

There was a rustle of plastic as Hubba-Hubba moved in his seat. 'Around eleven thirty.'

'Good.' I picked up my cup and took a gulp of coffee. 'I'll do the walk-past at twelve thirty a.m. I'm going to put the Mégane in the parking bay up on the road, and walk down to the marina via the shops, check out the boat, then back to the OP via the garden and the fuck bench, to clear the area in front of the OP.

'If the *Ninth of May* is parked up where it should be, the OP won't have to change.' I looked at Lotfi and he nodded slowly as he leant forward to pick up his brew. I described the OP once more, the higher ground above the fuck bench, the hedgerow, and the path from the marina to the main. I needed them to know my exact location so that if there was a drama they would know where to find me.

Lotfi looked puzzled. 'One thing I don't understand, Nick. Why would anybody write that on a bench?'

I shrugged. 'Maybe he's proud of his English.'

Hubba-Hubba joined in gravely as he filled Lotfi's cup. 'I think that whoever wrote that has had a very tall glass of weird.'

Lotfi's eyebrows disappeared under his shower cap. 'You've been watching too much American TV.'

Hubba-Hubba grinned. 'What else can I do while I wait for you to finish praying?'

Lotfi turned to me with a look of exasperation. 'What am I to do with him, Nick? He is a very fine man, but an excess of pop-corn culture is not good for such a weak mind.'

I started to go through the what-ifs. What if the boat wasn't there at all? What if the boat was there, but in a different position and I couldn't see it from the OP? What if I got com-promised by a passer-by in the OP? The answers at this stage were mostly that we'd just have to meet up on the ground to reassess. And if the boat didn't make an appearance at all, we'd have to spend all night screaming up and down the coast, checking out all the marinas – and, of course, Greaseball.

I swallowed the last of my brew and Hubba-Hubba picked up the coffee pot to give me a refill. There was a gentle click of beads as I continued. 'Phase two: the drop-off and the OP set-up. I want you, Hubba-Hubba, to walk along the main and past the OP at twelve forty with the radios, the pipe bomb, binoculars and insulin case. If the OP area is clear, I want you to place the bag in the OP, so it's there when I get back from finding the *Ninth of May*. Leave a Coke Light can in the top of the hedge to give me a tell-tale, then move back to your car and get in position for the stake-out. Where exactly are you going to be?'

Hubba-Hubba waved his arms about again to give me directions, as if I knew what was in his head and what he was pointing at. I was eventually able to establish that he'd found a place just past the marina, towards Monaco. 'There are vehicles parked along the coast, mostly belonging to the houses on the high ground.' He checked inside the pot to make sure he had enough of the black stuff to keep us going. 'The radio should work – I'll be no more than four hundred metres away.'

'Good news.' I had a brainwave. 'Wrap all my OP kit up in a large dark beach towel, will you?'

He looked puzzled, but nodded.

'Once I've found the boat I'll move back to the OP the same way that I walked in, but not before twelve forty, so the kit drop can take place. Once I'm settled in the OP I'll radio-check you both. Where are you going to be, Lotfi?'

He'd gone for the car park five hundred metres back into the town, on the other side of the marina from the OP. 'The one that looks over some of the marina,' he said, 'so the radio should work from there too – I'm in line of sight with you.'

It was a good position: in the dark it would be very difficult to see him, as long as he sat perfectly still and left a window open a fraction to stop condensation forming, and giving the game away. I'd told both of them to practise this when we first met up in-country. They'd spent a couple of nights not getting noticed in supermarket car parks, so they were well up to speed.

'Call signs are our initials – L, H and N. If I don't hear anything from you by one thirty, or you don't hear from me, you'd better move position and try to get comms. Come in closer if you have to. This job's going to be a nightmare with these radios, but it would be even worse without them.

'Once we've established comms I'll tell you if anything's changed – like, the boat isn't there – and we can reassess. Once we've done the radio check, and everything's fine, the OP is set, and no matter what happens we must never lose the trigger on the *Ninth of May*. Not even for a second. Lotfi, I want you to radio-check us every half hour. If somebody can't speak, just hit the pressle twice and we'll hear the squelches.'

I moved on to phase three. 'While we're all hanging about and getting bored, I'll be working out when to go down to the boat and place the device. I won't know when I'm going to do

185

it until I see what's happening on the ground. And I won't know where I'm going to place the thing until I know what the boat looks like. It might not happen tonight – they might have a rush of blood to the head and invite their mates round for a barbecue on deck, or decide to sleep under the stars. Or the boat next door might be throwing a party. But as soon as I'm ready, here's what I want you both to do.'

I covered all the angles, and finished by telling them what I had in mind if there was a drama, so we could get away quickly and, with luck, make it look like nothing more significant than an aborted robbery. We didn't want to put the collectors off their mission.

Lotfi and Hubba-Hubba were absolutely silent now. Even the beads were still. It was time for the difficult bit.

'OK, phase four, triggering the collectors away from the boat. We can't afford to lose them. We think we know the first location, but it means nothing – we're going to have to take them. I'm calling them Romeo One and Romeo Two, and so on as we ID the *hawallada*. I'll give them their numbers when I first see them. If they go towards Monaco, this is how I want to play it . . .'

I covered the details of the take of the collectors to the Palais de la Scala. Then I went through the actions-on in the event that they went towards Nice or Cannes, and finished my brew before confirming the major points.

'Remember that radio contact is vital, especially if I've had to follow them on to a train. If we have this all wrong and they go towards Nice and Cannes, I want you, Lotfi, to head straight for the Cannes location. Hubba-Hubba, you work your way into the city and take Nice. That way, hopefully, one of you will be at the collection point to back me up – if I manage to stay with them.

'If they go somewhere else altogether and we get split and lose comms, I'll have to assess the situation, see if I can do the job myself. Whatever happens, we'll meet back in our BSM positions again by 0030 Saturday morning. I'll radio-check at

0100. If there's been a fuck-up, we'll meet up on the high ground and sort ourselves out. Any questions?'

They shook their heads again, and Lotfi got cracking with the beads.

'Phase five: lifting the *hawallada*, and the drop-off. Getting the Special K into him is going to be difficult. I doubt if he'll take the injection lying down. Just remember, no matter what, he has to be delivered alive. When and how we do this is going to have to be decided by whoever is on the ground at the time.'

I was silent for a minute to let them take it in. 'Right, let's go through the DOP again.'

They knew where it was and how it worked, but I didn't want there to be any misunderstanding. 'Remember the tell-tale for the *hawallada* in position – the Coke Light can to the right and just under the recycling bin. Whoever is picking up the *hawallada* will remove it so it's clear for the next drop the following night.'

Lotfi started to pour everyone more coffee. I waved it away. I hated it when my pulse raced: there was going to be enough of that tomorrow, for sure.

'We have until four in the morning to make the drop-offs. I want to get rid of each one as soon as we've lifted him. That will give us time to get clear, and sort ourselves out for the next lift.

'We'll use frequency one for Friday, frequency two, Saturday, three on Sunday – just as well this job is only three days, we only have four frequencies.'

It got no more than a polite laugh from the two of them.

'We'll change frequencies at midnight no matter what is happening, even if we're still playing silly fuckers trying to lift the first *hawallada*. Remember, keep the radio traffic to a minimum and, please, no Arabic.'

Lotfi sparked up. 'Is it OK to come up on the net if we need to correct your English?'

I laughed. 'OK, but only in the event of split infinitives.'

They gave each other another squirt of Arabic, and both

smiled. When Lotfi turned back to me, I knew what was coming. 'On second thoughts,' he said, 'we won't be carrying enough batteries . . .'

'Very funny.' I reached over. 'Split this.' I gave him a smack on the back of the shower cap. 'Have I missed anything?'

We sat quietly, running everything through our heads, before I wound things up. 'I need you both to go and check out the other two *hawallada* locations before getting on the ground at BSM tonight. Get down to Nice, get down to Cannes, familiarize yourselves. But leave Monaco. I think we should only be going in there when we have to.'

As I went through all the timings again, I fished around in my bum-bag and got out my phonecard. They did the same. 'Zero four nine three.' I pointed at Hubba-Hubba.

'Four five.'

I nodded at Lotfi, who did his bit too. We went round and round with the telephone number until it was burned even deeper into everyone's memory.

We started to play the address game, exactly the same as we'd done with the pager number. I started off with the Cannes address, stopped half-way through and handed the baton to Lotfi, who finished it off, then started on the Nice address, pointed at Hubba-Hubba, who carried on. We played the game until we heard sirens in the distance – probably a fire engine and police escort about half an hour too late to sort out the burning car or maybe one of the apartments by now.

'This is now going to be the most dangerous period for us.' I leant forward, elbows on thighs, as the plastic crumpled and my hat bells gave a gentle ring. 'Up to now we've sacrificed a lot of our efficiency for security. From now on it's going to be the other way round. We'll have radios beaming out our intentions; we're going to have to meet up without a safe house; we'll be on the ground, vulnerable and open to discovery. Not only from the Romeos and the *hawallada* but from the police and the intelligence services as well.' I pointed to the shuttered window. 'Not to mention that lot, the third party.' The kids

188

screamed with excitement as they taunted the fire crew. It must be tough trying to hook into a hydrant while you're being pelted with dead pigeons. I wondered if they ever got used to it. 'They're the ones who'll be watching every minute we're out there. But if we're careful, by Tuesday morning we can all be back where we belong.'

I stood up and pulled the plastic away from my jeans as static tried its hardest to keep it there. Lotfi continued to watch me. 'And where do you belong, Nick? Maybe this is the biggest question.'

I somehow couldn't shake off his gaze, even though he still looked ridiculous in his shower cap.

'I mean for all of us.' He paused, choosing his words with care. 'I have been thinking about God, and hoping that he doesn't want us to die here, because it is for my family that I do these things. I'd rather be with them when he decides it is my time. But what about you, Nick?'

Hubba-Hubba rescued me. 'Take no notice. It's been this way with him since we were children.'

I sat back down to the jingle of bells and looked at each of them in turn. 'Of course, brothers. I should have realized . . .'

One thing I did realize was that we were moving into dangerous territory here. Standard operating procedure said that each of us should know nothing more about the others than we had to. Then I thought, fuck it. We were in dangerous territory already. 'How did you both get into this, then? I mean, it's pretty weird for a family man, isn't it? Is it an Egyptian thing, you all stupid or something?'

Hubba-Hubba smiled. 'No, I'm here to become an American. This time next month my family will be living in Denver.' He punched his brother on the arm in celebration. 'Warm coats and ski lessons.'

Lotfi looked indulgently at his brother as if he was an Andrex puppy.

'What about you?' I asked him.

Lotfi slowly shook his head. 'No. I'm going to stay where I

189

am. I'm happy there, my family are happy there.' He touched Hubba-Hubba on the shoulder. 'And he isn't doing this for warm coats and skiing lessons. He is a little like you: he likes to cover hurtful things with humour.'

Hubba-Hubba's smile evaporated. He glared at Lotfi, who just gave a reassuring nod. 'You see, Nick, we have an older sister, Khalisah. When we were all children she was whipped and kicked in front of us by the fundamentalists.' He cut the air with his right hand. 'Her crime against Islam? She was licking an ice-cream cone. That's all, we were just having ice-cream.' He had the mixture of hatred and grief in his eyes that only comes from seeing your own family hurt.

Hubba-Hubba rested his elbows on his legs and shifted his gaze to the floor.

Lotfi's face crumpled under his shower cap as he relived the experience. 'The fundamentalists shouted at her, screaming that it had lewd connotations. Our twelve-year-old sister was whipped with sticks – there, in the street, in public, then kicked until she bled.' He rubbed his brother's back between the shoulder blades. 'We tried to help, but we were just small boys. We were swatted away like flies, and forced into the dust while we watched our beautiful sister beaten. She still has the scars on her face, to remind her, every day of her life. But the scars inside are worse . . .'

Hubba-Hubba gave a low groan, and rubbed his face with gloved hands. He was breathing hard through his fingers as Lotfi rubbed his back some more, and comforted him with a stream of soft Arabic.

I didn't really know what to say. 'I'm sorry . . .'

Lotfi looked up at me, acknowledging my words. 'Thank you. But I know that you, too, have your sadness. We all need a reason to continue, and this is our reason for being here. We made a pact that day. We promised ourselves, and each other, that we would never again just lie there in the dust if one of us was being hurt.'

Hubba-Hubba gave himself a shake, wiping his eyes with

the back of his hands, and sat up as Lotfi continued. 'He will be leaving me soon for Denver. A new start for his family, and Khalisah – she is going also. But I am staying at home, at least until this evil is driven out. The fundamentalists, they are guilty of *shirk* – you remember what that is?'

I nodded.

'So you also remember I have a duty to perform for God?'

Lotfi fixed me again with his penetrating look. Not for the first time, he gave me the impression he could see right through me, and no amount of silly hats was going to stop him. A new start. Where had I heard that before?

25

FRIDAY, 23 NOVEMBER, 00:19 hrs

The fourways flashed as I hit the key fob of the Mégane and walked away from the parking space behind the OP. As I carried on down the road towards the marina entrance, I zipped up the front of my new jacket and shoved my hands into my pockets. There were several Snickers bars in each for later on, wrapped in clingfilm to cut down on noise.

A set of headlights swept the high ground ahead of me, the other side of the marina as they left the town, then cut into the night sky in the area of the car park where Lotfi's Ford Focus was going to be positioned. The vehicle continued down the dip, passed the marina entrance, then came uphill towards me, still on full beam, dipping briefly as it climbed past me. It was Hubba-Hubba's silver Fiat Scudo. He'd drawn the short straw with the sort of small van an odd job man would use. It had a sliding side door, plus two at the rear; on my instructions he'd had to spray out the windows in the rear doors with matt black car paint, and would have to scrape it off again before the van was returned to the rental company. We couldn't be sure of making a definite ID on the *hawallada* if we encountered a group of people handing over the cash, so we might have to lift a job lot of people, bundle them into the van, and let the warship sort it out. I bet they'd be able to sort the problem out in no time at all.

I couldn't see him behind the steering wheel because of the headlights, but I could read the first four digits of the rear plate as he went by. Tucked under that plate, as with all our vehicles, would be his spare key.

Silence returned, apart from the sound of water slapping against very expensive hulls and the clicking and clacking of bits of metal and ropes and all sorts of other shit as they rocked rhythmically at their moorings. A few lumpy clouds blocked out the stars now and then as they scudded across the sky.

I turned left at the mini-roundabout, and walked past the shopping parade towards the car park. There was still a light shining in the rear of one of the fancy restaurants, and the flickering glow of a TV set escaped from the gaps around the blinds of a cabin directly opposite, but apart from that everyone else in marinaland had thrown in their hands for the night.

I turned right at the car park and headed for pier nine, which was the second one on the right. In the dull glow of the overhead lamps that lined the edge of the marina, a sign told me I couldn't fish from here, and that the spaces were numbered forty-five to ninety.

From either side of me came the slap of water and the click of electricity meters as I passed the reversed-in boats. I was sure there was a better way of saying it, but Lotfi wasn't around to put me right. In my head, I ran through my reason for being here. I was looking for my girlfriend. We'd argued, and I knew she was on a yacht here somewhere – well, here or in Antibes, I wasn't too sure. But I was unlikely to be challenged: even if somebody saw me, they'd be much more likely to assume I was going back to one of the boats than getting up to bad things in the night.

A TV blared out of a white fibreglass gin palace the size of a small bungalow, gleaming in the darkness to my left. A satellite dish on the pier was collecting what sounded like a German programme, with aggressive voices barking out. People in the studio and inside the boat were laughing.

As I neared parking space forty-seven on my right, I found what I was looking for. The *Ninth of May* was a bigger and more upmarket version of the fishing boat from *Jaws*. Her name was painted on the rear in flowing, joined-up writing, as if it had been done with a fountain pen. She was registered in Guernsey, Channel Islands, and had a red ensign hanging off the back of a small sort of patio area. A diving deck jutted out over the propellers, with a foldaway ladder for swimmers to climb in and out of the water.

A short aluminium gangway, hinged at the back of the boat above the diving deck, was lifted clear of the pier by a pair of divots, as if they wanted a little bit of privacy.

A set of blacked-out floor-to-ceiling doors, with matching windows either side of them, preserved the anonymity of the main cabin. To their right was an aluminium ladder with handrails that led to the upper deck. From what I could see as I wandered past, there were two settees up there, facing forward, and a console, all covered with purpose-made heavy white plastic tarps. I supposed they'd whip these off for summer driving.

I concentrated for the time being on trying to take in as much information as I could without stopping or turning my head too obviously towards the target. I had to go to the end of the pier, glance at my watch, look a bit confused, then turn round and walk back. There was no other way to get off. The second time I caught the left-hand side of the boat, and saw light leaking from the two cabin windows. As I got closer there was still no noise but, then again, there wasn't a satellite dish and no TV cable running from the plastic casing on the quay; just water and electric.

It was twelve thirty-eight when I approached the shops. Hubba-Hubba should be nearing the OP. I decided to wait a few minutes to give him time to check the position and drop off my kit, before I moved up the concrete steps and checked out the front of the OP for myself on the way back to the road.

I stood against one of the louvred doors and listened to the gentle hum of a generator, feeling the heat seep through the slats as I had a good look at the top of the *Ninth of May* and worked out how I was going to get the device on board.

At twelve forty-three I walked up the stone steps to the flat roof and the fuck bench, following the pathway that led to the main drag. Once on the main I turned right, and saw a lone figure on my side of the road, heading towards Monaco. I knew it was Hubba-Hubba because he took small, jerky strides, almost as if he was wearing a pair of punk bondage trousers.

By the time I was past the Mégane he had disappeared into the darkness. I spotted the Coke can sticking out of the hedge, and, picking it up as I passed, I moved along the hedgerow about four or five metres before climbing over at what I thought was the same point I'd come out of on Wednesday.

Scrabbling on my hands and knees, feeling in front of me, I got to the bundle. I made sure I had eyes on the boat as I unknotted the towel. The *Ninth of May* was packed in among all the other boats like a sardine, but even in the gloom it was easy enough to spot, simply because I knew it was there.

The priority was to sort out comms; nothing was going to happen without them, apart from a fuck-up.

I wished we could have just used one of those antennae sticking out of the warship as a relay board. With that sort of help, we could have communicated safely and securely with anyone, anywhere in the world, even George. But you don't have that kind of luxury when you're deniable: you have to rely on emails, brush contacts and the Sony corporation.

I turned the volume dial to switch on the radio, then peeled back the strip of gaffer tape that covered the illuminated display, to check it was on channel one. The channel dial was also covered with gaffer tape, to ensure it didn't move. Hubba-Hubba would have checked all this before leaving the safe house, but it was now my radio, and time to check again. I slipped it into the inside pocket of my jacket, and put on the earpiece of the hands-free. The next item I retrieved and checked was the insulin case, before it went into my bum-bag.

A truck thundered past, heading east towards Monaco, as I checked the spare radio and the pipe bomb. It was still in its bin liner, to keep it sterile. Then I made myself as comfortable as I could against the hedge, making sure I could see the target through the V-shaped palm in front of me before getting a Snickers bar down my neck and checking traser. There were six minutes to go before the first radio check.

I watched the boat and generally sorted out my arse by shuffling left and right to make a small dip in the earth. It was going to be a long night. Then, checking the time once more, I unzipped my jacket and hit the radio pressle. 'Morning, morning. Radio check, H.' I spoke in a low, slow, normal voice. These radios weren't like military sets, which are designed to be whispered into. I'd only end up repeating myself, as the other two tried to work out what the mush in their ear was all about. I'd be wasting power and time on the air.

I let go of the pressle and waited until I heard a voice. 'H. OK, OK.' Then it went dead. I hit the pressle. 'That's OK to me. L?'

'I can hear you perfectly.'

'Good, good. OK, then. Everything is how it should be, the OP is set. I'll call you when I've worked out what I'm going to do. H, have you got that?'

I got two clicks.

'L?'

Click, click.

'OK.'

I zipped up my jacket and looked out at the boat, thinking hard about my options. It didn't take me long to work out that I really only had one. Swimming would be more covert on the approach, but once on the boat I would leave sign, and I couldn't guarantee it would evaporate by the morning. They might even come out during the night and see it. So it looked like the towel was out of commission tonight, which was good. I hadn't been looking forward to a dip anyway.

196

I decided simply to walk to the back of the boat, climb on board, and go for the padded seats on the top deck. At this time of year they wouldn't be used: the weather, and the reason for the visit, would encourage the Romeos to keep a low profile. The position wasn't perfect: the inside of the boat would contain the pressure wave of the high explosive as it detonated, just for a nanosecond, before it ripped its way out, shredding the superstructure, and whoever was on board, into thousands of tiny pieces. Even so, planting the device on the top deck would be good enough to take out the whole of the cabin, and the driver's seat below. If the blast didn't kill them, the shards of wood, metal and fibreglass flying through the air at supersonic speed would. I wasn't sure it would do enough damage to sink her, but no one inside would survive and the money would be shredded – and with it my fantasy of it washing ashore at my feet.

26

As I started to visualize playing Spiderman round the outside of the boat, Lotfi came up on the net. It must have been one thirty. 'Hello, hello, radio check. H?'

Click, click.

'N?'

I pressed twice, and Lotfi finished the check: 'OK.' It was good quick voice procedure, considering we hadn't worked together with radios before and they were used to gobbing off in Arabic over the net.

I pulled my knees up to my chest and rested my chin on them as I watched the silhouettes of the masts and continued visualizing getting on to the boat, moving around to the right-hand side, climbing up the aluminium ladder. I wasn't happy about it being right next to the cabin window, but at least there was a blind. I imagined that the sea covers were strapped down, so I thought I'd probably have to pull out the hooks from D-rings in the deck before pushing the pipe bomb into the gully where the seat and backrest met, in among the crushed crisps, melted chocolate and fifty-pence pieces.

Lotfi came back on the air at two a.m. and we all had a radio check. It was time to stop thinking about it and just get on with it. 'That's N foxtrot.' I was about to start walking.

'L, roger that.'

'H?'

I got two clicks from Hubba-Hubba.

I got up slowly and felt around the towel, brought out the plastic cylinder, still in its bin liner, then moved along the hedgerow and exited at the same place as I'd come in and walked down to the car. This time I put the key into the door, to try to cut down on the profusion of electronic signals flying around. High-frequency signals and electric detonators are not a good mix, so the more I could do without them, the better. I had to be quick off the mark, though, once the door was open, as the alarm started to count down with a steady sequence of bleeps. I had to get the key into the ignition and turn it the first two positions before the alarm activated and woke up the whole of BSM.

I got in on the passenger side and put the pipe bomb on the driver's seat. Then it was on with the garage gloves before opening up the glove compartment to switch on the only interior light I'd left working. I put the device on the drinks tray. Twisting and separating the two halves of the cylinder, I checked the clothes peg to make sure the plastic was in place before connecting the batteries.

Hubba-Hubba came up on the net. He was quite casual about it, but he had important information. 'Two cars, you have two cars.'

I immediately covered the light with my right hand and lay flat, my cheek resting against the piping of the driver's seat. I could smell the pick 'n' mix sweetshop aroma coming from the cylinder as the noise of engines got louder and light bathed the interior of the Mégane. Both vehicles carried on past, and as the sound of their engines died away I sat up again, checked the clothes peg and battery plastic yet again, and made sure that the fishing line was still held in place on the outer casing.

I hated this next bit.

There was nothing else I could do now; I'd checked

199

everything, but still checked it several times over again. Now I just had to go for it. Besides, if I'd made a mistake, I wasn't going to know much about it, because I'd be the one in thousands of pieces, not the boat.

I pressed down on the batteries with my left thumb, to keep them in place while I took hold of the plastic safety strip with my right thumb and index finger. I eased out the plastic, without breathing – not that it was going to help in any way, it just felt the thing to do. Once I had closed and twisted the cylinder tighter, the device was ready to be placed. I'd remove the final circuit breaker once I'd got it into position.

I closed the glove compartment and sank back into the darkness.

'L and H, that's me ready.'

I got an 'OK' from Lotfi and two clicks from Hubba-Hubba and waited were I was. After three or four minutes, I saw Hubba-Hubba to my right, his short strides taking him downhill towards the marina entrance.

I let him pass behind me, watching him in the side mirror, and very soon he got on the net. 'L, I'm nearly there. Acknowledge.'

Click, click.

Soon afterwards I saw headlights up on the high ground as Lotfi started down the hill. The headlights turned into the marina, then disappeared. Lotfi and Hubba-Hubba were moving into their positions, to cover me as I placed the device. Hubba-Hubba was foxtrot and staying near the shops, to warn me if anything was coming from that direction; Lotfi would stay with his vehicle and cover me from the car park. They were my eyes and ears while I concentrated on getting the device where it needed to be and not blowing myself up.

Leaving the bin liner, because I still had the gloves on, I shoved the device down the front of my cotton Puffa jacket and got out of the car. I moved on to the pavement behind the OP, for some cover between the hedgerow and the little bit of garden at the roadside, to check myself out. Then, using some of the insulation tape I'd kept in the bum-bag, I taped the earpiece around my ear. I didn't want it falling off and making a noise, either as it hit the deck or as one of the guys gobbed off at me while I was on the task.

I put the tape back in my bum-bag and made sure it was zipped up, then moved it round so it was hanging off my arse. I checked I had nothing rattling in my pockets. The Snicker bars were still there, so I zipped them closed, and jumped up and down to make sure that nothing was going to fall out.

I'd already done this before coming into BSM, but it was part of the ritual for a job, very much like checking chamber and checking the device. Check and test, check and test – it was my lifetime mantra.

Finally I made sure my Browning was going to stay where it was in my jeans and not fall into the water, and checked the hammer. When I'd cocked the weapon, I'd put the little finger of my left hand between the hammer and the pin, then squeezed the trigger so the hammer came forward under control but then stopped in the half-cock position, with the safety off. If I had to draw down, I'd have to make like Billy the Kid in a saloon fight, drawing and whipping back the hammer to its full cock position before I fired. Without an internal holster, it felt safer for me to have it like this as I was clambering around, rather than hanging next to my bollocks with the hammer back and a safety that could easily be flicked off.

Finally, I pressed each nostril closed in turn, and gave them a good blow. It's a pain in the arse trying to think and breathe at the same time with a nose full of snot. It would be back soon, it always was on a job, but I liked to start on empty.

As I set off down the road, I got out one of the Snickers bars, unwrapped the clingfilm and started to munch. It would make me look less suspicious and, anyway, I was still hungry.

27

There were too many boats blocking my view to make out the *Ninth of May*, and no sign of Hubba-Hubba as I carried on past the shops and into the car park, hands in my pockets, sweating up inside the plastic gloves. I took off my Timberlands and left them behind a wheelie bin at the end of the parade. The last thing I wanted when I got on the boat was them squeaking all over the deck and leaving tell-tale dirty marks.

Following the marina round towards the second pier, I checked my bum-bag to make sure everything was zipped up, then checked the Browning yet again to make sure it was good and secure. I walked casually but with purpose, a boat-owner going back to his pride and joy. I wasn't looking around me because there was no need: Lotfi and Hubba-Hubba were covering me, and if there was a problem, I'd soon know about it in my left ear.

I spotted Lotfi's Ford Focus nose-parked in a line of cars facing pier nine. I caught a glimpse of his face, illuminated by a flickering marina light, as I turned towards *Ninth of May*, then my brain started to shrink and focus completely on the target and surrounding area.

Light spilled out round the sides of cabin blinds to my left, and I heard the sound of German TV and real-time laughter once more.

I was no more than a few metres away from the target when a vehicle approached from the Nice end of the main. But it wasn't coming my way. Its engine noise dwindled and its lights faded as it headed on towards Monaco. I checked the device yet again, then the Browning and bum-bag, and risked one good look around me before crouching down behind the boat's utility stand. The meters ticked away like the crickets in Algeria.

All the blinds were still down, and I couldn't see a single light. It looked as if the Romeos had turned in.

It's pointless fannying around once you're on target – you're there, so you might as well just get on with it. Sitting on the edge of the pier, my hands gripping the base of the utility stand, I stretched my right foot across to the small fibreglass diving platform that overhung the propellers. My toes just made contact and I dug them in to get a decent purchase. I let go of the utility stand and extended my body like a circus gymnast, slowly pushing myself off the pier and transferring my weight on to the ledge. Every muscle screamed with the effort of controlling my movements so precisely that I didn't slip or bang into anything. The boat was large enough to absorb my weight; it wasn't going to start rocking just because I was messing about on the back end. The only thing I was worried about, apart from one of the Romeos suddenly deciding to take a breath of fresh air, was the noise the device or the Browning would make if they dropped into the water or clattered on to the deck.

I breathed through my mouth, because my nose was starting to block up again, and heaved myself on to the ledge. I hooked my little finger into the earpiece and pulled it away from my head, blocking the outlet in case one of the boys started to gob off on the radio. I needed both ears from now on. My throat was dry, but I wasn't going to do anything to moisten it just yet. It was more important to listen for a while.

There was no sound at all coming from this boat, apart from the gentle lapping of water against its sides. I could still hear the Germans' muted laughter. I replaced the earphone and raised my head, inch by inch, until I could see over the back of the boat. The patio doors were just a few feet away.

It's basic fieldcraft never to look over something if you can avoid it; always around or, even better, through. You should never cut a straight line, like the top of a wall, or the skyline, or the side of a boat. The human eye is quick to detect broken symmetry. My hands gripped the fibreglass as I raised my head, painfully slowly, hoping that the movement was disguised against the background of divots and the raised gangway. There was nothing: it was still clear.

I checked the device, Browning and bum-bag one more time, then got slowly and deliberately to my feet, lifted my right leg over the back of the boat and tested the ribbed decking with my toes to make sure I wasn't about to step on something like a glass or a plate. I put the rest of my foot down, gradually shifting my weight until my left leg was able to follow. I took my time, concentrating on the job in hand, not worrying about being seen through the patio doors. If I had been, I'd know about it soon enough. Better to spend time and effort on the job than worry about what might happen if things went pear-shaped. If they did, that was when I'd start to flap.

Moving to the right of the patio area, I eased myself up on to the right-hand walkway that led round towards the front of the boat, and to the ladder that would take me over the cabin and on to the upper deck. I was concentrating so hard that the rustle of my gloves sounded to me like a bush being shaken. I reached the ladder and placed my right foot on the first of the three rungs, applying pressure very slowly on the aluminium. The cabin window was no more than six inches to my right. I didn't want to use the handrail, to avoid strain on the rivets.

There was a metallic creak as I lifted my left foot on to the next rung. My mouth was open so I could control the sound of my breathing; my eyes were straining to make sure I didn't bump into anything. I kept moving, slowly and deliberately, all the time checking that the bum-bag, device and weapon weren't going to bounce on to the deck.

I eased my weight on to the third rung, then got my hand on the fibreglass deck and heaved myself upwards.

I found myself on all fours, on the top deck, as two vehicles came from the direction of Monaco and lit up the main, then vanished into the town. I got slowly to my feet, so there'd only be two points of contact above the sleeping people. It took me six slow, deliberate steps to reach the seats. Once there, I lowered myself on to my knees, and tried to find out how the covers were held down. There was a Velcro fastening down the sides. Undoing that would be a big no no, this close to the enemy.

I heard the sound of sliding doors, a burst of laughter, then German voices.

Lotfi got on the net. 'Foxtrots! We got foxtrots.'

I couldn't do anything but hug the deck, then inch my way, on my stomach, towards the protection of the seats forward of the driving console. I ended up over a sort of sunroof, a clear sheet of Perspex that would have looked directly down into the cabin if it wasn't for the blinds.

I rested my face on the Perspex and tried not to think about what would happen if the blind was opened. I heard the doors slide shut, and the sound of footsteps on the pier behind me. Then came the whimper of a dog, followed by a sharp, Germanic rebuke from its owner.

There was nothing I could do but wait where I was for the all-clear from Lotfi. I stuck my free ear to the Perspex to check for noises from below. There were none, and it was still dark on the other side of the blind.

I lay perfectly still, mouth open, breath condensing on the Perspex. Car doors slammed and engines fired up in the car park.

I stayed where I was, nothing moving but my eyeballs and the dribble spilling from the corner of my mouth, as I watched the vehicles leave in the direction of Nice.

I got a low whisper from Lotfi. 'All clear.'

I didn't double-click him in response: that would just create movement and noise. He'd see me move soon anyway. There was still no sound from below, but I wanted to get off this sun-roof. Having nothing more than a sheet of clear plastic and a concertina blind between me and a bunch of al-Qaeda was not my idea of fun.

I began to raise myself on my toes and the heels of my hands.

'More foxtrots, more foxtrots!'

I couldn't see what he was on about, but that didn't matter. I flattened myself once more. Then I could hear mumbling from somewhere along the pier. It sounded like more German.

'Two bodies on deck, smoking.'

I reached down slowly for my Sony.

Click, click.

We'd have to wait this one out. There was nothing I could do now but hope I wasn't seen.

I stayed exactly where I was, ears cocked, nose blocked, the left side of my face cold and wet. The mumbling was definitely German. I even got a whiff of pipe tobacco as Hubba-Hubba now got on the net. 'Stand by, stand by. That's four foxtrots towards you, L.'

I heard a double click from Lotfi as Hubba-Hubba gave the commentary. 'That's at the first pier, still foxtrot, still straight. They must be going for pier nine. N, acknowledge.'

I double-clicked gingerly. He was right, there was nowhere else to go, apart from one of the cars.

Lotfi got on the net. 'N, do you want me to stop them?'

What the fuck did he mean, stop them? Shoot them?

If they were aiming for any of the boats near me, I'd be seen. I could hear their footsteps now and the mumbles of a foreign language. They were definitely heading my way.

I reached for the Sony and clicked twice, and Hubba-Hubba came on the net immediately.

'H will stop them.'

There was a crash of breaking glass from the vicinity of the shops. A microsecond later, a high-pitched two-tone alarm split the night.

28

I froze.

A bright yellow strobe light near the *tabac* began to bounce around the marina. There was nothing I could do but hug Perspex, my pulse racing. The four foxtrots sparked up loudly in French, sounding surprised, while the Germans shouted urgently to each other.

I heard a rush of Arabic in the cabin below. Furniture was being knocked into. A glass was smashed. Lights went on. Through a tiny gap at the edge of the blind, I found myself looking straight down on to a stretch of highly varnished wood below the front window. A hand grabbed at things I couldn't see, and disappeared. A blue-shirted back came into view. They were already dressed down there. They'd probably been ready to do a runner. There was more gobbing off. They were flapping, thinking that whatever was going on outside was meant for them.

I heard an English voice, male and educated, very calm, very in control. 'Just let me check, just wait. *Let me check.*'

I saw a mass of curly black hair, and a wash-stained, once-white T-shirt. The hair was flatter on one side, probably from the way he'd been sleeping; its owner was peering under the front blind towards the shops.

There was movement in other boats, too, and lights coming on. A few people were venturing out to see what the commotion was all about. The strobe was still going for it big-time, and I kept rigid, my eye glued to the gap, trying to see through the condensation and dribble between me and the Perspex.

The man below me turned, and his face was highlit by the flashing strobe. It was Curly, for sure, the man at Juan-les-Pins and in the Polaroid; now I definitely knew where Greaseball was getting his information. George needed to know about this.

He was very skinny. His shoulder blades poked through his T-shirt as if he had a coat hanger in there. His big hair made his head look totally out of proportion to his body. He hadn't shaved for a while, and his slightly hooked nose and sunken eyes made him look as if he'd jumped out of a Dickens novel. He'd be the one giving Oliver Twist a hard time.

'It's OK,' he said, smooth as silk. 'It's just a burglar alarm. Things are cool . . .'

There was another flurry of Arabic. He was definitely the voice of reason. 'No, an alarm – it's just being robbed. You know, someone's breaking into the shop to steal, that's all it is, it's OK.' He moved back from the window and his face disappeared.

Was the alarm going to fetch the police? If so, how quickly? There was still talking and movement beneath me. It was an ideal time to get the job done. If I was wrong, and people saw me, I'd soon know about it. I got to my knees and wiped up what had fallen out of my mouth with my sleeve. Then I pushed the device under the covering and into the channel where the back of the seat met the backrest. I peeled back the insulation tape tab, and gave the fishing line a steady pull until the clothes-peg jaws released the strip of plastic and the two drawing pins connected. The circuit was complete; the device was armed. I pushed the cylinder in as far as my arm could reach.

The strobe was still going ballistic and I could hear people on other boats talking animatedly. It was starting to feel like some sort of yachting rave out there. I lay by the seats, not moving an inch, worrying about whether the kit at the OP would be found if the police decided to have a good look around. Biggest worry of all, though, was how to get off this thing before the *gendarmes* showed up.

About fifteen seconds later I knew it was too late. Two sets of blue flashing lights were heading down from the town. They arrived at the marina and turned right, towards the strobe. Below me, Curly started calming the Arabs down. 'They're just checking out the shop. Everything is cool.'

I watched as four uniforms got out of their patrol cars and inspected the shop-front, silhouetted in their headlights and flashing blues.

They were joined almost immediately by another set of headlights. The driver got out and waved his arms about, jabbering away nineteen to the dozen. Probably the owner, working himself up to a big insurance claim.

The police stayed for another twenty minutes, then the voices faded and lights started to go out all round the marina. Things went quiet in the cabin below me. At least they wouldn't be leaving without me knowing; this must have been the closest OP in OP history.

I lay there for another hour, glad of my new quilted jacket as I felt my extremities start to chill. I sat up slowly and checked around me. The marina was asleep once more. The *tabac* lights were on; it looked like the owner was guarding it for the night. I made sure that the vinyl covering of the settee looked exactly as it had when I arrived, then went back into Spiderman mode.

Less than fifteen minutes later I was walking along the pier towards the car park and Lotfi's Ford Focus.

I turned left, towards my Timberlands, and hit the pressle.

'L, stay where you are and keep the trigger. There's a change of plan. I'll let you know what later. Acknowledge.'
Click, click.

'H, check?'

Click, click.

'Meet me at my car.'

Click, click.

I got back to the bins to retrieve my Timberlands. As I headed back to the OP, I offered up a prayer to the god of wrong numbers that no one got through to the pager by mistake. At least, not until the three on the boat had done their job.

29

I had just started moving towards the stone steps when Hubba-Hubba came on the net. 'Stand by, stand by. Vehicle towards you. N, acknowledge.'

Click, click.

Not that I needed him to tell me. The unmistakable sound of a VW camper thud-thud-thudded its way around the edge of the marina. I sat half-way up the concrete steps and waited for it to park up, before moving towards the OP.

I followed the pathway until it reached the main, and turned right towards the Mégane.

Lotfi came on the net. I couldn't see Hubba-Hubba but I knew he was around somewhere. He wouldn't show himself until he saw me.

As I drew level with the car, I spotted him further up the road. I waited for him to join me, and we crouched in the shadows behind the hedge. 'What did you do that for?' I said. 'Getting the police down here could have been an absolute nightmare.'

He grinned. 'It stopped those people seeing you, didn't it?'

I nodded: he had a point.

'In any case, I've always wanted to do that.'

I nodded again: so had I. 'What did you use to smash the window?'

'One of the metal weights they use to keep the parasols in place. Those windows are quite tough, you know.'

'I need to ask you something.' I wiped my running nose. 'Is there anywhere in your area where I can send an email right now? It might be important. One of the guys on the boat was with Greaseball last night. He's a Brit, early to mid-thirties, skinny, long black curly hair. Looks like the guitarist out of Queen, you know who I mean?'

He ignored the stupid second question and thought for a few seconds about the first. 'The main station in Nice. They have some of those cyberpoints. There are maybe four or five of them. I think they lock the station at night, but I'm not sure. There are definitely two outside.'

I briefed Hubba-Hubba on what I had seen inside the boat, and told him to pass it on to Lotfi while I went to Nice. 'Tell Lotfi to keep a trigger until I get back. And if they move before that, you two just have fun!' I slapped him on the shoulder. I checked the pavement for people, then stepped out and went back to the Mégane.

Driving past the entrance to the marina and on up towards Lotfi's position, I listened in as Hubba-Hubba briefed Lotfi on the net, then started to work out the codewords I was going to need in the email.

I drove along the coast towards Nice. At this time of the morning the city was dead. A few cars passed me, and the odd loving couple or lost soul wandered among the brightly lit shop-fronts.

The main station was a grand nineteenth-century building, with plenty of modern steel and glass now complementing huge blocks of granite. The area around it was filled with the usual array of kebab stalls, sex shops, news-stands and souvenir shops.

Hubba-Hubba had been right: the station was closed, probably to prevent it becoming a homeless refuge at night. The two cyberpoints he'd mentioned were among a cluster of maybe six or seven brightly lit glass phone boxes to the left

213

of the main entrance. The only cameras I saw were focused on the entrance. I carried on past and squeezed into the only space I could see, down a side road.

The cyberpoint was exactly the same as the one in Cap 3000. I slipped on my plastic gloves, inserted my phonecard, got on to email.

I started to tap out with two fingers, gradually getting faster.

It was good to see you yesterday. Guess what? I think you had better move a lot faster if you want to get in with Susanna. There's this guy I've just seen with her. I don't know his name, but you might know him, he's got long, dark, curly hair. In his mid-thirties and English. Do you know him? Anyway, he's getting about quite a bit. I also saw him and Jenny together last night, which looked a bit suspicious as they obviously know each other very well, and it certainly seems that this guy tells Jenny everything. Did you know about this or is Jenny keeping that a secret from you? Sorry if this is sad news, but I just thought you'd like to know. Is there anything you want to tell me? If so I can come round after work tomorrow night. I would say have a nice day, but maybe not.

PS I gave your present to Susanna, she loves red.

I closed down and pulled out my phonecard. If George had anything new to tell me, or if I needed to change the plan, I'd pick it up at the DOP tomorrow night.

30

There was a sudden burst of static in my ear for the eight a.m.
check. 'Hello, hello – radio check.' As I reached inside my
jacket, I heard, 'H?' followed by two clicks. Then, 'N?' I hit the
pressle twice.

'That's all OK.'

The radio went dead. I brought my hand out of my pocket
and pulled up the zip. The coat had done its job well through
the night, and a couple of times I'd even had to undo the top a
little.

My face was greasy and my eyes stung, but my job was to
keep the trigger on the target boat and that was what I'd done.
There'd been no sign of life, outside or in.

First light was a bit later today because of the cloud cover,
and for the last hour or so a gentle breeze had been coming off
the sea and rustling the vegetation around me. It was going
to be a dull, grey, miserable day, not one that the postcard
photographers would be rushing to capture.

The traffic was starting to make its presence felt behind me,
and a shop's shutter rattled open below. I bet the *tabac* was
going to get one now.

The first thing I'd done on my return from Nice last night
was fold the towel and use it as a cushion under my arse. It

hadn't turned the OP into a hotel room on the Croisette, but it had made me quite comfortable. All my Snickers bars had gone, and I'd had a dump in the cling film. Lying next to it was my water bottle, full of urine.

I brushed my hair back with my hands and rubbed my eyes awake. Now wasn't the time to slack. I could hear laboured breathing: someone running, coming down the road to my left. He took his time to get to me, and I was amazed when he finally did: the wheezing and scraping of feet made it sound like he was about to have a heart attack.

There was general movement around the marina now, with quite a few bodies moving out of their boats. The crew of a rubbish truck were emptying champagne bottles and caviar tubs out of the two wheelie bins. I made a mental note to *really* find out who my biological parents were one day – I wouldn't mind finding out I belonged in a place like this, maybe even getting served in the Boston yacht club instead of just being able to work in it.

Birdsong had sparked up around me. I tipped over on to my side and supported my head with my right arm, stretching out my legs as I tried to restore some sort of feeling in them. I had a better view of the VW camper now. It was yellow and white, one of the newer, squarer-shaped ones, and all the windows were covered with aluminium folding blinds. They must have got their heads down as soon as the wheels stopped turning.

With just one eye on the binos, because I couldn't be arsed to sit up and use both, I watched the couple on the boat to the right of the *Ninth of May* emerge on deck. Hair sticking up, much the same as mine probably was, they did some boat stuff around the deck, their fleece jackets protecting them from the breeze. There was still nothing coming from the *Ninth of May*: the black blinds still covered the front window and the two on the side facing me. I ran the binos over the plastic covering on the top deck settees and the driving station. It was buckling a little under the breeze, but didn't look as if it had been disturbed.

I thought about what might be going on behind those blinds. Maybe they were already up, all three of them, just waiting to go and collect, lying in their bunks with time to kill, or memorizing street maps and bus and train timetables. Whatever it was, I wished they'd hurry up and get on with it. The longer they stayed there, the more chance I had of being compromised.

A very small, narrow Japanese van pulled into the car park and the old gardener I'd seen yesterday got out: he was dressed in the same baggy green overalls and wellies. He seemed more concerned about the camper than about his plants right now; he dragged himself towards it, looking like he was about to start an incident. Maybe campers weren't welcomed as energetically as everyone else was, according to the marina entrance sign.

When he got there, he shouted and banged on the side panel. One of the blinds went up and he carried on shouting and waving his arms as if he was directing traffic. He obviously got a satisfactory answer, because he went back to his vehicle with a bit more of a spring in his step. He opened the sliding door to reveal forks and spades and a wheelbarrow. The tools came out one by one, clanging as they hit the ground. I just hoped he hadn't woken up at three in the morning determined to get to grips first thing with that V-shaped palm up behind the fuck bench. Whatever he was planning, it wasn't going to happen yet. He looked as if he was going to take the first break of the day.

Lowering himself on to the sill of the sliding door, he tapped a cigarette out of a packet. The smoke was picked up and dispersed quickly by the breeze.

'Radio check. H?'

I unzipped.

Click, click.

'N?'

Reaching in, I double-clicked the pressle.

'Everything OK. Time to change batteries.'

217

He was right: we should start the day with fresh power, and I had to get it done before Old Man Titchmarsh dragged himself up here and started digging where he wasn't welcome.

I took the radio from my jacket, tugged the batteries off the gaffer tape, pulled off the battery cover and replaced them. I checked the display to make sure the power supply was on and I was still on channel one, then bunged the Sony back inside my jacket.

It wasn't that long before the sliding door to Old Man Titchmarsh's van was closed and he wheeled his way towards the concrete steps before disappearing into the dead ground below me at the start of the stairway. There was nothing I could do but stay where I was and just get on with the job.

The morning commute gathered pace on the main, and it wasn't long before OMT barrowed past me and the fuck bench, looking down at the camper and grumbling to himself. Maybe he hadn't been as firm as he'd thought. I soon heard metallic noises to my right as his tools were pulled off the wheelbarrow, and he started to dig in the sun-dried soil. If he saw me, I'd just have to play the bum and let him chuck me out. I could walk down to the marina entrance and maybe sit at the bus stop; at least I'd still have an OP on both exits. Then all three of us would have to take turns keeping that trigger until the Romeos moved. It would be a nightmare, but there was nothing I could do about it.

'Hello, hello – radio check.'

I put my hand in my jacket. It must be nine o'clock.

'H?'

Click, click.

'N?'

Click, click.

'That's all OK.'

The next three and a half hours were a pain in the arse. OMT seemed to spend more time smoking than he did gardening, which was fine by me because he took his breaks at the far end of the garden. Down in the marina, people wandered off their boats and returned with baguettes or bags of croissants; delivery vans arrived and did their stuff at the shops; cars drove into the car park and men with tool kits and overalls went to work on decks, rigging and other boaty stuff. I could hear a bit of music now and again from the restaurants, and the occasional loud voice or burst of laughter from customers in the *tabac*, punctuated by the smashing of more glass. The window-replacement boys must have been on site.

A small electric cart loaded with rubbish bins and brooms whined its way out of the dead ground in front of the shops and towards the wheelie bins where I'd hidden my Timberlands. OMT shouted down at the driver, who stopped and dismounted with a drag on his cigarette and a wave. His stomach looked about the same weight as the vehicle, which was probably feeling relieved to be rid of him. The bin cart driver cupped an ear towards the high ground of the gardens as the old boy gave him some verbal broadband, then turned back towards the camper with a determined nod.

The bin cart driver closed in on the VW, and repeated the performance.

There was a lot of thumping on the side of the van and what I supposed was the French for 'Get the fuck out of here, this isn't a campsite'.

The door slid half-way open and a woman with short dark hair and a black leather jacket appeared in the gap.

Words were exchanged, but whatever was said stopped the cart man in his tracks. He walked away from the camper as the sliding door closed.

My heart beat a little bit faster. This didn't feel right.

Old Man Titchmarsh called to him, wanting to know what was happening. The cart man beckoned him down the steps.

I hit my pressle. 'All call signs, this is N. There could be a problem. The yellow and white VW van that came in last night might contain another surveillance team. Roger so far, L.'

Click, click.

'H?'

Click, click.

'I'll explain more later. Nothing changes for us. Just remember your third-party awareness. If I'm right, there might be others out there. Acknowledge, L.'

Click, click.

'H?'

Click, click.

The woman had been fully dressed. Was that so she could get out of the camper fast if the shit hit the fan, and still have her weapon and radio concealed?

Either way, we still had our job to do. If they were after the *hawallada*, we just had to get there first. I reckoned George would be able to wring what he needed out of them a lot quicker than any law-enforcement agency.

The engine sparked up on the camper. It headed towards the marina entrance, with a man at the wheel.

'Stand by, stand by. That's the van now mobile, two up. A man with a dark ponytail and a woman with short dark hair and a black leather jacket.' The van went out of sight, following the line of the shop-fronts. 'That's now unsighted towards the marina exit.'

They both acknowledged with a double click, and it was no more than a minute before Lotfi came on the net with the van's progress. 'L has the Combi towards BSM, still two up. Now unsighted.'

I tried to convince myself that I'd been wrong about what I'd seen. But only for about three seconds.

OMT shuffled his way back up the hill and started digging away to my right as I got another radio check. It was twelve o'clock on the dot. 'Hello, radio check. H?'

Click, click.

'N?'

At almost the same moment, my eyes were sucked towards the rear deck of the boat. There was movement: a body appeared. It was Curly, still in his T-shirt and jeans, having a look around as he let down the gangway.

'N, radio check.'

Click, click, click, click.

There was a pause. He would only have been expecting two. 'Is that a stand-by, N? Is that a stand-by?'

Click, click.

He got the message. 'Stand by, stand by.'

31

Curly had finished pushing out the gangway, still in bare feet, as the Romeos I'd almost dribbled on last night appeared on deck. I couldn't radio Lotfi and Hubba-Hubba, as OMT was just a bit too close for comfort as he scraped about in the earth with his spade no more than four or five metres away. But Lotfi knew what to do. 'N, is there movement?'

Click, click.

'Are the Romeos still on the boat?'

I did nothing.

'Are they foxtrot?'

Click, click.

OMT was even closer than I'd thought. I could hear the rasp of a lighter.

The Romeos were now off the pier and had turned left towards the shops. I had a better view of them now. Both were in dark suits.

Lotfi got back on the net. 'Are there two of them?'

I clicked twice, raised the binos to my eyes with my right hand, and kept the left over the pressle as Curly hauled the gangway back in and disappeared inside the boat. I checked them out while Lotfi carried on asking questions. 'Are they male?'

Click, click.

Hubba-Hubba came on the net. 'H is mobile.'

Lotfi: 'Are they still in the marina?'

Click, click.

There was hesitation: Lotfi was trying to think of other things to ask so he and Hubba-Hubba could have a clearer picture of what was going on. But he still hadn't asked what they looked like. Finally, he got there. 'Are they Arab?'

Click, click.

I couldn't tell him right now, but they were also young, maybe in their early thirties, with short, well-groomed hair, white shirts, ties and black shoes. The shorter one, maybe five seven, five eight, had straight hair and a rounded, over-fed face. In his left hand he was carrying a Slazenger tennis bag, with a racquet in the outside pocket. The towelling round the racquet handle was faded and worn. They'd thought about ageing their collection kit, to make it look as normal as possible. They looked just like bankers off to the tennis club. It looked as if Greaseball's int was going to prove good: they would blend in perfectly in Monaco.

The second one was hands free and taller, maybe six foot, quite lean, with wiry hair brushed back off his forehead, a very neat moustache and a pair of aviator style sun-gigs. The Saddam look was obviously in this year.

I heard a vehicle drive into the parking space behind me, and a second later Hubba-Hubba got on the net. 'H is static behind you, N, and has the trigger on the main. I can give direction once they are on the main. N, acknowledge.'

Click, click.

As planned, Hubba-Hubba was coming in closer on the stand-by. That way, we'd have another person who could take the Romeos once they were out on the main, just in case I couldn't get out of the OP and do it myself.

The two collectors disappeared by the parade as Lotfi sparked up. 'N, are they still in the port?'

Click, click.

223

'Can you see them?'

Hubba-Hubba cut in when I hadn't replied after five seconds. 'H still has the trigger on the main.'

I waited for another thirty seconds, more than enough time for them to get half-way up the steps, if that was the direction they were headed. But there was a no-show as I still smelt OMT's cigarette on the breeze. I got up slowly on my hands and knees and gathered all my kit into the towel, including my little clingfilm package and the bottle of piss. Only after crawling to the exit point along the hedgerow did I risk getting on the net. My voice wavered as I tried to suck in air and move at the same time. 'OK, OK. They're both Arab, dark suits, white shirts, ties. The smaller one, Romeo One, is carrying a blue tennis bag, Slazenger. Romeo Two is taller, slimmer; sunglasses and moustache. H, acknowledge.'

Click, click.

'Is it clear? I'm coming out.'

There was a pause.

Click, click.

I stood up, jumped over the hedgerow. Hubba-Hubba had parked his Scudo my side of the Mégane, so he was shielded but could still look through my window to keep the trigger.

His window was half down, and he had his eyes on the exit. I walked up and made a show of checking my watch. 'The station, mate. Get to the station and be careful, keep an eye out for that van.'

He nodded, fired the ignition. 'Don't worry. Remember, Lotfi brings God with us.' He gave me a gleaming smile as he reversed back into the road. I dumped the kit in the Mégane boot, took over the trigger and prepared for the take. It was good to know that God was still on our team. We needed all the help we could get.

I closed the boot as Hubba-Hubba came back on the net, in a calm, low voice. 'Stand by, stand by. Romeo One and Two foxtrot, approaching the main from the entry road, about ten short.'

I looked down the road and saw the Scudo just starting to move uphill past the marina entrance.

'L, standing by.'

I gave my acknowledgement. *Click, click.* Bending down to check out a wheel on the side of the car away from the marina exit, I peeled the insulation tape off my ear and waited for them to appear on the main. Then I checked my Browning and bum-bag while I pretended to inspect the tyre tread, with both eyes on the marina exit.

Out they came. 'Stand by, stand by. N has Romeo One and Two. At the main. Wait – that's them now, left, towards the town. L, acknowledge.'

Click, click.

'H?'

There was nothing.

Lotfi came up: 'H, they're foxtrot, towards the town.'

There was a moment's delay before Lotfi came back to me: 'H acknowledged and everything looks OK. No Combi.'

I double-clicked. H was too far away from me, probably already at the station, but still within range of Lotfi, who was receiving both of us.

I let the Romeos settle down, and watched as they walked away from me, up the hill towards the bus stop. They both looked a little jumpy. Maybe they'd had too much coffee this morning. Romeo One kept changing hands on the bag and Two kept looking around him, not realizing he could do that by just moving his eyes.

I got on the net. 'That's approaching the bus stop on the left. Wait, wait. That's at the bus stop, still straight.'

'L, roger that. That's straight at the bus stop. H, acknowledge.'

One moved the bag over his right shoulder and glanced back. I doubted that he could see the wood for the trees, though: his nerves seemed to be taking over. I started to follow. 'That's N foxtrot and still has Romeo One and Two on the left and still straight, towards the town. They look aware, be careful. L, relay to H.'

I got two clicks before listening to a one-way conversation as Lotfi passed on the information.

If they'd stopped at the bus shelter, taking them towards Nice, I'd have got on at the stop before and Lotfi would have kept the trigger. If they were going towards Monaco and crossed the road to the other stop, Lotfi would have done the same and kept the trigger.

The trick was for each of us to know exactly where the Romeos were and what they were up to, so we could either jump ahead or hold back, and take these two without them ever seeing us. The more exposure we had to them, the more chance we had of getting compromised. We needed to be out of their vision at all times, because the mind stores everything. If they saw one of us today and thought nothing of it, maybe they'd make the connection tomorrow. One of us had to have eyes on the Romeos as much as possible, with the other two satelliting them, always out of sight, always backing the man who was taking, always being aware of the third party.

I lost them now and again as the road wound its way up to the high ground and into the town. But Lotfi had them in sight. 'That's Romeo One and Two, now passing me, still straight.'

I double-clicked, not knowing if Hubba-Hubba had done the same.

I checked my Browning was in position, and felt the bumbag to make sure the insulin case was still inside – even though I knew it wouldn't have unzipped the bag by itself and jumped out. I fished the MedicAlert out of my jeans and put it on to my left wrist to announce that I was diabetic and really needed to carry this stuff about with me.

As I got to the high ground, I caught sight of Lotfi's Focus tucked away well inside the car park. The Romeos were still ahead, partly shielded by the traffic. 'N has, N has Romeo One and Two. Still foxtrot on the left about five zero short of the station option. H acknowledge.' I smiled away to myself, as if I was talking to my girlfriend on my mobile.

Click, click.

'L?'

Click, click.

There was a junction right further up, where the station road ran down on to the main. A set of lights controlled the traffic.

The *pâtisseries*, news-stands and cafés were open for business. People were in line for a lunchtime sticky bun to go with their coffee taken at one of the outside tables.

'N still has, N still has foxtrot on the left, half-way to the station option. Do not acknowledge.'

I wanted them to listen, to cut down on time on the air, so I could just concentrate on the take.

'That's approaching. Wait, wait . . .'

I stopped and looked into a shop that seemed to sell just men's socks and ties. 'They're static at the crossing, they're at the crossing, intending the station. Wait, wait. It's a red man, wait out.'

I released the pressle and watched through the corner of the window as I agonized over my choice of Christmas tie, Santa or the Virgin Mary. Nobody gave Romeo One and Two a second glance, but to me they looked out of place. They weren't talking to each other; they didn't even look at each other.

A couple of families were also waiting to cross, with all the kids wearing Pokémon backpacks. I heard the beep of the pedestrian crossing.

'Stand by, stand by, green man on. Romeo One and Two crossing left to right, half-way.'

Once over the road they carried on straight up towards the station and disappeared. 'That's them straight and towards the station, unsighted to me. H, acknowledge.'

'H has, on the right towards the station, sixty short.'

The lights at the crossing had turned red again. I joined two women and more kids with backpacks. The kids were shoving baguettes down their necks as if they hadn't eaten since last Tuesday. Hubba-Hubba came on the net, and for the first time I had to put my hand over the earpiece as a couple of trucks screamed past. It was a big no-no, but I didn't have a choice.

'H still has, half-way to the station, still aware.'

The green man flashed and the beeps sounded. My new schoolfriends and I crossed. It was a good sign that the Romeos were aware. I hoped it meant they hadn't pinged us, rather than that they were in fact very switched on, and about to take us to an amusement park or shopping centre to fuck us about or, even worse, into an ambush.

I reached the other side of the road and turned uphill, leaving Hubba-Hubba to continue the take.

'H has, still on the right, approaching the station.'

The Romeos disappeared right, into the parking area in front of the station as Hubba-Hubba continued his commentary. 'That's at the station, wait, wait ... at the first set of doors. That's now complete and unsighted to me. I'm going foxtrot. N, acknowledge.'

Click, click.

He would now be taking a position that would give him a view of both the platforms, so we'd know whether they were aiming for Monaco or Nice.

I spotted Hubba-Hubba's empty Scudo van just past the entrance. He was out here somewhere, trying to get the trigger, making sure the Romeos didn't see him or, just as importantly, the third party who might wonder what this weird Arab bloke was up to.

The drivers at the taxi rank were still leaning against their Mercs, smoking and putting the world to rights. The multicoloured flower beds nearby were still getting a good sprinkling.

Taking my time, I wandered past the first of the two glass doors, hoping to get a glimpse of the Romeos, maybe by a ticket machine or the kiosk. But there was no sign of them in this half of the foyer, and I didn't want to walk in myself and risk being seen.

I plonked myself on the wooden bench outside, between the two sets of doors, hoping the train wasn't due just yet. 'H, can you see them?'

There was a pause. 'No, just the far end of the platforms. They could still be complete.'

Click, click.

A garage truck approached from my right, and I could hear it change gear through the radio as Hubba-Hubba spoke. He must be up there in the far car park. I decided I'd give it a minute or two to see if he pinged them; if not, I'd have no alternative but to go in. They should have bought a ticket by now and, with luck, would be out there on the platform.

I dug out my hundred-franc notes and stood up, making sure the zip of my bum-bag was still done up, and the Browning was still tucked well into my jeans.

I hit the pressle.

'N is going complete the station. H, acknowledge.'

Click, click.

'L, stand by.'

Click, click.

I walked through the second set of doors by the news-stand in case they were still on the concourse, and stepped around the little rat dogs that were still guarding the news-stand. My head was down, hat on, not looking for faces, just dark suit trousers. I couldn't see the Romeos anywhere. That was good, and that was also bad.

I stopped at the coffee machine and bought myself a cappuccino, then eyed up the snack machine and selected a couple of muffin-type things covered with sugary goo as the plastic cup fell into place waiting to be filled.

Hubba-Hubba sparked up on the net as I bent down and watched the brew fall into the cup and pulled the muffin wrapping apart with my teeth, getting the goo on my chin. 'That's both Romeos on the platform, your side, the station side platform.'

32

The dogs tied up by the news-stand gave me the evil eye as I reached inside my coat.

Click, click.

Some people bought tickets from the touch-screen machines, some headed straight through the double glass doors on to the platform, but there was no one hovering around like me, trying to shove the last of a muffin down their neck without getting most of the topping over their front, while attempting to keep out of the Romeos' line of sight. They were out there somewhere, the other side of the wall the coffee machine stood against. And, so far, it looked as if they were going to Monaco. They'd have to go over a footbridge for trains to Nice, Cannes and all stations to Marseille.

Four more people went through to the platform. They had to file between two steel posts about a metre high. There was a resounding clunk each time a ticket got fed into the slot and validated.

The coffee machine had finished clearing its throat. I took a sip from the steaming plastic cup as I walked over to the touch-screen ticket machines, and looked out on to the platforms to see if I could ping the collectors. The only people in sight were two train workers with peaked caps and beer bellies.

I touched the screen for a single to Monaco, then bought another to Cannes. I didn't know which of the three locations these people were heading for. They might even do all three today, or none of them. Perhaps they really were just meeting some of their mates for tennis.

If the destination was Nice, I'd just use the Cannes ticket and get off earlier. My tickets were still printing out as Hubba-Hubba came on the air. I could tell by the noise of traffic and his disjointed speech that he was walking fast. 'Too much third party, I'm going complete. They are definitely on the Monaco side, definitely on the Monaco side.'

I double-clicked him as I went and checked the timetables. The Monaco train was due in ten minutes' time, at twelve forty-one.

It would take much longer to get to Monaco by road at this time of day than the thirteen minutes it took by train, but Lotfi was waiting for me to press the button. The plan was that he'd drive to the underground car park by the Palais de la Scala and be ready to receive the two Romeos if I screwed up on the follow and lost them, while Hubba-Hubba tried to catch up. I needed the latter here for the time being, just in case the Romeos changed direction after Lotfi had taken off for Monaco. I made my decision.

I ran my finger down the timetable like a puzzled tourist. 'L?' I got two clicks. 'Go now, go now. Acknowledge.'

I could hear the engine already turning over while his pressle was down.

'L is mobile.'

He'd have just twenty minutes to get there. I hoped he didn't get caught behind a truck on the narrow road.

Hubba-Hubba kept it brief. He knew I was in the station, and might therefore be surrounded by people.

'H is complete and has the trigger on the station exit. Do not acknowledge.'

The timetable remained very interesting for a while as a middle-aged couple chatted with the guy at the news-stand,

and played with the demented little dogs, then I turned my attention to some ads for sun-soaked holidays in Mauritius for something like a thousand pounds a night, and decided that Cape Cod was more my kind of place.

The couple said their goodbyes to the guy and cooed over his dogs one last time before moving over to the glass doors and clunking in their tickets. As they passed through to the platform, I could hear the train, right on time. The rumble on the tracks got louder and the dogs growled as the train stopped with a squeal of brakes. I clunked my ticket and waited by the validation posts until I could hear electric doors slide open and people say their French goodbyes. Only then did I walk on to the platform, without looking left or right, and climb into the first carriage I saw.

From my forward-facing seat, I could see the backs of the Romeos' heads and the Slazenger bag on the rack above them through the interconnecting carriage doors. I sat and waited, ready to jump off again if they did. The doors closed and with a slight shunt the train started to pull out.

Hubba-Hubba came on the net. 'Are the Romeos on the train?'

Click, click.

'Are you on the train?'

Click, click.

'H is mobile.'

His foot was probably flat to the boards as the Scudo screamed towards Monaco.

The railway line followed the coast road, but there was no sign of Hubba-Hubba. It was going to be a nightmare for him to catch up; he'd just have to do the best he could.

There was no way I was going to walk into their carriage, in case we met in the aisle. One of them might be heading for the toilet, or simply moving away from where they'd got on, as I would in their position, to try to avoid surveillance.

I sat and watched the sea, and kept an eye on the vehicles we were overtaking on the road. With luck, Lotfi would be approaching the tunnels just short of Monaco.

As we neared Monaco, gracious old buildings with wooden shutters and ugly new ones blocked my view of the sea. Then we entered the tunnel that took us deep into the mountains. The train rattled on for a few minutes in darkness before emerging into the brilliant light of an immense underground station. The place looked like something out of a James Bond film, a huge stainless-steel and marble cavern.

The train slowed and a few people got up from their seats and gathered their bags and briefcases. I stayed put, looking out at the station. The platforms were clean and the marble highly polished; even the light fittings looked like they came from a Conran shop.

Carriage doors opened, and people dressed for work rubbed shoulders with Japanese tourists sporting their Monaco Grand Prix sweatshirts and Cannes baseball caps as they got out on to the platform and headed towards the front of the train. I, too, stepped out and followed the herd, the peak of my cap well and truly down as I checked around me.

I pinged them up ahead. Romeo Two still had his sun-gigs on, and One the bag over his shoulder. I got my gigs out and put them on my nose as well. Maybe sixty or seventy metres ahead of me were sets of escalators that led up to a bridge. The herd were moving up them and left, across the tracks, to the ticketing hall. I caught another glimpse of the Romeos doing the same. Romeo Two took off his glasses as they crossed, looking at everything but hopefully seeing nothing, as smooth announcements floated over the Tannoy system, and giant flat-screen TVs flashed train information.

We came into the ticketing hall: more acres of stainless steel and polished marble, still underground. All around me shoes squeaked and high heels clicked, to the accompaniment of coffee machines hissing and people jabbering to each other over espressos. The crowd was waiting for one of the many lifts to take them up to ground level. I didn't want to join them, no matter how big a crowd the lifts could accommodate.

With my left hand holding down the bum-bag and the pistol grip of the Browning, I pounded up the steel stairs, turning back on myself every tenth step or so. It was further than I'd expected, and I was starting to get out of breath. It hit me that I'd made a mistake: my chances of getting up there before the two collectors were slim. I could have gone faster if I'd used the handrail, but I didn't want to leave any sign. I pumped my arms back and forth, and kept going for it.

At last I saw daylight above me. Three more flights and I was at ground level. I saw the four aluminium doors for the lifts and a small group of people waiting. I walked into the entrance hall gulping in air, trying to calm myself down as the back of my neck started to leak. The glass and steel frontage of the small hallway looked out on a bus shelter my side of a busy road. I could see we were high above the principality, as I was looking out on to the Mediterranean, but there was no port. It must have been below somewhere.

The breeze blew in from the sea as I headed for the bus stop. My eyes darted about, looking for the Romeos. They should be going left, to the de la Scala.

I saw them then, at a corner about fifteen metres away to my left. Romeo Two was checking a small map as One looked about nervously and got stuck into a pack of Marlboro. I kept my back to them now, and walked directly to the bus stop, hitting my pressle. 'Hello, hello, is anyone there? This is N, anyone there?'

There was nothing. I gave it just under a minute, then spun round to face the road, hoping to see them in my peripheral vision. They were walking down the hill towards the casino and the general area of the Palais. I set off behind them, and immediately spotted two CCTV cameras. I hated this place: it was like an extra-large, extra-rich version of the *Big Brother* house.

I crossed to the right-hand side of the road, hoping to avoid them; the port was about three hundred feet below me. Huge grey clouds hung above us, cutting the tops off the mountains.

Hordes of trucks and motorbikes screamed up and down a road that had probably been built in the early 1900s for the odd Bentley or two.

The more we descended to the middle ground of the casino area, the taller the bank buildings became around us. Houses that had once been grand private residences were now plastered with brass plates. I could almost smell the big money deals going down behind their heavily blinded windows.

The Romeos consulted the map again before carrying on past the shiny Rolls-Royces, Jags and Minis lined up in the British Motor Showrooms, as One dragged on his Marlboro, sending smoke up above him before it got taken by the wind. If they were heading for the de la Scala, they'd have to cross over soon and turn off to the right. I stopped, stepped into the doorway of a bookshop, and got very interested in a French cookbook with a picture of a big sticky bun on its cover.

They crossed. I hit my pressle again, smiling away like an idiot chatting on his mobile. 'Hello, hello, anybody there?'

They must be heading for the de la Scala. They were now my side of the road and walking down Avenue Saint-Michel. I knew that because it was engraved expensively on a slab of stone just above my head, like all the street names here.

They committed to the right-hand bend of the avenue just fifty metres down the hill and became unsighted to me. Dead ahead of them now, about two hundred metres away, beyond manicured lawns, fountains and frost-protected rubber plant things, was the casino and its Legoland policemen. But they still had about another fifty metres until the end of Avenue Saint-Michel, where once more they had a choice of direction.

I got on the net again as I started to follow. 'Hello, hello, hello. Anyone there?' Still nothing.

33

I didn't want to stay behind them because I wasn't being pro-active. If I was going to be the only member of the team on the ground with the Romeos, I really needed to be doing Lotfi's job now, waiting for them in the de la Scala for the meet with the *hawallada*. But that meant jumping ahead, and if they went somewhere else once they got to the end of the avenue I'd be in the shit.

I carried on down Saint-Michel and talked to my imaginary girlfriend with a big smiley voice. 'Hello, hello, this is N.' Still nothing. Maybe they were caught in the traffic; maybe Lotfi was here but down in the car park. Whatever was going on, I had to make a decision.

I turned on to some steps that went directly downhill, to cut off the bend that they'd followed towards the casino. They led to an apartment block on the steep side of the road, and were well worn, which I hoped was going to prove it was a short cut.

I hurtled down them, past exotic plants and boring grey concrete blocks each side of me, keeping my left hand on the bum-bag and Browning and checking traser, as if I was late for an appointment, until I reached the road below. The casino was to my half-left about a hundred and fifty metres away.

Legoland policemen kept people moving so the Ferraris and Rolls-Royces had somewhere to park. The manicured lawns were being pampered by the sprinklers; directly left along the road, just under a hundred metres, was the junction with the avenue. I turned right, not checking anywhere because the Romeos could already be at the junction and heading my way. I continued to play looking at my watch as I hurried past fur-coated women and expensive shops.

By the time I rounded the corner to the de la Scala square, my neck was not just leaking but drenched with sweat. There was no sign of Lotfi anywhere on the grass, listening to my follow so he could decide when the time was right to go into the mall and get a trigger on the meet. The only people in sight were the orange-overalled, tree-cutting crew, having a brew on a bench. I tried again on the radio, but there was nothing. I'd just have to get on with it: I might be the only one here.

I started towards the glass doors of the mall, taking deep breaths to re-oxygenate myself, pushed through with my shoulder as I wiped the sweat with my shirt cuffs, and headed straight for the café, past the reception and the Roman marble entrance. The same immaculately dressed dark-haired woman was operating the desk, and still gobbing off on the phone. The same sort of people were at the café, too, talking discreetly into cellphones or reading papers. Some did both. I pulled up a chair to the rear of the outside tables and by the left-hand corner of the mall, so I was facing the reception but could also cover the exit by the dry-cleaner's.

I started to flap a little as I flattened my wet hair on the back of my head. What if the Romeos had gone elsewhere? Fuck it, I was committed now. I'd just have to wait and see.

The waiter who took my coffee order was more interested in watching a woman crossing her stockinged legs at one of the other tables than in my sweaty face. I took off my glasses and just hoped that one of the other two was nearly here. I needed some back-up desperately.

My *crème* turned up with a biscuit and a small paper napkin between the cup and saucer to take the spills. I handed the guy a fifty-franc note, not wanting to wait for a bill later. I needed to be able to jump up and go, without being chased myself for doing a runner. The change emerged from his money-bag and smacked down on the table just as Lotfi burst on to the net. He was out of breath and, by the sound of it, on foot and moving fast. 'Anyone, anyone, stand by, stand by. Anyone there? Stand by, stand by. They are in the square, Romeo One and Two in the square approaching the mall.'

I reached into my jacket as I took a sip from the napkin-wrapped cup.

The snarl of a chainsaw gave me a clue to his location. 'That's complete the building now, they're inside.'

Click, click.

There was relief on the air. 'Is that N?'

Click, click.

'Are you inside?'

Click, click.

'OK, I'll stay outside, I'll stay outside.'

Click, click.

The Romeos appeared at the bottom of the corridor and looked around, getting their bearings: they obviously hadn't been here before. They eventually walked up to the reception and studied the board. They stood for ten or fifteen seconds before their eyes seemed to lock on to the address they wanted: Office 617, the Monaco Training Consultancy.

I took another sip of coffee and watched between the heads of two women who were gobbing off in Italian in front of me, smoking themselves and anyone nearby into an early grave. Romeo Two had his gigs back on now. He took a pen from his inside pocket and used it to press the buzzer; I bet he'd used his shoulders to get through the door as well.

What now? What was I going to do if I was locked outside while they got directions from the receptionist?

Romeo Two bent down and I watched him say a few words

into a speaker by the buzzers – maybe a confirmation state-ment. Whatever it was, he was a happy man as he stood upright and gave Romeo One, who didn't look too certain about things, a reassuring nod.

They waited, not going into the Roman entrance just to their left, and then I realized why. I needn't have worried. There were cameras behind the receptionist's desk, and she would know what office they'd gone into. So they waited, admiring the Persian rugs in the shop opposite, perhaps wondering, like I had, why people would pay so much just for something to stand on. Their mums could probably knock them one up in a couple of weeks.

Lotfi came back on the air; the chainsaw fired up behind him, before turning into a high-pitched whine as it bit into a tree. 'N, radio check.' He sounded anxious, not knowing what was going on inside and needing a bit of reassurance.

I double-clicked him as the reception doors opened and out came a tall, dark-skinned man with black hair, greying at the temples in a way that made him look quite distinguished. He was about six foot and slim, not Arab, maybe Turkish, maybe Afghan. They didn't shake hands. He wore an expensive-look-ing navy suit, black loafers and a dazzling white shirt, buttoned all the way up, no tie. Maybe, like many people, he refused to wear one because it was a symbol of the West. Or maybe he was a fashion victim. I'd get the boys on the warship to ask him later.

They finished exchanging half a dozen very serious-looking words and started to walk back out of the door of the mall they'd come in through. I warned Lotfi. *Click, click. Click, click.*

Lotfi was straight back. 'Coming out?'

Click, click.

'Same doors?'

Click, click.

They disappeared from sight and, no more than three seconds later, the net burst into life once more. 'L has Romeos

239

One, Two and Three. They've gone right, your right as you exit. Towards the rear of the building.'

I got up from the table, and double-clicked him as I wiped the mug, keeping the napkin with me. As Lotfi carried on the commentary with the chainsaw in the background, I shoved the napkin into my jacket pocket, where it joined the muffin wrapper and plastic coffee cup. 'That's Romeos One, Two and now Three, foxtrot on the right, still on the right-hand side. About half-way towards the rear. They're not talking. Romeo One is still aware, they have quick feet.'

I pushed my way through the glass doors into the cacophony of traffic and chainsaw. I didn't bother to look for Lotfi. I knew he was there somewhere.

'Do you want me to stay here?'

I double-clicked him as I turned right, and followed on the same side of the road, putting my gigs back on.

34

They were now about two-thirds of the way down the narrow road leading to the admin area at the rear of the building, still not talking, but at least Romeo One wasn't looking around any more. He still had the bag over his shoulder and hung back slightly because there wasn't enough room for three abreast on the pavement. They'd chosen a good route, avoiding cameras; the only bits of people control were the two-foot-high steel bollards stopping people parking on the kerb. By Monaco standards, it was all quite relaxed.

They turned right at the corner and disappeared from view. I quickened my pace to get eyes on in case they disappeared completely through a door. I hit the pressle. 'That's all three Romeos right, to the rear, temporary unsighted.'

I got two clicks from Lotfi; I didn't know if he could see and it didn't really matter, so long as he knew what was going on. There was also a possibility that Hubba-Hubba could receive but not send as he made his way to us.

Reaching the corner, I crossed the road and began to hear what sounded like a supermarket trolley round-up. Steel containers on wheels were being shunted backwards and forwards from a lorry backed into the post office loading bay. Once I was on the far pavement I turned right, just in time to

241

see the three of them passing through a steel door next to a garage shutter alongside the loading bay.

My mind raced as the door closed. It must be the exchange – unless this was a car park and they were about to leave. 'L . . . Hello, L.' It was hard to keep my happy smiley face as I chatted on my hands-free. 'Are you near your car?'

'Yes, in the car park, in the car park.'

'OK, mate, go complete . . . and static outside the car park. All three Romeos are unsighted in a garage, I have the trigger. You've got to be quick in case they go mobile. Remember your third party.'

I got two clicks as I passed the post-office van and the mail-trolley pushers, then an anxious voice. 'Hello, N, hello, L? Radio check, radio check.'

At last, Hubba-Hubba.

I hit the pressle. 'This is N. L's here too. Where are you?'

'Near the casino, I'm near the casino, I'm nearly there.'

'Roger that. That's Romeo One, Two and now Three unsighted at the back of the building in the last shuttered garage before you get to the post office loading bay. I have the trigger, acknowledge.'

Click, click.

'OK, stay complete and cover the square, able to take in all directions. L is going complete now. I'll trigger them away if they go mobile.'

Click, click.

'L, where are you?'

No reply: he was probably down in the car park.

'That's H static on the square. Can take in all directions. N, acknowledge.'

Click, click.

Seconds later Lotfi came back on the net, and I could hear the Focus's engine closing down in the background. 'Hello, N, hello, N. That's L static on the car park road, covering away from the square.'

'Roger that, L. Stay where you are. H is here, and is covering

242

the square and can take in all directions. N still has the trigger, no change. L, acknowledge.'

Click, click.

By now I was at the mall entrance near the dry-cleaner's and there was a loud hiss of steam from a pressing machine. 'L, I want you to describe Romeo Three to H. Acknowledge.'

Click, click.

There was nothing else I could do now but keep the trigger on the shutter and listen while Lotfi told Hubba-Hubba what our new best mate looked like.

I watched the letters and parcels being taken backwards and forwards in the carts. Keeping the trigger was so important that I'd have to risk exposing myself out here in full view of the postal workers, and so close to the women in the cleaner's, but thankfully out of sight of the camera on the corner of the building.

I leaned against the wall and checked my traser. I wasn't interested in the time, just in making it look as if I had a reason to be there. There was another loud hiss of steam from the pressing shop, and then a small group of people came out of the exit. I had to brass it out. Security was definitely getting sacrificed for efficiency.

A couple of minutes later there was movement.

'Stand by, stand by, Romeo One and Two foxtrot. Wait . . . that's Romeo One and Two both carrying bags. Wait . . .' I started to smile, as though I was listening to a good story on the mobile. 'That's both Romeos now foxtrot right, towards me. Romeo Three still unsighted. He must still be inside. I have to move. Wait out.'

I turned and walked into the mall with the big smile still fixed on my face. 'That's Romeo One and Two unsighted, stay where you are. Both stay where you are. L, acknowledge.'

Click, click.

'H, can you get a trigger on the mall entrance?'

'H already has the trigger and can see the road from the rear of the building.'

Click, click.

Both exit points from the shutter, plus both entry points back into the mall, were covered if Romeo Three moved on foot. But it was what we'd do if he went mobile that worried me.

As I bent down I took particular interest in the china shop window across from the dry-cleaner's. Painted plates and silver cutlery gleamed under the brilliant display lights and I waited to see what the two Romeos were doing. It was just a few seconds before I caught a side view of both of them quickly passing the mall's glass doors, going on to the junction below the camera. They had two bags now, each with a tennis racquet in the side pocket. The second bag must have been inside the first to give it bulk, and now it just looked like they were two mates on their way to a friendly game.

I got back on the road, hoping that the Romeos weren't waiting at the junction. Tough shit if they were: I was committed now and had to get a trigger on the shutter in case Romeo Three went mobile. I needed to get a vehicle ID and direction for Lotfi and Hubba-Hubba, who would then be on their own.

I'd got myself out on to the other side of the mall door, looking right quickly by the camera junction – no Romeos – then left towards the shutters, as my earpiece burst into life. 'Stand by, stand by! H has a possible Romeo Three foxtrot towards the square, that's half-way . . .'

He double-clicked as I shot back in through the door, past the cleaner's and china shop, towards the café with a third party smile. 'H – stop him. He mustn't get back to the office. Stop him!'

I got a double-click just as I followed the mall corridor right, passed the café and headed for the other exit. If Hubba-Hubba didn't stop him, I would have to in the corridor. As I passed the marble entrance and carpet shop, my left hand started to unzip the jacket so I had an easier draw down on the Browning. I had a hot, tingling feeling, and was sweating again. If we didn't act fast we could lose him upstairs, maybe for ever. I wanted him lifted and dropped off as quickly as possible. We couldn't afford to wait around here: security was tighter than a duck's arse.

Barging my shoulder against the mall door, I shot back out on to the road facing the square and the chainsaw crew. Hubba-Hubba stood on the pavement to my immediate right, with an enormous smile all over his face, just about to shake the hand of his long-lost friend, Romeo Three. There was a burst of French between them before the Arabic started. *'As-salaam alaykum.'*

Romeo Three looked perplexed, but went through the motions and raised a hand to Hubba-Hubba's. *'Wa alaykum as-salaam.'*

Passers-by took no notice as the old friends met on the street, and Hubba-Hubba initiated a bit of cheek-kissing. As I approached, the *hawallada*'s eyes darted nervously between the two of us. Hubba-Hubba greeted me in Arabic, all smiles, and put a very firm arm out to bring me into the group and let me know he was running this bit. The *hawallada*'s hand was large but his shake was weak and soft. Hubba-Hubba carried on gobbing off and gesturing towards me, accompanied by nods and smiles. Romeo Three didn't look so happy, though. *'Allah-salaam alaykum.'* I reciprocated. *'Wa alaykum as-salaam.'* But I left the kissing business to Hubba-Hubba.

As I broke off with the handshake, Hubba-Hubba embraced us both, and steered us back towards the rear of the mall, still jabbering away in Arabic and talking about the old days.

Romeo Three's eyes betrayed a mixture of fear, puzzlement and pleading. He was flapping big-time, but he was too scared to do anything about it, not that he had the opportunity. Hubba-Hubba kept both of us tightly in his arms as he continued to gob off, smiling and nodding like a game show host. I smiled back and nodded at the *hawallada*. Whatever was being said was obviously doing the trick, for Romeo Three turned the corner without protest, just resignation. We stepped aside as the post truck thundered past.

We stopped next to the shutter, and Romeo Three fumbled

through his bunch of keys. With Hubba-Hubba's help and support, he finally inserted the right one into the cylinder lock and opened the metal door. Acting the gentleman, Hubba-Hubba ushered him inside and followed a step behind.

I entered the cool darkness last. There was hard concrete beneath my feet, and a strong smell of paint. Romeo Three started begging. The only word I could make out sounded like 'Audi'. I pushed the door closed and hit the light switch on the left-hand side of the steel frame with my elbow. I could now see what the *hawallada* was babbling about. A French-plated metallic silver Audi A4 was parked and filled most of the space in here.

Hubba-Hubba stepped alongside him just as he was turning towards us and slammed his right hand over Romeo Three's mouth. The keys slipped out of his hands and fell to the ground with a jangle. Pulling his head back, and hooking his left arm around his neck, Hubba-Hubba went down with him on to the dusty concrete, grazing the skin on his face, their clothes covered with dust.

Muffled screams escaped from the jerking body as he kicked against the side of the car in his struggle to get out from under Hubba-Hubba. The Egyptian looked like he was trying to wrestle a crocodile, and responded by forcing Romeo Three's head more firmly into the concrete to the sound of both of them snorting for oxygen.

I was already down on my knees, opening up my bum-bag and extracting the insulin pen as the *hawallada* fought non-stop to free himself, and Hubba-Hubba did everything to keep his face down and his arse up.

'That's good, mate, keep him there, keep him there.' I dug my right knee into his left thigh. His cologne filled my nostrils and I saw a gold Rolex glint on his wrist. This boy had obviously never seen what a traser could do for you.

I clamped the plastic needle cover between my teeth, and put all my weight on to his thigh, so I could get to the injection site before spitting it away. I could feel his wallet in the back pocket of his trousers as I used my free hand to push down on his arse, trying to keep it still.

As I fumbled with the button to pull it out, there was a hiss of air brakes and another truck started to back into the post office loading bay.

35

I whispered urgently, 'For fuck's sake, keep him still!'

The sound of the two of them fighting for breath as they heaved about on the concrete was almost as loud as the rattle of containers and banter between the postal workers.

I threw the *hawallada*'s wallet on to the ground and sat on both his legs, right behind his knees so his kneecaps were pressed into the floor. It must have hurt, but he was flapping too much to notice. I stabbed the pen into the upper right quadrant of his right buttock and pushed into him hard, pressing down the trigger at the same time. There was a faint *ping* as the spring pushed the larger than normal insulin needle through his clothing and into the muscle mass. I held the pen there, pushing down for ten seconds as instructed, as the sound of angry, frustrated breathing fought its way through Hubba-Hubba's hand.

We both held him down for the minute or so it took for his struggles to subside. Very soon, he was en route for the K hole.

I got to my feet. Hubba-Hubba still held him down until he'd stopped moving completely. I reloaded the pen by unscrewing it and replacing the cartridge and needle. After picking up the spat-out needle cover, I packed everything away in the bum-bag and fished out the nappy pin from my jeans as Hubba-Hubba disentangled himself and brushed himself down. The carts outside were still being filled, to the sound of a lot of French banter.

Hubba-Hubba picked up Romeo Three's keys and talked slowly and softly to Lotfi on the net, telling him what was going on as he inspected the fob.

With the opened nappy pin in my hand, I leant down, forced open the *hawallada*'s mouth, and pushed it through his bottom lip and tongue before fastening it and clicking down the pink safety cap. His muscles were completely relaxed by the ketamine, and we couldn't risk him swallowing his tongue and suffocating. There was also the risk of him vomiting as he came round from the drug and if that happened at the DOP with no one else there, he might choke on it. The pin would keep him safe until he reached his new home. Meanwhile Lotfi had got the news from Hubba-Hubba, and I heard him give a double click.

Our new friend was probably having his near-death experience by now, looking down at us both and thinking what a pair of arseholes we were.

The Audi's yellow fourways flashed as Hubba-Hubba pressed the remote and the locks clunked open.

I thumbed through the wallet and found that our new mate's name was Gumaa Ahmed Khalilzad. On the whole, I preferred Romeo Three. Pulling at his sideburns and fiddling with the nappy pin, I got no reaction. Then I put my ear to his mouth to check his breathing; it was very shallow, but that was what we'd been told to expect with this stuff.

What I wasn't expecting were the two thick, banded wads of hundred-dollar bills Hubba-Hubba held in each hand as he walked back from the Audi.

I took one bundle off him, and threw it down inside my jacket and sweatshirt. 'A little commission he skimmed off the top?'

Hubba-Hubba nodded in agreement as he slipped his bundle down his shirt.

He looked at me expectantly. 'What do we do now?'

249

A quick look at traser told me it was three thirty-eight, a couple of hours or so before last light.

The banter from the postal workers ebbed and flowed as I went through the options. Hubba-Hubba knelt down and pulled out a crisply laundered white handkerchief from Gumaa's now dirt-covered navy jacket. There was no way I could get Hubba-Hubba's or Lotfi's wagons in here. They wouldn't fit in the garage, and they couldn't just back up to load him in with people so close.

I watched as Hubba-Hubba tied the handkerchief around Gumaa's head like a blindfold. It wasn't to stop him seeing, but to protect his eyes. He had lost control of his eyelids as well as his tongue, and they might easily open during transportation to the DOP or during his wait there for pick-up. We needed to deliver him in a reasonable condition so that the interrogation could start as soon as he came round, and not after he'd had emergency treatment to remove two inches of lollipop stick from his eyeball. We'd planned to use gaffer tape from our cars, but you can't win them all.

I was going to have to drive the Audi out of Monaco with Gumaa in the boot. There was no other way.

Hubba-Hubba looked at me expectantly. I gave him a nod and hit my pressle. 'L?'

Click, click.

I could hear vehicles, and people talking around him. The chainsaw had stopped. 'Are you still complete?'

Click, click.

'In the same place?'

Click, click.

'H is going mobile first to clear the DOP. I'll then come out on to the square, turn left, and pass you in Romeo Three's car, a silver Audi. He'll be with me. I'll count down to the junction and then to you. You then back me, OK?'

Click, click.

'Good. We'll then make our way to the drop-off, just as planned.'

Click, click.

'Remember, you are Romeo Three's protection.'

At last he was able to come on the air. 'Of course, of course.'

I nodded at Hubba-Hubba. 'We'd better get him in the boot.'

He went round to the driver's seat and there was a clunk as the boot opened. With me lifting his legs and Hubba-Hubba gripping him under his armpits, we lugged Gumaa over to the Audi and lifted him in. We were now vulnerable; him to getting the good news from a tail-end crash, and us to being compromised, so Lotfi would try to stay behind me, close enough to stop anyone getting between us in the traffic. As we laid Gumaa down, I took off his jacket and wrapped it round his head as a cushion, then pushed him on to his side so he could breathe better, adjusted the handkerchief and threw the wallet back into his pocket after wiping it free of prints. It was part of the package for the boys on the warship.

Hubba-Hubba stood there waiting for the green light. 'Not yet, mate. We need to make this look like a hire car.' Fortunately there wasn't much to rearrange, just a plastic air-freshener on the rear parcel shelf, shaped like a crown, and some French and Arabic newspapers on the seat. They all went into the boot before it got closed down.

I looked at Hubba-Hubba. 'First thing, how do I get out of here?'

He pointed at a red and a green button to the side of the shutter.

'OK, mate, go and clear the drop-off. I'll come in via BSM, and radio check you to make sure everything's clear up there.'

He nodded and walked to the door as I half sat in the Audi, turned the key and watched him disappear into the street, closing the door carefully behind him.

'That's H foxtrot. L, acknowledge.'

Click, click.

The engine ticked over gently and exhaust fumes filled my nostrils as I moved over to the electric doors, waiting to be cleared by Hubba-Hubba.

There were still voices outside and I could just hear the chainsaw rev up once more in the distance. It was now magnified in my earpiece as Hubba-Hubba came on the net. 'N, it is all clear, it's all clear.'

Click, click.

I hit the shutter button with my elbow and the electric motor whined. As the steel door squeaked its way up, I slipped my gigs on to my nose and pulled my peak down low.

Reversing out, I had to stop parallel with the truck to close the shutter, before heading for the square. Hubba-Hubba was on his way to the drop-off. 'H is mobile. L, acknowledge.'

'Roger that, N is mobile.'

The Audi was an automatic, so it was quite easy to keep my right hand on the pressle.

'That's approaching the left-hand bend ... at the bend towards the square ... half-way ... approaching.' I hit the junction. 'Stop, stop, stop. Silver car.'

'L has, L has.'

The black Ford Focus was up the road to my left, just past the entrance to the car park and facing away from me. There was no need to carry on with the countdown: he had me. I turned left and Lotfi slotted in behind.

We wound our way back to the casino, down the hill towards the harbour. Traffic was heavy but steady as people began to head home from offices and banks, clouds of cigarette smoke and bad music billowing out of their open windows. Higher up, much bigger clouds, dark and brooding, gathered in the mountains.

We crawled around the harbour, with Lotfi protecting the rear of the Audi from impatient commuters.

Motorcycle police were directing traffic on a four-way junction not far from the tunnels. A truck in front of me eventually got the wave and turned right. I followed as Lotfi hit the net. 'No, no, no, no, no!'

As the message sank in I saw Lotfi in my wing mirror, heading straight on. There was a series of short, sharp whistle blasts

252

from one of the policemen now behind me. He was wearing high-leg riding boots and a sidearm, and was waving me to a halt. Another policeman kicked up the stand on his bike, and my mind raced through the options. It didn't take long; I didn't really have any. I had to bluff it.

If I put my foot down I probably wouldn't even make it past the other side of the tunnel. I took a deep breath, accepting my big-time fuck-up, checked my Browning was covered, and pulled over as a few trucks moved out into the centre of the road to pass the knobber who didn't know where he was going. The policeman approached and I pressed the down button on the window, looking up at him, my face one big apology. He still had his helmet on, a BMW lid, the sort that you can pull up the face. He said something in French and pointed back to the junction. His tone was more exasperated than aggressive.

I stammered, 'I'm sorry, officer, I . . .'

The bags under his eyes drooped as he looked down at me with an expression of unutterable weariness. 'Where are you going?' Perfect English.

'To Nice. I'm sorry, I'm a bit lost and I missed your signal . . .'

His expression told me he'd been dealing with dickhead Brits for years. With a resigned nod, he walked back towards the junction and beckoned me to reverse. A dozen horns were leant on as he held up the traffic with a leather-gloved hand and pointed me in the direction Lotfi had gone. I gave him a wave of thanks and tried to avoid the angry glares of the other drivers.

As I pulled away I saw Lotfi on foot to my left, coming uphill towards the junction. His arms were crossed and inside his jacket, which meant only one thing. He had drawn down in case he had to get me out of the shit the hard way. He spotted me and turned on his heel as I got on the net. 'L, where are you parked? Where are you parked?'

The roar of the traffic filled his mike. 'On the right, not far. Down on the right.'

'OK, I'll wait for you, I'll wait for you.'

Click, click.

I drove down the hill, looking for the Focus. It felt really strange knowing that someone had actually been coming to help. Nobody had done that for me since I left the Regiment.

I saw his car in a small layby in front of some shops. I pulled in about four cars back, and waited for him to get back behind the wheel. I watched him approach in my rear-view, and felt a surge of gratitude that I realized was close to friendship. It had been my fuck-up; he didn't have to come back and help, but he had been prepared to put his own life at risk to do so.

He walked past me, not giving the Audi a second glance, and as he waited for a line of cars to pass before opening his door, I wrote myself a mental Post-it to find a way of thanking him.

36

The Audi and the Focus merged with the traffic as we flicked on our lights to drive through the tunnel. Two Legoland police and three more in riding boots, astride their machines, were on duty at the roundabout the other side, checking tax and insurance discs as the traffic filtered past them. The flow speeded up now, as most of the traffic turned up to the A8, wanting to get straight home rather than waste time winding along the coast. I was trying to think what to do now that there was an extra vehicle in the plan.

It was starting to get dark, so the headlamps stayed on. Pinpricks of light were scattered all over the populated slopes to our right, but as the mountains got higher, they thinned out.

It wasn't long before we arrived at BSM and passed my Mégane behind the OP and then the marina entrance. I knew I wouldn't be able to see the *Ninth of May* from the road, but couldn't resist a look anyway before checking the rear-view mirror for the hundredth time to make sure Lotfi was still behind me. I got on the net. 'H, radio check, radio check.'

I got two low and crackly clicks.

'You are weak. Have you checked the drop-off?'

The clicks were still crackly.

'OK, change of plan, change of plan. I still want you to

cover me, but in my car, cover me in my car. Roger so far.'

Click, click.

'I need you to get rid of the Audi after the drop-off. Lotfi will back you, and take you back to your car afterwards. H, acknowledge.'

Click, click.

'L, acknowledge.'

Click, click.

'Roger that. Just carry on now as planned. Do not acknowledge.'

I carried on along the coast road, Lotfi still behind me; I could see his dipped lights in my rear-view, but I had no idea where Hubba-Hubba was. It didn't matter: we were communicating. We eventually reached the junction that led to Cap Ferrat, and then, no more than two minutes further on, rounded a sweeping right-hand bend and the bay of Villefranche stretched out below us. The warship was lit up like a Christmas tree about a kilometre offshore, and a dozen yachts twinkled away at their moorings. I didn't have long to take in the picture-postcard view before stopping at the junction that took us to the DOP. I waited with my indicator flashing for Lotfi to overtake, then followed him up an incredibly steep series of hairpin bends. The road narrowed, with room for two cars just to inch past each other. Lotfi's tail-lights disappeared ahead of me every now and again as we wound our way up the hill, past the walls and railings of large houses perched on the mountainside, then steel crash barriers to stop us driving over the edge.

Our destination was Lou Soleilat, an area of rough brush and woodland, situated around a big car park-cum-picnic area lined with recycling bins, where the Coke Light marker was going to be placed to show that there was a *hawallada* ready for collection.

The pick-up team, probably embassy or naval personnel, would drive past the picnic area from the opposite direction, from Nice. If the Coke can was in position, they'd throw it away with the rest of the crap they'd be dumping for cover, and continue downhill about five hundred metres to the DOP, pick up the *hawallada*, and continue to follow the road down to Villefranche and the warship.

The picnic area had been cut into the woods and laid with gravel. Wooden benches and tables were sunk in concrete for those Sunday afternoons with the family. I supposed the bottle banks were just there so the local fat cats could drive up in their overpowered 4x4s and dump a week's worth of empty champagne bottles, and feel they were doing something for the environment.

We carried on until we were about four hundred metres short of the drop-off point, then I turned off into a small parking area while Lotfi headed on beyond the DOP to the picnic area. There was room for about six vehicles; it was used by people during the day while they took their dogs for walkies in the woods, and at night by teenagers and philandering businessmen for a different kind of exercise altogether. There were enough used condoms scattered around the place for an army of dogs to choke on. Whatever, it was too late for dogs and too early for any backseat stuff, so I was alone.

As Lotfi disappeared into the darkness I hit the lights on the Audi, letting the engine tick over. My head fell back on to the headrest for a few seconds. I was fucked: my brain hurt just thinking about what I was going to do next.

Lotfi's job at the picnic area was to warn me if anything came from his direction as I dumped off Gumaa, and to leave the Coke Light marker once the job had been done. Hubba-Hubba would be joining me here soon, and he would cover me from this direction.

It wasn't long before Lotfi came on the net. 'That's L static in the car park. There are two other vehicles, with a lot of movement in a Passat. The occupants are being very energetic with their map-reading. The Renault next to it is empty.'

I double-clicked. I'd obviously been wrong: it wasn't too early for that sort of stuff. Maybe they'd just fancied one more for the road before they went home to their respective partners.

While I waited, I got out the pen, hoping that whoever was picking up Gumaa would be driving past at intervals during the night, and not only just before first light. It wouldn't be good if he woke up in the tarpaulin thinking, what the fuck am I doing here with this pin in my mouth?

I couldn't hear any movement from him yet, but he was going to need another burst of Special K to keep him floating, or whatever he was doing in the back there.

Headlights approached from down the hill and turned into the parking area. As they bumped over the gravel I recognized the Mégane. Hubba-Hubba pulled up level with me and powered down the window. I did the same and leant over my passenger seat to talk to him. He looked eager for instructions.

'Would L'Ariane be a good place to burn this thing out?'

It needed to be somewhere that wouldn't arouse too much attention, not for three days anyway, and the estate seemed a safe bet.

He thought for a moment, his fingers drumming on the steering wheel. 'I think it would be, but I need to wait until much later. It's too busy there at the moment. Maybe past midnight some time. Is that OK?'

I nodded. All I wanted was to make sure there were none of my prints or DNA, or anything else, to connect us to this job. I said, 'Make sure you lose the plates as well, mate.'

Hubba-Hubba smiled just enough for me to make out the whiteness of his teeth. 'Of course. I'll give them to you as a souvenir.' He jerked his head at the rear of the Audi. 'How is he?'

'Haven't heard a word. He's going to get the good news with the pen right now, just in case he's got a long wait.' I felt for the boot-release catch and got out into the fresh and rather nippy air. The light came on as I opened the lid, and there was a heavy smell of exhaust as the engine ticked over. I could just make out his face from the boot light, and it was obvious the movement of the car, or maybe his own efforts, had done him no favours. The nappy pin had ripped some of his lip and tongue. He was still breathing; blood was bubbling from the corner of his mouth and on to the handkerchief that had slipped down his face, and one glazed and dilated eye was open.

I pulled his eyelid down and pushed the handkerchief up over his eyes once more before turning him over a bit. I pressed the pen against his arse and pushed down the trigger. He was going to wake up thinking someone had implanted a golf ball in his cheek. Not that he'd be worrying about it that much when he saw he was in the steel hull of the warship with a roomful of very serious heads bearing down on him.

I shut the boot, packed away the pen as I coughed out the exhaust fumes from my lungs, and walked over to Hubba-Hubba. 'What did you say to him earlier on? You know, to get him into the garage.'

He smiled even more, pleased that I had asked. 'I told him I wanted to go back to where he'd just come from. He asked me why, and I told him I wanted the money. He said he didn't know what I was talking about. So I insisted.'

'How?'

'It was easy. I introduced you as the man who cuts off the heads of the *hawallada*, and promised that if he didn't hand over the money you'd do that to him. I told him that we all have very thin skin.'

No wonder he hadn't been too keen to shake hands.

Hubba-Hubba finished the story. 'At first he kept saying he had no money. I knew that – he had just handed it to the Romeos. I just wanted to get him off the street so we could lift him. But then he started to say that I could have the money, that he had it in his car. It was pretty good, no?'

'For a beginner . . .' I grinned back at him. 'Listen, thanks for getting us all out of the shit this afternoon. It was really quick thinking.'

He took his hands off the wheel momentarily in surrender. 'It was nothing. He had to be stopped. Besides, it was you that was going to cut his head off, no?'

Now there was something he wanted to say. 'About the money . . .' He touched the lump in his chest. 'What are we going to do with it?'

'Split it three ways. Why not?'

He didn't like that. 'We can't, it's not ours. We must put it with the body and it'll be taken to the ship. If we keep it, it's stealing. Lotfi would agree with me.'

If we handed it back, it would be lost in the ether. I shook my head. 'Tell you what, keep hold of it and we'll decide what to do on Sunday. You never know, there might be a lot more of this to worry about in the next two days.'

Before he could say anything more, I explained how I was going to carry out the Gumaa drop-off.

Hubba-Hubba had something else on his mind. 'We got away with it, didn't we?'

'One down, two to go. I'm going to check the bins later in the morning to see if they've shed any light on the Greaseball and Curly connection. It'll be about five-ish and I'll need Lotfi to take the trigger, same place as this morning, when I'm ready. You never know, you might get your chance to sort out Greaseball after all.'

That made him happy.

'Make sure Lotfi knows what's happening, and tell him we still need that God of his for another couple of days. After that we'll be in the clear, so he can have the rest of the week off.'

'I'll ask him.'

'Good. Come on, give me a hand.'

We lifted Gumaa out of the Audi and replaced his wallet before transferring him into the boot of the Mégane. It took about two or three minutes for us to gaffer tape his hands and feet, then join all four limbs together. I then taped his eyelids down correctly as Hubba-Hubba gave Lotfi a sit rep before going back to the Audi with a new phrase to add to his list. 'One down, two to go,' he said, and gave a quiet chuckle as I got into my Mégane.

'That's N mobile to the DOP. L, acknowledge.'

260

Click, click.

I took the money out of my sweatshirt and placed it under the driver's seat, hoping that maybe a little might find its way back to the US with me.

37

With the brake and reverse lights cut-out on, I backed out into the road with just a gentle red glow of the rear lights. There was no white reverse and no bright red as I put on the brakes to change into first before heading uphill.

The DOP was about four hundred metres to my left, at the end of a small grassy track that went in about eight metres before being chained off. It looked as though it had been that way for years. Just the other side of the chain, old fridge-freezers were piled on top of each other as the ground sloped downhill, and there were enough bulging bin liners to feed the incinerator by the safe house for a year.

Lotfi came on the net. 'Stand by, stand by. There is movement between the cars. Engines on. N, acknowledge.'

I double-clicked and slowed.

'Both cars are mobile. Wait, wait . . . at the main . . . wait . . . one left, one right towards you, N, towards you. Acknowledge.'

I double-clicked again, hit the brake and clutch and waited for the headlights to get to me. As long as no one else was coming from behind I'd be OK. Within seconds, twin beams swept over the high ground then hit me full on as the vehicle crested the hill. Whoever was in the car would never be able to

make out whether I was static or not, and it saved me having
to pass the drop-off, turn round at the picnic area and try
again.

I saw the faded, hand-painted sign nailed to the tree. It
probably said the driveway was private property and dumping was illegal, so fuck off. I didn't much care. It was my
marker to turn my lights off and take my time in the dark. Foot
on the brake continuously, I drove slowly over the hard mud
ruts up to the chain.

'That's N static. No one acknowledge.'

They knew where I was and I wanted to cut down time on
the air and get on with the job. The track was lined with fir
trees and thornbushes, plastered with wind-blown refuse.

There was no time to fuck about.

With the engine and handbrake on I climbed out and opened
the boot, making sure the Browning was tucked well into my
jeans and the bum-bag was done up.

Gumaa was a lot heavier than he looked when only one
person was doing the lifting, and I banged him about a bit as I
tried to loop him over my shoulders. I eventually got his taped
and trussed body into a sort of fireman's lift.

Once I'd got my legs over the drooping chain, I moved out
of the line of sight from the driveway and in among a couple of
ripped open bin bags, an old mattress with protruding springs,
and a very ancient tarpaulin. I dropped Gumaa on the tarp, and
pulled him on to his side so he could breathe easier. Finally I
checked that he was still alive, before wishing him well on his
onward journey with Ketamine Airways, and folding the
decaying canvas over his body to keep him warm.

I reversed the Mégane back out on to the track, and turned
downhill. 'That's drop-off complete. H, acknowledge.'

Click, click.

'L, don't forget the marker.'

Click, click.

Passing Hubba-Hubba's parking area, I got back on the net
once more. 'That's N now clear. Refuel, get some food. And

remember to change channel. If I don't hear anything before one thirty, I'm going to move my car into position, and check out the boat, OK? L, acknowledge.'

'Yes, mother hen.'

'H?'

'Cluck cluck.'

One down, two to go. I could almost hear Hubba-Hubba repeating it to himself, and having another little chuckle.

As I turned the first of the string of hairpins that led back down to the glittering patchwork of Villefranche, I threw the muffin wrapper and all the other crap I'd been collecting during the day into the passenger footwell. On the main drag, I headed right, towards Nice, stopping to fill up and buy two egg baguettes, a can of Coke Light, some bottled water and a few more Snickers bars for the OP.

Curiosity got the better of me as I neared Villefranche. I still had time to kill before returning to the *Ninth of May* so I parked for a while in a line of vehicles tucked into the side of the road, still facing towards BSM and just short of the DOP junction. The baguettes were cling-wrapped and sweaty, and the Coke was warm. It looked like I'd been a fridge too far.

As I munched, I watched the lights of the warship glittering on the water below me. It was just after eight when I'd finished, and the road was still fairly busy. I settled back, feeling greasy, full of Coke Light, damp bread and not-too-fresh egg. My eyes were stinging, but once I'd pushed the seat all the way back things started to get more comfortable. Checking that the doors were locked, and the Browning secure, I eased the hammer away from the patch of raw skin on my stomach where it had been rubbing, and made sure that my window was open a fraction to let out condensation, then closed my eyes and tried to doze.

My head jerked up again less than a minute later as a car heading towards me seemed to slow as it neared the junction, but went straight on.

Next time I looked, traser told me it was eleven forty-eight.

A very noisy Citroën had made its way down from the high ground and was waiting to join the main. The street lamp just short of the junction illuminated an old man hunched over the wheel with a cigarette in his mouth. He wasn't too sure when to move out, even though there wasn't much traffic. When he finally went for it, I saw why. With a grinding of gears and a flapping of fan belts, he laboured his way towards BSM. I wondered how he was ever going to make it back up the hill. I'd seen flashier motors used as chicken coops.

I changed batteries on the Sony, momentarily peeled off the gaffer tape and switched to channel two. I'd watch the junction until about one o'clock, then go back to the marina, get into position, and wait for the other two, who'd be at least another couple of hours.

My bacteria takeaway was starting to make its presence felt; the atmosphere in the Mégane smelt like gorilla's breath. I hoped I'd be needing a dump before I got into the OP, rather than after.

At twelve fifty-six, I saw headlights coming downhill. A small, dark-coloured Renault van, the sort a tradesman would use, came into view. It was two up, and I was sure I knew the head behind the wheel.

They checked the main and turned right, no indicators, towards me and Nice. As they passed under the street light I got a better angle from my semi-prone position, and pinged the driver. He'd had a different top on the last time I'd seen him, but it was definitely my mate Thackery. I didn't get to see his companion that close, but he, too, was young.

As soon as they'd passed, I popped my head up and watched them turn left, down towards the bay. I didn't envy Gumaa what was going to happen next.

I jumped out of the Mégane and crossed the road, watching the headlights bounce off the houses along the narrow streets, sometimes losing them altogether as the van continued downhill. Eventually it reached sea level, and disappeared into one of the buildings by the water's edge.

Today had been a success. We'd achieved the mission. But we hadn't had much choice. I couldn't see George being too understanding if we hadn't brought him Gumaa. 'But, George, we really had a good trigger and the follow was, frankly, excellent. It was the French getting in the way that messed things up for us. Never mind, I think we've learnt a great deal today and we can do a lot better next time . . .'

I walked back to the car, feeling a sense of satisfaction. The other thing I was feeling, as I pulled the seat up into the driving position, was a nagging sensation in my bowels. Turning the ignition key might have disguised the noise, but it hadn't hidden the smell. I powered down the window and made my way to the picnic area to see if there was anything for me from George, having learnt one big lesson. No more dodgy egg baguettes.

I turned into the junction and headed uphill, reasoning I might as well check the recycling bins now to see if anything had been left for me, and save time and fucking about later. I was going to the same place that I'd collected the insulin packs and explosives from. The marker was the same Coke can. It would be left in position if something was there for me, and I would remove it once I had picked up.

I drove past Hubba-Hubba's cover position, then the drop-off, and on to the picnic area. My headlights hit the recycling bins and two huge green plastic bottle banks, each with a large steel ring poking out of the top. The Coke Light can was still in position just under the forward right-hand corner of the nearer one.

There were no other vehicles in sight, so I parked up on the mud and gravel just past the bins, and turned off my lights. I pushed my hand underneath the one to the left of the Coke can, and felt for the broken brick that would be there if I had a message. Bingo. I dragged it out, a lot lighter than an ordinary brick, then took the can as well.

I turned the car round and headed back the way I'd come, wanting to be clear of the area as fast as I could. Once back on the main I turned left, towards BSM, leaving the warship lighting up the bay behind me. At the layby behind the OP, I closed down the Mégane, then got out my Leatherman and started to dig into the brick with the pliers.

The centre had been hollowed out, then its contents plastered over. I pulled out the cling-filmed package and unravelled it, at the same time brushing the plaster dust off my clothes. Inside was a sheet of A5, covered in tight print. I opened the glove compartment and laid it on the drinks tray. There was no introduction, just the message.

George did know about the connection between Curly and Greaseball. It also seemed the *Ninth of May* was well known to the French police. They suspected it had been used more than once to ferry heroin from here to the Channel Islands.

Curly's actual name was Jonathan Tynan-Ramsay, and he originated from Guernsey. I didn't give a fuck: he was going to stay Curly for me. He had a list of minor drug offences, and had been on court-imposed drug rehab programmes, which he'd failed to complete. He'd eventually served five years in jail in England for his part in a paedophile ring, and left the UK after being put on the sex offenders list. He had lived in France for the past four years. He and Greaseball were members of all the same clubs. The sort of clubs Hubba-Hubba wanted to put a bomb under.

George finished with a warning. The local police were taking an interest now that the *Ninth of May* was on the move; it had last been seen in Marseille three days ago. The police didn't know what had happened in Marseille, but George reckoned it had picked up the Romeos from the Algiers ferry, and now the police were waiting to see where it popped up again. It was just routine, he said, but be careful.

I tore the message into bite-size pieces and started chewing. As I headed back down the mountainside, I wondered why the fuck George hadn't told me all this in the first place. There'd been enough opportunity.

38

SATURDAY, 24 NOVEMBER, 01:38 hrs

I passed Lotfi's vehicle position in the hotel car park and could see nothing out of the ordinary. Below and ahead of me was the marina, and quite a few of the boats were still lit up. Driving down to the entrance, I saw nothing to get me worried, nothing parked up near the bus stops, no bodies mooching around. I carried on up to the layby behind the OP. It was empty, no sign of Hubba-Hubba's vehicle. Good man: he had thought about the third party, parked elsewhere and walked over to pick up my Mégane.

So far everything looked normal – which didn't mean a thing.

A vehicle approached from the other direction, passed me, forgetting to dip its lights, and carried on. I followed the line of the mountains towards Monaco, not wanting to park up behind the OP now in case the van was back: it'd make too much noise this time of the morning. The marina lights in my rear-view mirror disappeared as I completed the corner and drove into the darkness. Eight or nine vehicles were parallel parked in a layby ahead. They probably belonged to the cluster of houses above me on the steeper ground – apart from Hubba-Hubba's Scudo. I pulled in at the end of the line.

I got out, checked my bum-bag, and moved the Browning

hammer away from the sore, which had started to bleed. From the back of my Mégane, I retrieved the towel, emptied out the cling-film-wrapped dump and urine-filled water bottle, and replaced them with my fresh supply of water and Snickers bars.

I locked the Mégane, slung the towel and its contents over my left shoulder, and started back down to the OP with my cap firmly on my head to keep me warm later on.

There were just one or two lights on in the houses way up the hill; other than that the mountain was asleep.

An animal scurried away from me as I approached the entry point in the hedgerow. I had a quick look round before climbing over and following the hedgeline on my hands and knees until I reached the V-shaped palm shrub.

I sat there for a while and tuned in, then got the binos out of the towel. They worked well as a night-viewing aid with a little help from the dull lighting around the marina. I started with pier nine, but couldn't be sure that the *Ninth of May* was still there. A boat was parked up in its position, but it didn't seem to have the same silhouette. The binos were inconclusive; they were good, but not that good.

I'd have to go down to the pier to confirm physically, and do it straight away. There was no point sitting waiting for first light, only to find that the thing wasn't there.

I scanned the general area through the binos for the van. There were about a dozen vehicles in the car park, only two of them vans. These were right next to each other, and parked facing the boats. The one nearest me had some signwriting on that I couldn't make out from here. Worryingly, both had a good view of pier nine.

Leaving the towel and its contents behind, I crawled to the exit in the hedgerow but, instead of going through it, carried on for another twenty-five or thirty metres as a vehicle moved into the marina. I turned downhill towards the Petite Afrique beach. There was no pathway, just scrub and dry earth all the way down to the sand.

Once I hit the sand I got up and walked to the car park. My detour meant I was approaching the vans from the rear, on the assumption that if anyone was inside them they'd be concentrating on the target.

I passed the swings and climbing frame, using the huge piles of sand as cover but walking normally, as if I was taking a short cut back to my boat. It was pointless getting tactical and running, crawling, ducking, all that sort of stuff. I was out in the open and, no matter what I did, I would be seen when I crossed the flat, open expanse of car park, if not before.

My Timberlands slipped and slid as I negotiated the sixty-odd metres of beach; then I hit the heat-cracked tarmac of the car park. I checked inside the cars as best I could, to see if any heads were pulled back in their seats, with their car windows open just an inch to prevent that ever compromising condensation. The odd vehicle still moved to and fro along the main, and I heard laughter from the far side of the marina. As I got closer to the car park I could see the silhouette of a couple kissing in a saloon to my right, near the bin area, but that was all. It was probably the vehicle that had come in while I was moving down here. I didn't think I'd seen it there before. I sauntered along until I got between the two vans. Once there, I stopped and listened, standing as if I was taking a piss. If there was surveillance, it would probably be in the unmarked one. The other was too easy to spot with such a VDM – visual distinguishing mark.

There was nothing I could do but stand there and listen. I put my ear gently against the side and opened my mouth to cut off any cavity noise, but heard nothing. I did the same with the other one, but again, nothing. It would look highly suspicious to anyone watching, a guy putting his head against a couple of vans, but I didn't have any other options.

I must have been there for about three minutes, hearing nothing but the gentle lapping of water against boats, and the odd clanking of the rigging.

A vehicle screamed along the main towards Monaco as I

stepped out on to the pier. I wasn't concerned about the kissers: they had other things on their minds, and might be there all night. The Germans weren't dreaming of life on the ocean wave along with everyone else around here. Their TV was still going full blare as I passed, but it was the last thing on my mind by then. I had a horrible, empty feeling in my gut. I took a few more steps and stood, looking foolishly at the washing that hung along the back of a boat called the *Sand Piper*, which was parked where the *Ninth of May* should have been. I stood there like an idiot, willing my boat to materialize, hoping I was about to discover I was on the wrong pier. But it wasn't to be.

Fuck – now what?

Spinning on my heel, and quickening my pace, I checked further down the pier, just in case it had been shifted a few spaces. I went back and checked the first pier. No luck. I was going to have to search the whole fucking place: I didn't know how the system worked, maybe they'd been moved to another parking place, or they had a technical problem and were parked up alongside the workshop the other side of the marina. I wanted to cover as much of the area as I could, in as short a space of time as possible, but I couldn't run. There was still third-party awareness to think about.

As I made my way back towards the shops I delved into my bum-bag for the phone card and started to recite the pager number to myself. 04 . . . 93 – 45 . . . Fuck, what if they'd left for Algeria already? What if Greaseball had been wrong, and there was only ever going to be one pick-up? My mind raced. The tennis bags had been big enough to hold at least a million and a half dollars between them, more than enough to pay off a coachload of relations.

Shit, shit, shit.

Clenching the phonecard in my fist and reciting the number like a madman, my eyes darted everywhere, still in hope of spotting the boat. My plan now was to work my way methodically around the whole marina. There was no other way to confirm whether the boat was there or not. I walked past the cars that were parked to my right, but kept on looking out to my left, at the boats.

Two bodies stepped out from the kissing car. There was a challenge from the driver. *'Arrêtez! Arrêtez! Arrêtez!'*

I carried on walking, my hands in my pockets, eyes down at the concrete. I wasn't going to stop, but I didn't know what I was going to do. Water was behind me: the only escape was forward, past them and up to the main.

The driver, a man, was about six metres away and came out past his car, blocking my path, his door left open. *'Police! Arrêtez!'*

Now the other body, a woman, emerged, leaving her door open as well. She ran behind and past him, and carried on down to the quay, maybe to make sure I didn't jump in. Her black leather jacket glinted dully under the lights.

39

The man's voice was very calm. As he moved forward I could see his ponytail. *'Arrêtez, police.'*

I kept walking, head down, and did my best to look confused. I didn't want to open my mouth unless I had to.

The woman moved in step with him, following the waterline no more than two metres behind. She kept at an angle to her partner so she had a clear field of fire. The man kept gobbing off in French as he got closer to me, moving slowly, like a stalking cat, bending his legs and hunkered down a bit, treating me as if I was an unexploded bomb with a tremor switch. The woman sensed this was wrong: I hadn't stopped. Never taking her eyes off me, she moved her right arm, pulling back the jacket to get to the pistol somewhere on her hip.

No more than three metres separated us now. I stopped as I heard the squeak of leather as the woman's pistol came up. I hadn't exactly helped calm the situation down by not talking to them or looking as if this had never happened before. Her hair flicked up as she jerked her head around, checking everywhere to make sure I was alone, before getting eyes quickly back on me.

Ponytail moved forward while she stood her ground, covering him. He had a couple of days' stubble to go with his hair.

He thrust his ID at me with his left hand. A National Police badge, looking very much like a sheriff's star with the word 'Police' set in a blue centre.

'*Police*,' he said, in case I had trouble reading.

He flicked the fingers of his right hand upwards, but at first I didn't understand the gesture. Then I twigged; he wanted my hands out of my pockets and up where he could see them. His eyes never left mine, looking for signs that I was going to try something. This guy was really experienced; he knew that eyes give away an action a second before it happens.

He gestured upwards again with his right hand. '*Allez, allez.*' He wanted my hands in the air, or on my head, I wasn't sure which.

What the fuck was I going to do? Jump into the water and swim for it? To where?

He was just a pace away as my hands went up on to my head. He was pleased with that and continued to talk to me in confident, subdued tones as he closed his ID and shoved it between his teeth.

She was still static at the water's edge, behind him and to my left.

Ponytail closed in and ran his left hand over the front of my jacket. His right hand was still free to draw down if necessary. Encountering the Sony, his eyes narrowed. He breathed through his nose, kept the ID in his mouth, and gave a muffled but calm, '*Pistolet.*'

Even I knew what that meant, and the woman moved in closer until she was at right angles to me. I could almost feel her tongue in my ear as she whispered something along the lines of 'Move and I'll kill you'.

She was too close. You should never be within arm's reach. I had to do something, anything, before he got down to the Browning.

He started to pull on the zip of my jacket, yanking it with such force that it snagged about a third of the way down and I got tipped forward.

It was time to act.

His eyes were still staring into mine. My hands were still on my head and my left elbow was level with her pistol. Taking a slow, deep breath, I counted to three, then forced my arms forward to push the muzzle away from me. She shouted out, as if Ponytail didn't know what was happening. I made a lunge to the left and body-checked her, toppling her into the water.

Ponytail came at me. I tucked my head in and got my forehead into his face. There was a crunch of bone on bone and he dropped to the ground. I followed, my head flashing with pain. It felt like I'd headbutted a wall.

He arched his back, trying to draw the weapon, which he had holstered behind his right kidney, as Leather Girl splashed about below us. His jacket fell open. I saw a mobile phone clipped to an inside pocket. It was quicker to get to than my Browning or his pistol hand. Grabbing the phone upside down in my right hand, I knelt astride him and stabbed at him, using the stubby antenna like a dagger blade, stabbing into his shoulders and chest. I didn't want to kill him, but I needed to fuck him up for long enough for me to get away. He screamed in pain and I felt his blood warm on my hand as my own ran into my eyes. The pain in my head was a nightmare. I kept on stabbing, maybe six or eight times more, I wasn't counting. Fuck him and his weapon, I just wanted to make some distance between them and me. Scrambling to my feet, I ran towards the concrete steps.

Ponytail cried out in pain as he writhed on the ground behind me, and I could hear people calling out from the boats in a cocktail of languages. I wasn't too worried about the girl. When she got out of the water, she'd stay with him, sorting him out. It might have been worse. I might have gone for his face or throat.

I was taking the steps two at a time when Lotfi's voice burst in my left ear. 'Hello, N – N, radio check.' Almost simultaneously, I saw headlights coming from the direction of the town, down towards the marina entrance. I jumped over the 'I fuck girls!' bench and hit the Sony pressle as I stumbled into the scrub. 'Keep going, we have a drama, do not stop. Go to H's vehicle. You'll see mine there, wait there, wait there. Acknowledge.'

Click, click.

Mud caked my bloodstained right hand, as well as the mobile. Lotfi's lights continued on past the entrance and passed me as I grabbed the towel and the OP kit and scrambled along the hedgerow, leaving the screams and lights going on in boats behind me.

As soon as I was out on to the road I started to sprint uphill as fast as I could, ready to leap back over the hedge as soon as any vehicle came along the road. My throat was bone dry and my lungs hurt as I sucked in oxygen and pumped my free arm to get me up the hill and past the bend. I found Hubba-Hubba and Lotfi waiting in the Focus, lights off and engine on. Lotfi unlocked the doors as he saw me approaching.

I jumped into the back. 'Let's go! Drive towards Monaco and get off the main – quick as you can, come on, let's go, let's go!'

The Focus revved up and we screamed away from the kerb as I tried to catch my breath.

I shoved the mobile with the OP kit in the towel, wiping the mud and blood from my hands as I did so.

'The boat – it's gone. At least, I think so. I only got to check two piers. The van, it was definitely the police. I've been stopped by them.'

They didn't look at all happy.

'It's OK, I think they just want to know what the boat is up to. The guy who owns it is a drug smuggler, small-time, that's all.'

I finished wiping my hands as the Focus hit the first of the hairpin bends, and stuck the corner of the towel on the split in my forehead, just inside my hairline.

Hubba-Hubba's mind was already jumping ahead. 'The device . . . if they are on their way to Algeria, we must stop it now.'

'It's an option. We could make the call, if it's still in range. But we've got other things to consider first. It could have moved to a marina along the coast, so the Romeos can still make their collections. As far as they're concerned, yesterday was a success.'

Lotfi changed down to get up the incline.

'Look. Maybe the alarm and the police scared them last night. Maybe Greaseball is wrong and they move each day . . . maybe it is still down there . . .'

I had regained my breath now. Leaving my head, I fished inside the towel and brought out some water to finish cleaning my hands and face as well as getting some down my neck. 'Perhaps they've pinged us and moved, hoping to shake us off for the next two collections. Maybe they've even prepared an ambush in case we find them again.'

I much preferred the first two possibilities. Lotfi's face was set in a frown as he concentrated on the road. 'If we call in the device now, we might stop them getting to Algeria. But what if they're still here? Not only do we fuck up the mission, we might kill real people, and that's something we're here to stop. So, I reckon, forget about the police, forget about the boat missing. These things can be dealt with. We're here for the *hawallada*, remember? One down, two to go.'

I leant back in the seat. 'Look, we are in the shit, and right now checking the marinas seems the best way of getting out of it. What do you think?'

It was pointless me telling them what I wanted to happen. Playing the dictator always leads to a gang fuck. You've got to bring people along with you. They looked at each other, mumbling away in Arabic, then both nodded.

'I have already been to the bins and got more information about the guy I saw with Greaseball on Wednesday night and on board last night. The *Ninth of May* belongs to him. He's a small-time dealer and another fucking paedophile. Him and Greaseball are mates.'

I could hear heavy, angry breathing from both of them.

277

'I know how you feel, but we have to cut away from that and get on with the job. Remember what we're here for. We've got to find the boat. If we have that, we have *hawallada*. We have to keep focused.'

I let it sink in, which gave me time to think. There wasn't really a plan: it was just a matter of getting out there and finding the boat. If not, we were going to have to stake out both Nice and Cannes tomorrow, and hope they came to us.

'OK, we have to check every marina in our areas. I'm going to see what Greaseball knows. We'll meet at six a.m. in the parking area Hubba-Hubba uses to cover me at the DOP. I want to get together while it's still dark, so if we've found the boat again, we can get an OP in to trigger the Romeos before first light.'

They nodded.

'If anybody doesn't make it to the meeting place, for whatever reason, the other two must carry on with the job.'

I continued my quick change-of-plan briefing as it bubbled up in my head.

'Anyone who doesn't make the meet this morning is to stake out the Nice address. See if you can raise anybody on the net. If not, tough. We all meet up again, twelve thirty tomorrow morning in the same parking area, whether or not we've dropped another *hawallada* off first.

'If we don't find the boat, we're going to have to put triggers on the Nice and Cannes addresses and hope they turn up to collect. We do that for two days, and if no luck, that's it, we'll have fucked up. Any questions?'

Lotfi raised his right index finger. 'What if only one of us makes the meet tomorrow morning?'

My stomach rumbled. 'The one who makes it has the choice. Put a trigger on the Nice addresses and carry on as before, or just bin it and go home, accept the failure.'

Hubba-Hubba's eyes scoured the coastline. 'It's got to be here, it's got to be somewhere,' he muttered. 'We can't let the money leave.'

Lotfi gobbed off in Arabic and I got just one of the words. *Allah*. He turned to me as Hubba-Hubba shrugged his shoulders and looked back out to sea. 'I'm sorry, Nick, I forget. I was saying that he is not to worry. If God wants us to find them we will, and he will protect us, believe me.' His eyes shone with conviction.

I hoped like hell he was right.

40

The Focus drove around for another twenty minutes up on the high ground. At one point the autoroute was visible in the distance; white light, not too much at this time of the morning, moved in both directions.

We came back down the mountain to the cars. We had to get on with the search, and had to take the chance of getting closer once more to the marina, no matter what was happening down there now.

Lotfi changed down again as we took a steep right-hander.

'Anyway, the Audi.' I chanced a smile in the silence. 'How did it go?'

I drank some more water as Hubba-Hubba gave a grin that glowed in the light from the instrument panel. 'We burnt it near the incinerator.' By the look on his face, Lotfi had enjoyed himself too. 'There was another dead vehicle already burning there, so we just joined the party.'

The main was clear and we parked up where we had started. As I gathered up my towel, the smell hit them. Lotfi quickly opened the door to get out. Hubba-Hubba thought it was funny but got out all the same, for health and safety reasons. He turned back and whispered, 'Is that, how do you say, a "silent but deadly"?'

I got out of the car on Lotfi's side. As he locked up he muttered, 'He really has been watching too much *BB and Blockhead*.'

Hubba-Hubba shook his head slowly. 'Butthead – *Beavis and Butthead*.'

I checked traser and it was three fourteen as I drove through Cannes, stopping two or three times after turning a corner to see who followed. Just short of Greaseball's apartment off Boulevard Carnot, I turned three sides of a square, but nobody came with me. Finally, I parked about half a K from his flat and walked in.

I pressed the buzzer for about two minutes and eventually got a groggy, crackly answer. I knew exactly how he felt. '*Comment?*'

'It's me. I want to talk to you. Open up.'

He was confused. 'Who? Who's me?'

'Somebody you met in Algeria, remember?'

There was a pause. 'What?' He coughed. 'What do you want?'

'Open up and you'll find out.'

The speaker went dead and was replaced by the high-pitched buzz of the electric latch. I moved towards the stairs, taking my time to minimize the squeaking of my Timberlands on the fake marble, and didn't push the light switch to help me up the stairs. The Browning came out and I pulled back the hammer to full cock and pushed the safety catch up with my thumb, ready to take it off at a moment's notice as I slowly climbed.

Standing in the stairwell on the fourth floor, I listened with my right ear at the doorway out into the corridor, my mouth open to lessen the noise of me catching my breath. There was nothing. I moved into the hallway with the pistol at my side. I got to Flat 49 and tapped gently on the door, standing to the left of the frame so I could see into the flat as soon as it opened. There was the rattle of a security chain, then the squeak of hinges.

He looked scared but a bit out of it, dark rings beneath his glazed eyes. He staggered a little as he led me into the living room. The glass patio doors and shutter were closed, so the smell of cigarettes was overpowering. Fully dressed, he stood by the coffee table, taking nervous sips from a small bottle of Evian. A used syringe lay on top of the table, next to a foil card of oblong-shaped pills.

His hair was greasy as always, but now sticking up. His red-striped shirt was creased, with the tail hanging out. Judging by the scrunched-up pashmina on the settee, that was where he'd been sleeping.

'Is there anybody else here?'

'No, there's no one. What do you want? I have told you everything—'

I put the Browning muzzle to his lips. 'Shut the fuck up.' I nodded towards the door that divided the living area from the corridor into the bedroom and bathroom, then stepped back and closed the front door with my arse. 'Go on. You know what to do.'

'I tell you, there is no one here. Why would I lie to you? Why?'

He held out his arms in submission and swayed a little.

'Just do it.'

After two attempts he recapped the bottle, chucked it on to the settee, and walked into the corridor. I moved behind him, clearing the flat. Nothing much had changed: everything was still in a shit state. We came back into the living room and he sat down, slumping into the cushions.

'Where's the *Ninth of May*?'

His brain wouldn't compute. 'It's where I said it would be.'

'No, it isn't. It was there yesterday, but now it's moved. Where has Jonathan taken the boat?'

He looked totally confused now. 'He? Who? I don't understand what you—'

'Jonathan Tynan-lah-di-fucking-dah-Ramsay. I know all about him, what he does, what he's done, who he's done it with. I even saw you with him Wednesday night. The Fiancée of the Desert, Juan-les-Pins, remember?'

I bent down, looking into the wall unit for the Polaroids, but they were still nowhere to be seen.

I straightened again. 'You hearing me?' I pushed up his chin and finally got to look into his eyes. 'I have no time to fuck about. Tell me where the boat is.'

He looked genuinely puzzled and very worried as he slumped back into the settee. 'I don't understand, I don't know what you're saying. He should—'

'It's very simple,' I cut in. 'The *Ninth of May* has left Beaulieu-sur-Mer and I want to know where it's gone. Back to Marseille? '

I wanted him to know I knew a lot more than he thought.

There was no more time to waste. I was losing valuable minutes. I went to the kitchen and used the muzzle of the Browning to rummage in the drawers. I picked up a plastic-handled bread knife and came back into the living room. He pushed himself back an extra three inches in the settee. He was paying a lot of attention to me now.

'I'm going to ask one more time. Where is the boat?'

He hesitated, then began to stutter. 'I don't know . . . it should be at the port. It isn't going to Marseille, that was just to pick up the two guys from the Algiers ferry. No, no . . . Beaulieu-sur-Mer . . . that's what he—'

He was rubbing his face now with both hands, leaning forward and resting his elbows on his legs. 'It should be there, I . . .'

I didn't try to get eye contact again, just pushed him back into the back cushions and pointed the knife at his face. He needed to see it.

'Listen carefully. If you don't know where it is, you're no good to me. I don't give a shit how important you think you are to other people. To me you're nothing, and I'd rather have you dead than able to talk about me, if you ever live long enough, pumping that shit down you.'

His dopy eyes rolled towards the syringe and pills. 'Please, I don't know anything. The boat should be at the port. The boat was there. I swear, you will make a great mistake, I am protected, I—'

'Shut the fuck up. You've got fifteen seconds left. Tell me where the boat is.' I shoved the Browning into my jeans and checked traser. 'You saw how messy this gets . . . especially if this thing isn't sharp enough.'

His eyes were jumping around in his head. He was losing it, big-time. 'I swear I don't know, please . . .' His hands suddenly came up, as if he'd had a revelation. 'Maybe he's gone back to Vauban . . .'

'Antibes?'

'Yes, yes. Maybe he's moved back there . . .'

I knew this place, I knew Vauban. It was a massive marina in the old town of Antibes, about ten minutes' drive from Juan-les-Pins. I pointed the knife back at him. 'Why there?'

'It's always there, in the port, that's where he lives. He told me he would go to Beaulieu-sur-Mer for three days with those guys. I swear this is the truth, I swear . . .'

'Where in Vauban?'

'With the fishing boats.'

I reckoned he was scared enough now to be telling the truth. Sweat poured down his face as he leaned forward, nervously pushed a tablet through the foil and bunged it down his neck, then fought with the Evian bottle top. I watched as he swallowed it like a gulping dog, hands shaking so badly the water ran down the side of his stubbly face.

He fiddled with the foil, as if making up his mind whether to take a second for luck.

'Is everything still going to plan?'

He looked up at me, his voice trembling as much as everything else. 'Yes, yes, everything. I'm sure. I don't know why the boat has moved. I didn't speak with Jonathan since he returned from Marseille with the collectors on Wednesday. He stopped at Vauban with those guys for a few hours, to meet me and try to persuade them to stay there. That was when I learnt the addresses of these *hawallada*. You have to believe me. If the *Ninth of May* has moved, that is where it will be, by the fishing boats. Jonathan will not be letting anyone down, there will be a reason for him to leave.'

I looked down at the crap he had on the table. He knew what I was thinking.

'You're disgusted. Everything I do disgusts you.' He waved the card at the syringe. 'You think this is heroin, or maybe a little mixer, something like that?' He held up the tablet that he'd just pulled out with his shaky thumb and forefinger. 'This, my friend, this is saquinavir, an antiretroviral . . .' His whole demeanour had changed. I didn't know whether he suddenly just didn't give a fuck, or if the chemicals he was taking had made him a bit soft in the head. He put the pill into his mouth, but didn't follow it with any water. It rattled against his teeth as he spoke. 'How times have changed. I take it for keeping slim at the gates – for as long as I can. The syringe, that is for my pain. These are the only drugs Jonathan and I take these days.'

He tilted the last of the Evian into and around his mouth before collapsing back into his sleeping position on the settee.

'The police were at Beaulieu-sur-Mer. They were looking at the boat before it disappeared.'

He smiled weakly to himself and moved his head to get more comfortable in the pashmina. 'He told them he didn't want to leave Vauban, he told me at dinner, but that's what they wanted, so . . .' He shrugged his visible shoulder. 'He is my friend, I know him. He must have moved back home to make things look more normal. Yes, that's what he has done. The boat would have been watched because it has moved such a small distance. The police, they know these things, the boat is known to them. But those two guys, they don't know that.'

He smiled to himself once more and rubbed his eye like a child.

He might be right. Curly might have used the Romeos'

freaking out as an excuse to move back to where he felt safer.

Greaseball looked up at me, red-eyed. 'Do you know why it's called that?'

'What?'

'The ninth of May, 1945. The day Guernsey was liberated from the Nazis. Jonathan's a very patriotic boy.' He was definitely in a world of his own; maybe the pills were making him ramble. He sighed and a little stream of saliva dribbled down the side of his face. 'It is going to be our liberation.' He took a deep, whistling breath through his nostrils, and his eyelids drooped. He gave himself a small, secret smile. 'Not sad for long. No, no, no.'

'Both of you planning to go out with a bang, are you?'

'Bien sûr, mon ami. That's the only thing that keeps us alive. I know you want to kill me. But I don't care what you think. Fuck all of you. All of you are hypocrites. You find us disgusting, yet you use us if it suits you. You give me immunity for what we have done.'

'Fucking boys, you mean? Does he still do it? You take him to Algeria with you?'

'And more, and more.' His eyes were almost shut now, and he was dribbling big-time. Whatever he'd been pumping into his veins over the years had cost him several billion brain cells. 'You don't like me and I don't like you. But I've still given you what you need. You know why? Because we do have something between us. We both hate al-Qaeda.' He tried to stare at me with glazed eyes, but he was just off-line. 'Are you surprised? Why else do you think I am doing this? Why do you think I told them I could organize the collections? I have made them a fortune from heroin here, and what do I get?' He threw his arm out, pointing at the flat. 'So, you see, we are the same, you and me. You don't like that, do you?' He gave up trying to lock on my eyes and turned over.

I opened the door with my sweatshirt cuff and left him to his dreams. I only wished I could have helped him on his way.

286

41

Antibes and its harbour, Port Vauban, is Yachting Central for the Mediterranean. A third of the world's megaboats are based on the Riviera, and the majority of them are parked in this one port. Here, even boats with a helicopter on the deck are sneered at by those on Millionaires' Row, where the smallest looks as if it's owned by Cunard.

The support services for all these thousands of pleasure craft make Antibes an all-year-round town, not a sleepy, seasonal place like Juan-les-Pins or any of the others along the coast.

I passed the nondescript apartment blocks that had spread out of the old town like a wave, swamping everything in their path, and as I neared the port the streets began to narrow and the buildings got much older. There were just inches each side for manoeuvring past rows of scooters and cars, all of which looked abandoned rather than parked. Maybe the mayor awarded a weekly prize for the most artistic parking arrangement.

The Romans had built Antibes into an important town, but in the seventeenth century the public baths, aqueduct and open-air theatre had been torn down and the stone used to build its defences, including a fort to protect the port where Napoleon was once imprisoned. All that was left of the old city wall was a few hundred metres that faced the port.

The old town proper was picture postcard stuff, apart from the Christmas lights taped on to windows and straddling the streets. Tall, shuttered buildings lined the streets, with washing strung on lines between them. I drove through a small archway set into the old wall, which was maybe ten metres thick. The other side and ahead of me was a forest of masts, illuminated by the harbour lights. To my left was a car park that followed the wall until it ended, maybe two hundred metres away. To my right, the wall continued, and rows of small fishing boats were parked up in the water. Behind them, small market stalls waited empty to sell the day's catch. If Greaseball was correct, then somewhere among the fishing boats, in the poor man's area, was the *Ninth of May*.

The car park was virtually empty, and not a VW camper to be seen. Not that I expected to see it: if the police were here, they certainly wouldn't be using the same vehicle. Keeping a constant speed, I checked out the car park opening times before turning left, back into the old town, parking in the first space I could find.

If there was a French trigger on the *Ninth of May*, they'd ping me as well if I used the car park. Just like the Romeos, I always wanted to be behind them, out of their field of view. I'd abandoned my jacket and cap after the gang fuck at the marina and cleaned myself up a bit before putting on the new green baggy sweatshirt I'd bought at Cap 3000 during the brush contact yesterday.

Before getting out I checked the Browning and the bum-bag for the umpteenth time before following the wall townside back towards the port. To my right was a line of small restaurants and cafés in the shadow of the massive blocks of granite or whatever it was. They were closed for the night, their outside furniture stacked, wired and padlocked to the ground.

I headed past the archway towards the stone steps up to the ramparts, so that I could get a better view of the boats.

Once through an alleyway between the wall and a closed-up

bar, I emerged into a small, cobbled, tree-lined square that had made many a postcard photographer's day. As I started up the steps, I looked at the sky. The clouds had gone and stars were out, twinkling as best they could against the manmade stuff thrown up from the town and harbour.

I stopped about four steps before the top to check out the ramparts. Along each side of the wall was a three-foot-high parapet, which must once have run its entire length. Now, it was blocked in both directions, leaving quite a large area for people to use as a viewing platform. To the left, the wall over the archway was blocked by a rusty wrought-iron gate and railings, and to my right it had been made into a small car park. How they got up here was a mystery, but I saw three empty cars and a Renault van. The van was a dark colour, and had been reversed against the parapet. Its rear windows looked down over the port.

I moved back down the stairs a little, into dead ground, and sat on the steps. A dog started to yap somewhere in the old town and a moped rattled along the cobblestones below.

There was only one way to find out if the van was occupied or not. I stood up and climbed to the viewing area. The van had a sliding door on its passenger side, so I kept to the right-hand side of it, in case it suddenly opened to reveal a bedraggled, short-haired woman in a damp leather jacket.

As I approached, I could see that the driver's cab was blocked off from the rear, screening the interior. I'd have expected a vehicle like this to be full of old newspapers and drinks cans, even an air-freshener hanging off the mirror, but there was nothing.

I got on the right side of it, between the flush body panel and a BMW, before standing still, doing my open-mouth trick, and waiting.

The dog sparked up again. Still I waited, and maybe three or four minutes passed before there was movement. The steel creaked just a little; maybe they were changing over the trigger; but enough to tell me there were people inside.

I moved forward, closer to the parapet, but not beyond the line of the rear windows, to look down at the quay. I couldn't help but smile as my eyes followed the line of boats below me. There, tied up next to the first of a whole row of bigger boys, a fifty-foot monster called the *Lee*, was the *Ninth of May*, looking as if it was hiding behind its mother's skirts.

Like the owners of plenty of other small craft here, Curly had made the place look just like home. The quay behind boasted an array of very weathered garden furniture.

I studied the settee cover on the top deck, and it looked much the same as when I'd left it. There were no lights on board and the blinds were down.

I turned slowly, walked back to the steps and down into the square, leaving the police to it as I thought through potential exit points for the Romeos. They'd have to come along the quay, past the fishing boats and stalls, until they got to the road through the archway. They could then go straight, following the wall on either side until it stopped, then uphill, out of the old town, towards the railway station. The other option was to turn left through the archway and head for the bus station through the old town. Neither was more than ten minutes' walk away.

According to traser it was three fifty-eight. I still had time to do a more detailed recce of both, and work out how I was going to get a trigger in on the boat without getting pinged by the police. I crossed the archway, staying out of sight on the town side of the wall, and went to check out the rail option first. I thought about the two, maybe three people inside the Renault. Chances were, they had a camera mounted, ready to take pictures of the boat as soon as there was movement on board. Like me, any food they had with them would have been removed from its original noisy packaging, and wrapped in cling film or a plastic bag. Their toilet arrangements would be a little better than mine, though: they might even have stretched to plastic jerrycans. The inside of the van would be protected to cut down on noise. Maybe the floor was covered with soft gym mats and the wall padded with foam. They'd certainly be wearing trainers or soft shoes.

But even so, at night, with hardly any ambient noise to drown their gentle movements, thank fuck I had heard them.

42

It was six thirty-three when I arrived in Hubba-Hubba's car park, three minutes late. The other two vehicles were already there, parked together, with no one else around. It was far too dark to walk the dog, and the sex would have happened hours ago.

Once I'd closed down the Mégane, I started towards Hubba-Hubba's Scudo. The cab windows were slightly open, and the engine was off. I heard a gentle click behind me as Lotfi closed the door of the Focus. We approached the van together and as we climbed in through the side door the ribbed steel floor buckled gently under our combined weight. Hubba-Hubba turned round in the driver's seat to face us both. I slid the side door back so it closed gently, and before anybody said anything I gave them a thumbs-up in the dull light of the glove compartment bulb. 'We've got the boat back. Greaseball gave it to me and I have checked, they're in Antibes.' Two very relieved people gave big sighs and gobbed off to each other in Arabic. 'But we do have a problem: the police are there.'

I described the boat's exact location, then the position of the Renault van, and the layout of the surrounding area. 'The only way I can see us getting a trigger on the target is by having someone in the back of this thing.' I looked at Hubba-Hubba as they exchanged more Arab stuff and sounded quizzed. 'Where are the blankets to cover the *hawallada*?'

He tapped the rear of his driver's seat. 'Under here.'

'Good, I think it'll work. Basically, one of us needs to get in the back of this wagon, and stay there all day if necessary, watching the quay by the fishing boats and the archway so we can trigger the Romeos away. We need to play about with the back of this thing a little bit, but the first thing we need to do is choose the right man for the job. Hubba-Hubba, congratulations.'

He didn't make any sounds of concern.

'Don't look so happy. You're just about to find out what it's like to be holed up in the back of one of these things all day, looking through a small aperture waiting for the target, knowing that if you take your eyes off the trigger for just a second, you could miss what you've been waiting hours to see.'

Lotfi knelt up and forward and shook Hubba-Hubba's shoulder, obviously pleased it wasn't him. 'That's not a problem for this man. He's the smallest, of course he should do it.'

Hubba-Hubba said something back that didn't sound too pleasant. I couldn't do anything but smile because I didn't know what Lotfi was on about. To me they looked like they'd both come out of the same mould.

I took a breath to gather my thoughts. 'OK, then, first things first.' I was waiting for Lotfi to get his beads out and, sure enough, I heard a click. 'Ground – you've just had it. Remember that the bus and the rail stations are a lot closer to the boat than they were yesterday. That's good for us, as it's easier to take them, but it's bad if they've decided they can trim their timings and get there just in time to jump on and go. So we've got to be on the mark and right on top of them.

'The boat is in exactly the same condition as when we last saw it: the blinds are down, everything is buttoned up on the device. There's no reason to believe it's been moved, or that the Romeos have gone.'

Lotfi's mind was elsewhere. 'What about the police, Nick? What about what happened to you? Do you think they have made a connection between you and the boat?'

'I really don't know. We just have to focus on what we're doing. Nothing has changed for me. We have a job to do, an important job. The police are at Vauban – so what? They're here for the boat, we're here for the *hawallada* and the cash. If we do our job properly they won't even know we exist. When, or if, they do, that's when I'll start flapping. It's a tall order, but we don't have a choice.'

Lotfi gently tapped his brother's arm once more. 'But Nick and I, we are taller.'

He was clearly very pleased not to be going in the back of the Scudo.

'Situation. Greaseball and the int from the recycling bins both said the police presence could just be routine, because Curly's used the boat to smuggle heroin.

'And because it's moved about quite a bit these last few days, the police have taken an interest. It went from its normal parking place in Vauban to Marseille to pick up the Romeos from the Algiers ferry, then back home to Vauban, then to BSM. I reckon they moved back because of the alarm last night. The Romeos were spooked big-time, and I think Curly used it as an excuse to scurry back home.'

Hubba-Hubba adjusted himself in his seat. 'But why use a boat that is known to the police? That's crazy . . .'

'Fuck knows, mate. I asked Greaseball and he said the Romeos didn't know the boat was known, and laughed. Maybe him and Curly were so desperate to make a few dollars they just forgot to tell them that the *Ninth of May* had form. Who knows, who cares?'

Lotfi did. 'Why, if they are getting paid for helping the Romeos, does Greaseball become the source?'

'That I don't know. What I do know is that he's protected, so he probably has no choice – and maybe he thinks he'll get to keep some of the money. '

Neither of them could keep a straight face as Lotfi gave out a low, '*Booooom.*'

I grinned too. I couldn't agree more. 'It's just a shame that Greaseball won't be on board when we make that call.'

Hubba-Hubba looked as disappointed as I felt.

'So, I reckon that if they don't know the police have eyes on them, we've got to assume that everything from the collectors' point of view is still going to plan, and they're off to Nice tomorrow.'

I pressed on. 'Enemy forces. We now have Curly on the list and, of course, the police. Also, don't forget our last enemy. Watch your third-party awareness . . .

'Execution general outline. Phase one is getting this van in position, which has to be pretty soon, before the car park fills up, so we've got time to manoeuvre you into a good spot before it gets busy. Phase two, triggering the collectors and taking them to Nice, or wherever they're going to go. Phase three, the lift of the *hawallada*, and the drop-off. Phase four, setting up for the last collect in Cannes.'

I saw Lotfi's fingers getting ready for the next few clicks. 'Phase one, positioning the van.' I explained that I needed the Scudo to nosey-park in one of the spaces near the archway so that the rear door windows faced the fishing boats, with Hubba-Hubba already in the back and Lotfi driving. 'You guys need to meet up somewhere near the rail station.' I pointed at Lotfi. 'Leave your car there, then drive Hubba-Hubba into position. The car park barrier comes down at six, so make sure you leave the parking ticket in the cab with some cash. Work out where you're going to leave it in the vehicle, but leave it out of sight. And remember, there could be eyes looking at you from inside that Renault.'

I turned to Hubba-Hubba. 'For the same reason, just be careful and don't rush coming out of the back of here. You can have a practice later. Make sure you have the trigger on the quay, and be able to give direction if the Romeos are foxtrot or even

295

mobile at that archway. Who knows? Curly might have a car and give them a lift.'

Hubba-Hubba nodded intently.

'So then, phase two, triggering the collectors. On the stand-by from Hubba-Hubba, I want you, Lotfi, to cover the rail station. You don't have to be on it physically all the time; you can be hovering about having a coffee somewhere, doing whatever you want to do, but make sure you have eyes on it within a minute. And, of course, make sure your car is nearby so you can react to whatever the Romeos do. I'm going to be doing the same, but at the bus station.

'Phase three, taking the collectors to the *hawallada*. We're going to have to do exactly the same as we planned before, and that's why Hubba-Hubba needs to be in the back here, because I want us all in our own vehicles today. Does that make sense?'

Hubba-Hubba nodded at Lotfi, pleased there was a tactical decision behind my choice.

I ran through all the RV drills if we got split during the take. They were the same as yesterday's, but I covered them anyway.

'Any questions?'

None.

'Phase four, the lift and the drop-off. Same as yesterday. We don't know where the *hawallada* is going to be, we've just got to think on our feet. If there's one of us, if there's three of us, it doesn't matter. Whoever's there will just have to improvise. The most important thing is, we must get these people. I've got two cartridges left for my pen, so I'm going to need a spare from one of you. We can redistribute the stuff tomorrow.'

Lotfi fished in his jacket pocket.

'Any questions? All right, service and support. Remember the radio frequency change at midnight. Remember fresh batteries. Remember full fuel tanks. Remember the pager number. And please, Lotfi, put in a good word with God for us again.'

He shrugged his shoulders. 'There is no need. I already have.'

'Then ask him if he wants to give us a hand sorting out the arrangements.'

Hubba-Hubba sparked up. 'We are going to prepare it here?'

'Why not? It's as a good a place as any. Besides, it won't take more than half an hour. All we have to do is use one of the blankets to cut off the rear from the cab, and make a small aperture through the paint on one of the rear windows. Easy.'

We sat in the dark now that Hubba-Hubba had closed the glove compartment.

'But the problem there is,' I poked Hubba-Hubba in the shoulder, 'no matter how small the aperture, there is always the risk of compromise. Kids are a nightmare: they always seem to be exactly the same height as the aperture. And when they've thrown a wobbler at their mother, they'll always stop and turn just in time to notice half an eye looking out at them from a hole in the van parked next to them. That normally freaks them out and they scream – which, of course, pisses the mother off even more, and she doesn't believe the kid's story of eyeballs looking at them and drags them away.'

Hubba-Hubba conferred with Lotfi. He looked confused. 'Nick, what is a wobbler?'

'A paddy.' He still didn't get it.

Lotfi gobbed off some Arabic as Hubba-Hubba nodded intently.

I leant forward and poked him in the same spot once more. 'And that's the least you'll be wanting to throw after a few hours staring out of the back of this thing.'

43

We all exited the Scudo.

'Lotfi, I need you to keep a lookout on the road while I sort out the back with Hubba-Hubba, OK?'

'Of course.' He walked to the parking area entrance as we put the van space light back in place to see what we were doing, and started to use gaffer tape to fix up one of the dark patterned, furry nylon blankets Hubba-Hubba had bought so that it hung from the roof just behind the two cab seats.

Hubba-Hubba was leaning in from the left, and me from the right, as he whispered questions about his new job to the sound of gaffer tape being pulled away from its reel. 'Won't my eyes be seen from outside if I'm looking through the aperture?'

'No, mate, it doesn't work like that if we do it correctly. It'll be pitch black inside here if we seal the blanket down the sides. You just need to keep your head back a bit, especially if there's a kid throwing a wobbler next to you.'

'What about noise? What if I have to move, what if I get a cramp?'

'That is a problem, mate, because if you move too fast the wagon can rock. The slightest movement can be detected. Even when these things are purpose-built inside a van. If you have to, just do it really slowly. You must keep the noise down in there.

'Normally these vans would be lined with foam, stuff like that, to absorb the noise. But for you there is going to be jack shit. You'll just have to take your boots off and lay out the spare blanket.'

'Jack shit . . . Jack shit. Yes, I like this saying.'

'And talking of shit, don't. Sorry. No food, just water, you can't afford to need a dump.' I explained the logistics. 'Make sure you take some empty bottles to piss into. Dumping is going to make too much noise, too much movement, and you won't be able to keep the trigger. And you can't just dump in your jeans, because you need to get out and join in the take.'

Hubba-Hubba couldn't resist. 'Have you ever had to dump during one of these triggers?'

'Twice. Once on purpose, because there was nothing I could do about it. I was just about to trigger someone and I couldn't hold it in any longer. It didn't matter, because I wasn't in the take, just the trigger, so I was going to be driven away.'

Another length of gaffer tape was ripped off the roll. 'And the other?'

'Let's just say it was lucky I had a long coat on.'

The blanket was now hanging from the roof and we were starting to tape down the sides. Even with half of it hanging down and the rest gathered on the floor, I could make out the picture I was faced with in the dull light. 'Where the fuck did you get this?' I pulled out the blanket from the bottom to expose the remainder of the furry dogs playing snooker.

'They were all I could get in the time. . .' He giggled as he realised how stupid it looked, and I couldn't help but join in.

I forced myself to get serious. 'Where's your spray paint?'

'In the passenger door compartment.'

'OK. You need to seal off just a little more down your side.'

I climbed out of the van and walked round to the right hand door, to the sound of ripping gaffer tape as he got to work. By the time I had got round to the back again, Hubba-Hubba was sitting on the side door sill.

'What we need to do now, mate, is scrape a small hole at the bottom of the right hand window, in the left hand corner. That way the aperture is roughly in the centre of the rear, and you'll get a better perspective.'

I shook the paint can and the ball bearing mixer inside rattled about. 'Keep it in the back in case you need to make it smaller once you're in position.'

Less than five minutes later, and with the use of Hubba-Hubba's thumb nail, it was done: a nice little scrape, a centimetre long, ran along the bottom of the right hand window.

'Once you've triggered the Romeos, just crawl under the blanket, check first it's clear, and climb out. You've got the Renault to think about, and we might as well keep the blanket in position seeing as it's so interesting.'

Hubba-Hubba stayed in the back as I got out and slid the side door shut, and the interior light died. I moved to the driver's seat and could hear him moving about inside.

I opened the glove compartment for some light. 'OK, mate, have a go at getting out.'

He started to worm his way under the blanket, trying to keep low. When he was half way, he stopped and fished down the front of his shirt, pulling out his charm. 'It keeps doing this.' He lay where he was, checking the clasp.

'H, can I ask you a question?'

He looked up, surprised, and nodded.

'I think I understand Lotfi but,' I indicated his little beaded palm, 'where does this fit in? Are you religious – you know, a paid-up Muslim?'

He concentrated once more on his repairs. 'Of course, there is only one God. To be a true Muslim doesn't mean we all have to be like Lotfi. Salvation is attained not by faith but by works.' He took the charm to his teeth, biting down on the metal before fiddling with it some more.

'You see, when I die I will be able to say the Shahada with

the same conviction as he will. Do you know what I am talking about?' He raised his head again. 'You heard the old guard say it in Algeria. *"La ilaha ill-Allah, Muhammad-ur rasul-ullah."* For you, that means: "There is no God but Allah, and Muhammad is the apostle of Allah." That is the Shahada, the first and greatest teaching of Islam. I just said that to you with true sincerity, and that is what makes me just as good a Muslim as him.' He fastened the chain, and gave it an experimental tug.

'When my book of destiny is weighed it will show God that I was also a good man, and my reward will be the same as his, crossing the bridge to Paradise. Our Paradise is not like yours – a cloud to sit on, a harp to play – it is a perfumed garden of material and sensual delights, surrounded by rivers and fountains playing. Sounds good, yes?' He put the charm back around his neck. 'Lotfi would be able to tell you what Suras that is in. But before I get there, I have to live this life.' The charm was now securely back on and he lifted it up for me to see. 'And this gives me all the help I need.'

He replaced the chain around his neck before finishing his crawl up into the passenger seat.

'What does Lotfi think of all that?' I was puzzled. 'How come you two are so different? I mean, you with the charm and him with the Qur'ān?'

He smiled as he fought with the seat, jerking himself forwards, trying to get the thing to move as he pressed down on the seat adjuster, so there was more room to crawl into the cab. As the seat finally gave in, I could see where he had hidden the cash from Gumaa. 'We were both at a Muslim school together – you know, sitting there cross-legged on the floor, learning to recite the Qur'ān from memory. I would have been like him, if it wasn't for the fact that the words just fell out of my head as quickly as they tried to put them in. So I was thrown out of school and our mother taught me with my sister. Our father had died of TB, years before.' He looked directly into my eyes. 'You see, going to a religious school is not just about faith. For a family cursed by poverty, it is a way out –

301

boys are fed and cared for. Our mother saw it as the only way for us to survive.'

'But how did you learn English? I mean, most people in your shoes are still—'

He laughed gently to himself. 'You know, the first pair of shoes I ever had were from Lotfi. They were given to him at school.' His smile turned to an expression of infinite sadness. 'Our mother died a few months after Khalisah was beaten. She never was the same after that – none of us were.'

He put his hand on my shoulder. 'But we stayed together, Nick. That is because the inheritance our mother left us was love for each other. We are a family first, no matter what disagreements we may have, no matter what pain we may suffer. Because we have love.'

I thought a bit about my inheritance, but decided to shut the fuck up.

He tapped his chest. 'He hates this. He says I will not go to Paradise, but to Gahenna, hell, instead. But he is wrong, I think.' His eyes sparkled. 'I hope . . .'

He paused for a moment, but I kept silent. These boys were making a habit of saying stuff that came a bit too close for comfort.

'Lotfi is not right about everything, but neither am I. And it was Lotfi who gave up what he had to take us both to Cairo, to our aunt, and to school. That's why I speak English. We are a family, Nick. We learnt long ago to meet in the middle, because otherwise the family is lost. And we had a promise to keep, that we made as children.'

He dug into his jeans pocket before pointing a clenched fist at me.

'What is it?'

'Ketamine, you needed some more, no?'

44

The square was near the bus station in the new part of Antibes. I sat in my car in a roadside parking space with my hat and sunglasses on and listened to the two of them as they put the Scudo in place, Hubba-Hubba giving Lotfi instructions as he manoeuvred the wheel. 'Back, back, back, stop, stop.' I'd asked them to communicate in English so I knew what was happening. Finally everything was to Hubba-Hubba's satisfaction. 'H has the trigger. I can't see the target, but I will be able to give a stand-by as soon as they move along the quay, and can give direction at the archway. The Renault is still on the wall. It's dark blue. N, acknowledge.'

I put my left hand down to my jeans belt and hit the pressle. 'Roger that, that's N foxtrot. L, be careful.'

'Roger that. That's L, foxtrot to check the obvious.' He was on his way to confirm the *Ninth of May* was still there. Just because the police were, it didn't automatically mean the boat was. The only way for him to do that was to go up on the wall where the van was, or hug the port side of the wall so he was in dead ground to the van along the quay. But that would take him in direct line of sight to the boat. He opted for the wall and brassing it out. He wouldn't be there for more than a minute, and it had to be done.

I got out of the Mégane and bought myself a twenty-four-hour parking ticket. The last thing I wanted was to come back here and find the car had been towed away. I had also learnt a lesson yesterday when I should have pre-bought tickets in both directions in case the timings were tight for the Romeos when they caught the train, and there wasn't enough time to get a ticket without them seeing me. I wasn't making the same mistake today: both Lotfi and I had paid a visit to the station earlier this morning.

I left the parking ticket on the dashboard and glanced down at traser: seven forty-seven. Dodging the dog shit, I headed across the square in search of a café. I was ready for some coffee and croissants. It was going to be a sunny day; the birds were singing in the morning's first light, traffic was moving, people were going to work, most with sunglasses on, and a lot with small dogs in tow.

Several of the cafés were open, their canvas or plastic awnings out to shade the handful of customers who were already getting stuck in to the coffee and newspapers.

I walked over the square towards a large corner café that was all glass front, with huge patio doors and wicker chairs outside, and ordered a large *crème* along with a couple of croissants, paying for it there and then in case I got a stand-by. It was time just to sit and relax in the shade until Hubba-Hubba gave us the hurry-up.

Lotfi came on the net just as the croissants were put on the table. He was walking: I could hear French conversation and the beep of a scooter in the background. 'This is L. The obvious is still static, blinds down, gangway up. H, N, acknowledge.'

I put my hand down on the Sony and waited to hear the double-click from H before I gave mine.

Lotfi came back. 'I'm going for coffee. H, what would you like – cappuccino?'

There was no reply to that – or, at least, not on the net.

Cars trundled around the large grass- and tree-covered

304

square. The sore on my stomach was trying hard to scab but the hammer on my Browning wasn't going to let it. No matter, two more days and the weapon could go into the sea. I felt into my hairline above my forehead; at least a scab had sealed the headbutt split.

I drank coffee and watched doorsteps being washed, and rat dogs being walked by their owners and having a dump everywhere they could. I could sit here for an hour or so and no one would see it as anything out of the ordinary.

I started to think about the police but cut away quickly. If they planned to do anything we would know about it soon enough. And there was fuck all we could do about them in the meantime.

I stretched out my legs under the table, and thought about Hubba-Hubba cramped up in the back of the small van. Although Lotfi and I were covering the two stations, we also had to make sure we were close enough to give him support if someone fancied getting their hands on a new van for minimal outlay. We'd have to get in there quick, mainly to help Hubba-Hubba, but also to salvage the operation.

The sun rose gradually over the buildings and began to warm the right side of my face. I took another sip of coffee and dunked the end of a croissant.

Lotfi was exactly on time with the eight o'clock call. 'Radio check. H?'

Click, click.

I could hear a dog barking in the background. That was all they seemed to do around here, bark and crap. I'd not seen one chase after a stick.

'N?'

I reached under my new green Cap 3000 sweatshirt and double-clicked on my belt, then sat back, stubbed at the croissant crumbs on the napkin with a coffee-wet finger and waited for the stand-by.

Another twenty-seven minutes passed and I was waiting for Lotfi to start the next radio check. Hubba-Hubba came on the net, his voice agitated. 'H has lost the trigger . . . There's a truck in the way. H has lost the trigger. N, L, acknowledge.'

I hit the pressle. 'Roger that. N's going for the trigger. L, acknowledge.'

Click, click.

I got up and started to move as I wiped my cup and took the napkin. Nearly running through the old town, I climbed the stone steps in the small, cobblestoned square. As my head got level with the concrete between the two sides of the ramparts, I saw the Renault, still reversed against the wall, now with a Skoda parked to its right.

Two other people were up there with me, old men waffling to each other by the rampart overlooking the port, where the wrought ironwork met the stone. I hit the pressle before I got too close as I took the last few steps up on to the wall.

'N has the trigger. N has the trigger. H, acknowledge.'

Click, click.

I got up top and looked out over the port, between the van and the Skoda. I gave myself some time to admire the effect of the dazzling sun bouncing off the water around so many hulls. If Hubba-Hubba had any sense, he'd be using the time to rest his eyes.

I checked that the blinds and gangway were still the same, then down over the wall and left, into the dead ground, to make sure the Romeos hadn't decided to move out in the minute or so it had taken to regain the trigger, and weren't walking along the quay. I could see the Scudo, reversed into a space so that the rear blacked out windows faced towards me. The vehicle blocking Hubba-Hubba's view was a small, refrigerated van picking up crates of fish from the boats. I got my eyes back on the *Ninth of May* as a passionate conversation was developing on the other side of the police van, and saw movement on the *Lee*. Three kids, aged from ten to twelve, were doing boaty jobs on the deck. Two adults, whom I presumed were their

306

parents, were in chairs at the back, drinking coffee.

Still playing the tourist, I stared out at the fort overlooking the mass of masts and glittering hulls. In less than five minutes the fish van was on its way back through the archway. I moved back towards the steps. 'Hello, H, that's the truck clear. Acknowledge.'

I stayed up top, waiting for Hubba-Hubba to take over as the two old men sauntered past behind me, their arms flying around as they put the world to rights. They disappeared down the stairs with their dogs in tow. I suddenly felt naked, with my back to the van and no one else here.

'H has the trigger. N, acknowledge.'

Click, click.

I'd finished my bit of tourism and headed back to the steps, wondering where I'd go now for another brew.

Three paces down I got *click, click, click, click* in my earpiece. I smiled, slowed down and hit the pressle. 'Is that a stand-by from H?'

Click, click.

Shit, they were early.

'Are they both foxtrot?'

Click, click.

'Are they dressed the same as yesterday?'

Nothing.

'Are they carrying a bag?'

Click, click.

Then he came on the net. 'Romeo one has the same bag. It's full. They're both wearing jeans.' The net went dead momentarily. 'That's approaching the archway.'

I stayed put, smiled some more, and sat on the stone step. 'N can take, N can take. L, where are you?'

'Nearly at the station, nearly there.' His voice merged with the passing traffic.

'H still has Romeo One and Two, at the archway . . . Wait . . . wait, that's now crossing the road, towards me. They're staying this side of the wall.'

The radio went dead as I started down the stairs again into the square and right towards the archway. If they had a camera in the Renault, I bet it had been snapping away big-time.

45

I got to the arch and waited for information. It wasn't long before Hubba-Hubba came back on the air. 'That's Romeo One and Two in the car park, following the wall and unsighted to me.'

I went through the archway, turned left, and could see their backs immediately among the lines of vehicles.

'N has Romeo One, Romeo Two foxtrot. Half-way along the old wall, generally towards the rail station. L, acknowledge.'

An out-of-breath Lotfi did just that. 'L has the trigger on the station.'

'Roger that, L. Romeo One, black leather jacket on jeans, carrying the bag. Romeo Two, brown suede jacket on jeans. L, acknowledge.'

Click, click.

'That's both Romeos now temporary unsighted.'

I moved to the right as I passed Hubba-Hubba's blacked out windows, trying to get a better view now they were hidden by some coaches.

'Both Romeos still temporary unsighted, still generally towards the rail station.'

There was nowhere else for them to go just now, unless they could walk through walls. Hubba-Hubba would be crawling his way under the snooker dogs now and moving out of the car park so there would be no delay when he needed to go mobile. He had better do it right. The van could see him from up there.

They appeared the other side of the coaches.

'Stand by, stand by. N has both Romeos approaching the end of the wall. No one acknowledge.'

I started to cut in left, towards the wall now, so I'd be more or less behind them when they hit the end of it, with freedom to go in any direction. Romeo One was clearly nervous.

I hit the pressle. 'That's at the end of the wall and still straight, generally towards the station. Approaching the first option left – they are aware. No one acknowledge.'

I was now behind them by about thirty metres as they passed boat kit and insurance shops before stopping at the junction to let a vehicle out. 'That's held option left, still intending straight, towards the station.'

They carried on over once the vehicle had passed. 'That's now foxtrot still straight.'

Getting to the junction myself, I overheard a voice straight out of *EastEnders* as a crew-cut thirty-something with a black nylon Docklands bomber jacket gobbed off on his mobile. 'I don't fucking care. What's the matter wiv you, you deaf or somefink?' Further down the junction a Brit-plated truck with pallets of Happy Shopper goods was being unloaded for 'Geoffrey's of London', a shop that seemed to supply baked beans and plastic cheese to the huge numbers of Brits who worked on the boats.

I got back on the net. 'That's Romeo One and Romeo Two still foxtrot, approaching the main before the station. L, can you at the main?'

The last leg of the route was uphill and they would be unsighted to me for far too long once they crossed the main as it was higher, dead ground to me.

He could. 'L has, L has. Romeo One. Romeo Two. At the main, they're crossing, approaching the station.'

The Romeos were unsighted to me now as I moved uphill

and the traffic screamed past in both directions above me. The station was the other side of the main. In front of it was a bay for taxis and a small car park.

'That's H now complete. N, acknowledge.'

Click, click.

Lotfi kept up the commentary. 'That's approaching the station.'

I got to the main and also watched them while I waited for the green man and Lotfi kept gobbing off on the net. 'That's both Romeos complete the station, unsighted to L.'

The green man flashed, the bleeps cried out, and the traffic stopped reluctantly. I gobbed off and smiled as if I'd just heard a joke on the phone. 'Roger that. N will take. H, go now, mate, go now. H, acknowledge.' I got a double click and hoped I'd done the right thing by taking a chance and sending him straight on to Nice. This surveillance stuff wasn't a science, and decisions had to be made on what you knew at the time. All I knew was that the traffic was horrendous and the train would get there far quicker than any road vehicle, and I needed someone else there to back me. If I'd made a mistake and they were going for Cannes, or anywhere else for that matter, Lotfi had better be able to fly in that Focus of his and keep up with the train.

The old station had undergone quite a renovation within the last couple of years. It had retained its original shape, but the inside looked very modern and clean, with glass everywhere, glass walls, glass counters, plate-glass doors. As I went in, the Romeos weren't to the left by the ticket machines, or to the right where there was a small café and news-stand.

Four kids were smoking round one of the tables, listening to dance music on their radio. I could see a section of both of the platforms and the two tracks between. Time in recce is seldom wasted: I knew the platform nearest me would be going towards Cannes. What I was hoping was that both of the Romeos were going down into the tunnel to the left, and would emerge on the far side platform, which would mean they were off to Nice.

I got on the radio as I checked the timetables. 'That's the Romeos on the platforms. L, can you see them?'

'L's foxtrot.'

I waited in the cover of the station listening to an NRG Radio jingle booming out from the café area.

Lotfi came on the net. 'Stand by, stand by. L has the two Romeos on the far platform. They're static the tunnel exit. N, acknowledge.'

Click, click.

The framed and Perspex-covered timetable on the wall said the next train for Nice was at nine twenty-seven, stopping at Gare Riquier, just seven hundred metres or so from the target shop on Boulevard Jean XIII. Maybe I'd made the right choice in sending Hubba-Hubba there, after all.

I waited near the timetable and listened to the high-caffeine breakfast show blaring from the radio. I didn't want to move anywhere else now, because if I crossed the concourse towards the café the two Romeos would be able to see me.

Posters carried pictures of happy families going on trains and really enjoying themselves, all with unnaturally perfect teeth. I studied them for a couple of minutes before Lotfi came back on. 'Stand by, stand by. Train's approaching, no change on the Romeos. I'm going complete. N, acknowledge.'

Click, click.

The train entered the station from the direction of Cannes. The dirty blue and aluminium carriages squeaked to a halt. I ran out on to the platform, turned left, and headed for the tunnel. Through the grimy glass of the carriages I followed the two Romeos' dark faces as they waited to step aboard with the dozen or so others alongside them.

I raced down the steps and along the dimly lit tunnel, passing the people who'd just got off the train. It looked perfectly natural in this environment: who didn't run to catch a train?

Taking the steps two at a time and making sure my peak was down low, I didn't look at their carriage, but carried on and entered the next one along. Taking my seat immediately to keep out of the way, I kept an eye on the tunnel just in case they'd changed their minds, or were putting in some anti-surveillance. The train doors closed before it shunted forward and off we went as I tried to control my breathing. 'L, we're mobile. Go for it now, go! Acknowledge.'

Click, click.

He'd be hitting the coast road on his way to Nice, hot on the heels of Hubba-Hubba, who should have been at least a third of the way there by now.

I couldn't see the Romeos through the glass of the connecting door this time, but I'd be able to see if they got out at one of the four or five stops on the way.

We emerged from the shade of the station building and the morning sun burned through the glass, making me squint, even with my sun-gigs and hat on. I just sat there and watched the Mediterranean go past as we travelled the twenty minutes towards Nice.

Gare Riquier wasn't like the station at Antibes, an old building made new: it was still old, an unmanned pick-up and drop-off point for commuters.

The two Romeos disembarked along with a woman in a big flowery dress, dragging a tartan shopping trolley behind her. Both now with gigs on, they walked out of the station and left towards the busy road, which was the main drag I'd used to get up to L'Ariane and the safe house. I followed them out. The main was about forty metres away, and the noise of traffic was almost deafening. Trucks, cars and scooters fought for space on the tarmac in both directions as their exhausts hazed the air. The Romeos stopped about half-way, dug out a map from the side pocket of the bag, and got their bearings. If they were going to the target shop, it would be left at the main, straight on for about four hundred metres, then right on to Boulevard Jean XIII. I waited by a wall smothered in spray-painted graffiti in both French and Arabic. I imagined the good news was that they all fucked girls, but I couldn't be sure.

313

The Romeos put away their map and turned left at the main, under the railway bridge, before crossing over and heading north along the right-hand side of the street, maybe to keep in the shade, maybe because they should be turning right eventually anyway. Romeo One had the bag over his shoulder and was still looking like a cat on hot bricks as he checked left and right of him, still seeing nothing. They carried on past rows of low end cafés, banks and shops, everything that fed the east side of town, all very much the poor relations of their counterparts in Cannes or downtown Nice.

Smaller roads fed the main from both sides and the odd tree stuck out along the pavements. But instead of grass around them, there was just mud and windblown McDo cartons, dog shit and butt ends. It was a lot easier to do the follow here than it had been in Monaco; one, because there was less CCTV to worry about, and two, because there were many more people moving around in all directions. Wherever they were heading, they were obviously late.

I tried a radio check but there was nothing from either Lotfi or Hubba-Hubba. I wasn't expecting there to be, but it would have been nice if they'd been here somewhere to back me.

They crossed several small junctions on the right, then stopped at a larger one that had lights, waiting with the impatient herd, which was growing as vehicles hurtled past and air brakes hissed. There were a lot more brown and black faces here than in Monaco, and the two Romeos weren't getting a second glance. They took the opportunity to check their map again, while I took particular interest in the range of mattresses in the window of a waxy pine bed shop. They should be turning right at the next junction, which was a crossroads, to get on to Jean XIII. From there the target shop was roughly three hundred metres up the boulevard on the right.

46

Romeo One still looked around as if he was expecting the sky to fall on his head. He lit up as Romeo Two went back to the map.

The green man flashed and they crossed. I gave another radio check before following on behind. 'Hello, anyone, this is N. Radio check, radio check.'

Nothing.

They turned on to Jean XIII and became temporary unsighted. I quickened my pace and fought with the flow of pedestrian traffic to get eyes on again as French and Arabic music fought its way out of cafés and cheap clothes shops. It was risky to do so this early in the take, because of third-party awareness. No matter where you are, someone is always watching. But I had to get in there, I had to keep on top of them, being so close to the target and *hawallada* whom we still had to ID.

I started across the road at the junction with Jean XIII, dicing with the traffic. A scooter had to swerve to get out of my way. The Romeos were still foxtrot towards the target, still on the right. I got to the other side, turned right, then had them once more. Being on the opposite side of the road gave me a better perspective of what they were up to than if I'd been directly behind them.

The shops were all selling pots and pans, pedal bins and bundles of brightly coloured plastic coat hangers, and the Romeos mingled well with the early shoppers who'd just stocked up on toilet cleaner and bin liners.

The net burst into life. 'That's H turning on to the boulevard. Radio check, radio check.'

It was a relief to hear his voice. I hit the pressle on my Sony. 'N has Romeo One and Romeo Two on the right on the boulevard. They're at the Café Noir, on the right. H, acknowledge.' Just as I released the pressle, I saw his Scudo pass me.

'H has, H has. I'm going for the trigger.'

I double-clicked him as I continued taking the Romeos. Both of them were checking shop numbers to the right and left of them. We came to a small street market selling fruit and veg, and the Romeos disappeared now and again between barrows of apples and melons and street traders sounding like French Del Boys.

I gave a running commentary for Hubba-Hubba and also, I hoped, for Lotfi, who at some stage was going to rejoin the net and would need to get up to speed on the situation. 'N still has Romeo One and Romeo Two. On the right at the fruit market, still straight, towards the shop. H, acknowledge.'

Click, click.

Ten seconds later he came back on the air. 'That's H static, thirty metres past the shop on the right. The target is a fabric store, one old man, Arab, white shirt, buttoned up, no tie. That's H foxtrot.'

I double-clicked him. The Romeos had stopped at a small junction and were still checking numbers. Romeo One scanned the crowd of shoppers as Hubba-Hubba came back up on the net.

'H has the trigger. N, acknowledge.'

Great news. 'Roger that. Romeo One, Romeo Two, still on the right, approaching the end of the market. Can you after the market?'

There was a gap while Hubba-Hubba worked it out.

Click, click.

'Roger that. That's ten short, still on the right.'

I shut up now and waited for Hubba-Hubba to see them. They passed the last stall and had gone no more than three or four paces before he was back. 'H has Romeo One, Romeo Two.'

Now I could drop back a little and let Hubba-Hubba take them into the shop. 'That's now fifty short, still on the right.'

I could still see the Romeos, but the fact that Hubba-Hubba had the trigger gave me the freedom to think about what I was going to do next. I just hoped that Lotfi got here soon.

'That's twenty-five short, still on the right, checking numbers. They're slowing down, they're slowing down.'

I kept my head low as I listened, pretending to window-shop as the world passed by. There was no need to look directly at the targets. I was being told what was going on, and it would be a nightmare if we had eye to eye.

'That's approaching the target. Wait, wait. That's at the target, going complete . . . that's complete the target. They're talking to the white shirt. Wait, wait.' The cry of a baby and a flood of female Arabic burst over the net. I heard their waffle get weaker: he was walking away from it. 'H is foxtrot, I can't hold the trigger, I can't hold the trigger.'

I quickened my pace.

'Roger that. N going for the trigger. You take the rear, acknowledge.'

Click, click.

As I got nearer I could see what the problem was. Hubba-Hubba was crossing from left to right over the road just past the target: he'd been lurking in a doorway, which two head-scarfed women with long coats and a pram were trying to get through.

He reached the junction, which was two shop fronts to the left of the target, and disappeared. His route would take

317

him round to the rear of the shops and the wide alleyway.

Security was now definitely being sacrificed for efficiency as I stopped to have a look at the display outside a hardware shop. Ladders on the pavement leant against the wall, and brooms and brushes sprouted between the rungs. No matter; at least I could see the shop. 'N has the trigger.'

Click, click.

I could also see the conversation that was happening between the unknown in the white shirt and Romeo One and Romeo Two. When that finished, they started to walk towards the rear of the dimly lit shop. I had to take off my glasses so I could see inside clearly. It looked almost empty, with not much more stock than a few rolls of multicoloured fabric lining the walls. They passed a long glass counter with lengths of cut material all over the place, then another man emerged from the rear internal door with a group who'd been standing in the shadows.

'Stand by, stand by. Unknowns on target.'

Then I realized they weren't unknown. It was the man with the goatee I'd seen get out of the Lexus on Wednesday night in Juan-les-Pins, and go into the Fiancée of the Desert. His smaller, bald-headed driver was standing to his right, still looking bored.

Goatee leant forward and spoke into Romeo Two's ear without any greeting. I got back on the net. 'That's a possible Romeo Three. Tall, Arab, black on jeans, and goatee beard, with three or four unknowns.'

There was a little more movement in the gloom. My view was abruptly blocked as a truck rumbled between us. By the time it had passed, everybody was starting to pile back through the internal door.

'They're heading to the back of the shop,' I said. 'That's all three Romeos unsighted, could be coming your way. H, acknowledge.'

'Nearly there, I'm nearly there. Wait out.'

It had to be the *hawallada*. They were whispering the password.

I moved away from the hardware shop. It was pointless being exposed to the white shirt who had now returned to the glass counter. I could still keep the trigger from a distance. I turned back the way I'd come, making sure I could still see the place.

'Hello, this is L. Radio check, radio check.'

Relief wasn't the word for it as I felt for the pressle and stopped by the door of a flat, behind a news-stand. 'N has the trigger on the shop. Where are you?'

'Approaching the target from the main.'

'Roger that. Wait.'

I kept my eyes on the shop as a group of teenagers in the world's baggiest jeans ambled past with Walkmans in their ears and cigarettes in their hands. It gave me time to think before I hit my pressle.

'L, sit rep. I have the trigger front. Romeo One and Romeo Two are complete the shop with a possible Romeo Three. Arab, tall, black on blue and a goatee. H is foxtrot and getting the trigger rear. Go static and stay complete in case Romeo Three goes mobile. L, acknowledge.'

Click, click.

As soon as that finished, Hubba-Hubba came on the net. 'H has the trigger.' I heard him trying to control his breathing so he could be heard clearly.

'N, acknowledge. N, acknowledge.'

Click, click.

'That's L static. First junction past the market and can take in all directions. N, acknowledge.'

Click, click.

I guessed he was on the junction facing the boulevard now to be able to do that, so he could come on to the avenue and turn left, right, in all directions.

Hubba-Hubba started to give plate checks in case any of the vehicles behind the shop went mobile with the possible *hawallada.* 'White Mercedes van, Zulu Tango one five six seven. Large scrape on the left-hand side. Blue Lexus, Alpha Yankee Tango one three. Highly polished.'

I was right, it was him.

'Stand by, stand by – movement by the vehicles.'

The net stayed open for a few seconds and I could hear Hubba-Hubba's laboured breathing and the rustle of his clothes before it went dead. There was a long pause and I could feel my heart go up a gear as I waited for the next stand-by to say vehicles had gone mobile. Lotfi would be doing the same, and his engine would be running in preparation. The world just walked on past as we both waited on Hubba-Hubba.

The net crackled into life. 'That's an Arab, short, fat, brown wool on jeans. Foxtrot from the shop. Wait . . . He's going to the Mercedes, he's heading for the van. Wait . . . wait . . . no good, I think he's seen me, he's using a cell. That's me foxtrot. Lost the trigger, lost the trigger.'

I hit the pressle with my eyes still on the front of the target. 'H, go complete. Stand by to take anything that goes mobile. L, go—'

Two guys exited from the front of the shop. The expression on their dark-skinned faces said they were on a mission.

'Stand by, stand by. That's two unknowns from the target front, both Arab and black leather. That's right, towards the junction. H, go complete, get out of there. H, acknowledge.'

Click, click.

Lotfi burst back on the net. 'L is mobile.' His voice was tight with tension and I understood his concern.

The two guys from the shop had reached the junction and turned right. I hit the pressle. 'That's the unknowns now right at the junction, unsighted, towards the rear. H, acknowledge.'

Hubba-Hubba's voice was a whisper. 'H has the two unknowns, I can't move yet. Engine on, engine on the van.'

He was close, I could hear it.

'That's—'

The next sound was of Hubba-Hubba resisting and Arab voices shouting. There was lots of grabbing going on around the Sony as it crackled like a forest fire.

Fuck. It had gone noisy.

47

Shit, shit, shit!

I sprinted across the road, not bothering to look out for traffic. My right hand forced the Browning down into my jeans to stop it falling out, and my left held the earpiece in place. My whole being was focused on that corner, two shops to the left of the target. I got that familiar feeling in the pit of my stomach, the same sensation that always came when shit was on. I'd had it even as a kid, running away from the bigger boys who wanted to beat me up and nick my dinner money, or from an angry shopkeeper whose stuff I'd tried to lift. It was a horrible feeling: you know there's a drama, you wish it wasn't there, you know you've got to do something about it, but your legs just won't take you fast enough.

I turned the corner but saw nothing except a few people standing maybe twenty metres further down on the other side of the road. All eyes were turned to the alleyway. Screams still came over the net, mixed with shouts and the sounds of a struggle. Everything was in Arabic but none of it was from Hubba-Hubba. Then I heard him in the background. He was in pain, he was getting filled in, he was getting subdued.

My mouth was dry as I drew down and, alert to the third party, kept the weapon by my side. I turned the corner into the alleyway, not bothering to clear it. There wasn't time.

I was too late. The Merc van was bouncing over the potholes away from me, with one of the unknowns trying to close the rear door. More Arabic commotion streamed over the net. Even if I'd spoken the language I wouldn't have been able to understand what was being said – it was so confused and loud. But for sure Hubba-Hubba was in there. I caught a glimpse of his trainers; he was fighting back as two guys climbed on top of him, trying to keep him down in the back.

The left door was already closed, the small window covered by black plastic. The second door was pulled shut from inside; that, too, was covered. I kept running towards the rear of the shop.

The Lexus was still there. The back of the shop was closed down. Shit, who to go after, Hubba-Hubba or the *hawallada*?

Lotfi swung into the alleyway like something out of *Hill Street Blues*. Somebody somewhere would be getting on a phone to the police. I motioned with my hand, trying to get him to slow down, to stop. The vehicle nearly somersaulted over its two front wheels as he hit the brakes. His eyes looked frenzied. The growing crowd on the road turned and gawped.

Jumping out, Lotfi had his pistol up, ready to fire.

'Keep it down, for fuck's sake!' I pointed along the alleyway, which was now clear. 'The van, black plastic covering the rear windows. He's in the back. Go, go, take it.'

I turned to run back the way I'd come, shouting at him as he jumped back into the Focus. 'I'll give you directions at the boulevard, go to channel four, channel four. Go, go, go!'

I disappeared left around the corner, going back towards the boulevard. Fuck the third party now. People everywhere were stopping to rubberneck.

I got down to the corner and looked left. The van had slowed as the traffic hit the vegetable market. I turned the dial on the Sony to four and hit the pressle as I sucked in oxygen. 'L, they've gone left, they've gone left towards the main. L, acknowledge, acknowledge.'

The Focus screamed into view at the junction, Lotfi still playing cops and robbers. He was going to have to slow down before he had a crash or ran somebody over. Either would stop him being able to take. He was looking frantically left and right, trying to see where the van had gone, then looking down, probably having just remembered to change channels. I kept on sending. 'They've gone left, they've gone left towards the main.'

He didn't reply, but he must have heard me because the Focus screamed round towards the market, braking hard as the horn screamed out at people trying to cross the road in front of him, then hurtled down towards the mass of fruit buyers.

I turned right and had gone maybe twenty metres up towards the Scudo when I got a blast of screaming and ranting in my ear. I couldn't understand any of it. 'Slow down, slow down! Say again.'

I got to the wagon and started to pull at the soft steel numberplate at the rear, feeling for the key and fob taped behind it. Lotfi carried on trying to get the message across; he'd slowed down but the voice was still very high-pitched, he was really hyped up. 'L has, L has! Past the market straight for the main. They're going for the main. N, acknowledge, acknowledge.'

I double-clicked, not wanting to talk yet, in case he got more sparked up.

By now I'd extracted the key fob and hit it to release the central locking. I jumped in and began turning the Citroën round so I could back Lotfi. A cluster of third party watched; at least two were on mobiles. This was a weapons-grade screwup.

Forcing the Scudo round into the traffic and driving down towards the market, I checked my decision to go for Hubba-Hubba. It must be right: Lotfi wouldn't help me lifting Goatee. But deep down I knew we wouldn't get Goatee either way; he would be well and truly going to ground now. The job was destroyed, and I would be, too, if I got caught by the police. But what could I do about it? Abandon the two of them and just head for the airport? It was tempting. I instinctively moved my hand down to the bum-bag, making sure my docs were still with me. I could just turn round and drive straight to Nice airport, get the first plane out of here . . .

Lotfi had calmed down a bit when he came back on the net, trying hard to keep the speed and tension from his voice. 'L still has, L still has. They are approaching the main, lights are green, lights are green. No indication. Wait, wait. They're intending right, that's now right on the main, towards the autoroute. Acknowledge, acknowledge.'

Click, click.

By now I was half-way down the market. I couldn't see Lotfi ahead of me and just hoped that he was still with them and hadn't got held by the lights. I couldn't guarantee it, because he was too sparked up to give me a full commentary.

I tried to anticipate. The main drag went on for about a kilometre and a half, until it took a sharp left-hander at the bridge over the railway lines from the freight depot. If the van went that route they'd eventually hit the feeder road that followed the river towards the autoroute at the north end of town, where the safe house was.

'L still has approaching the freight station.' Despite his efforts, he was still hyped up, talking an octave above his normal voice, but at least I could understand him now.

I reached the main on red, getting right up close to the car in front in case it was a short light.

'That's now at the freight station still straight towards the autoroute. N, acknowledge.'

'Roger that, I'm held at the main.'

Click, click.

They changed. All the cars in the queue made it through, and I turned right, following Lotfi, trying to get closer and back him as he carried on with the commentary. 'That's approaching the swimming pool on the right.'

I heard the hiss of an artic's air brakes over the net.

'That's now at the swimming pool. Still straight, speed forty, forty-five. N, acknowledge.'

'Roger that, N's mobile.'

Click, click.

Railway lines appeared on my left, running into the freight station just ahead. I couldn't be that far behind them. The swimming pool was maybe three hundred metres further on and I was travelling at roughly the same speed as them in the flow of traffic.

All of a sudden I got a frenzied, 'Stop, stop, stop! That's at the lights before the railway bridge. The van's five vehicles back, I'm four behind that, lights still red. N, where are you? Where are you?'

I held down the pressle. 'The swimming pool, not far.'

'Roger that. Stand by, stand by. Lights green. Wait, wait . . . Now mobile. That's left over the bridge. Wait, wait . . . Stand by. They are going . . . Wait, wait. That's them in the right-hand lane . . . intending right, they're going to the autoroute. That's them now towards the autoroute, they are following the river to the autoroute. Acknowledge, acknowledge. N, acknowledge. Where are you?'

Click, click.

He was starting to get sparked up again as he took the van over the junction. The important thing was that he knew I understood where he was and he knew I was behind him somewhere.

The railway bridge traffic lights were about a hundred metres ahead of me as Lotfi resumed his commentary. 'Speed, sixty, sixty-five. Half-way to the autoroute turnoff. N, where are you? Where are you?'

It was time to talk, now that he'd finished manoeuvring around junctions, and was on a straight drag.

'At the bridge lights, and held.'

'Roger that, speed no change.'

They were on the dual carriageway towards L'Ariane, the

autoroute way above them and ahead, on the viaduct. If they carried on straight this side of the river, they could take the ramp for Monaco and Italy, or cross the river and head for the Cannes and Marseille ramp. I didn't care which one; it'd be much easier to take them up on the autoroute, fuck the toll booths and cameras now.

Lotfi had more to say. 'Approaching the bridge over the river, on red. We're going to be held.'

Good, I could catch up. Cigarette smoke billowed out from the car in front, and its radio blared as we waited for my lights at the railway bridge to change. 'N's mobile.'

'Roger that, N. That's at the lights, intending left. They're going to cross the river, they're going to cross the river.'

I turned right on to the fast-flowing road and the riverbed to my left. Ahead of me were the other two vehicles. I could see the autoroute viaduct ahead and accelerated up to ninety Ks, trying to close the gap. 'Stand by, stand by, lights to green . . . that's left over the river, left over the river. N, acknowledge.'

Click, click.

Lotfi's voice was still high-pitched, but slower. 'That's half-way over the bridge. They're intending right, they're intending right, not for the autoroute, intending right towards L'Ariane. N, acknowledge, where are you?'

48

Click, click.

Lotfi came back. 'Stop, stop, stop. Held at the lights, still intending towards L'Ariane. The autoroute traffic now is moving on. We are held. N, they are definitely intending right. Acknowledge, acknowledge. Where are you? What if they go into the mountains?'

It was still not the time to talk to him yet. *Click, click.*

I got my foot down and tried to make up the distance. If the van carried on further north, past L'Ariane and the built-up area, the roads became very narrow and wound up the mountains on either side. It would be hard to follow a target in that sort of terrain even with a four-car team, let alone two. It would need both of us to keep on top of the van, changing positions often so the same vehicle was never behind the target for long. At the same time, we'd have to keep close to each other, because once we got up into those hills there was no telling if we could keep communications. If the van became unsighted, we'd have to split up and look in different directions to try to find it, which would totally screw everything.

Lotfi came back on. 'Stand by, stand by. Lights to green. They're mobile, right, towards the incinerator. N, acknowledge.'

Click, click.

'Roger that, approaching the bridge, approaching the bridge.'

'Roger that, N. Still towards the incinerator. Speed four five, five zero. Increasing.'

'Roger that, roger that, I'm at the bridge, at the bridge.'

Click, click.

I turned on to the bridge and followed the line over the stony riverbed. The viaduct and the incinerator funnel towered into the sky to my right. I turned right, past the filter light, and as I followed the other side of the riverbank, I could see Lotfi's Focus about four cars back from the Merc van. Lotfi was regaining control once more. 'That's half-way towards the incinerator.'

'Roger that. N's backing. I'm now backing. Acknowledge.'

'Good, good, that's approaching the incinerator. Wait, wait, at the incinerator, still straight. Now straight towards the apartments.'

Click, click.

Lotfi was sounding a lot better now. 'That's approaching the apartments. Wait, wait. Past the first option left, speed six five, seven zero. It looks like they're not slowing down around here. N, acknowledge. N, acknowledge.'

'Roger that. That's me at the incinerator.'

'Roger that, N, that's past the second left, wait, past the third. Still straight, they're still going straight, speed no change.'

Driving past the incinerator, I saw the burnt-out shell of the Audi in the dead ground to the right of it, and the skeleton of a van a few metres away that had also been torched.

'That's now past the apartments, still straight. They're heading north, it looks like they're heading out of the city, speed no change. I'm going to need you soon to take. N, acknowledge.' He was getting sparked up again.

Click, click.

'That's now approaching the bridge on the right. Brake lights on, brake lights on! Intending right, intending right, they're going back over the river. That's now right on to the bridge. N, acknowledge. N, acknowledge.'

Click, click.

Looking along the line of the rocky riverbed, ahead of me I could see the van crossing the bridge from left to right, with the Ford Focus directly behind. Lotfi came back. 'Half-way over the bridge brake lights on, brake lights on, intending left.'

I could see the the van's rear indicators flashing.

'That's now over the bridge, they're intending left into the industrial area. I'm going—'

'Don't go with them, don't go with them! Acknowledge, acknowledge. L, acknowledge. Don't do it.'

The van disappeared as it took the first left just over the bridge. The Focus went straight as Lotfi told me what he could see down the option. 'That's the van at the horse, at the horse. They've gone straight, into the industrial area beyond the horse, somewhere to the left. I'm unsighted.'

'Roger that. N is checking, N is checking. L, acknowledge.'

I got a double-click as I saw him take the next turning left and disappear. I got to the bridge and turned right, and got a burst of air brakes and flashing headlights from an approaching truck as I crossed his front.

I didn't want Lotfi to go in there. Going into a closed area was dangerous and it might be a trap. Or they might just be stopping in there to see if anyone was following.

I was about half-way over the bridge when I heard, 'L's foxtrot.'

'Roger that. That's me on the bridge.'

As I reached the other side of the rocky riverbed I looked into the first option left and could see the horse he'd been on about. Down on the left-hand side of the road was a thirty-foot-high stone monster, prancing on his hind legs, Roman fashion. It was to the left of an entrance into what looked like a decaying light-industrial estate. To the left of the gate was a large, rundown brick warehouse with a faded, hand-painted sign running the full length of the wall, announcing it was a *brocante*, selling second-hand furniture and all sorts. There was a line of vehicles parked into the wall. Fuck it. I turned, crossing over the traffic and headed to the left of the horse and the vehicles.

The road quickly became a mud-caked, potholed nightmare with puddles of diesel and muck. At last I saw Lotfi in my wing mirror, walking down towards me from the bridge road. I swung left by the horse and backed up against the brick wall of the warehouse, in line with the other cars. It was out of sight of the industrial estate entrance, in case I was being watched, and it looked natural. I was just your everyday furniture buyer.

Lotfi was just a few metres short of the estate gates, and was going for his pistol. If he'd seen me, he certainly wasn't coming over to join me.

I powered down the window and waved to him from the Citroën like a long-lost friend, smiling and gesturing for him to cross over. It didn't look as if it was working. All I could hear was the noise of traffic rumbling over the bridge and the hissing of air brakes. He looked over to me and must have had a change of heart, because he ran reluctantly towards me, avoiding the potholes as I held out my hand in welcome from the window for the benefit of any third parties. He played his part in the pretence, but his eyes were still dancing around just like they'd done in Algeria.

I tried to calm him down and glanced at the pistol. 'Put that away, mate, get in the car.'

He ignored me.

'Get in the car.'

'No, come. That is wasting time. We've got to go and get him. Now.'

I started to plead with him through the window, and both of us had smiles on as his eyes screamed round like a pair of Catherine wheels.

'We just can't go in like that.' I gestured for him to get into the wagon. 'Look, we don't know where they are, how many of them there are. It could be a trap. Come on, get in the car, let's take our time and we'll all get out of this alive.'

But Lotfi wasn't having any of it. 'He might be dead soon. We have to—'

'I know, I know. But let's find out where he is first, so we can work out how to get him out in one piece.'

'I will not leave my brother behind.'

'We're not leaving anybody behind. Just get in the car. We've got to stay calm and work out how to get him out. Come on, you know it's the right thing to do.'

He thought about it for a couple of seconds, then walked round the front of the Citroën and climbed in beside me. He stared at the rocky riverbed to the right, where the wall of the *brocante* ended. I left him to it, changed channel back to two and listened in case Hubba-Hubba was sending. There was nothing coming over the air at all, so I switched it off and removed it from my belt as Lotfi checked chamber.

'I cannot wait any longer, he could be dead any minute. Are you coming with me?'

I turned to a heavy, nostril-breathing Lotfi, who was trying to calm himself down as he stared into my eyes. I couldn't make out whether he really cared if I went with him or not: he was going anyway.

'You know this is fucked up . . . You don't know how many there are, you don't know what weapons they have, you don't even know where the fuck they are. You are going to die, you know that, don't you?'

'God will decide my fate.' He turned for his door handle.

I hated this shit. I should have just cut away and headed for the airport back at the boulevard. Fuck it. I started to suck in my stomach so I could draw down the Browning. I tapped his arm with my spare hand to get his attention before nodding at the radio. 'We can't use these things any more, mate. They might start scanning channels on Hubba-Hubba's. Let's just hope they didn't switch to channel four and listened to us flapping on the way here, eh?'

Lotfi turned and gave me a smile as I pulled back the hammer from half-cock and checked chamber. My head was spinning. Why was I doing this? 'Thank you,' he said quietly.

'Yeah, right. Kismet my arse. If I'm going to die I might as well make sure a couple of those fuckers come along with me – so they can get their books, whatever they're called, weighed.'

He finished checking that his magazines were correctly positioned on his belt carrier before looking up at me as I did the same. 'Destiny – their books of destiny. You know exactly what it is called.'

'Come on, then, let's get—'

Lotfi's eyes darted beyond me and he sank back into his seat. Instinctively, I followed.

'Lexus.'

I heard a vehicle crunch over the gravel filling some of the potholes on the road towards the industrial estate.

'Two up in the front.'

I looked, but now being side on I couldn't see who was behind the darkened rear windows. Baldilocks was definitely driving.

'Romeo Three, with the Goatee, I saw him in the same restaurant as Greaseball the other night. I don't know if they met or what, but . . .'

The vehicle had gone past the gates and I jumped out of the Scudo, shoving away my Browning.

'Come on, we can do this without getting killed now, we have time.'

Lotfi ran round the vehicle to make up the distance with me as I headed towards the rusty, sagging chain-link gate that hadn't been closed in donkey's years. I kept to the left against the brocante wall for a little cover as I passed the gate. Lotfi had caught up with me, and he still had his pistol out. 'Put it away,' I snapped. 'Third party, for fuck's sake.'

Leaving him a few steps behind to sort himself out, I kept walking. In front of me was a ramshackle collection of buildings, at least thirty, probably forty years old, some of brick or stone, some of a corrugated fibre. Pipes that ran between the buildings had been lagged and painted with tar, and held together with bits of chicken wire. Skips were overflowing all over the place. Stacks of old tyres had collapsed across the diesel-infected tarmac that long ago had lost its straight edges and was starting to merge with the mud. There was even an old stone farmhouse and barns, which had long since given up the struggle against the encroaching *banlieues*.

I inched forward, using the wall, trying to look as normal as I could. Then, as I reached the end of the wall of the *brocante*, I saw movement to my left. The rear of the Lexus was disappearing inside a tall brick building. I held out my hand behind me. 'Stop, stop.'

I leant back against the wall, just as a train came into the station off to my right, beyond the estate. The screech of its braking wheels drowned out the clatter of the roller shutter as it crashed down behind the *hawallada* and his men.

49

I took my gigs off for a better look at the building and put them into the bum-bag.

The estate consisted of six or seven worn-out structures spread around the edge of a large open square. The target building, which I hoped the van had driven into, was in the left-hand corner furthest away from us. It was about forty metres long and twenty-five high, and constructed of dark, grimy brick. There were no windows on the front elevation, just the rusty shutter in the left third, tall enough to take a truck. The roof was flat, with lines of triangular glass skylights sticking up in the air like a dinosaur's fins, or something in a Lowry painting. Two other buildings – a converted stone barn, and the old farmhouse – formed the left side of the square and met the back of the *brocante*. Just beyond them was the river.

Lotfi was trying hard to control his breathing; he had his mouth closed and pulled in air heavily through his nose. The veins throbbed in his temples as his eyes stayed glued to the building. 'He knows I'm coming for him,' he said. 'He's waiting for me.'

He started to move forward and I held out my arm to stop him, looking around anxiously for third party. It was midday, people were on the move, traffic hummed up and down the main. 'I reckon nothing's going to happen to him just yet, mate. Goatee will want to know what all this means – that's why he's here, it must be. We have time now to do a little planning.'

I made an effort to get eye to eye with him, but he was too focused on the building. 'We won't be able to get in there anyway – look, there are no windows this side, no possible point of entry. Just those shutters, and they're down and locked. And even if we could get in, we haven't got a clue how many players are in there . . .'

Lotfi's gaze was still locked on the building as he lifted his hand to cut off my objections. 'None of that matters to me. God will decide the outcome. I've got to go.'

'We'll both do it. Look, if God's going to decide what happens, let's give him a hand here and do a recce, give him something to work with.' I managed eye contact, and he sort of smiled. 'You might be in the good lads' club with him, but I'm not sure I am.' I tilted my head to indicate the way we'd just come. 'Let's look round the back.'

There were two elements to this now. The first was to get Hubba-Hubba out in one piece, the second was to lift the *hawallada*. We still had a job to do. If we did it right, maybe we could achieve both – but not if we just went for it like Lotfi wanted to.

We turned right, passing the Scudo, and walked along the front of the *brocante* towards the fenceline just as two happy shoppers tried to fit a couple of chairs on to the roof rack of their Nissan. I hoped we could work our way along the riverbank, passing the barn and the farmhouse, get behind the target building, and see what we could see.

As we took a right again at the far end of the *brocante*, we were confronted by a dry, worn mud path that seemed to run the whole length of this side of the industrial estate. It was about four metres wide, in the space between the river and the buildings, and strewn with rubbish and dog shit. The remains of a chain-link fence ran parallel with the riverbank to our left. Old concrete posts were still standing at five- or six-metre intervals, but the wire was either rusty and pushed down, or missing altogether. About a hundred and fifty metres away on the other side of the river was the busy main that followed it, and a cluster of blocks of flats that looked as though they'd wanted to join the L'Ariane club, but couldn't afford the membership fee.

I walked slightly ahead of Lotfi, following the natural path rather than kicking through all the decayed Coca-Cola cans, old cigarette packets and faded plastic carrier bags. About a hundred metres ahead of us was the solid brick side elevation of the target building, easily the tallest structure in the estate. We followed the path past the end of the *brocante*, and now had the solid stone back wall and terracotta-tiled barn immediately to our right and traffic screaming over the bridge behind us.

A group of half a dozen women suddenly appeared from another path at the rear of the target building. I looked back at Lotfi to make sure he'd seen. His weapon was out again, down by his leg.

'Put that fucking thing away, will you?'

The group were headscarfed Arab women weighed down with overloaded plastic bags. They didn't turn left to come down towards us, but carried on straight, through the fence-line. They didn't give us as much as a second glance as they began to pick their way across the dried-up riverbed. It looked as if they were heading to the flats on the other side of the river, and couldn't be bothered going all the way down to the bridge.

The farmhouse was derelict, and graffiti-scrawled steel sheets barred anyone getting in through the windows that faced the river. Somebody had started a fire against the steel-covered doorway; black scorch marks stained the stone and the paint had blistered off the steel. We continued, trying to look as normal as possible as we negotiated the remnants of a dis-embowelled mattress lying across our path.

We turned right, behind the target, and on to a track that was just as well-worn and covered in litter. Instead of a fence on my left, there was now a stone wall about ten feet high. I could see

337

straight away that there was nothing at the rear that would help us gain entry – no vents, no windows, just more unrelenting brick.

Lotfi came up level with me. 'This must be a short cut to the station.'

'What are you on about?'

'There's a railway station just the other side of the buildings, at the end there. That's where I've parked.'

We carried on, following the rear of the building; there was still the other side elevation to check out. At the far corner, about forty metres along, I finally found something useful, a window frame set into the brickwork. Lotfi and I exchanged a look. 'See? I told you it was worth it.' At last I got another smile.

The window was metal-framed, with a single glass panel that opened outwards – not that it had been opened in years. The frame was rusty, and covered with cobwebs and grime. The glass was heavy-duty, frosted and wired, but there was a small wind-activated plastic ventilator fan, about four inches in diameter, cut into its centre. The main problem was going to be the two bars on the other side that I could see casting dark vertical shadows against the glass.

We carried on the five or so paces to the end of the building, and both leant against the wall, trying to look as if we were having a casual chat while I took a look round the corner and back into the estate. On this side, there was nothing but brick once more. Past the far edge of the building, I could see the gate off to the left, and beyond that traffic buzzing along the bridge road.

Lotfi lost patience and started walking back to the window. I followed, glancing down the track towards the station, then back at the river. 'Listen, mate, nothing's going to happen to him yet. He knows you're coming, he'll hold on. We've got to do this right.'

He was now inspecting the window. 'The only way is up,' I said. 'What do you reckon? Shall we go and see what we're up against first?'

Lotfi wanted to go through the window. I shook my head. 'It could take far too long. Better to use the time climbing up there. Maybe there's a skylight open or something.'

He surveyed the window once more, then the twenty-five metres of climb, before nodding reluctantly. 'Let's do it. But, please, let's hurry.'

'One of us at a time, OK? It's old.'

He checked that his weapon wasn't going to fall out, and I did the same. I started to climb the rusty downpipe, hot from the sun. It shifted as it took my weight and there was a small shower of rust flakes, but there was nothing I could do about that. I climbed with no great technique, apart from pulling down on the pipe as opposed to pulling out. I didn't know how good the fixings were, and I was not sure I wanted to find out.

My hands eventually got to the top and I thrust my forearms on to the flat roof. My shoulders, biceps and fingers ached from the effort of climbing, but they needed to produce one last burst of energy. I heaved and clawed my way upwards and across, until I could eventually roll on to the rooftop. It was hot bitumen and gravel, almost molten under the sun. It burned into my knees and the palms of my hands as I swivelled round to look down at Lotfi.

As I leant out, I could see beyond the industrial estate, in all directions. We were overlooked in the distance by the flats across the river and a few houses on the high ground this side but, apart from that, there should be no problem with third party. I hoped none of the tenants decided this was the time to test out a new pair of binoculars.

I could see the railway station – a small one – less than a hundred metres away to my right. A well-worn path led to it from the rear of the warehouse, through a gap in the fence, over the line, and into the parking area. I could just make out the shape of Lotfi's Focus estate in a line of vehicles near the road.

The railway line ran parallel to the river, and there was a

339

level crossing just past the entry point to the estate that Lotfi must have belted over before turning left and parking.

Lotfi's grunts became audible above the drone of traffic as he climbed. Two hands appeared at the top of the pipe and I pulled on his wrist as he gripped me. I heaved him over and we both lay on the flat roof, getting our breath back. I closed my eyes against the sun, and felt the heat of the roof burn through my sweatshirt and jeans.

I rolled on to my front, my clothing pulling at me as the bitumen tried to make it stay where it was. After checking that my Browning was still secure, and not covered in tar and grit, I crawled on my hands and knees towards the line of six sky-lights in the centre of the roof. Even from here I could see they weren't frosted and wire-meshed, just clear but grimy. Some of the panes had cracked, and many were covered in pigeon shit. It didn't matter: it was a way in.

As I crawled, with Lotfi just behind, the hot tarmac sub-stance beneath the gravel slowly moved under the weight of my elbows, toes and knees. Then its surface split, like the skin on old custard, and I sank a few millimetres into the black stuff.

I noticed that my shadow was more or less under me, and a quick look at a now tar-covered traser told me it was after twelve thirty. The sun was high, but all the same I'd have to be careful as I stuck my head over the glass that I didn't cast the world's biggest shadow across the floor below. Shape, shine, shadow, silhouette, spacing and movement are always the things that give you away.

I headed for the second skylight from the left, because there was glass missing from it. I was no more than a metre away when I heard a scream from inside, louder than the drone of the traffic and the blast of horns and air brakes.

Lotfi heard it too, and scrambled past me to get to the miss-ing pane.

I put my hand up. 'Slowly, slowly. Remember your shadow.'

He nodded and moved his head up gently, trying to get his

face against the hole. His nose was doing all the breathing now, and his sweat-covered face was screwed up in anger.

I went to the left of him and, with bitumen-covered fingers, rubbed the grime slowly from the glass to get a better view.

50

Years of pigeon shit hung from the steel roof supports like grey icicles. Then, down at ground level, among the old faded newspapers and lumps of rubble, I saw why Lotfi's breathing was suddenly a lot more agitated. Romeo Two was on the concrete floor, naked and covered in blood, getting kicked to bits by the two unknowns I'd seen come out of the shop and walk to the rear, the ones who must have lifted Hubba-Hubba. They still had their black leather jackets over jeans. I couldn't see any weapons on them.

There was movement from Romeo Two. He was trying to crawl towards the Lexus, parked next to the Merc van, which was two up, opposite the shutter at the far end of the building. Blood dripped off his moustache and mouth as the two unknowns just followed him, kicking, and having a good laugh. They pushed him down on to the ground, then kicked him again, turning him away from the vehicles. The engine sparked up on the van and it drove slowly to the shutter. The passenger got out and pulled on the chain. He climbed back in and the Merc disappeared, while one of the black leather jackets lowered the shutter.

Below us, in the middle of the building, were two vehicle-inspection pits and two sets of concrete ramps. Romeo One and Hubba-Hubba were inside one of the pits, also naked. Ripped clothes were strewn around on the concrete, probably having been checked inch by inch for tracking or listening devices. Blood had dripped from their faces on to their sweat-drenched bodies. They were kept in the pit by what looked like a heavy old iron gate from a stately home, maybe bought from the *brocante* next door, which had been dragged over the top of it.

Hubba-Hubba sat cross-legged in one corner, his head down. His blood-wet hair was matted and glinted in the sunlight. I couldn't see his face.

Sweat dripped into my mouth as I took in the scene. Goatee stood above them on the gate, shouting and poking them with a broom handle, as if baiting a couple of pit bulls before the Big Fight.

All the faces below me were Arab. Baldilocks was leaning against a concrete ramp in a baggy blue short-sleeved shirt and black trousers. He took a long drag on a cigarette and swapped funnies with the fat van driver, who had a brown pullover stretched over his gut. I thought that he had been the one to spot Hubba-Hubba at the rear of the shop, as the Romeos prepared for loading inside. But none of this made sense. Why lift him, and why lift the Romeos?

Lotfi was inches from me now, his eyes fixed on the pit. Hubba-Hubba's head was still bowed. He wasn't reacting to the blows, just rolling with them, taking the pain. Romeo One was on his knees, begging Goatee for mercy. What he got instead was another burst of good news from the broom handle.

Lotfi turned to me, his face determined. 'He's waiting for me.'

I nodded. 'Not long now, mate. Go beyond the skylight, see if there's a trap door.'

He took another long, hard look at his brother before crawling backwards and making his way to the other side of the roof. Maybe there was a fire door, with a steel escape ladder attached to an interior wall. It wouldn't help us much: we'd be spotted at once coming down it. But at least it got Lotfi out of the way for a while. I didn't want him sparked up any more than he was already.

As I listened to the screams and shouts I looked around below me. The building was just one big open space, and had obviously once been used as a garage workshop. I was lying with my head towards the shuttered entrance at the far end of the building. There was nothing behind it now, apart from the Lexus. It looked as though it had been the vehicles' holding area, before they were brought over to the inspection pits and ramps for repair in the middle. At the other end, the ground-floor window was hidden by two Portakabins, which stood at right angles to each other in front of a rough, whitewashed breezeblock cube, no more than eight foot high, which jutted out of the corner. Unless Lotfi came up with something magical, the only way in was through the shutter, or that window.

Goatee stepped off the gate and barked an order at the boys by the ramp. Baldilocks and Van Man threw down their ciga-rettes, walked over to the pit, and dragged the ironwork gate to one side. When there was a big enough gap, Romeo Two was herded into it by the black-leather brothers.

Hubba-Hubba didn't react as the newcomer fell in beside him and the gate was dragged back over. But the reunited Romeos gobbed off to each other and did some more begging to the people above.

A mobile phone rang. A couple of them reached into their pockets, but it turned out to be Goatee's. He flipped it open, and did a bit of business as the other four congregated by the ramps. Cigarettes were passed round and lit as Goatee carried on his conversation in what sounded like French. There was even a little laughter from him as he walked towards the shutters.

Goatee had a big smile on his face, and waved his left arm gently back and forth as he talked. He was maybe in his early forties, with a short, very neat hairstyle that made him look even more like George Michael today. His body language was cajoling, and he kicked small imaginary footballs against the wall as he moved.

Lotfi appeared from the other side of the skylight on his hands and knees, shaking his head as he closed in on me. He stared down at Hubba-Hubba, then shifted his attention to Goatee.

'It's a woman,' he whispered. 'He says he'll be home late, there is lots to do.'

And then, as if a switch had been thrown, the phone was thrust back into Goatee's pocket and he strode back to the pit. The smile had gone.

The two Romeos were on their knees, beseeching him in rapid Arabic. I turned to Lotfi. 'What are they saying?'

He put his ear to the hole instead of his eyes and plugged the other one with his thumb as a jet passed overhead and vehicles raced about us, his face screwed up in concentration. While I waited for him to work it out, I moved the Browning to the back of my jeans and turned the bum-bag round, letting my front sink into the bitumen. It didn't make much difference, I was already covered in the stuff. I felt as if I'd been crawling in hot volcanic mud.

'They don't know who my brother is. They've never seen him before.'

I watched Goatee light a cigarette while he glowered at the two men gibbering on their knees below him, picking off some tobacco that was left on his lips.

'They're saying they're just here to collect money from three locations. One yesterday and two today. They don't understand what's happening. They know nothing apart from where to collect the money.'

He had the same thought as I did. 'Nick, two collections today?'

Shit! I glanced over to him, then back at Goatee, who was holding a hand out as Van Man brought over Hubba-Hubba's yellow Sony. He brought it up to his mouth and mouthed, 'Bonjour, bonjour, bonjour,' with an exaggerated sneer.

He flicked his unfinished cigarette into the pit and crouched over Hubba-Hubba, shouting questions. There was no reaction at all from the Egyptian. 'He wants to know who he was talking to on the radio.' Lotfi wiped sweat from his face. 'He wants to know who we are, where we are, what we're doing.' And then, strangely, Lotfi smiled. He looked me in the eye. 'He won't say a word, Nick. He knows I'm coming.'

Hubba-Hubba was still facing the bottom of the pit, not responding. Maybe Lotfi was right: he actually did believe. Goatee got pissed off at the lack of reaction and hurled the Sony at the gate. Shards of plastic and electronic components showered into the pit like shrapnel. Then, in what looked like an explosion of frustration, he forced the broom handle down on to the base of Hubba-Hubba's neck with both hands. Hubba-Hubba just took the pain and went down, his blood-stained head falling into Romeo Two's lap.

Lotfi stared down as Goatee screamed into the pit. He was looking far too calm. It was as if he had a plan. 'What else are they saying, mate?'

Lotfi closed his eyes and cocked his ear to the broken pane. 'He doesn't believe the Romeos. He says it doesn't matter who is telling the truth and who is lying. It doesn't matter if he kills them and he is wrong. Someone else will collect the cash.' He opened his eyes again and looked at me. 'It is now time, Nick.'

I nodded back. 'We only have the window to—'

Lotfi jerked away from the glass and up on to his knees. Wiping his hands on his jeans to get the bitumen off, he nodded over towards the gate. The heat burnt into my palms as I put my hands into the black stuff and pushed myself up to see what he'd seen. He was already crawling towards the downpipe.

A Peugeot estate with police markings and blue light bar

had stopped at the junction opposite the line of cars in front of the *brocante*, where the Scudo was parked. It was three up, and the front passenger was on the radio.

51

I had to assume the worst: that third-party calls earlier had alerted the police about the Scudo and these three boys were just about to get a promotion. They'd find the radios and the boot set-up, and the cash under the seat – together with enough fingerprints to keep them dusting for weeks. The first thing they'd do was look for us around here.

I checked Lotfi's Focus. Nothing was happening there, but it wouldn't be long before it did after his cops-and-robbers impersonation. I couldn't help thinking that maybe it was God's way of saying, 'That's enough of a recce for me today, now just get on with it.'

Still trying to work out how we were going to do it, I decided to take one more look down into the building before I went to join Lotfi. I hadn't reckoned on things getting worse. Goatee was still on the gate, but the boot to the Lexus was now open and Baldilocks was handing him a red plastic fuel canister. The can was then held up, like a bottle of wine at a restaurant, for the three in the pit to see.

Hubba-Hubba finally looked up. The charm had gone from his neck. There was no reaction at all: he just took the shouting, and bowed his head once more. He was waiting for Lotfi to come. But in the meantime he was preparing to die.

Lotfi was nearly at the corner of the roof as a train squealed into the station. He stopped at the parapet, waiting in case anyone took the short cut. By the time I had reached him, the train had left. Should I tell him what I'd seen? What would it change if I did? We were still going to have to get down and try to make entry through that window. Would it help for him to know that his brother was on the verge of being torched – especially if it turned out we couldn't get inside?

Lotfi checked for people crossing the railway line. 'All clear. Ready?'

I nodded, checked my Browning and bum-bag, then clambered over the parapet, scrambling down a bit too fast. Slivers of rust sliced into my hand, but my pain was nothing compared to Hubba-Hubba's. As soon as I hit the ground, Lotfi started to follow.

I switched the bum-bag and Browning from my back to my front once more and took my Leatherman out of its belt case. I wanted the weapon back where it normally sat, because it was an instinct to draw down from that position and I got the feeling I'd be needing it.

Lotfi landed beside me as I opened the blade of the Leatherman. Reaching up on tiptoe with my left hand and pushing up with my free hand on the concrete window sill, I started to stab and cut into the plastic fan casing.

Lotfi was against the wall, keeping watch. It seemed a good idea to prepare him for failure. 'If we can't get these bars off, the only way to go in is through the shutter. We wait for someone to come out, or maybe the van to come back, then—'

'God will decide what we can and cannot do, Nick. It's in his hands.' He didn't look at me: his eyes stayed fixed towards the track.

That was all well and good, but what if God decided it was time to light up the pit?

I lifted out the centre of the four-inch-diameter fan and tried to look through at the bars beyond the now grimy, bitumen-smeared glass.

349

Fuck it, I had to tell him.

'Before we left the skylight, I saw Goatee waving a fuel can at the three of them in the pit. You know what that could mean, don't you?'

His expression didn't change. His eyes still didn't leave the track. But he did have his beads in his left hand, threading them between his fingers and thumb, one by one. 'Yes, I do know what that means.' His voice was unbelievably calm, unbelievably collected. 'Let's just carry on.'

I needed help to get my hand through the hole. 'Give us a leg up, mate.' I lifted my right foot, and he cupped his hands. We both grunted as I stretched out my arm and he pushed up against the bricks.

I got a glimpse of urinals as I reached through, and at the fourth attempt I managed to pull down the rusty window latch. Not much happened. The frame was so old it had been glued in place by years of weather. I lowered myself back to the ground and used the Leatherman blade to prise open the frame.

There was no noise from inside, which was good: if we couldn't hear them, chances were they couldn't hear us. I just hoped none of them suddenly decided they wanted to take a leak.

Pushing at the bars was no good, they were solid, but I used them to pull myself up the extra foot so I could see what was going on. They were secured by three straighthead screws, above and below the frame, driven through two strips of metal that were welded on to the bars.

I dropped back to the ground and got out the screwdriver of the Leatherman. 'You know we still need to get the *hawallada*, don't you, as well as Hubba-Hubba? We've already lost the third one, and without these people we don't get to the ASUs. We need them – you know what's going to happen if these ASUs aren't jumped on?'

'Nick, I understand the importance. You forget, my brother and I volunteered.'

His expression was so calm it was unnerving. He really did believe in right and wrong, and all that Kismet stuff. 'You also know it's finished, after this? We are compromised to the police, we have missed the other collection. Let's just get both of them out, drop off the *hawallada*, and get the fuck out of this country. OK? No revenge shit, it'll take too long.'

I pulled myself up again, using the bars, and managed to half sit on the sill so I could get to work with the screwdriver. At least the stained toilet and two dust-filled urinals had no smell, just dried cigarette butts, from the eighties probably; the filters gathered around the drain holes were faded white with age.

Layers of paint covered the screw heads near the ceiling, and I had to dig them out first with the blade before I could get the screwdriver to bite. It eventually started to turn after the head had twice slipped out of the groove and scraped my knuckles.

The first screw came out and I handed it to Lotfi and stayed silent as I got to grips with the remaining ones. There was too much to think and worry about. I glanced at Lotfi, still calm, watching up and down the path. Me, I was flapping a bit, but ready to go for it so we could get the fuck out of France before the police got hold of us.

I didn't bother with the bottom screws, just prised the bars downwards. Then, getting out my Browning and turning my bum-bag round to the back of my spine again, I went in head first, belly-flopping on to the toilet, using the two urinals as support to stop me falling on to the floor and making noise.

I could hear voices the other side of the door.

Lotfi followed me through, closing the window behind him but not pulling down the catch.

The door was an overpainted cheap interior one, with an old, brushed-aluminium handle. The gap at the bottom was too narrow for me to look through, but the screams and shouts didn't leave much to the imagination. At least I couldn't smell petrol or burning yet.

Lotfi also got his ear to the door. 'They're begging them to stop – we must hurry now.'

'We need to spread out so we can cover them all. I'll take the left, using the Portakabin that side as cover. You take the right, using the other one.'

One of the Romeos screamed so loudly it sounded as if he was in here with us. Lotfi got very sparked up, his eyes flashing once more the same as they'd done in Algeria. I put a hand on his shoulder. 'Me left, you right, and this God of yours knows I'm with you, yeah?'

As he nodded, both Romeos cried out again. I pulled the hammer back from its half-cock position on the Browning and checked chamber by gently pulling back the backslide just enough to see the brass of the round in position. Then I pushed it back into position.

Lotfi was doing the same as I checked my bum-bag for the last time and wiped the sweat from my eyes with a bitumen-stained hand.

Slowly, I pushed down on the door handle and it gave way with the smallest of squeaks. I didn't want to burst in. I wanted us to get in as far as we could, using the Portakabins as cover, before it went noisy.

There was a little resistance from the hinges, but I managed to pull it towards me an inch as Goatee's shouts and the screams from the pit increased. My view was mostly obscured by the Portakabins, but between them to my half-right I could see the concrete ramps. And no one was there any more.

52

I couldn't understand the Arabic, but I could tell the difference between begging and demanding. Lotfi's hard-set jaw told me that for him every word mattered.

I just had to assume that they all were at the pit; there was nowhere else for them to have gone, unless they were bumming around in the Portakabins or giving the Lexus a polish.

Change of plan now that I couldn't see anyone. I visualized how I would go straight through the gap in the two Portakabins to the ramps, so I could use them as cover while I dominated the area. None of them would be able to outrun Mr Nine Millimetre.

That would give Lotfi a chance to move in and lift Hubba-Hubba, and once that was done, there would be three of us to get Goatee into the car and get the fuck out. And that was about as far as I got. We'd just have to get in there with the maximum amount of speed, surprise and aggression, weapons up, making sure they didn't have time to draw down. Only Lotfi's God could tell where things went from there.

I moved my head back so I could whisper to Lotfi. 'Change of plan, I'll head straight for the ramps and—'

A piercing scream forced its way through the gap in the door.

Lotfi jumped up, pushing me over. Pulling at the door, he drew down his weapon before hurling himself into the warehouse, screaming Arabic, running straight through the gap between the Portakabins then turning right, to the pits, and disappearing from view.

I followed, safety off, screaming at the top of my voice, joining in with everyone else now as the noise echoed about the building. 'Hands up! Hands up! Hands up!'

I'd taken only three steps into the warehouse when there was a loud *whoosh* from the other side of the Portakabins to my right, then agonized screams that drowned every other sound.

I emerged past the Portakabins to see the group to the right of the blazing pit staring open-mouthed at us. We both screamed louder, trying to overcome the noise from below us as the flames shot higher than our heads.

Baldilocks was in position to draw down, but couldn't decide whether to do so or not. He looked at Goatee. He was looking at me. I stayed static, weapon up, out in the open.

Lotfi had reached the pit, his screams now just as loud as those of the burning men.

I kept my Browning up, pushing down with my thumb on the safety. 'Hands up! Hands up! Hands up!'

The black-leather brothers were trying to work out whether to take a chance and draw down, I could see it in their eyes. I felt the heat on my face as I moved in closer, to get better shots, never crossing my feet over as I moved, wanting to keep them apart so I had a constant, stable platform to get some rounds off on target. I didn't have that many to fuck about with.

Lotfi, on his knees by the pit, roared with all the air in his lungs as he battled with the hot, heavy iron gate, trying to drag it just a few feet.

Hands flailed from the flames below. Disembodied, high-pitched screams filled the building.

Above ground, the group's eyes were still darting everywhere, at the pit, at me, at each other. I moved towards them more and with each step the stench of burning flesh became stronger than the fuel's. It was tempting to do all four of them, but Goatee was in the middle of the group. I needed him alive.

Lotfi yelled for his brother, fighting the flames, fighting the gate.

Where was Van Man?

There was movement to my right and I was too late.

The piece of scaffolding swung in hard. I felt a crushing pain in the right side of my chest and the Browning flew from my hand. I lost all the air from my lungs before hitting the concrete.

Between the flashes in my head I could see Lotfi lying on the floor, gripping a charred hand that strained up through the bars of the gate. The flames were beginning to die. Even if his brother hadn't burned to death, he would have been asphyxiated long before now.

Lotfi bellowed like a wounded animal, a long, drawn-out, pitiful howl of despair. His sleeves were smoking and burnt away, and his hands and arms were blistering. Bodies moved in and he was kicked away from the gate, but it wasn't physical pain that was causing his anguish.

My glimpse of him lasted a second more, before feet rained in on me too. I could do nothing more than curl up, close my eyes, grit my teeth, and hope it would stop very soon.

Angry Arabic echoed round the walls. The kicking stopped. Hands grabbed my feet, dragging me on my stomach and chest towards the pit. Lotfi's screams got closer. I pushed down on the heels of my hands to try and keep my face from being grated along the concrete floor and felt the skin of my palms coming away.

I opened my eyes in time to see the charred but still recognizable bodies in the pit, and the smouldering paint on the gates. My legs were released, my bum-bag got pulled off me and I was pushed against the right-hand Portakabin. Lotfi was frogmarched over to join me and forced on to his knees. All four of them stood around us, letting off a good kick now and again. The hem of Baldilocks' trousers was just inches from my face. I could smell cologne and cigarettes, and heard heavy, laboured breathing as one of them gobbed on to my neck.

Lotfi seemed oblivious to the state of his arms and hands. His skin was hanging off him like potato peel, some flakes red, some black. His watch and MedicAlert looked as if they had sunk into his grotesquely swollen wrists. The raw skin on my hands, ingrained with grit, was incredibly painful, but nothing like he was going through.

A pain in the right of my chest was as much as I could bear. I had to take rapid, shallow breaths, and each one felt like I was being stabbed.

Lotfi caught my eye and started rocking slowly backwards and forwards with his arms out so he didn't touch them, just taking the pain. 'I should have—'

He got a kick that rolled him off to his side. They closed in on us again just as Goatee pushed his way through the crowd. They gave him some space as he looked down just a few feet away from us, having nearly recovered his breath. In his left hand he held our passports. The four behind him were already counting out our cash. In his right hand he held an untipped cigarette, unlit, and a disposable lighter. Eyeing us both with mock concern, he placed the cigarette between his lips and clicked the lighter twice before he got a light. His watch, a very slim gold thing, glinted in the sunlight.

He hadn't bought his clothes at a street market either. The black shirt looked quality, and his jeans had an Armani label on the back. He smelt of expensive cologne and as he smoked I could see well-manicured nails. The fingernail on the little finger of his right hand was much longer than the rest, to the point where it nearly started to curl. Maybe he played the guitar, or perhaps he just didn't like using a spoon to scoop up his cocaine.

He traded stares with Lotfi while I cleared the snot and blood from my nose on to the concrete and my jeans. Hubba-Hubba lay less than fifteen feet away from his brother, yet Lotfi gazed at his killer as if he was studying a painting. I was

356

impressed. I'd known a few people over the years who could keep their head in a gang fuck, but this was something else.

Goatee looked down at us and breathed deeply, before kicking Lotfi in the leg. 'Do you speak English too?'

Lotfi nodded, his gaze never wavering.

Goatee took another drag of his cigarette. When he exhaled, the halo of smoke danced in the sunlight above him. 'I suppose you are the people on the other end of the radio?' His tone was icy. He was waiting for an answer, but Lotfi wasn't giving, and he was right, but only up to a point. This wasn't the time to answer questions, it was the time to start begging for our lives.

I wiped another fistful of snot and blood off my nose, then went for it. 'Look, I don't know what the fuck is going on here.' I nodded in the direction of the pit. 'We were just told to follow those two. We thought they were moving heroin to the Channel Islands. Someone there was worried it was going to affect his business. Whatever's going on here, we don't need to know. What the fuck, we can just walk out of here now and forget the whole thing . . .'

I knew I had lost him on the first few words. He didn't even look at me, but remained staring at Lotfi, and took another drag before gobbing off at him in Arabic. Lotfi replied with three or four sentences, which meant nothing to me. I just knew Goatee was getting fucked off by him big-time.

Goatee forced a lungful of smoke out through his nostrils as he turned to face me. 'What does it matter? I do not care who you are. If you came to steal from me, or you didn't, it matters not.' He flicked the ash over towards the pit. 'They are dead. You are dead. I still have the money, and I'll simply wait for another collection. I can't afford to take chances. I don't care what's happened. God understands, God will forgive me.' He turned to Lotfi. 'No?'

There was no reply.

Goatee took another drag and turned back to have a word with the black-leather brothers. Lotfi's lips started to move; he put his head down and rocked backwards and forwards slightly. I didn't understand all of it but certainly got the *'Muhammad rasul-ullah'* bit.

The Shahada; he was preparing for death.

He might be ready to meet his maker, but I wasn't.

Goatee heard Lotfi too, and turned his head round to watch, before shrugging his shoulders and throwing both passports towards the pit. They landed on the gate, one falling down on to Hubba-Hubba's black and red charred body. Goatee walked away and yelled stuff at the other four.

Lotfi's eyes followed the black-leather brothers, one of whom carried the empty petrol container, as they walked towards the Lexus. If God was on our side, he needed to get his finger out of his arse and do something pretty quick.

One of the brothers sparked up the Lexus while the other pulled on the chain to open up the grease- and grime-covered shutters. The vehicle reversed, then turned to face the exit as the *hawallada*'s mobile gave another ring. He opened it up and headed towards the other side of the building. The Lexus went through the door and disappeared. Van Man started closing the shutter as Baldilocks kept watch on us, sunlight bouncing off his sweat-covered head.

It was a very short phone call: I got the impression that Goatee was telling her he might be back in time for tea after all, but not to keep calling him at the office. Whatever we were going to do, we had to do it before the Lexus got back. I looked over at Lotfi and his eyes were still locked on Goatee. Blood dripped from his nostrils, bubbling as he prayed.

Goatee put the phone in his pocket and walked back over to us. He'd almost reached us when two shots rang out outside. Van Man let go of the chain. The shutter stopped rattling, about two feet from the ground, as they all drew down and Van Man dived to one side of the entrance.

There were more shots, followed by shouts and the revving of engines, then the screech of brakes and the sound of a collision. Baldilocks froze, looking to Van Man for some kind of clue about what the fuck he should do next.

There were more single shots. Van Man took a quick look outside. 'Police! Police!'

Goatee barked instructions at them both. Lotfi had stopped in mid-prayer. The light was back in his eyes. He glanced across at me with a look that said, 'You see, Nick? I was right. God's come to the rescue.'

I gave him one back that said, 'Let's get the fuck out of here, and let's do it now . . .'

He launched himself at Goatee, as the pain in my chest disappeared and I wrapped myself around Baldilocks before he had the chance to switch himself back on. I hung on to him like a drowning man, trying to keep his arms down and the weapon out of the way. I kept pushing him back, moving my legs as quickly as I could to keep him off balance. The pistol clattered to the concrete and we crashed into the ramp, then fell to the floor, me on top, still wrapped around him. The pain returned, big-time. My ribs felt like they'd been given the good news by a jackhammer. I fought for breath. I heard myself scream as he squirmed under me, his pistol just over a metre away.

It was a Beretta, and the safety catch was still on. My brain shrank. That weapon became my whole world.

I fell sideways, arm outstretched, but Baldilocks managed to slow me down, grunting with the effort, dragging at my leg, pulling at my sweatshirt, trying to beat me to it.

The muzzle was facing us; my hand was no more than six inches from it. I could feel his fingers scrabbling at me, trying to climb over me. But I was there, no pain in my hands now, gripping it to my chest.

I couldn't breathe. I couldn't suck in any air. Trying to turn the thing round, I got it in my right hand. He was now on top of me, forcing the weapon down between me and the concrete. My ribcage started to collapse. I pushed up with my arse, trying to make space under me, trying to spin the weapon round, stripping the skin off my knuckles.

He grabbed my throat. His teeth bit into my shoulder.

I felt his laboured breathing on my neck.

If I didn't get some air into my lungs soon, I was going down. Starbursts of light flickered across my eyes. I needed oxygen, my head was about to explode.

More gunshots outside.

I got the weapon in my hand, but his weight was still pressing down on me too much to move it.

I twisted left and right, jerking up and down, trying to create a gap so I could free my hand. He bit harder, his hands shifting from my throat to my arms.

I rolled on to my right side, got the Beretta into his biceps, and fired. He shrieked and sprang off me, clutching the wound, wriggling like an eel. I could see bone and blood as I lay there trying to breathe.

Lotfi was lying by the pit, a few feet from Goatee. Both were curled up, both leaking blood.

Sunlight poured in through the gap underneath the shutter. Shots ricocheted off the steel as Lotfi crawled over to the *hawallada*. I screamed at him, 'No, let's go, let's go!'

He'd got on top of Goatee and was forcing the pistol into his face. Fuck him, we'd never get him to the DOP anyway. 'Just do it, let's go – come on! *Come on!*'

He looked over at me, his face covered with blood.

'Come on! Do it! The window!'

Sirens wailed. Rolling off Goatee, he lifted the pistol to fire at Van Man, who was still at the shutter, but he was in shit state; it would be a waste of rounds, and he knew it.

The weapon came down as I moved to the cover of the Portakabins, my head swimming, vision blurred, eyes wet with pain. 'Come on, kill him,' I croaked. 'Let's go!'

We had to get out of there before the police threw a cordon around the estate.

Lotfi hauled himself on to his knees, clutching his stomach. 'Take him, take him now . . .'

He was still scarily calm.

'Fuck him. Let's go!'

'No, I need revenge, you need the *hawallada*.'

He staggered to his feet and stumbled towards Baldilocks, firing two rounds into him as soon as he was close enough. One exited his head at an angle and ricocheted off the ramp.

As he headed for Van Man, I shuffled forward and got hold of Goatee by the feet, dragging him behind the Portakabin. His head bounced on the concrete as he tried to keep his hand over the gunshot wound in his stomach. His black shirt, wet with blood, glistened in the sunlight.

I stopped at the toilet door. I couldn't catch my breath, everything was too painful. But I had to keep dragging. Somehow, I got to the window. Blood streamed from my mouth as I bent down and tried to get Goatee on to my shoulder.

I had to get on my knees to do so, then haul myself upright on one of the urinal pipes. He gave a whimper as I stopped to chug up and gob out another mouthful of blood, before trying to shove him out through the window.

53

He fell out of the window head first, gasping in pain as his shins scraped against the metal rim of the frame, before he hit the ground with a crump and a muffled cry.

I followed, trying to keep my weight off my chest as I wormed my way through, fighting to stop myself shouting with pain. I finally tumbled down beside him on the dried mud of the track. Sirens wailed in the distance. I got to my knees, trying to suck oxygen into my lungs without moving my ribs. Every intake of breath still felt as if I was being stabbed. I was sweating all over, the pulse throbbing heavily in my neck.

On my knees, I lifted Goatee by the armpits, manhandling him back on to my shoulder. I struggled to get myself upright, using my legs to push, and my free hand to claw my way up the wall. I tried to take deeper breaths, but the effort just made me cough up more blood that in turn blocked my nose.

As I stumbled towards the railway tracks and Lotfi's Focus, the sound of sirens got closer, coming down the main behind me and following the river.

I made my way to the end of the building and peered round it, towards the estate entrance. The white police patrol car was blocking it. The Lexus had smashed into its rear, spinning it round in its attempt to get away, and ending up off towards the farmhouse in the right-hand corner.

I couldn't see any sign of the black-leather brothers, but the three policemen were bobbing and weaving on the far side of the patrol car. Their main attention was towards their left and the farmhouse area.

Lotfi appeared in the open ground, staggering towards the police with his weapon dangling in his hand. They started screaming orders at him as he made his way slowly towards their line. He was buying me time to get away. The gap between this building and the next was about two metres; after that I'd be in cover right down to the railway tracks. He raised his hands as more orders were screamed at him, but held on to the pistol. He moved forward, blood drenching his clothes, taking his time to come level with the Lexus, making sure they were following his every move.

Would they spot me as I crossed?

Lotfi moved to the right.

I tried to fill my lungs, adjusted Goatee on my shoulders as Lotfi moved to the right, towards the farmhouse, firing at the black-leather brothers who were over there somewhere, firing back.

I went for it.

Sirens seemed to be coming from everywhere. I couldn't tell if I'd been seen or not as I crossed. It didn't really matter. All that did was getting to the car.

I lurched along the path, a stone building to my right and the brick wall to my left, bumping into both. My vision was blurred; I was feeling dizzy, I needed more oxygen, but it just hurt too much to fight for it. I heard a fusillade of shots from the police that seemed to last for ever. If it meant they were still shooting at Lotfi as he ran out of rounds and went at them with his bare hands, I could only hope his end came quickly.

The track disappeared into a cutting, which was lined both sides with bushes and caked with drinks cans and cigarette packets. The cutting was no more than five or six metres deep on each side, but that would be enough to hide Goatee in while I went to get the Focus.

I scrambled and slid down towards the railway. Goatee was making spasmodic attempts to free himself, but they only lasted a few seconds. He lost it once more and slumped on to me. I could feel his blood soaking into my bitumen-covered sweatshirt and mixing with my own sweat. His beard rubbed against my right forearm as I struggled to keep him in position.

Signs that probably said 'Do not cross here' were nailed up to warn users of the dangers of this rat run. I picked my way carefully over the stone bedding, then crossed the tracks. My nose was still blocked, and by the time we were on the far bank my mouth was full of blood again, making it hard to breathe.

I couldn't muster the strength to get him up the other side of the embankment. I tried, but we fell together on to the dry earth path just a metre up the bank. Sirens were directly above us, on the main beyond the station. It was decision time.

I lay there in much the same condition as Goatee, both on our backs and desperately trying to take in oxygen. He mumbled to himself then screamed out. I swung a clenched fist to make him shut up, hitting him somewhere in the face. I wasn't too sure where, because my eyes were still wet and blurred, but it seemed to do the trick.

I rolled on to my front and crawled over him, leaving him where he was, and headed slowly up the bank, finally coming level with the cracked and potholed tarmac of the packed car park. The station itself, a dirty cream brick building, was immediately to my right. I lay there for a minute, fighting for breath, and against the pain that each breath brought with it. Blood continued to pour out of my mouth each time I coughed.

Craning my neck around the tyres of the car nearest me, I spotted the Focus, parked facing the road about fifteen metres away, its tailgate towards me. People had stopped, trying to see what was happening, and were getting on their mobiles to tell their friends about all the excitement. More police cars swooped into the area, one passing left to right on the main.

There was nothing I could do to hide myself. I just had to go for it, and get us both into the Focus before there was no way out.

It was fuck-it time again. I got up and staggered towards the black estate car, squinting in the sunlight, trying to walk upright and stop myself coughing, and failing at both.

I burped up some more blood and gobbed it out. I was going to need to control my breathing soon, and McDonald's came to my rescue. A bin to my right was overflowing with McDo burger containers and grease-stained brown paper bags. I picked one up, tipped out the used napkins and ketchup sachets, and shoved it into my back pocket.

It was then that I heard the gentle thwack of rotor blades up above me somewhere. I couldn't be arsed looking up, just focused instead on the car.

The glare of the sun made my eyes water even more as I bent down and started to pull at the thin rectangular numberplate. With the key and fob in my hand, I pulled myself upright to go round to the driver's door, and found myself face to face with a skinny, middle-aged black woman with a freckled face and multicoloured dress. She stood on the pavement by the Focus with two carrier bags of shopping. She just opened her mouth and stared at my bloodstained, bitumen-streaked sweatshirt, and at the blood and snot all over my face.

54

The fourways flashed as I hit the key fob. I grinned at her like an idiot, not having a clue what to say.

Half climbing, half falling into the driver's seat, I settled for a smiley '*Bonjour*', and, to my amazement, she just replied in kind and carried on walking. Maybe she saw blokes like me every day round here.

I closed the door on the stifling heat and smelly plastic of the interior and started the engine, checking the fuel gauge as I did so. It was just over three-quarters full. Good skills – he'd filled up at every opportunity.

I tried to turn my head to find the closest gap to the path, but the searing pain in my chest made me think again. I couldn't get a lungful of air. It seemed to be going into my mouth all right, in short sharp gasps, but nothing would go down. I was starting to hyperventilate.

I reached into the back of my jeans, pulled out the McDo bag, and got it over my nose and mouth. With both hands cupping it in position, I concentrated on breathing slowly in and out a few times, puckering my lips. It was a bit juddery, but I managed to get at least half-lungfuls before holding my breath for just a second, then exhaling slowly.

Leaning forward over the steering wheel with the bag over

my face, I repeated the cycle. My eyes flashed up as a red *pompiers* ambulance passed me on the main. This just wasn't happening quickly enough. I was fighting to draw oxygen, but I wasn't getting anywhere. And then, painfully slowly, I started to succeed. The bag collapsed half-way, then filled out again. It was a big effort and took me several attempts, but at last I got things under some kind of control. That was all I could do for now; I really needed more time if I was to get my breathing back to anything like normal.

I reversed the Focus out of its space, scraping it along the Peugeot next to me, and carried on backing into the gap nearest to where I'd left Goatee. The heels of my hands stung as the raw skin ran over the hot plastic of the steering wheel, smearing it with blood.

Leaving the engine idling, I got out once more, opened the tailgate and scrambled down the bank. He'd shifted on to his side, and was curled up in pain. I got him on to my shoulders once more, and began to work my way up the bank. His weight pressed against my lungs as I moved up the hill, and I couldn't stop coughing.

Still more sirens – in the distance, but closing in.

When I finally got on to level ground, I felt like cheering. I reached the car and tipped Goatee into the boot just as the helicopter closed in. There was next to no resistance from him as I pushed and bent his legs to fit him in. I checked that the back tray came down flat and closed the tailgate, pushing down on whatever bit of him was in the way until he moved it. Back in the driver's seat, I got the bag over my mouth once more, trying to regulate my breathing before I made my move. My eyes were still watering, my head banged, everything was blurred.

The quickest way out of the city was north into the mountains. I turned the ignition and rolled out of the car park. The sun was still fairly high and to my left.

To help relieve the pain, I had to lean my body left or right rather than turn the wheel with my hands. I caught sight of my face in the rear-view: I was really fucked up. I screwed it up further to try to keep the sweat out of my eyes as I moved into the traffic.

I carried on out of the city, concentrating on the road ahead as best I could. Wiping my eyes with my sleeve didn't seem to make much difference. Goatee found another little burst of energy, kicking out at the back and screaming, then went quiet again.

The road narrowed and we were soon climbing steeply. The pain in my chest was too bad for me to change gear, and I had to stop in a layby to let a small convoy of cars pass before they got terminally annoyed at my snail's pace. I used the opportunity to take controlled breaths into the bag, the paper inflating and deflating like my lungs weren't.

I didn't know where I was, but the sun was still to the left of me. I was definitely moving north. There was no way I was going to take the risk of driving back into the city, just to get on to the main drag that I knew led directly to Villefranche. I was going to do it cross-country.

I stayed in the layby for maybe ten minutes, breathing into the bag. Now that I had time to do it properly, I was able to breathe back in the carbon dioxide that I needed in my blood to relieve the symptoms. Willpower alone wouldn't have done the job: I needed the bag to break the cycle of hyperventilation. I knew I must be in shit state for this to be happening.

Breathing a lot better but still in small gulps, I thought about how I was going to get to the DOP. From here, I knew that as long as I kept the sun on my left, to the west, the coast would be behind me. I'd chuck a right at the first opportunity, and head east, with the sun behind me, paralleling the coast. That way I'd be able to bypass the city. When I chucked another right, heading south, I'd eventually hit the sea. With luck, I'd be able to sort myself out from there.

I rejoined the road, keeping in first gear, only changing up into second when the engine was screaming. There was another outburst from Goatee in the boot and I turned on the radio to drown the noise. It was monotonous, rapid dance music, but at least it was louder than he was.

Even if I got Goatee successfully to the DOP, I didn't know what I was going to do next. There was no way I could go to a hospital. No identification, no money, no nothing – I'd be picked up in minutes. What had happened down in the industrial estate would be a massive deal, even for such a rough *banlieue*. The police heli was up: they'd be looking for runners. TV and radio would carry saturation coverage any minute.

I had no chance of getting out of this. The police would find my docs in the pit soon enough, and then I'd really be in the shit. I couldn't run to the American consulate. They'd fuck me off at the door. The only chance I'd have would be to jump over the wall, giving myself up to someone inside the compound. Even then they'd probably chuck me out. I could try making a run for Italy, but I'd still be in the same boat.

I worked my way up on to the high ground, leaning on the wheel to take some of the weight off my chest. The coughing persisted, and the knifelike pain came back each time my body tensed as I tried to stop it.

The only chance I had was to get on board that warship. It didn't matter how I did it, even if it meant posing as one of the *hawallada*. Only the warship guaranteed medical attention, and offered the possibility of escape.

I drove with the sun to my left for what felt like hours. I still didn't know where I was because I'd been concentrating too much on other things. I eventually took a junction right, which led into a narrow lane with steep, rocky sides, dotted with clumps of grass and the odd stubby tree. I was heading east now; the sun half blinded me in the rear-view mirror. The dance music banged out, and the boot tray gave a jump now and again, not quite in time with the beat. I didn't have a clue how far inland I was, but I knew I was paralleling the sea and was some way above Nice.

I was feeling more and more exhausted. I'd gone on maybe another hour. Any road south would do me now. I found one and, with the sun to my right and getting lower, began my descent towards the coast.

The rapid breathing returned, and I had to pull in at the roadside and get the paper bag on to my face. The radio boomed, and Goatee gave the back tray another couple of kicks as I puckered my lips and kissed air.

55

I gobbed out some more blood and covered my mouth and nose once more with the McDonald's bag, but it was getting wet from me dripping into it every five minutes, and wouldn't be good for much longer.

After about fifteen minutes, the hyperventilation had eased and I threw the bag back on the passenger seat. The road ahead swam in and out of focus. All I knew was that as long as I kept heading south, towards the sea, I could sort myself out and get to the DOP.

As darkness began to fall, I found myself on an avenue of large houses set well back from the road, at the end of which was a sign that told me Villefranche was to the left, and Nice to the right.

The volume of traffic increased, and I had to concentrate even harder as the headlights came on and the wipers failed to shift the smear of insects on my windscreen. In just a few more Ks I was approaching the picnic area. I stopped by the bottle banks, and levered myself slowly out of the car, letting my arms take my weight. The car park was empty, but I left the music on to cover any noise Goatee might make. Opening the rear passenger door, I bent down to retrieve a full can of Coke Light from a six-pack in the footwell, and shoved it under the right corner of the nearest bottle bank. My chest felt like a knife thrower had used it for target practice as I pushed myself back up.

Back behind the wheel, I felt under the dash for the brake and reversing lights cut-out, pressing down on the brake so the rear of the wagon was now a blaze of red. It was in the same position as on the other two cars so that everyone knew where to find it, just like the keys. My fingers found the switch, and the gentle glow from the tail lights returned in the rear-view mirror.

I circled the car park and headed downhill, eyes peeled for the DOP driveway. If I missed it, I'd have to go into Hubba-Hubba's old holding-up point, then make my way back uphill, and I didn't want to do that if I could avoid it. Every movement was agony.

I kept the vehicle lights on full beam and let the car just coast on its brakes, leaning on the wheel to relieve the pain. I turned off the radio to help me concentrate. There was no sound from the boot.

At last I saw it. I moved into the oncoming lane, killed the lights, put the Focus into first and managed to make the sharp right turn on to the track. My chest burst into flames again, and I coughed blood on to the dash.

The rusty chain was padlocked to a wooden post at either end. I put my foot down. I hit it dead centre and the Focus lunged forward, but then stopped, throwing me against the steering wheel. The engine stalled.

My chest was agony. I coughed up another mouthful of blood and mucus and reached for the soggy McDonald's bag. When my breathing had slowed, I lowered the window, listening for vehicles. There was nothing; I moved the gearshift into reverse, checked there was no white light behind me, backed into the road, and tried again, this time with more revs.

The post ripped out and I braced myself and braked, not wanting the Focus to go all the way down the hill just yet. I turned off the engine, put the handbrake on, and pressed the

372

boot-release catch before stumbling outside. Shoving the wet McDonald's bag down my sweatshirt and using the car to support myself, I waded through a river of broken boxes, empty cans and burst bin liners.

The light came on as I lifted the tailgate. Goatee was still out of it, just a limp bundle. I got hold of his feet and swung them out, bent down and half lifted, half dragged him out on to the ground. It was just as well there was no resistance from him: I wouldn't have been able to fight back.

I made my way back to the driver's seat, released the hand-brake and gave the Focus as much of a push as my grating ribs would allow. It rolled slowly forwards, gathered a bit of momentum, and carried on down the slope until it hit a barrier of old washing machines. It hadn't gone far, but was out of view of the road, and that was what mattered.

I turned and limped back to Goatee, got my hands under his armpits, and dragged him on to the canvas tarpaulin to the right of the driveway.

A car came downhill from the picnic area, bathing the road-side and bushes in light. I waited for the sound of its engine to die, then pulled him over on to his side to make sure he didn't choke on his tongue. He curled up like a baby. I sat over him; I tried lying down, but it was just too painful.

Coughing out more blood, I checked traser. It was just past seven o'clock: it could be hours before we got a pick-up. Goatee's condition was a worry. I wasn't sure he was going to make it. Come to that, I wasn't too sure about myself.

I lifted the corner of the tarpaulin and covered him, trying to maintain his core temperature. I tried to get some of it over me as well, but it hurt too much to pull it any further. I started to hyperventilate again with the effort and the McDonald's bag finally fell apart as I tried to breathe into it again. There was nothing I could do but use my cupped hands. I rested my elbows on my knees for a moment, but that was too painful.

More vehicle lights bathed the skyline intermittently for the next hour or so, then I heard a diesel engine coming down the hill. I listened and hoped it would stop at the driveway, but no such luck. It passed and the lights disappeared. I checked traser again. Only ten minutes had passed since the last time I'd looked.

Goatee retched, and I heard a splash on the tarpaulin. He wheezed and fought for breath, then coughed again and I felt warm liquid on the hand that I was using to support myself.

Two or three more vehicles passed in each direction as I just sat there, cross-legged, trying to keep my trunk upright, wishing my life away because I desperately needed Thackery to turn up and get us out of here. Goatee moaned gently below me; now and again his body twitched and his legs pedalled on the tarpaulin, but at least his breathing was more regular than mine.

Suddenly, soft bleeping noises filled the air. I wondered if I was hallucinating. It took me several seconds to realize they were coming from Goatee's mobile. He started to straighten out his legs, mumbling to himself in Arabic. I lay down next to him, feeling in the dark, finding his hand as it tried to find his pocket. I pulled it away weakly.

'Fuck you,' he grunted. There were only a few inches between our faces now and I could smell his rancid breath. Mine was probably no better.

I dug into his trouser pocket with my left hand and pulled out the mobile. It had stopped ringing, and Goatee was whining in Arabic, I thought more in anger at not being able to take the call than from the pain.

'What you saying?'

I could hear slurping as he opened and closed his mouth a couple of times before muttering, 'My wife.'

I opened up the phone and a dull blue display glowed in the dark. 'Tough shit.' With the blood- and bitumen-covered thumb of my right hand I tapped in the digits 001, then the rest of the Massachusetts number.

It would be afternoon in Marblehead, and she should be home. She had to be – it was her day to look after the B-and-B.

It rang three or four times, then I heard her voice. 'Hello?'

'Carrie, it's me. Please don't hang up.'

'Oh.'

'I need help.'

'I've been telling you that for months.' Her tone changed. 'So, Nick, where do we go from here?'

'Listen, I really need your help.' I tried to stop myself coughing.

'Are you OK, Nick? You sound . . . have you got somebody with you?'

'Yes, I have.' I hesitated, then realized I had no choice. 'Look, I'm still working for George.' I moved the phone away from my mouth, and this time coughed up some more blood.

'Nick?'

'I'm all right. I need you to call your dad for me. Tell him I'm coming in with today's collection, and the collection is ready now. Tell him we both need medical attention, and quickly. Can you do that? Can you contact him?'

'Sure, his pager. But—'

'Please, just make the call.'

'Of course.'

'Please do it now – it's important.'

'Nick?'

'I've got to go – just do it now, please.' I hit the off button, but kept the power on in case the phone had an access code.

Goatee coughed and cleared his mouth before speaking. 'Your wife?' He lay there waiting for a reply.

'You're dying. People are going to pick us up soon and try to save you, but that's only because they want you alive. They want to know what you know. After that, I don't know what happens, but it's not going to be good.'

There was a pause. He didn't say anything, but I could hear his head moving up and down on the canvas and the smell of his breath came and went in waves.

'Me, I'm going home. That's the end of it, apart from the fact that somebody stitched both of us up. Those two you lifted in

375

the shop, they were the real collectors.' I could hear his head move again. 'We were there to follow them, to get to you – and then do exactly what I'm doing with you now. So my job is done, but my two friends are dead. And so are yours, and chances are you'll never talk with your wife again. Tell me who you saw in Juan-les-Pins Wednesday night, and what they said.' I let it sink in a little before continuing. 'Look, you're fucked, but I can do something for both of us.'

A vehicle passed by, up on the road, so I let my words sink in a little more. 'You've got nothing to lose, you've lost it already.'

He gave what sounded like a sob, then made an effort to pull himself together. He turned his head towards me, and the rancid smell returned. 'He said he knew that the collection was taking place today . . . He said the collectors were not the real guys. They were coming to steal the money, but they were coming with the correct code. He also told me that there would be other guys out there following them as protection.'

'What did this man look like? Was he white? Black?'

'Arab.'

'With long, greying hair?'

'No, no. Greased back.' He coughed, and I heard liquid in his throat. 'I had to do what I did. Surely you understand that? Just tell me your price and let me go. I'll pay you money, more than you can imagine. No one will know what happened. You can say I escaped. How much do you want?'

My mind was on other things. I'd heard all that crap a million times before, over the years. I thought about the first time I'd been to Greaseball's flat. He hadn't been expecting me, and that was why he'd tried to hide the tennis bags. I'd thought he was trying to stop me seeing the syringes when he kicked them under the bed, but that wasn't it at all: he was going to collect the money in them. There were even a couple of racquets out on the landing. Their plan couldn't have been simpler: they were even prepared to sacrifice this collection so they could hang on to the other two, Monaco and Cannes.

376

I opened up the mobile once more, mentally reciting the pager number. The first four numbers toned out from the phone, then I stopped. What if they were still in the harbour, or anywhere near real people? I couldn't do that. I had to stop the money movement, but it was my anger dialling, not the job. I could get something organized from the warship. After all, they had enough technology on board to find anything, anywhere.

I kept the phone in my blood-stained hand as Goatee stirred again. 'Please tell my wife . . . please call her.'

I thought about lying to him to make him feel better. Then I thought about Hubba-Hubba's charred hand reaching through the wrought-iron gate. I turned to face him again in the darkness. 'Fuck you.'

He didn't reply, just coughed up even more blood than I had and started to breathe very quickly and shallowly. I forced myself up on my arse to relieve some of the chest pain, and felt myself breathing out of rhythm. I cupped my hands over my nose and mouth.

Another vehicle roared up the hill and I checked traser. It was eight twenty-seven.

I slid my way down again, and lay next to Goatee.

All I could do was wait now, try to control my breathing, and hope that we were going to get picked up before both of us were dead.

56

Another vehicle swept down the hill, but this time slowed as it neared the entrance to the track.

Whoever it was came to a complete halt, with his engine ticking over. I heard the high-pitched whine of the vehicle reversing; then a mixture of red and white light swept across the bank of bin liners beside us. There was just a second's silence before the doors swung open. There was something about their echo that made me think van, not car. It must be them. Then the crunch of footsteps headed my way as red light now fought its way past the collapsed chain barrier.

I didn't move a muscle. Maybe it was just somebody about to do some late-night fly-tipping. If it was Thackery, he'd know where to find us: I didn't want to spook him, in case he and his mate were armed. I wanted to get into the back of that wagon in one piece.

Goatee stirred, and I leant over and cupped my hand over his mouth. I realized that I still had the phone in my other, and slipped it into the pocket of my jeans.

Two silhouettes appeared in front of the gentle red glow, weapons already drawn down, and picked their way through the rubbish. The one on the right saw us first. 'Shit! We've got two!'

The other one closed in and gave Goatee a kick. I didn't know whether he was looking for a reaction, or if it was just for the hell of it.

The *hawallada* responded with a dull moan and curled up even more. I didn't want any of that: I didn't know if my ribcage could take it. I looked up and kept my voice very low. 'He's the one you're here for. He's got a gunshot wound to the abdomen.'

The shadow leant towards me.

'I'm the one who delivered him. The man—'

The punch flattened my nose against my face. My eyes watered, and white stars flashed inside my head. I lay there, just trying to get my breath back, as a hand ran over my body, checking for weapons. The phone was found and confiscated.

The other did the same to Goatee, then they both picked him up and carried him by his arms and legs to the van, beyond the bushes. I hoped they were going to come back for me, but just in case, I struggled up on to my hands and knees and started to follow.

My route was paved with rusty cans and broken glass.

I got to the track as the two shadows reappeared. I held up my hands, taking the pain in my chest. 'I'm one of you,' I gasped. 'I need to get to the ship.'

They closed in and I got a very thick New York growl in my left ear. 'Shut the fuck up.' Hands gripped me and half lifted, half dragged me into the back of the van. The pain was unbearable but I wasn't complaining. One of the shadows got in with us and the door closed. In the gentle red glow from the rear lights, I could see him ripping apart the Velcro fastenings on a trauma pack. As we started to move, he turned on the interior light and I saw Thackery's face at last.

He completely ignored me, concentrating on Goatee in the mix of white and red light from the rear units exposed in the back as we bounced our way back to the road.

He was wearing much the same gear as he had in Cap 3000. I tugged at his jeans. 'It's me. Cap 3000, remember?

The brush contact, the colour was blue. It's me . . .'

He ripped open the plastic wrapper of a field dressing with his teeth.

'Do you recognize me?'

He nodded. 'You OK?' He sounded like one of Dolly Parton's backing group.

'Not sure.' I dribbled some blood down the front of my sweatshirt, as if to show him what I meant. We headed steeply downhill and encountered the first of the hairpins.

Thackery held the dressing in place over Goatee's gut, and manhandled him over to look for the exit wound. Not finding one, he started to wrap a bandage aggressively around the *hawallada's* stomach. 'What the fuck's going on here, my friend? Some buttons got pressed and we were told to do the pick-up quick as we could.'

The driver hit the brakes. Thackery held Goatee in place and I put my hands on the floor of the van to steady myself as we took another sharp right-hander, and lost some more of the now drying top layer of skin from my palms. 'There's been a fuck-up. I need your help.'

He continued bandaging, checking Goatee's tongue wasn't blocking his airway. 'Hey, man, I don't know what this is about, and I don't want to know. We know nothing, we just do what we do.'

More red light bled into the white as the driver hit the brakes for the next hairpin.

'I need you to go to the port at Vauban.'

'All we do is pick up and drop off, man. Don't even have comms with the guys down the hill.'

'Look, the men who killed the rest of my team – they've got the money, they've got the boat. We have to stop them, or all this has been for nothing. They don't know it yet, but the guys down the hill need to know where it is. That's why I'm here, that's why you got the fast ball for an early pick-up. We need your help, there just isn't time!'

He finished dressing the injury and stared at me intently.

380

I explained about the *Ninth of May*. 'I need to know if it's still there. If not, bang on other boats, wave our weapons around, shout – do whatever we need to do to find out what's happened to it.'

He hesitated, and got back to checking Goatee. 'How do I contact you?'

'You got a cell?'

He nodded. 'In the front.'

'Keep mine, and I'll take yours. Find out what's happening in Vauban, then call your own phone.'

He nodded and slid back the hatch on the bulkhead. 'Hey, Greg, we have a situation here. We have to kick ass in Antibes after the drop-off.'

I looked through the hatch as we continued downhill. We'd already crossed the main drag, and were heading into Villefranche. People were out and about, restaurants were open, neon was flashing.

Then, to our left, I saw the warship, still lit up like a Christmas tree in the centre of the bay.

Thackery's phone was passed back and the hatch closed. He turned it on before handing it to me.

Greg banged on the bulkhead and Thackery said, 'We're here.'

The vehicle came to a halt, then moved on another ten or fifteen metres before stopping again. An American voice echoed outside, 'Lights.' Thackery opened the rear door and disappeared left as the last of the fluorescent strip lights flickered on along a wall. We were in a stone building with a high terracotta roof; I couldn't see anybody, but there were more American voices around the van as they closed in on Thackery.

'We got two guys.'

Thackery didn't fuck about. 'The one in the sweatshirt covered in tar is one of ours. He's injured. He needs to talk to whoever is in command here. There's more going down, he'll explain. The other guy, the pick-up, has a gunshot wound to the abdomen. Looking pretty bad. Look, we gotta go, he'll explain.'

A radio crackled and a slick East Coast voice started relaying the information to the ship. Three or four people appeared at the back of the van, led by a black woman with Venus Williams hair, and a sheet of paper in her left hand. She was dressed as if she'd stepped straight from a Gap window, apart from a Glock .45 on her right hip.

'Your name?' She was from the South, too.

'Nick Scott.'

'What did you deliver yesterday?'

'A man, Gumaa . . . Gumaa something. Guy in a blue suit.'

'What's the next authentication colour?'

I didn't want to fuck this up. I tried to get my brain in gear. Blue was the brush contact, and red was the Nice email.

'White, it's white.'

'OK.'

She moved out of the way as Goatee got lifted out by two men in jeans and safari jackets with pockets full of shiny scissors and other medical kit.

She reappeared, and I saw that the paper she held was a printout of my Scott passport photograph. 'You OK?'

'You in command?'

'No. He's on board. He knows you're here.'

One of the safari jackets cut in. 'Has he been drugged?'

I shook my head and looked back at the woman. 'I need to get over there.'

It was pointless talking to her. I didn't know how far down the food chain she was, and to relay stuff just wastes time – which was something we didn't have.

As soon as Goatee had been lowered on to a stretcher, a young guy got a line into his arm and attached to a bag of fluid. Two others tended the gut wound.

Venus held out her arm to me. 'Can you move?'

I nodded and eased myself down on to the concrete, clutching Thackery's cellphone to my chest in a vain attempt to ease the pain.

I could see now that we were in a boathouse. A grey Navy

launch with a hard top was waiting at a jetty. The place echoed with low but urgent voices and the sound of feet on concrete as the stretcher was taken on board.

Venus put her arm round my waist to help me to the launch, but it wasn't the kind of help I needed. I could almost hear my ribs grating against each other. 'It's OK,' I gasped. 'I'll sort myself out.'

There was a shout from somewhere behind me. 'Lights!'

We were thrown into darkness as a set of well-oiled shutters was lifted and the van reversed out. The shutters came down again and the neon flickered back to life.

Keeping my back as straight as I could, I hobbled towards the launch. Venus went to lock up and sort things out. No one was remotely concerned about my condition. It was Goatee they were here for.

I pressed a button on Thackery's phone to illuminate the display. The signal strength was fives.

I stumbled aboard like an old man and sat on a hard plastic bench while Goatee got the five-star treatment. He had an oxygen mask on now, and was having more trauma care than a major RTA.

We were ready to go. Venus hit the switch again as another set of shutters opened seawards.

The launch started up, smothering me with diesel fumes, then reversed out into the bay as soon as she'd jumped on board.

As we gathered speed, the line of restaurant lights along the quay receded. I went back to staring at the phone screen, willing the signal to stay strong, and hoping that Thackery and Greg weren't screaming towards Antibes at warp speed, risking a crash or getting pulled by the police.

57

The side of the warship loomed high above us. A rectangle of red light glowed at us from the top of a gangway, about six or seven metres above the waterline. At the bottom of it two shadows stood ready to receive the launch. Two black and businesslike RIBs [rigid inflatable boats], each with two huge outboards, bobbed up and down on the swell beside them.

The launch's props powered down, and we came slowly alongside. The two guys grabbed our side rails. They were dressed in dry bags and black woolly hats, and had rolled-up life preservers around their necks. Venus got to her feet as they pulled us alongside. 'Come with me.' She nodded down at the stretcher. 'Where he's headed, you don't want to go.'

I left Goatee to his fate, and made my way up the gangway behind her. I was feeling weak and nauseous, and salt water gave the good news to my hands as I tried to get a grip on the guardrail.

Wrapping my arms around my chest like a cold child, I stepped into the red glow. There was a gentle hum of radio traffic, and murmured exchanges among the dozen or so bodies crouched in the small, steel-encased holding bay. They were all in dry bags, unzipped to let in some air. Next to each man, a Protect helmet, the sort canoeists wear, rested on top of a black nylon harness, holding magazines for the 10mm version of the Heckler & Koch MP5. All wore leg holsters with .45 Glocks. The red light was to protect their night vision; something was going to happen out there in the dark and, by the look of things, it was going to happen soon.

One of the bodies stood and spoke quietly to the woman. Her name wasn't Venus, it was Nisha.

Then he turned back to the group. 'White light, people. White light.'

Everybody closed their eyes and covered them with their hands as he threw the lock on a bulkhead door and pushed down the handle. White light poured in from the corridor, drowning the red. I followed Nisha; as the door closed, we stood blinking in a corridor lined with some sort of imitation wood veneer. There was complete silence, except for the gentle hum of air-conditioning from the ducts above us. Our rubber soles squeaked on the highly polished lino tiles as I followed Nisha along the corridor, expecting a squad of imperial stormtroopers to appear at any moment.

I kept unwrapping an arm, checking the phone. The signal bars suddenly disappeared. 'Stop!'

She spun around. 'What's the problem?'

'I can't go any further.' I started to turn back towards the red room. 'I haven't got a signal. The two guys in the van, they're heading to Antibes – there's a boat, we need to know where it is. I need a signal.'

'You talking *Ninth of May*?'

I nodded.

'We got it. Left Vauban a couple hours ago.'

'You're already tracking it?'

'We'll hit it just as soon as it crosses the line into international waters.' She turned back the way we were heading. 'Come on. Someone is waiting to talk to you.'

We came to another veneer-covered steel door, with a stainless-steel entry system alongside it. She tapped in a code, there was a gentle buzz and she pulled it open for me.

Banks of radar and computer screens glowed at us from three sides of the room. This had to be the ops centre. Maybe a dozen people, all dressed in civilian clothes, talked quietly into radios and to each other as they studied the screens.

The room was small, maybe five metres by five, with wires gaffered to the floor and wall; this wasn't a permanent fixture. A large command desk dominated the centre of the space. A grey-headed forty-something in a green polo shirt stood by it, poring over charts, mapping and photography with two more serious-looking heads. All three grasped mugs of steaming brew, and none of them looked up.

As Nisha and I approached, I could make out satellite images of Vauban and BSM, and then an enlargement of my passport picture.

Greyhead finally acknowledged our presence. He raised a pale, overworked, acne-scarred face.

Nisha moved over to one of the computer screens. 'You in command?' I asked.

He gave me the once-over. 'You OK?'

I shrugged.

He nodded in the direction of Nisha, who was now holding a phone. 'I wouldn't keep him waiting.'

'Who?'

He didn't answer, but I didn't really need him to. As he turned and told someone to get me a medic, I dragged myself over to Nisha, eased myself down into a padded swivel chair, but couldn't stop another spasm of coughing. Stuff came up, but there was nowhere to gob it, so I pulled out the neck of my sweatshirt and used the inside. I wiped my mouth on my sleeve before taking the phone. I put the mobile on the desk top; there were two signal bars on the display.

'Nick?' It was George. 'Where are the—'

'The collectors? They're dead. It's not them on the boat, I reckon it's—'

'Stop. I need two things right now. One: where's the rest of the team?'

'Both dead. The police will have the bodies by now . . .'

'You sure they're dead?'

I took a long, slow, painful breath. 'I watched one die, and heard the other.'

'Good. Were you part of the incident in L'Ariane?'

'Yes.'

'Good, we can contain that.' I heard him turn away from the mouthpiece and speak to the people around him. This was a deniable operation: they were making sure every track that could lead to us had been blocked. Lotfi and Hubba-Hubba were no longer assets. They'd been written off George's balance sheet.

I could hear murmurs of approval from the voices around George as he finished passing on the great news.

'OK. Two: is the device still onboard? Our people are going to intercept.'

'Listen, George, it's not the collectors on board. I just told you, they're dead. It's the source and Ramsay. They got the team and the collectors killed, and they've taken the money.'

'We know, son, we found out yesterday. They won't get to keep it for long.'

We found out yesterday? They knew? Why the fuck hadn't we known?

'What? We could have done things differently . . . the other two could still be alive.'

'I keep telling you, son, I don't tell even God everything. Now, is the goddamned device still in position? They don't know it exists yet – they need to know if it's still there.'

I shook my head in disbelief. 'What's happening? You lifting them?'

'All we want is the money.'

'You're just letting them go? They got our guys killed—'

'OK, son, this is how it goes down. It's over. They go free, we get the money, we get the *hawalladas*, you get a medic, and a good night's sleep.'

'My team are dead, George. You're letting the fuckers go?'

He didn't even pause to draw breath. 'I have other plans for those two. Don't mess up on me now. You have everything to lose, and nothing to back up with.'

I remained silent for a moment. I thought about the boys on the RIBs giving Greaseball and Curly a big kiss on both cheeks and waving as they disappeared into the night.

George seemed to be reading my mind. 'Son, do I need to worry about you?'

'No, George,' I said. 'I know what I've got to do.'

'Good. Tell them about the device. We'll meet soon.'

The phone went dead and I gave Nisha back the receiver. 'There's an explosive device on board.'

She turned to Greyhead. 'Simon, we definitely have a device on board.'

He looked up sharply from his desk.

'On the top deck, a plastic cylinder tucked into the settee behind the wheel. There's no anti-handling device . . . just twist the cylinder, take the two AA batteries out and it's safe. I'll draw a picture.'

Nisha was already fetching me paper as the information was passed down to the red room via one of the radio operators.

One of the medics arrived as I started sketching a diagram of the device and its location, trying not to smear it with too much blood.

Greyhead had other things on his mind. 'Stand to, the crews. The *Ninth of May* . . . Looks like they've stopped hugging the coast and are heading out to sea. Should be over the line in twenty-five.'

The red room would be a hive of activity now as the crews pulled on their chest harnesses, made ready their weapons, and finally put on their Protects and life-preservers.

As I sat there, trying to cut away from my anger, the theme tune to *Mission Impossible* struck up. Heads spun to see which shit-for-brains had brought a cellphone into the ops centre.

I pressed the green button and immediately got Thackery hollering in my ear. 'It's gone, the boat left!' I heard the kids from the *Lee* in the background. 'There were two on board, the guy who owns the boat, and his friend . . .'

I looked around me as things started getting more intense. The crews were in the boats, ready to go. 'Stand down, mate, it's all been taken care of.'

'What?'

'It's all been taken care of, stand down. Thanks, mate, thanks.' I hit the end-of-call button, then finished the drawing and handed it to Nisha.

I sat in the swivel chair as Greyhead confirmed the crews were ready in their boats. As soon as they had the drawing, he'd give them the go. 'Contact thirty-three minutes.' He wanted to make sure they were in international waters.

George was right, of course. This was going to be a long war, and Greaseball would be even more useful in future. Now they'd stolen from al-Qaeda, George had both of them tightly by the bollocks, and could point them in whatever direction he pleased, as long as HIV didn't get them first.

'Contact twenty-nine minutes,' a voice called out from the radar screen.

I wondered what was happening on the *Ninth of May*. Curly would probably be doing the driving, leaving Greaseball to pull the cork on a bottle of good champagne. Next stop, maybe, some boy town Greek island and the start of their own big bang theory.

The ops room continued to follow the progress of their two crews.

'Same heading. Contact twenty-one minutes.'

But then my smile disappeared. So what if they lost the money? They'd still be alive: they'd still get to go wherever it was they were heading.

As the medic lifted my sweatshirt and started to have a good look at what was left of my ribcage, I pictured Lotfi and Hubba-Hubba in their Marigolds at the safe house, having a good laugh as I gave them my jester impression. They had saved my life, and kept their promise to each other.

Now it was time for me to keep mine to them.

I started pressing the buttons with my right thumb as the medic dug into his bag. A gentle beep sounded each time I hit another digit of the pager number, willing it still to be in range.

Suddenly the answering service was gobbing off to me in French. I didn't understand a word it was saying, but I knew what it meant: 'Wait for the tone, then tap in the number that you want the pager to display. After that just hit the star button.'

I waited for the tone, and did exactly that, just hitting the eight button a few times, then the star. I pushed the phone against my ear and held my breath.

We had done our job, and done it well; so fuck George, and fuck everything he had for me.

A few seconds later the answering service came back to me, and this time I understood every word.

'*Message bien reçue.*'

EPILOGUE

WEDNESDAY, 5 DECEMBER, 10:28 hrs

The coast road north ran parallel with the rail track out of Boston. I watched from the carriage as it cut through the icy marshland. The day was dull and grey, the only burst of colour a huge Stars and Stripes in the distance, fluttering from a flag-pole at the point where the earth met the sky. I wondered how cold my reception was going to be at Wonderland – or if I was going to get one at all.

The other passengers on the aluminium commuter train still looked at me as if I'd just escaped from the local nuthouse, maybe because I was in the same greasy, unshaven state as last time, maybe because I still had traces of bruising, and the cuts on my hands and head had not yet healed. I was too exhausted to worry.

The front pages of their papers still carried pictures of troops in Afghanistan, where the Taliban were now on the run. 'Inside the Manhunt' read the cover of *Time* magazine, and Bin Laden's face stared out at me through the cross-hairs of the art department's sniper rifle.

I hadn't seen George yet, and still didn't know what was going to happen to me. My big hope was that I'd find a pass-port in my Christmas stocking, but I wasn't holding my breath.

The train rattled on across Rivere. Every time I did this

journey I felt as though I was in the middle of an American history lesson: everywhere you looked there was something to remind you that the Brits had had their arses kicked here a couple of hundred years ago. I remembered telling Carrie, 'We'll be back as soon as the lease runs out.' It had seemed quite funny at the time, but I couldn't raise much of a smile right now: I was too busy wondering how much Brit arse was going to get kicked today.

The warship had weighed anchor within hours of the *Ninth of May* exploding, after Greyhead's boat teams had finished trying to make sense of the fireball they'd seen in the distance as they closed in. Once we were within reach of the western Italian coast, I was shoved on a heli.

The headquarters of the US 16th Air Force, based at Aviano, was about an hour and a half from Venice, but I missed out on the sightseeing. My three days there were spent in a featureless admin block, getting debriefed by two men and a woman to the roar of F-16 fighters and a coffee percolator whose power kept cutting out. At least the coffee was hotter on the flight back to the States, courtesy of the USAF.

They told me George had gone ballistic about Greaseball getting the good news. I spent a bit of time describing how the device worked, but couldn't for the life of me explain what had caused the detonation. Maybe a wrong number? That had always been a worry.

They nodded, then moved on, but I wondered how long it would be before George took a long, hard look at Thackery's phone records. Whatever, I would just have to play dumb: it was one of the things I was really good at.

Being holed up at Aviano at least gave me time to rest my two broken ribs, with some help from a shedful of codeine and sleeping upright on a settee.

Gumaa and Goatee hadn't been so lucky. They'd wasted no time in telling the interrogation team who their contacts were in the US, and a bunch of six-man ASUs, one living in the

Detroit area, had already been covertly rendered. There would be more to come: the two *hawallada* were giving out information faster than Bloomberg.

The Detroit ASU had planned to drive to the Mall of America in Minnesota. Seven times larger than a baseball stadium, with more than forty-two million visitors every year, it was the perfect target for a dirty-bomb attack. Their plan was pretty much along the lines George had feared. All six were going to move into the mall at different times, through different entrances, on to different floors in different sections. They had aimed to detonate themselves at exactly two p.m. on 24 December. The place would have been filled with tens of thousands of shoppers, kids in line for Santa, all that sort of Christmas stuff.

I thought Lotfi and Hubba-Hubba would have been pretty pleased to have got in the way of that. I just wished they'd been here to celebrate.

Their bodies were probably still in a morgue in Nice. No one was going to come forward to claim them; they'd probably be burned, or buried by the French in paupers' graves. I hoped that they'd both be getting their little bit of the Paradise Lotfi had spent so much time talking to God about, and that they'd been able to look down on the *Ninth of May* with a big smile on their faces as it got the good news.

I thought about the three of us fucking about with the hats in the safe house, and Hubba-Hubba with that evil eye thing around his neck, and couldn't help but smile. Then, from nowhere, I could hear his voice as clearly as if he was sitting next to me: 'He hates this. He says I will not go to Paradise . . . But he is wrong, I think. I hope . . .'

I hadn't been able to stop thinking about their sister, Khalisah. What would she and their families do now? They'd be needing money. I didn't know how these things were done: would George see to it that they were looked after? He'd have to, surely – he'd have a hell of a job recruiting more Lotfis and Hubba-Hubbas if they discovered their families wouldn't be

393

taken care of if everything went to rat shit. But there was no way I could trust him, even if he said he would. I'd do something about it myself. The Mégane would have been towed from the square in Antibes by now, but with luck the money we'd taken off Gumaa would still be under the seat. It wouldn't be much, but it would be a start . . .

The bridge over the Saugus river took us into Lynn. We were nearly at Wonderland. Last time I'd come up this track I'd looked forward to a new job, a new life. But what now?

I didn't even know if she was going to take the day off work to meet me. But if she didn't, I'd just go and sit on the doorstep until she came home. There were some things I needed to say, and thought she needed to hear.

Hubba-Hubba had helped make my mind up.

He'd been sitting in the cab of the Scudo, repairing his evil eye.

'We are a family first, no matter what disagreements we may have, no matter what pain we may suffer . . . We learnt long ago to meet in the middle, because otherwise the family is lost.'

I couldn't be a student or a bartender – or anything else, for that matter. I couldn't do anything other than what I did. Sure, I didn't much like a lot of the stuff that went with it. But she had once said to me that she didn't care what I did, as long as I was good at it. Well, this was what I did, and I was good at it. And, thanks to my two friends with the Marigolds and the shower cap fetish, I'd realized I was working for something I believed in. The people I cared for lived in the country I had played a small part in protecting, and for once in my life I felt good about what I had done. And if the angels did come down and weigh my book of destiny for a laugh, then maybe there'd be a page or two of good stuff for them to read.

Maybe Carrie would read it too. Maybe I could tell her about Lotfi and Hubba-Hubba and Khalisah, and we could take a few steps towards the middle. People can stay together if they

394

really want to, even if there's a whole lot of shit going on around them. I knew that now: I'd seen it happen.

The train came to a halt and people stood and reached for their hats and coats, and gathered up their bags of Christmas shopping. The automatic doors drew back to reveal the signs for Wonderland station.

I stepped out of the carriage. It was as cold as it ever was, and the wind was bitter. I zipped up my fleece jacket, and joined the throng heading for the barrier.